The Journal

Rhonda Brown

authorHOUSE®

AuthorHouse™
1663 Liberty Drive
Bloomington, IN 47403
www.authorhouse.com
Phone: 1-800-839-8640

First published by AuthorHouse   10/7/2010

ISBN: 978-1-4520-8182-3 (sc)
ISBN: 978-1-4520-8183-0 (e)

Printed in the United States of America

This book is printed on acid-free paper.

For Steve, Roger, and Tyler…with love.

ACKNOWLEDGMENTS

Love and thanks to our sisters, Cheryle Ehmke, Linda Strause, and Sandy Tower, for reading our book, finding our mistakes, and for encouraging us to continue writing. Also, many thanks to Cheryl Knueman, Diana Schutz, Heather Isaac, Sally Haines, Trish Lipp, and Vivianna Ehmke for their friendship and support.

Thanks to Kathy Seal, our spiritual mentor, for keeping us on God's path. Thanks to Wayne and Barb Pruett for their insights on ranching in the Santa Cruz Valley. Thanks to authors Susan Tornga and John Lyman for their sage and counsel.

At lastly, thanks to Aunt Rubie, who at 83 is still gracious, beautiful, and still believes in me.

Chapter 1 – *Sam 1979* – The Birth

Lying in the bed of the large private birthing room, trying to remain calm between contractions, Sam thought about the baby she would soon meet. She knew without a shadow of a doubt that her baby was going to be very special, had known it from the minute she'd discovered she was pregnant. She knew, too, trusting the sixth sense that rarely failed her, that it would be a daughter.

She had waited impatiently for almost nine months, and now, happily, the wait was coming to an end. She was actually about three weeks shy of her given due date, but that just meant she would see her daughter sooner than originally planned. She was not worried; babies were born early all the time and she had complete confidence in her obstetrician.

She was wishing she had someone to share this experience with. Michael was out of town, having assumed there was no reason for him not to attend the three-day conference when his wife's due date was still so far away. She mentally replayed the conversation they'd had yesterday morning.

"Please, Michael, don't go," she had begged. "Dr. Lee said the baby is already moving into position so I could go into labor at any time now. I really want you with me if that happens." As she said this she'd leaned into him, put her arms around his neck and laid her head on his shoulder.

Unmoved, Michael had reached up, circled her wrists with his hands, and took them from his neck as he stepped back from her, barely concealing his impatience. He'd taken her hands in his.

2 | Rhonda Brown

"Look, Sam, you know how important this deal is. Besides, you aren't due for another three weeks, and you could even go past your due date. I'll be back in three days, so stop worrying."

Having firmly stated his position, his voice had softened and he'd leaned forward to peck her on the forehead, as if to say, "that's a good girl," before dropping her hands and then turning back to resume packing. Knowing it would do no good to argue, Sam had simply sighed and sat down heavily on the side of the bed.

"I told you so," she mumbled now under her breath. It brought little satisfaction, however, since Michael was not there to hear her. Neither did she say it when she'd called to leave him a message that she was on her way to the hospital.

She had also left a message for her parents with the housekeeper at their ranch but did not really expect them to act on it. Her mother, Etta, was probably in her sitting room, drunk as usual, or passed out by now. Her father, Jose, could be anywhere, as long as it wasn't in the immediate vicinity of her mother. Sam and her father had never been close, so there was no reason to expect him to rush to her side to hold her hand while she was in labor.

Her grandparents, Maria and Big Jose, would come, she knew, the minute they returned to the ranch today from their month-long vacation. They would not have expected this development so they had left for their long-awaited trip with excited anticipation when Sam was less than eight months into her pregnancy. She laughed to herself to think of how guilty Maria would feel upon arriving at the ranch and receiving the message Sam left for her. She just hoped they'd get here before the baby did.

Thinking of how happy Maria would be over the birth of the baby led to an ache deep in Sam's heart, knowing that her other grandmother, her beloved Maman, would never see this child. How Maman would have loved her new great-granddaughter, Sam mused. She had such happy memories of her own childhood with her French grandmother and she knew her daughter would have enjoyed growing up with that wonderful woman as well. But that was not to be.

I wish Honey was here to hold my hand she found herself wishing. Then, as often happened when she thought of her best friend, she heard the answering comment in her head: *Yes, Sam, you know I would have been there if you hadn't changed the plan by starting labor early. But not to worry, I'm with you in spirit, as is Maman. Now get to work and bring that baby girl into the world.* Comforted, Sam thought how nice it was that she and Honey could communicate telepathically.

When another contraction clinched her abdomen with the now-familiar rhythmic pain, Sam grabbed at the sheets for something to hold on to until it passed. Even through the intense labor, she felt excited and assured herself that this was going to be one of the happiest days of her life. As the contraction eased, she glanced at the only visitor she'd had so far; someone she wished was anywhere else. It was Winifred Fitzgerald Maxwell, Michael's mother. Having her here was like having no visitor at all.

Winifred, dressed in her most fashionable luncheon attire, had breezed into the room earlier – an hour ago, two maybe? – Sam had lost track of the time. Her mother-in-law had rushed through the door and began to speak at the same time, announcing that she'd had to cancel her lunch date with a very important Los Angeles socialite in order to be with Sam. She was not gracious about it.

"Now don't take this the wrong way, Samantha dear, but I am not here to help or to assist you with this labor. God forbid I should be expected to *coach* you or any other such nonsense. I am only here because Michael called and begged me to come after he received your message. He said something about giving you moral support, whatever that's supposed to mean. Anyway, I'll be right over here if you need me, not that I think you will. I simply must apologize again to Audrey for leaving her at the Beverly Hills Hotel the way I did, and I have several other important calls to make."

All of this had been said without a pause, and having stated her position, Winifred turned to look for a telephone. Noticing that there was one located on the far side of the room, she'd rushed over to grab it and started punching numbers with her perfectly manicured fingernails. Sam, who had not uttered a word, had felt dizzy and out of breath just listening to her. Winifred had been on the phone continually since then, apparently unaware that her daughter-in-law's labor pains were increasing in intensity and frequency. It would not have occurred to her that Samantha would, heaven forbid, actually *need* her.

It was not a surprise that Winifred was only there because of

Michael's request. Sam knew that Winnie – as she secretly called her mother-in-law in her mind, knowing the regal Winifred would feel insulted to be referred to by any nickname – would not even walk across the street to help her in a crisis unless she was forced to, much less coach her during labor. She was convinced that the snobbish Winnie felt childbirth was a disdainful task only peasants should have to endure. Sam would not have been the least bit surprised to learn that rather than having carried and given birth to Michael herself, Winifred had instead hired someone else to take care of the unpleasant business of pregnancy and childbirth.

The thought made Sam smile briefly before the next contraction hit. It was so strong it jerked her upper body to a sitting position. She lay back again as it eased, but did not have time to wipe off the perspiration that was running from her forehead into her eyes before another agonizing pain hit. She was groaning softly – heaven forbid that she should disturb Winnie's important phone conversation – when the OB/GYN nurse in charge of her room entered to check her progress.

"Oh my," the nurse said after lifting the blanket to peer between Sam's legs. "Honey, you'll be having this baby soon. *Very soon.* You just hang on a few more minutes while I get your doctor in here. It's almost time to start pushing." With that she replaced the blanket, gave Sam's leg a pat, and flashed a sweet motherly smile before turning to hurry out of the room.

Sam took the nearly non-existent time between contractions to glance toward Winnie. Her mother-in-law had not directed a single word to her following the grand entrance and speech upon her arrival and for this Sam was extremely grateful. The continuous low-pitched drone of Winnie's conversations in the background was all she could tolerate in her current circumstances. Soon another contraction started, and Winnie was no longer one of Sam's concerns.

The nurse returned, bringing the obstetrician with her. Dr. Lee smiled at Sam and picked up her chart. While the doctor reviewed it the nurse pulled back the blanket once more and put Sam's legs into the stirrups. Dr. Lee then pulled up a short stool and situated herself between the legs that were now shaking with each pain.

"Okay, Sam, you can start pushing with the next contraction." She glanced around the birthing room. "Michael isn't here yet?"

Sam didn't bother to answer as another wave of pain washed over her. The nurse lifted her shoulders and held her in a near-sitting position when the doctor ordered, "Push now Sam." She didn't have to be told twice, as there was nothing she could do to prevent the overwhelming need to push. Giving in to the pressure in her abdomen, she pushed as hard as she could.

"One more, as hard as you can, and that should do it," Dr. Lee urged. "The baby's head is already out, just need that last push to get the shoulders out."

The doctor was right. One more was all it took. Sam felt instant relief and heard a pop as the baby slid out of her body and into Dr. Lee's waiting hands. She struggled to sit up, then fell back, wondering why she felt so light-headed. She wanted to see her beautiful baby; she wanted to hear her first cry and see her angry little face. Silence. *Why isn't she crying?*

"Dr. Lee," Sam cried weakly as she started to panic, "what's wrong? Why isn't my baby crying?"

The obstetrician didn't answer. The nurse clipped the umbilical cord and cut it, then looked over to see the baby, a broad smile on her face. She loved newborns. Soon, however, the smile slowly disappeared and a curious frown appeared.

"What is that?" she whispered.

It was at this point that the pediatrician, Dr. White, entered the room. She walked over to see the baby and stopped without saying a word. The baby still had not cried.

"Dr. Lee," Sam tried again, noticing how quiet the doctors and the nurse were. She was exhausted from the effort of childbirth and it was increasingly difficult to make herself heard. "Is my baby okay? What's happening? Say something!" Her voice was barely above a whisper.

Her arms began to shake and no longer had the strength to hold her up. She fell back, frustrated at her inability to make herself heard. In her head she felt herself scream *I want to see my baby, now*! even as she fought to keep from giving in to the fog that was beginning to envelope her. However, her words were not voiced, and the medical personnel in the room were not paying attention to her.

"Doctor, please, let me have the baby," Dr. White finally said. "I need to clear her passages and get her breathing, and to examine her."

Winifred had been standing with her back to the room while she continued to talk on the phone. Now, however, the sounds of the other voices caught her attention and she turned around. Seeing the others in the room she hurriedly ended her conversation and rushed over to see what all the commotion was about. She peered over the shoulder of the doctor who was holding the newborn baby. Then, after taking one long, increasingly baffled and then horrified, look at her granddaughter, she fainted.

This spurred the medical personnel to action. The nurse bent down to check on Winifred, while the pediatrician reached to take the infant from Dr. Lee. When the obstetrician continued to stare at the baby in her arms, Dr. White became insistent.

"Dr. Lee, please give the baby to me and see to Mrs. Maxwell. She doesn't look very good."

Reluctantly, Dr. Lee gave the baby to Dr. White. She then turned to Sam slowly, unsure of what she should say, but soon was yelling loudly instead.

"Samantha, Samantha." She received no answer. "Nurse, call a Code Blue."

Sam heard low voices. At least she thought it was voices. She tried to listen, but the rhythmic beeping of the machines near her head interfered with being able to clearly discern what she was hearing. She was so tired, and felt so weak. Where was she? Were the voices in her head?

She tried to open her eyes but her eyelids remained closed. Finally, with much effort she was barely able to lift her lids a tiny slit. The room appeared to be almost completely dark, or maybe it was her imagination because she just couldn't get her eyes to open any further. Neither could she move her head, so her vision was limited to the area in front of the bed. She didn't recognize the room, what little she could see of it, but knew she was lying in a bed.

Sensing that someone was standing next to her, she tried to speak, but like her eyes, her mouth didn't seem to want to work, so the words were only in her head. She was so thirsty and desperately needed some water, but couldn't ask. After what felt like a super-human effort she was able to move one finger on one hand. It was then that she felt a soft touch on that hand.

"*Mi Hija*, I am here. It's your Maria."

Maria? Sam's brain tried to process that information. How could Maria be here? *Maria? It is really you?* Sam knew she had not spoken the words aloud.

As she felt herself slipping into a fog a thought came to her that she needed to ask Maria something. But what was it? Then she smelled chorizo cooking and heard bacon sizzling. Just relax, she told herself; she would lie here a few more minutes before she got up.

Oh yes, now she remembered, she wanted Maria to tell the story about the time…

CHAPTER 2 – *Maria 1962* – The Savior

On most cool summer mornings in Arizona 11-year-old Samantha Luna Lopez loved to lay in bed with her windows wide open. She enjoyed listening to the comforting and familiar noises: the creaking of the windmill if there was a breeze; the horses neighing to each other in the corrals or stables; the moaning and groaning of the old ranch house as it expanded and contracted. Best of all she loved the soothing sound of Maria singing in the kitchen below while making breakfast. The wealthy Luna family might own the Hacienda de Luna but Maria Carmen Lopez claimed its kitchens.

Maria was proud of the addition to the original ranch house, added some time in the early 1900's when the ranch was about 100 years old. In the years since then there had been some remodeling done to modernize slightly or to enlarge the space. In spite of the various updates, however, the kitchen had purposely maintained the southwest charm of the original ranch house. It had been featured in more than one issue of the Tucson Lifestyle magazine.

She often stood quietly in the huge, pleasant room that she referred to as the 'Big Kitchen' and thanked the Blessed Mother for bringing her here. She would gaze around the room, her eyes resting on, and loving, everything in it. There was a massive river-rock fireplace at one end that was large enough inside for an average-sized man to stand upright. A long buffet-style serving table ran the entire length of an adjacent wall, and opposite that were bright yellow cabinets topped with colorful Mexican tile, two giant stove tops with a large grill between them, and an old double porcelain sink, all remnants from the original kitchen.

These were some of the items and architecture that neither the Luna family nor Maria could bring themselves to replace, so they were always incorporated into each remodeling project.

Above the cabinets were nothing but windows and these, along with pale yellow painted walls, gave the kitchen a warm glow on sunny days. On those cloudy or dreary rainy days when there was no sun coming through the windows four gigantic chandeliers that were built from horseshoes and cow horns provided the necessary light.

Wide oak planks covered the floor and were worn to a smooth, almost white finish by the ranch hands' booted feet over the years when they strode back and forth between the serving table and the narrow pine dining table. The table was so long it filled the entire center of the kitchen, and could comfortably seat 20, maybe 30 people if necessary. Several wooden benches and assorted chairs flanked both sides of the old table.

Double saloon-style swinging doors led to a large baking room – formerly the original kitchen, now the 'Small Kitchen' in Maria's mind – that accommodated a large walk-in combination refrigerator and freezer located on one wall. A stone oven in another wall was still used to bake bread over live embers, as well as flour and corn tortillas. Baking in here kept the big kitchen cooler, especially in summer. A roomy walk-in pantry was located off still another wall and held months' worth of foodstuffs. Since the nearest store was over forty miles away Maria didn't want to be caught short

A door next to the baking room led to a service closet where many shelves and cabinets held a myriad of items: good china as well as more delicate china and stemware, lacy tablecloths and napkins, and fancy, gleaming silverware pieces. These items of expensive dinnerware would never see Maria's kitchen table. They were only used in the hacienda's formal dining room.

Maria's kitchens produced two kinds of food: spicy and spicier. Not a soul complained, however, as Maria's meals were delicious and filling, and well-known in the Santa Cruz valley. Not only did the family and the ranch hands look forward to the meals created by her, but neighbors and business connections never turned down an invitation to a meal at the hacienda.

This morning, as on every other morning, the ranch hands appeared at the kitchen door promptly at 6:00 a.m., after some early-morning chores had been taken care of, and dutifully wiped their feet before traipsing into the big room that was filled with enticing smells. Good-natured chatter did not disguise their anticipation of a delicious breakfast.

Sam's bedroom, situated directly over the big kitchen, carried the sounds of the ranch hands as they greeted Maria with either "*Buenos dias*" or "Good morning." Sam could hear the scraping of the benches after they had filled their plates at the serving table and then took their places at the dining table. She heard bits and pieces of their conversations while they ate, many of the words muffled when they spoke around the food in their mouths: "ride out to…"; "…break that horse"; "…mend the fence along the lower forty." The snatches of familiar early morning conversations that were necessary to keep the ranch running smoothly were comforting to the young girl. Her world was secure.

This particular morning, as soon as the slamming of the back door signaled that the ranch hands had left the house and Maria and her helper were starting to clean up after them, Sam jumped out of bed to hurriedly dress. Her usual weekday outfit consisted of a white T-shirt topped with a shabby and frayed too-small cowboy shirt and paired with old Levis that sported ragged holes in both knees. She pulled on her worn boots that were becoming too tight. Almost twelve years old, Sam seemed to be growing taller and filling out more every day. She needed to remember to tell Maria or Maman that she needed new boots and a couple of new shirts. If she told her mother, she'd just get a smile and hear "Sure, Darlin'," but the new clothes would never materialize. She was better off saying something to either of her grandmothers.

Once dressed, Sam dashed into her private bathroom and rushed through the routine of brushing her thick, curly hair, and then her teeth. She hated the sprinkling of freckles across the nose that was reflected back at her in the mirror. There was nothing she could do about them, though, so after rinsing her mouth she merely flipped off the bathroom light and hurried back into the bedroom. She grabbed a new leather journal from the top of her dresser, and then ran out the bedroom door and down the hallway that was beautifully paneled in knotty pine. Her steps slowed to a halt at the top of the giant staircase. The polished banister led to a huge great room below, and was a constant temptation, one which Sam could not resist if she thought she could get away with it.

She took a quick look toward Poppie's door, just in case he was still in his room. She really didn't expect him to be. After all, it was long past 4:30 and he was usually up and out before 4:00. He needed to make sure that the ranch foremen had everything coordinated and under control and that his own never-ending bookwork was brought up to date. A lot of hard work and constant surveillance went into running a ranch smoothly.

She wasn't taking any chances. The last time he had caught her, and she still remembered the tongue lashing she had received. However, this time it appeared that he was out of the house. No Pop in sight, no noises coming from his room or light under his door. Satisfied that she was in the clear, she climbed onto the gleaming banister, folded her long legs behind her and glided backward down to the bottom. She jumped off with a loud thump as she reached the banister's end.

"Carino, sabes que tu poppie no le gusta que hagas eso," Maria scolded from the kitchen. Sweetheart, you know your father does not like you to do that.

Sam ran into the kitchen, wrapped her arms around Maria's thick waist, and answered, *"Si, por lo que no vamos a decirle, ?no?"* Yes, so we aren't going to tell him, are we?

Maria hugged her back and laughed. "English, *Mi Hija*, English. You know I need to practice my English. And don't you go changing the tune."

"Subject, don't go changing the subject. Where's Big Jose?" Maria and Big Jose, as everyone but Maria referred to her husband – she always called him My Jose, as if that was his full given name – were as much a part of Hacienda de Luna as the horses and grasslands. They had lived there since long before Sam was born.

Before Maria could answer Sam snatched two pieces of bacon and a slice of toast from the old serving buffet. She carried the food and her journal to one end of the long, now-empty kitchen table. Munching on the toast, she glanced up at Maria with her pencil poised over a clean page of the open journal.

"You promised to tell me the story of how Pancho saved you and Big Jose," she reminded Maria. "I'm ready now."

"*Si, si, pero yo se` que usted ha oi`do que historia miles de veces,*"Maria answered. She rolled her eyes toward the ceiling for emphasis before placing a glass of cold milk on the table next to the impatient child.

"No I haven't heard it a thousand times," Sam answered in English, and she mocked Maria good-naturedly by rolling her own eyes upward, then laughing. "Besides, it will be good practice for you to tell me again, in English. I want to write it down this time."

"Okay, okay. You and your writings," Maria muttered as she moved to the sink and started washing the dishes. She began her story.

"30 years ago, when My Jose and I were married for a little more than a year and I was big *embarazadas* – I mean pregnant – with Little Jose, we decided to come to *Estados Unidos*, the United States. We wanted to have the baby here so he could be an American citizen. We wanted to make a good life for our child and things were so hard, so bad in Mexico. We loaded up our old truck with everything we owned and drove all night. We crossed the border just south of Naco. The moon was so bright, it made such a beautiful picture. It was a good omen, we told ourselves.

"That old truck was as burdened and full of our things as my stomach was with your father. I felt every bump in the road, and we just crossed the border when my pains began. I didn't tell My Jose right then. He was worried enough already about the border patrol, and finding a place to live and a job to provide for us. I clutched my rosary to my breast and prayed to the Blessed Mother to help us find shelter, a place where I could safely give birth to our child. Oh, *Mi Hija*, the pain became so bad, and with each bump it grew worse.

"I was barely 17 and my husband was 20. He was so tall, dark and handsome. He was skinny, but that did not matter. When he looked at me with those big beautiful eyes that were as black as coal my heart would just melt. It almost felt like it would stop beating altogether. And he had thick eyelashes that any woman would envy. Oh, but that is another story for another day, when you are older.

"After crossing the border we took the back roads, trying to get to my sister Lucy's house outside of Tucson before the sun came up. We did not want to be stopped by the border patrol. My pains were getting stronger and stronger. I knew we were lost out there in the middle of the desert when our truck just stopped. There was barely any light in the sky, so the air was still cool. But it was June and I had heard of people crossing in the desert in the summer, only to die under the Arizona sun. I was so frightened. I knew My Jose was also frightened, but of course he was a man. Men had to protect their women and pretend that everything was okay.

"When I tried to get down from the truck I could not move because the pain was too great. Then my water broke. 'Jose, our baby wants to be born,' I tried to tell him. 'He wants to come out into the world now.'

"My Jose just stared at me. 'Now, Maria? Can you not wait awhile yet? Please try to wait,' he begged me.

"I would have laughed if I could. However, your father, Little Jose, just did not want to wait any longer, and the contractions were becoming stronger.

"'Yes, Jose, now,' I managed to tell him through the pain. Although I was the fourth oldest of twelve siblings, and I knew what needed to be done because I watched my mother give birth many times, it was much different when I was the one who was having a child. Between each pain I would give instructions, hoping that together we would be able to do this.

"I asked him to bring the big blanket from the trunk in the back of the truck, and then help me down. In those days your grandfather "moved like the rabbit." He found the blanket and was back to open my door just as another pain started, and this one was so hard that I lost my breath. I grabbed his hand for strength…"

"She grabbed it so hard she almost broke all of my fingers," a voice interjected as Sam's grandfather walked into the kitchen. With a broad grin he scooped his loving wife into his arms and whirled her around before setting her down again. He was still handsome, still skinny, and also still 'moved like the rabbit.' At 50 years old, his dark hair was beginning to turn gray and made him look very distinguished.

"Jose, *tu me bajo, ahora mismo*," Maria scolded. You put me down right now.

Sam knew that Maria loved every minute of Big Jose's teasing. She knew too that they loved each other more now than they did 31 years ago when they married. It made her feel happy to watch them. However, she was anxious to get back to the story so she could finish writing it down. She did not want Maria to be distracted by her husband's teasing.

"Maria, what happened then?"

"Well, I was not so fat then, even though I was heavy with your father. So my strong husband just picked me up like I was a feather, and laid me down on the blanket," Maria started to continue.

Before she got any further, however, Big Jose grabbed her again and hugged her tightly. "But I like you better now, *mi amor*. There's more of you to love." He looked at Sam and winked.

Maria hit him playfully. "Why are you here, in my kitchen? Why are you not working?"

"Because I just needed a little kiss," he answered, still holding her in a tight embrace. Now he kissed her full on the lips.

"Oh, you. You go back to work," Maria laughed. She was blushing slightly as she said this, and backed out of his embrace to flap her apron at him. "Shoo. Sammy wants to hear the rest of my story."

"As if she has not heard it 200 times already," he said, grinning at his granddaughter. He ruffled Sam's curly sun bleached hair and kissed Maria once more, on the cheek this time, before starting for the door.

"I'll be back to see my favorite girls later," he promised, and blew them both a kiss before disappearing through the doorway.

Sam sighed. "Maria, when I grow up, I want to marry a man who loves me as much as Big Jose loves you."

"Yes, *Mi Hija*, do not settle for anything less. If a man does not love you above everything else, there will be trouble." Sam knew by the sad look on her face that Maria was thinking about Mama and Poppie. This was something she didn't want to think about right now. Instead, she wanted to see the smile on her grandmother's face again, and was eager to hear the rest of the story

"So what happened next, Maria? You were on the blanket by the truck, and…?"

"*Si, si…*"

"So there we were, the sun was just coming up, and I was praying to Our Blessed Mother. I knew that something was wrong; the baby was not coming like he should. I kept pushing, the need to do this was very strong, but nothing was happening. There was no baby trying to make his way into this world. My Jose was so scared.

"'What should I do, Maria? Tell me what to do to help you,' he was pleading with me.

"I was too weak to answer him, and I could not think of what to do. All I could do was pray. So I prayed and pushed. 'Oh, Mother,' I prayed, 'please, please help us. I do not want to die here in this strange place. I do not want to lose my baby or My Jose.'

"It was then that we heard the thunder of a horse's hooves, and we saw a great cloud of dust. A rider was racing toward us, like he was being chased by a runaway fire that was coming too close, or by a herd of stampeding cattle. As he came closer we could see that he was not being chased at all. It was as if he knew we were in trouble and he rode up and stopped in front of us. Then he jumped off his horse and knelt down beside me on the ground.

"The rising sun was behind his shoulders and head, surrounding his long brown hair, almost like a bright halo. His shirt was white with loose, flowing sleeves. I looked into his piercing blue eyes, and I remember thinking that the Blessed Mother had heard my prayers and sent her Son to help us.

"This man who came to our aid nodded to my frightened husband and spoke to me in perfect Spanish, although I thought that maybe he was a gringo. 'Everything is going to be okay,' he assured me. He then looked at My Jose and told him what he must do.

"'Sir, I need a clean blanket or cloth, even a shirt, anything, as long as it is clean. Also, get my canteen from my saddle, please.'

"This man spoke without hesitation and with authority in his voice so my husband did not question him, he just turned to do as he was asked. The man then turned to me again and his voice was gentle.

"'I am going to look to see what is happening. You must trust me, okay?' He waited for me to nod and then he lifted my dress; he only took one look before he said, 'Your baby is breech, turned the wrong way.' Then he glanced at My Jose who was back again and, still in his gentle voice he said, 'I will try to help the baby come out.'

"Nodding gratefully, my husband agreed. 'Do what is necessary, but please, do not let my Maria or our baby die.'

"'Maria, is it? That's a beautiful name.' he said, trying to calm me, I know. Then he rinsed his hands with some of the water from the canteen and put one hand on my stomach.

"'Now, Maria, I don't want you to push anymore, okay? I'm going to put my hand inside you and turn the baby so I can pull it out. It will hurt, but only for a short time. Soon your new baby will be lying in your arms.' Glancing once again at My Jose, he asked, 'Sir, what is your name?'

"'Jose.'

"'Okay, Jose, good. Now, when I pull the baby from the womb you need to be ready with the clean cloth and the water. Are you ready?'

"'I am ready.'

"The man put his hand inside me and I was thinking I would die from the pain. 'Maria,' he said to me very softly, 'stay with me. Relax as much as you can, that will make it easier. We're almost there.'

"I felt him pulling and I felt the baby leave my body suddenly. The pains were already beginning to lessen. The man handed our new baby to his father and I heard the most beautiful sound, it was like music in my ears. It was our baby's strong, and very loud, cries.

"'It is a son, Maria. We have a son. Thank you Mother, and thank you too, mister,' My Jose said. He was smiling down at Little Jose, who was cradled in his arms.

"Then he looked at this man who had saved me and our son.

"'How can we ever repay you? We don't even know your name,' he said, still smiling.

"The man also smiled, and his was like the brightest sun.

"'Pancho,' he answered. 'My friends call me Pancho. And I have a feeling we are going to be great friends.'"

CHAPTER 3 – *Pancho 1925 to 1932* – The Early Years

Francisco Luis Luna – Pancho to his family and friends – was 20 years old and had reached the towering height of 6'5". One would think that there was not a person alive who could intimidate him. Yet, when confronted by his tiny 4'9" mother, Carmen Teresa Gonzales Luna, he appeared to shrink in size. He would stand in front of her and not utter a word when being reprimanded by the shrew that was his mother. The manners he had been taught as a child kept him from walking away from her tirades; he just stood there until she was finished. He'd discovered long ago that the more passive he was the less time would be spent being subjected to her blustering criticisms.

Carmen was not a nice person. From his early childhood Pancho remembered her yelling: she yelled at him; she yelled at his father, Luis; she yelled at their servants; at their lawyers. To those who interacted with her on a daily basis it seemed she never stopped yelling. The only time there was any peace was when she was sleeping, or there was someone she wanted to impress within earshot. She was completely controlling, not above embarrassing people in order to make sure her demands were met. Since not one person had ever tried to defy her, least of all her family members, there was no reason to change.

Because his mother had always been this way, Pancho just spent his days working the family's vineyards and trying to stay out of her way. He did not try to improve on the wine-making business that brought in his family's fortune; his mother would never have listened to him anyway. He was, if not content, at least patient enough to suffer in silence. He promised himself that some day he would marry and move away from his mother's house, and then he would have all of the peace and quiet he wanted. He would be the master of his own household, answering to no one. Until that day he would continue to endure her tirades and her demands.

One memorable evening Carmen was hosting a dinner party to celebrate Three King's Day. Her guests included Mario Ortega, the owner of the Ortega Vineyards, the most famous wine-making operation in all of Spain, and his daughter, Yolanda. There were also other neighboring vintners and close friends present. The massive oak dining table accommodated twenty and each place was occupied. The food was plentiful, the wine flowed, and everyone appeared to be enjoying themselves. Various diners around the table were engaged in conversations with their immediate neighbors, other diners with those directly across the table.

When the table was cleared of empty dishes and glasses, and guests were enjoying an after-dinner liqueur or more wine, served along with strong, black coffee, Carmen stood up at her place at the head of the table. She smiled at her guests, raised a crystal wine goblet, and asked for silence.

"I have an announcement," she began when all heads were turned toward her. Her guests looked expectant, her son confused. He was unaware of any recent news that would require a formal announcement.

"I am proud to announce that my son, Francisco, is engaged to marry Yolanda Ortega. I am very pleased to be welcoming Yolanda into our family. Congratulations to the happy couple." With this, Carmen took a sip of her wine, set her goblet on the table, and began clapping. Her guests followed suit; Pancho did not.

Seated at the opposite end of the table, the alleged bridegroom-to-be stared at his mother. His expression clearly showed he was caught by surprise. Slowly he turned to look at Yolanda, seated halfway down the table on his right. *Did she know about this?* She had bowed her head and was staring down at her lap. He could see that a slight tinge of color had crept into her cheeks. Her father, seated at Carmen's left, had clearly known what was coming. He was beaming and clapping loudly.

Unable to find his voice for a moment, confused thoughts raced through Pancho's mind: *Marry Yolanda? Not even consulted?? Where had this come from?* He didn't love her, in fact he hardly knew her. His mother had never spoken to him of such a union. Slowly, anger began to boil from deep inside. The usually passive son became livid. This time his mother had gone too far. To announce his engagement to a virtual stranger, without even consulting him, was more than he would accept. She underestimated him if she thought he would calmly participate in an arranged marriage. She was in for a surprise.

As the applause ebbed, Pancho stood and held up his hands for silence. With his mouth a grim line, his eyes blazing, he shot his mother an angry glare before softening his gaze to look around at the sea of faces watching him. There was a moment during which the only sound was that of the fire crackling in the room's ornate fireplace. When he was able to bring his temper under control he smiled politely and addressed the guests seated around the table.

"I must apologize for my mother. She has been misinformed and spoke in error. Yolanda and I are not engaged to be married." Then, his voice gentle, he looked directly at the girl who had not raised her head. "Yolanda, I am truly sorry for any misunderstanding." Without another word he wadded his satin napkin into a ball and tossed it onto the table. Then, with a slight bow to all assembled he strode from the room with quiet dignity. Mouths agape, all heads turned to watch his exit.

The only noise to follow this pronouncement was a gasp from the other end of the table. As one, all heads now turned to Carmen, who was still standing but leaning on the table, as if for support. Without a word she picked up her wine and practically gulped the remainder of the contents before slamming it back down on the table. The stem broke, but she did not appear to notice. She had still not uttered a word. Her guests tried to remember a time that they had ever seen her speechless before. None could. No one noticed the color that had deepened on Yolanda's cheeks while she continued to stare at the hands that were clenched tightly in her lap.

Pancho had changed out of his evening attire and was throwing clothes into a suitcase when his mother stormed into his bedroom without knocking. She had never knocked before entering his room, and saw no reason to start now. She stood just inside the threshold, hands on her narrow hips, and fire spitting from her eyes. Her ramrod stiff posture and imperious voice made her appear much taller than she actually was.

"Just what in the hell do you think you are doing, Francisco? How could you embarrass me like that, in front of our guests? Of course, you are going to marry Yolanda. She is a lovely girl, and I have decided she would be the perfect wife for you."

Pancho stopped, turned slowly, and stared at his mother.

"And you saw no reason to consult me? I'm sorry, Mother, but I refuse to fall in with your plans this time. I am almost 21 years of age and I am no longer taking orders from you. In fact, I have decided to leave. I will be gone within the hour." He resumed packing.

It was obvious she expected him to accept her word as law as he always had. The amused expression on her face when he finished speaking told him just how ludicrous she thought his declaration was. He turned his back; he no longer cared what she thought.

"Are you crazy or just stupid?" she laughed. "If you leave here you leave with nothing. Do you hear me? Nothing! It's time you stopped this nonsense about leaving. I won't hear any more about it."

When he continued to pack his clothes without answering, her laugh turned to a sneer and she actually growled as she marched to the bed and sent the half-packed suitcase flying. Expensive, custom-made clothes were now strewn all over the polished tile floor.

"As you wish, Mother," Pancho replied quietly. He dropped the shirt he had been about to add to the suitcase on the floor instead, where it landed on top of the scattered clothes. He then walked over to his armoire, took out his wallet and put it in the inside pocket of the leather jacket he had donned when he changed from his black suit. Turning, he started to walk around her, toward the door, then stopped and looked at her sadly. His voice was still quiet when he said, "Have a good life, Mother."

Not believing that he would actually leave, Carmen grabbed at her son's arm but he wrenched it away and continued toward the door.

"Pancho, stop," she pleaded as she stumbled over his clothes while trying to follow him. She now looked her size, tiny and pathetic. Her voice had lost its commanding timbre and now became wheedling. She had found that sometimes that worked. "Please don't leave, I'm…"

He spun around, interrupting her. "Sorry? For what, Mother? Sorry that *you* have once again embarrassed *me* in front of my friends and colleagues? Sorry that you also embarrassed Yolanda? What dowry did her father promise you? A quarter ownership in the Ortega vineyard? A half, maybe? You are always sorry when it suits your purpose. Actually, I'm the one who is sorry, Mother. Sorry that it had to come to this. You have gone too far, and I will stay here no longer."

As he walked out the door and started down the staircase she ran after him, screaming, "Okay, leave. But don't come crawling back. You're just like your father, worthless. You are not welcome here again," she spat. In her fury she did not think about the guests downstairs that could hear everything.

Once again Pancho stopped. Slowly he turned, his hands fisted at his sides. "Call me anything you want, Mother. I don't care. But don't spew your ugly words to me about my father. Not ever again." He slowly walked toward her. "He was a kind and decent man who, God help him, loved you; although exactly why, I'll never know. And as far as being just like him," he now stood over his mother's shaking figure, "I'll take that as a great compliment."

His mother sank to the floor, her façade switching once again, to self-pity this time. Sometimes that worked when apologizing did not. "He left me too," she cried holding her head in her hands, waiting for her son's sympathy.

He had none. "He died, Mother. He died of a broken heart. And while he may not have died by your hand, you killed him just the same." His anger toward her could turn to hate if he was not careful. "You killed him a little every day, with your scorn and your demands, and with your lovers."

He retreated once again to the stairs. At the bottom he ignored the guests who by now were milling around near the landing. They clearly didn't know whether to leave or wait to bid their hostess a polite farewell. When Pancho noticed Yolanda crying in her father's arms he stopped. Laying a gentle hand on her shoulder, he spoke softly to her, "Yolanda, I'm sorry, truly sorry. I swear I knew nothing of this."

Carmen, leaping up, ran to the top of the grand staircase. Ignoring the audience below, she shouted after her departing son. "You'll be back," she spat at her only child. "You Luna men always come crawling back." The shrew was back.

Anyone who was not familiar with her strength, her determination to rule might think she was losing her sanity as she screamed down profanities in her frustration. Her guests, however, did know her well and thus simply waited for the opportune moment to make their exit. Inwardly, in spite of their expressions of polite disinterest, most of them were cheering for Pancho, happy someone stood up to Carmen at last.

Pancho dropped his hand from Yolanda and strode with purpose out the front door. He could no longer stand to be in the same house with his mother. He wanted to be out of the range of her voice, which was still screaming after him, now from the porch.

"Fine, leave me. I don't care," she screamed hysterically, her face beet red with anger. "Leave, I don't need you, you ungrateful bastard. I don't need anyone."

Upon reaching the stables Pancho saddled his horse and left. The only things he took with him were his rifle, his bed roll and a canteen of water. He did not look back.

After several hours of riding, Pancho reached the boundaries of his mother's property and reined in his horse. He looked long at the ornate *Las Viñas de Luna* insignia which announced the entrance to the Luna Vineyards. It sat proudly above a massive black wrought gate.

Pancho knew this would be the last time he would pass through that gate and he was both sad and excited. He dismounted and turned toward the land that he had worked since he was a child. He closed his eyes and inhaled deeply. He would miss the beauty of the land, but mostly he would miss the smells of the vineyard: the fresh scent of early morning dew on the grapes, the musty smell of the dark, rich fertile soil after a summer rain, the delicate fragrance of the grape blossoms in the spring, and the lush, pungent aroma of mashed grapes at harvest.

He opened his eyes and reached for his canteen. After quenching his thirst he remounted and walked his horse through the gateway. Once on the other side he spurred his horse to a gallop. As he moved further away from his mother's land, he felt as if a burden had been lifted from his shoulders. He was free, eager to be the man his father would have wanted him to be. *I'm sorry, Papa, that I could not be that man on the land you loved.* Thinking this brought a sad smile to his face.

He wondered, as he often had, what would cause a kind, gentle man like his father to marry a cold, unfeeling woman like his mother. Did they actually love each other at some time in the early years of their marriage? Was it a different woman who had made his father an offer he couldn't refuse, and then had married him? What had happened to change her into the shrew who would remind her husband almost daily that he owed her, that without her money he would be nothing?

Pancho knew that the beautiful countryside with the perfect soil for growing grapes had once belonged to his father. However, after a long drought, when all looked lost, his mother had appeared and had persuaded him to sell to her before it was too late. In the end it was Gonzales money that had saved the vineyard. Maybe it had been the love of the land that kept his father tied to the woman who did her best to emasculate him. The words that Pancho had heard many times in his life replayed in his mind, and he hated that he couldn't banish them from his memory.

"Without my money, Luis, where would you be?" He could hear her sneer at her husband. "My money saved the land that you would have lost," she would remind him with a smirk. "It bought new vines when yours were withered and dying from the drought and brought men to work them when your workers left because you couldn't pay them. My money paid to have the water brought in to make them thrive, and to restore the soil. It paid to bring the villa back to its rightful splendor. My money did all that, Luis, not yours. The only smart thing you did was to sell me the vineyard and the villa. Without me and my money you would have nothing now."

Invariably his father would simply smile and quietly reply, his voice respectful, "Yes, I know, my love. I am a lucky man to have such a generous wife."

It sickened Pancho even now to remember the verbal abuse and that his father did nothing to stem it. He had often wished his father would stand up to her, but he never did. Suddenly, he realized he had been doing the same thing, unconsciously, while his father was alive and even after he was gone; it was easier than arguing with her. Now she had gone too far and he was leaving this land he had worked and grown to love. But he no longer cared. He would make his life somewhere else. His father, buried in the family plot, had also loved the land, the vineyards, and the villa. He was at peace now and would never leave, and it was fitting.

Francisco Luis Luna left Spain at twenty years old to become a man, to start a new life, in a new land, in America.

During the next five years Pancho traveled throughout the United States. He was searching for just the right place to settle, to start a new Luna empire. He would know it when he saw it. One thing he knew from the beginning was that he would never grow grapes. Wine did not flow through his veins, as his mother loved to remind him when he was growing up. Perhaps cattle, he thought more than once during his search. *I will find the perfect land and I will raise and sell cattle.*

Although he had left home with only the clothes on his back and enough money for his passage to America in the wallet he had taken from his armoire, he was not penniless, contrary to his mother's threats. He had a trust fund from his grandfather Gonzales that he could draw from when he turned 21. One that, luckily, his mother could not touch. It was not as large as the Luna fortune that had grown steadily over the years under his mother's careful management, but it would be enough to buy a decent-sized property and give him a new start. He simply had to decide where.

He was well educated and knew the value of hard work and perseverance. Unlike his father, who had lost his fortune by overextending himself right before three years of severe drought, his grandfathers Luna and Gonzales had managed their fortunes well and carefully. By following their examples Pancho knew he could be successful. He vowed to be cautious, to always be prepared for the unexpected. He had money enough, if he was careful, from the sale of his horse before sailing to America, and from the odd jobs he performed during his travels to keep him from starving until he was old enough to access his trust fund.

On August 20, 1930, the search was over. Pancho stepped off the train in Patagonia, Arizona, and slowly turned in place to view the magnificent Santa Cruz Valley with its vibrant blue sky, its ochre-colored mountains, and its lush green landscape. The view from the train that had brought him here had consisted mostly of desert across Texas and New Mexico. Now, taking in the mountains, the trees, the beautiful sky, he knew he had found his new home.

He bought a horse, a bedroll, and enough supplies for a week, and then set out in search of the perfect property. On the second day of his quest he came upon the Johnson Ranch.

The Johnson Ranch had been in John Johnson's family for many years. When John died, however, he was a confirmed bachelor and he left no heirs. Situated in the piedmont of the Santa Rita Mountain range, the vast 750,000 acres had fallen into probate and was held by the state for back taxes. Instantly falling in love with its rolling grasslands and beautiful mountain views, Pancho bought the property without checking out the ranch house, barns, stables, and numerous out buildings. *So much for caution.*

When the listing agent protested that there were buildings to see, Pancho told him it was the land that was important. Buildings could be repaired, torn down, rebuilt, whatever was necessary. Without the perfect land, buildings did not matter.

"First things first," he assured the frustrated agent who wanted the young man to see all the ranch had to offer. "What I need are ranch hands, cattle, horses, and a good vet. Can you point me in the right direction?"

"As a matter of fact I can. If you don't mind checking out the vet first," the agent smiled, "I'll take you to meet my brother. He's the best animal doctor around these parts." So it was that Pancho met and hired Dr. Carl Bowman, who immediately asked to be called "just Doc."

The evening after the papers were signed that deeded the land to Francisco Luna, Doc rode along to see the buildings that his brother had been so anxious to show Pancho. The ranch house was called the Johnson House. As they rode west toward the main house the view was breathtaking. The sun was just starting to set behind the Santa Rita Mountain range that framed the magnificent two-story structure.

It was the beauty of the sunset that held Pancho in its grasp. He had never seen such an unusual blend of colors: blues, pinks and oranges all streaking horizontally across the sky behind the majestic mountains caused him to hold his breath. He would soon learn that Arizona had some of the most spectacular sunsets to be found anywhere. Doc, who was used to such glorious palettes of color, watched his new friend with amusement at the look of awe that was etched in the big man's face.

After drinking in his fill of color, Pancho lowered his eyes to the structure in the foreground of this scenic vision. The two-storied ranch house was made of tongue-and-groove wooden siding that had originally been painted a brilliant white. It now looked nearly gray from years of neglect, but that did not deter from the architecture and could readily be remedied. What caught his eye was the porch that wrapped around the front and both sides of the building. *The perfect place to sit and relax after a hard day's work*, he thought to himself.

The second story boasted a balcony that stretched across the front, where he assumed the bedrooms were located. The windows on the second story were flanked by faded red shutters. The metal roof that reflected the rays of the setting sun was the color of aged copper. The house was not on the grand scale of the *Villa de Luna*, in which he had spent his first twenty years, but that was unimportant. It had a grandness of its own, and could be made even more so if he wished. A new coat of paint, for starters, would go a long way to restoring its previous splendor.

He would change its name to *Hacienda de Luna* and this would be his home for the rest of his life.

During the two years after Pancho purchased his land, he'd turned it into a smooth-functioning operation. In addition to hiring Doc he had also hired several of the hardest-working cowboys in the area; he bought and bred a top-of-the-line herd of longhorns; he had almost completed the much-needed restoration on the magnificent old ranch house. He had been busy, and he was very pleased with the results.

Pancho loved his land. He often packed his saddlebags with the necessary provisions and stayed out on the range for days at a time. He referred to these trips as his 'rounds,' so-called because he would ride around his vast property inspecting fences for damage, making sure the ranch hands who lived in the far-reaching areas of the immense acreage were well provisioned, and checking on the welfare of his ever-increasing herd of longhorn cattle.

On a morning when he had been out on the range for five days he was looking forward to hot food, a hot shower and a soft bed. He was about a mile east of the hacienda when he spurred his horse to a run, his stomach screaming for a hearty breakfast. The last thing he expected to see, as he rounded a bend in the road about a quarter of a mile from his objective, was a dusty and overloaded faded red pickup truck that looked as if it had traveled many miles before breaking down. On closer inspection he noticed a very nervous-looking young man pacing back and forth beside an even younger-looking woman who was lying on a blanket on the ground. What caused him to urge his horse even faster was that she was in obvious pain. He guessed, from the worried look on the man's face, and from the size of the mound the woman was clutching with both hands, that she was in the final stages of childbirth.

Coming to a stop near the couple, he jumped from his horse to offer his help. Not wanting to show his uncertainty in a situation he had never before encountered, he did what his grandfathers had often advised him to do in all situations: "Take control no matter the situation. Always act as if you know what you are doing even when you know nothing. Never show fear, and people will always respect you."

Following this advice, Pancho knelt beside the woman. He ordered the young man to bring clean blankets and water. From the look of relief on the man's face Pancho felt he was probably relieved to have someone take over. The husband clearly had not known what to do, and was happy to let this stranger, who appeared to know what he was doing, take over. He couldn't know that Pancho had never delivered a human baby.

Pancho had helped Doc deliver breeched calves dozens of times, and after checking under the woman's dress he could tell that this baby was most certainly in a breech position. He did his best to reassure both mother and father that everything was going to be okay. He knew he would have to turn the baby before taking it from its mother's womb and that it would be painful for her. He explained the situation to the nervous young man and promised to try to help the baby into the world.

After washing his hands in the cool water he said a silent prayer, took a deep breath, and reached into the birth canal. He spoke to the woman, Maria, he had learned, and asked her to try to relax as he reached for the infant inside. He felt her cervix expand as he inserted his hands, and he wrapped them around the tiny form that he encountered.

He took another breath and slowly began to turn the baby as he had done with calves. While he worked he continued to speak softly to Maria, trying to help her relax as much as it was possible to do, with two big hands inside of her. Eventually he was successful, and he pulled the infant from the warmth of its mother's womb.

He cleared the mucus from the child's mouth and eyes and held up the newborn, a boy, for the new parents to see. As the father, Jose, reached for his son he laughed at the angry-sounding cries coming from this baby who had not needed to be spanked in order to draw his first breath.

After introducing himself to the couple and explaining that they were actually on his land, Pancho took the new family to the hacienda. The three adults felt comfortable with each other from the beginning, and after offering them a permanent place to live and work, the Lopez family became valued and loved members of the Luna family. Maria was the sister Pancho had always wanted, and Big Jose the little brother. And Little Jose, well, Little Jose would always be like a son…

CHAPTER 4 – *Sam 1979* – The Fog

As she tried to climb out of the fog that continued to surround her, Sam fought against a vague memory of terror and of agonizing physical pain. But she couldn't remember the basis for this memory. The physical pain was now gone, but there was something that still tugged at the edge of her mind. *What is it? Why can't I think clearly?*

In spite of the effort it took to open her eyes she managed to get them half opened, a little more than before. Her head still would not move so she looked around only as far as her eyes would allow. She was lying in a darkened room that felt familiar. She had been here before. As she directed her glance around the room she noticed a few moving shadows. *Were some of these shadows in uniform?* She wasn't sure, but she felt no alarm at their presence, not like they were there to harm her. She tried to turn to her side in order to have a better look, but she was so weak her body would not cooperate. Exhausted from the attempt, she gave up.

While she lay wondering what was happening to her, something just out of reach was trying to grab her memory in spite of the gray fog. She closed her eyes again, discovering that made it easier to concentrate. There was something about a baby. *Was it her baby?* The answer was so close, right there on the edge. She felt she could almost physically reach out and grab it.

I'm here dear one. Through her confusion she didn't realize that the voice was not audible, but in her mind. All she knew was that she was drawn to it and that it was gentle and soothing. It was so familiar and it was filled with love. She wanted to open her eyes to see who was speaking, but she felt instinctively she would see no one. Just as she knew the owner of the voice was someone precious to her. With this realization came an ache that was almost pain, the ache of missing someone who was lost to her.

Maman… my baby… something wrong… As quickly as they came the thoughts drifted away again without completing the picture she was mentally struggling to construct. She was so tired, she needed to rest. With her eyes still closed to the dark a picture barely formed in her mind she began to drift off once more.

Her last thought before giving in to the fog was of her grandmother. Her beloved Maman…

CHAPTER 5 – *Fina 1932 to 1955* – The Bad Dream

"Sammy, *ma chere*," Maman crooned softly, "wake up, wake up. You were having another bad dream."

Fina, Samantha's gentle French grandmother, knew from experience how to bring the child out of a nightmare. It had to be done carefully, so as not to frighten her any more than the dream already had. Even though she was calmed by the soothing voice, when at last Samantha opened her eyes, she was shaking, almost uncontrollably.

"Oh, Maman, it was horrible," she started to explain, with a trembling in her little four-year-old voice. "I was in a hospital and there was this mean old woman in the room, and I was in a lot of pain. I was having a baby, a beautiful girl. I couldn't wait to see her, to hold her. But then, after she was born, there was something wrong. It was something bad, Maman. They wouldn't let me see her or hold her. And they wouldn't tell me what was happening to my baby."

Fina wrapped her arms tightly around her granddaughter, trying to soothe her shivering body. She stroked Sam's forehead, pushing the sweat-drenched curls out of her eyes. "Hush, hush *mon petit papillon*, my little butterfly, it's over now. It's over, hush," she whispered as she rocked the tiny body gently back and forth. Her strong, tanned arms were calming the child now, as they always did whenever she was troubled.

While Sam was telling her grandmother about her nightmare someone else turned on the bedside lamp, keeping it low so that it would not hurt the little girl's eyes. Her father's parents, Maria and Big

Jose, were standing on the other side of the bed looking worried, and dressed in their nightclothes. So too, Sam now noticed, was Maman. Her screams – for she knew there were usually screams when she had a bad dream – must have woken everyone up. There was no sign of her screams having disturbed Mama or Poppie, however. One glance told her they had not rushed to her room as the others had.

She was not surprised at the absence of her parents at her bedside. She hadn't really expected to see them. It was always Maman, Maria and Big Jose who came rushing in to wake her and calm her down. Her parents were never there for her when the bad dreams came, or even any other time she may need them. With the instinct of the young, she knew they never would be.

The young girl's shivering was down to an occasional shudder. She snuggled closer to Maman, drawing on her warmth and familiarity. Maman always made her feel better after a nightmare.

"Stop thinking about the dream now, *ma chere*. That is all it was, just a bad dream, there was no baby," she said quietly, trying to convince her granddaughter there was nothing real about the dream.

Sam was not surprised that her grandmother knew what she had been thinking: that the dream had seemed so real; that she had felt such a strong desire to see and to hold her baby daughter. Yes, Maman had certain gifts, one of which was knowing what others were thinking. The girl would not accept that her dream was not real, however.

She looked up at the face that she loved. "But Maman, it *was* real, and my baby had something wrong with her. Can't you tell me what it was? You know everything. You can *see* things. Please tell me what was happening to my baby in the dream."

The wise woman inwardly released a sigh because she knew Samantha would not give up until she had answers to her questions. Her inquisitive mind was one of the things Fina treasured most about her precious granddaughter; she just wished that *now* was not one of times she wouldn't give up. She relented, knowing there was no other choice.

"The Veil, *ma chere*. She was born with a veil covering her face. There was nothing *wrong,* she was not hurt, it would just look strange to someone who had never seen one. She is a very special baby. But that is not something a little one like you needs to worry about right now.

You need to go back to sleep. Maman will lie down with you and hold you until you can sleep again."

As she gently pushed Sam to lie back, she looked up and her eyes met those of her friends. They exchanged concerned glances before Maria bent over the bed to kiss Sam's forehead.

"Your Maman is right, *Mi Hija*, do not worry about the dream. You will feel better in the morning." Then she patted Fina on the shoulder before turning to Big Jose. "Come, my husband, we should return to our bed. The rooster crows early and I need my sleep."

"*Si,* we both do." Big Jose reached for his wife's hand and gently drew it to his lips for a tender kiss on the backs of her fingers. He then released it and knelt to kiss Sam's still slightly damp forehead.

"I love you, *mi Niña*, and sweet dreams."

Then he too patted Maman's shoulder. "We love you too, Fina. Samantha is lucky to have you." Together the couple turned to leave the room, as Fina crawled under the blankets and hugged the child close to her. Already Sammy had fallen into an exhausted sleep.

"You will be alright, Fina?" Maria turned back to ask softly, concern in her voice for both her friend and the little girl.

"Yes, yes, you two go back to bed. The rooster does crow early and we all need our sleep." This was said quietly, in order not to wake the sleeping child. The two women smiled at each other before Maria and Jose, their arms around each other's waists, slowly made their way back to their bedroom.

Long after the others had gone to bed Fina lay awake next to Sam. She wasn't sure if she was more frightened for her granddaughter, or for the great-grandchild yet to be conceived. At last, as she was falling asleep herself, she whispered to her God, "*Le voile, c'est un don ou une malediction?*" The veil, is it a gift or a curse?

In the morning Sam seemed to have forgotten all about the nightmare she'd had just hours before. She was her happy, carefree self as she raced into the kitchen for her ritual breakfast with Maria. She was singing a French song as she entered the kitchen. It was one that Maman had taught her.

Maria didn't understand the words of the song, but she liked the happy-sounding tune. The fact that Sam was even singing at all was a good sign. Sometimes, after a bad dream, and last night's was *muy malo*, very bad, Samantha would be listless and docile for days. She couldn't be coaxed into eating, and would be afraid to fall asleep at night, afraid of terrors that would take her to strange, scary places located in some future time. She would talk about people she didn't know, and things she didn't understand.

Maria was thankful that today was not one of the bad mornings after. She silently prayed, *Thank you Blessed Mother, for protecting our precious little one. Give her bad dreams to me instead, por favor.* Then, satisfied that all was well, she lifted and kissed her mother's crucifix that hung on an old antique chain around her neck and tucked it inside her blouse to lie against her ample bosom. She forced a bright smile to her face before she turned from the sink to greet the cheerful child.

"Good morning, sweetheart, how is our little butterfly this beautiful morning?"

"Wonderful my dear, sweet Maria. *?y usted?*" came the answer as the little girl hugged Maria's leg and smiled up at her. "And you?"

Maria laughed. Sam had started talking in complete sentences before her first birthday. Now, at barely four years old, she often mimicked the adults around her.

"I am good my butterfly. What would you like for breakfast? Eggs and bacon?"

"Yes, thank you," Sam responded politely as she backed away. "But we need to hurry. Maman is going to show me some of her herbs that she uses for headaches, and I don't want to be late."

Then Sam raised her hand, placed the back of it to her forehead in a dramatic imitation of a near-swoon, and said in her practiced Southern drawl, "I do believe I feel one comin' on now, so perhaps I should retire to my room."

"Samantha Grace," Maria scolded, while trying not to smile, "it is not respectful to mock your poor mother." The doting grandmother turned her back in order to hide the smile that just wouldn't be kept at bay. Sam's imitation of her overly-dramatic mother was so perfect that Maria could have closed her eyes and sworn it was Etta in the room. She didn't think the child was aware of her mother's *real* illness, she was just repeating what she had heard her mother say many times.

"I'm sorry, Maria," Sam apologized. "Please don't be mad at me.

I was just teasing, honest." She hated it when anyone was angry with her.

"It is okay, my love, I forgive you. Eat your breakfast. Maman will be waiting for you in her gardens."

"Okay, but do you still love me?" She hugged Maria again, tightly.

"Of course, *Mi Hija*, now and forever." She said this as she hugged her granddaughter back, kissing the top of her head. "Now sit down and eat your breakfast before it gets cold."

Sam did as she was told, gobbling her breakfast before taking her dishes to the sink. She hugged Maria one last time on her way out of the kitchen, calling cheerfully from the doorway, "Love you, Maria, see you later my dear."

Maria laughed at Sam's use of grown-up language, then called after her, "Ask your Maman to try to do something with your hair *Mi Hija*. And I love you too."

Sam's long blonde hair, sun-streaked and curly, had a life of its own. Regardless of how the adults might try to tame it, to force it to conform to a manageable style, it would burst free of constraints to produce a riot of wild curls around Sam's pretty face and trailing down her back. Thinking shorter was better, her fast-growing hair was cut when she was two. The result resembled a clown's curly wig, pointing in all directions at once. Grown out now, it was still a daily battle trying to tame it.

The young girl ran happily to Maman's gardens, kicking up dirt and singing as loud as she could on her way. Nearly out of breath when she arrived, she spotted the familiar wide-brimmed gardening hat just past the rose bushes. She was happy to see that her grandmother had not yet reached the herb garden. She came to a stop in front of the older woman and gave a small curtsy and a big smile before greeting her beloved Maman.

"I am here, *Madame*, at your service."

Fina was on her knees, pulling at the stubborn weeds that plagued all of her gardens. She turned to Sam with a smile, not letting her concern about how Samantha would be after last night's nightmare show on her face.

"Good day to you, *Mademoiselle.* How are you this lovely morning?"

"Wonderful, thank you. I am ready to help you in the herb garden now." There was a gleam of anticipation in the girl's dark green eyes. Her most favorite thing in the world was helping Maman with the gardens.

If Sam's unmanageable hair was a curse of her short existence, her eyes were a blessing. They reflected her moods, whether happy or sad, and were the windows to her pure soul and kind heart. Depending on what she was wearing, on her mood or even on the weather, her eyes could change from a dark, emerald green to a dusky brown, or even to a crystal clear blue. Fringed with silky black lashes, her round eyes were the perfect complement to her slightly upturned and freckled nose and her tiny bow-shaped lips. Hers was the face of an angel on a child of four, but would be the face of a goddess at maturity.

Today those eyes carried the sparkle of innocence and excitement. There was not a hint of the upset of the previous night. Relieved, Fina relaxed and pulled the girl to her for a big hug. Her face was buried in a mane of curls that smelled of sunshine and sweet little girl. The lingering aroma of strawberry shampoo, from a formula that Fina herself had concocted, also filled her senses. Pulling back she took in the wild halo of curls that decorated the angelic face.

"Oh, the beast is wild today, no?" she said of her granddaughter's unruly head of hair.

"Yes, I know, but just this once can we let it be free?" Sam pleaded with her grandmother as she hugged her back. When she pulled back to gaze at Maman, she unconsciously slipped into an imitation of her mother's southern drawl, forgetting Maria's earlier admonition to be kind. Tossing the long locks with a shake of her head to emphasize her request she added, "It so hates to be caged."

Laughing at her precocious one, Fina did not scold. Instead, she acquiesced, "Well, okay, just this once. Now help me with these pesky weeds, and try to keep your wild mane from getting in your way. When we're finished here then we will go to the herb garden."

Each of them was lost in thought as they worked side-by-side for the better part of an hour. Then Fina stood and brushed her gloved hands against her dirty white overalls while she surveyed their efforts. At last she announced, "Good enough. We can move to the herb garden, but first I must have a cool drink. I get so parched working in the morning sun."

Hand-in-hand, they turned and walked toward the nearby beige building that was called the Garden Room. Colorful and welcoming, it offered a haven from which one could choose a garden view to enjoy from the four-sided wrap-around porch: the rose garden, the vegetable garden, the butterfly garden or the herb garden. Each view was soothing and was often accompanied by a cool Santa Rita mountain breeze, even on the warmest summer day.

After washing up at the sink inside the woman and the girl each selected a root beer from the refrigerated cooler, and then chose to relax in the brightly-painted rocking chairs facing the butterfly view. It was with peace and contentment as she rocked back and forth that Fina relived bittersweet memories of the day she first saw this beloved building, 23 years earlier.

Francisco "Pancho" Luna, the man Josephina Grace Marionneaux had recently married, was anxious to show his new bride the present he had built just for her. She had arrived at the hacienda that day and after dining with Maria in the kitchen they went to the master bedroom where her bags had yet to be unpacked.

"Put your walking boots on Darling," Pancho had ordered, eager to show his bride the rest of the ranch that was now her new home. As he said this he grabbed her around her tiny waist and lifted her off the floor in a gentle bear hug.

"I've got something to show you, it's sitting out back on another part of the ranch."

Fina laughed and kissed the top of her husband's long, shaggy light brown hair as he held her high in the air.

"There's more? I can't believe there is more to see than all this. The house is so huge, I'm afraid to leave this bedroom or I will need breadcrumbs for a trail so I can find my way back." She laughed once more and chided, "But before I can see more, you will have to put me down."

Pancho laughed and lowered his bride to the floor. "OK, Darling, you win. But hurry so I can show you what I built for you. It was built with all the love in my heart. I hope you like it, because it will probably last far longer than the 50 or 60 years I plan to be married to you."

Fina had stiffened imperceptibly at Pancho's words. She could never tell him what her psychic abilities let her see: they would have less than twenty years together. She had learned long ago not to question fate, but to live life to the fullest every minute. She lived, not in fear of the unknown, or even of the known, but in love. And her deep and abiding love for her beloved Pancho overshadowed any doubts about the wisdom of marrying him, knowing their life together would be cut short. Putting this knowledge out of her mind, she gave him her brightest smile, her bright green emerald eyes shining with love.

Pancho had felt the brief stiffness before she relaxed, however, and was concerned. "Fina, are you cold? You seemed to shiver there for a second."

Still smiling, she answered huskily, her voice heavy with a sadness that she knew Pancho would mistake for desire, "No, I'm fine. In fact, are you sure you want to show me the surprise now? Can't it wait awhile?" She had a sudden need to hold him.

"No, my love. As much as I want to make love to you again and again, I'm afraid if we start that we will not leave this room until morning. It won't take long and then we can come right back. Now, find your walking boots and we'll go."

He patted her perfectly-shaped bottom as she turned to find her boots. Sighing with happiness and with lust, he watched her search through her suitcases that had been deposited on the bedroom floor. Oh, how he loved this beautiful and mysterious woman.

Soon, boots were found and donned and they clasped hands as they walked out of their room. Fina admired the great room that they walked through to reach the front porch of the old ranch house. Then her breath caught at the sight of the late afternoon sun, its brightness diffused with streaks of dark and light pink threading through fluffy clouds as it started its descent. With the peaks of the Santa Rita Mountains outlined against the colorful sky she thought she had never seen anything as beautiful. God had painted the perfect landscape.

It would start to become dark soon so they didn't linger to appreciate the splendor before them. Hand-in-hand they stepped off the porch and headed down the path that would take them to Pancho's surprise.

After a moment Fina glanced sideways at her husband. "Do you know the thing I love most in this world, next to you, that is?"

Pancho pretended to be deep in thought, rubbing his chin with his free hand. "Maria's cooking?"

They had feasted earlier on one of Maria's 'simple' dinners, and Fina had made a friend for life when she paid her a sincere compliment with the comment, "Your Mexican food is more delicious than anything I have ever eaten." On their way back to their bedroom after they had eaten their share of the spicy meal, she had whispered to her husband, "And I thought Cajun food was hot. My mouth is still burning. But it was soooo good."

Now, she laughed at him, "Well maybe Maria's cooking is a very close third, but second, next to you, is the vast expanse of sky here. Not just the gorgeous sunsets like this one, but any time of the day. Whether it is cloudy, clear, sunrise, high noon, or sunset, you have to believe there is something bigger than us out there. Something divine, holy, mystical even. I hardly ever looked at the sky in Baton Rouge. It was so often rainy or dark and cloudy, and you could not see for miles as you can here in Arizona."

"While I agree with you, there is something that is even more beautiful to me, *mi amor*. Something that is more brilliant than the sunsets and more mysterious than the expanse of Arizona skies. What I find the most beautiful in all the world is the love in your eyes when you look at me. It was worth the wait now that I have found you when I see my love for you reflected back at me." Pancho stopped their walking long enough to bend down and kiss her lightly on her pale pink lips.

"Why, Francisco Luis Luna, I do declare, that's almost poetic," Josephina Luna responded to her husband as she pretended to swoon.

It was then that he turned her around for her first glimpse of what he called the Garden Room. Beige in color, with Peacock-blue shutters on the many windows and gaily-colored rocking chairs just begging to give comfort, it was a building that she knew instantly would bring her pleasure for many years to come.

"Maman, Maman," Samantha repeated. She was standing in front of her grandmother's rocking chair and tugging at her hand. Still getting no response, she reached up and lightly rapped on the woman's forehead. "Knock, knock. Is anybody in there? Come back."

Brought back to the present, Maman apologized, "I am sorry, my pet, but sometimes a woman can get lost in her past. I didn't mean to ignore you."

Finally having her grandmother's attention, Sam placed her hands on her narrow hips as she'd seen Maria do countless times when she was about to give a lecture over some minor offense that had been committed. She then heaved a sigh as if the weight of the world was on her tiny shoulders. Satisfied that she had conveyed her frustration, she lifted a hand to shake an index finger at Maman. This was another of Maria's many habits, and Sam used it to scold the older woman, almost as if she were an equal.

Not only was the child mimicking Maria's stance, she was quoting, almost verbatim, a conversation that Maria and Fina had had more than three years ago. "Pancho would not, I repeat, NOT want you to be alone for the rest of your life. You need to pick a new husband from the pack of men that follow you around the ranch like bees follow the honey." Finishing her scolding, Sam's hands moved back to her hips once more.

"Samantha, darlin', where did you hear that?" Surprise and amusement at the admonishment coming from the small child had Fina's southern drawl creeping into her voice.

Shrugging her shoulders at her grandmother's question, Sam answered, "Oh, I don't know, Maman. I think I dreamt it once. Anyway, I know you were thinking of Papa Pancho and you always look sad when you think about him. Today is not a day to be sad. Besides, I want to ask you something."

With this said Sam sat down once more on the red rocking chair facing the butterfly garden and picked up the root beer she had laid on the yellow side table. She took a deep drink and started to rock gently, her forehead furrowed as she thought about the question she wanted to ask.

"Sure, my own little butterfly, what is it? You look so serious."

"How come I don't have the 'gift'?" Sam stopped rocking and turned to look at her grandmother.

"And why do you think you don't have it?" Maman answered the question with one of her own.

"Well, I guess mostly because I have never healed anyone like you do, and I don't always know what people are thinking. Some of the time I do, but not very often."

Fina closed her eyes and rocked quietly without saying anything for several minutes.

"Maman, are you in the past again?" Sam whispered.

"No, my child, I'm just thinking about the best way to answer your question. Actually, everyone does have the gift. It's just that, well, they don't always know that they have it, or if they do know, they don't know how to develop it properly. You see, it's all in the knowing."

She paused and thought some more before she continued. "Sometimes people know and use their gift from the time they are born. Or sometimes they learn to use it later, when they are older. Sadly, most people never learn how to use it. The gift can be different with each person. Like you said, some people heal, some people hear things, and some people see things in their dre…."

Sam interrupted, perhaps afraid to hear the rest, "What about you, Maman?" Rocking again, she asked, "When did you know?"

"Me? I knew even before I was born. I have always known."

Now Sam was the one who closed her eyes and rocked.

"*Ma chere,*" Maman said after a few minutes, her rocker keeping pace with the little girl's rhythm, and her hand gently patting Samantha's as she spoke, "it is okay to be afraid. Most of the time the gift is a good thing and you can use it to help many people. But I will be honest and tell you this because I know you are old enough to understand: sometimes you will see and feel things you would rather not know."

"Like my dreams, Maman?" Sam whispered so softly that Fina had to bend closer to hear, "and like my baby?" She had stopped her rocking chair again, but kept her eyes closed.

"Yes, my pet, like your dreams, and like your baby." Fina said, stopping her own rocker. She then scooped her precious granddaughter onto her own lap, holding her close while they rocked as one, each with her own thoughts. No further words were needed.

CHAPTER 6 – *Fina 1915 to 1923* – The Rubies

Fina – born Josephina Grace Marionneaux on April 1, 1915 – was named for her great grandmother, and like that ancestor, she was gifted.

As far back as the family tree had been traced the 'gift' had been passed from one generation of Marionneaux women to the next. The women on this tree only had daughters, and once in each generation a *chosen* one was born. The chosen daughter was always left-handed and had both the *sight* and the ability to heal. If this child was also born with a veil – or, as it was called in medieval times, a *caul* – which was a thin filmy membrane, usually a remnant of the amniotic sac that covered a baby's face at birth, the family knew the caulbearer would be an extremely gifted and a powerful psychic, seer and healer. Fina was born with a veil.

Both Fina's mother and her grandmother were chosen daughters, and this was rare for three direct descendants. They were both named Rubie Grace Marionneaux and were known as 'the Ladies' or 'the Miss Rubies.' Individually Fina's mother was called Young Miss Rubie and her grandmother Old Miss Rubie.

Most Marionneaux women did not marry; those who did retained the Marionneaux name. While the husbands were shown on the family tree they rarely had longevity and did not play prominent roles in the families. Marriage was not considered necessary and all illegitimate offspring were shown sprouting from the mother only. Fina and her two older sisters, Monique and Helena, never knew their father. They did not deem it necessary to ask questions and their mother never volunteered any information about him. He did not appear on the Marionneaux family tree.

The Miss Rubies were well-known for their special gifts. Their fame extended to all borders of the state of Louisiana and beyond, and people would travel many miles for one of their readings or their healing treatments. These the women performed in their home without charge. Though they never requested compensation, offers of repayment other than monetary were never refused: a cow, a sack of potatoes, material for a new dress, a room painted or a garden weeded. If the locals wondered how the Marionneaux women survived without any visible means of support their questions were never voiced and their curiosity went unsatisfied. If asked, the women would have replied, "God provides a way where there is none." And so it seemed that God did indeed provide. The Marionneaux women somehow always had food on their table, clothes on their backs and the taxes were always paid on time on the ancestral home located on the outskirts of Baton Rouge.

Viewed from the outside, the white rambling old plantation house boasted a wrap-around porch and was graced with massive carved pillars. Several floor-to-ceiling windows filled the width of the home.

Inside, to the left of the enormous entry hall, was a large parlor used for healings. The room was anchored by a dark parquet wood floor and kept dimly lit by the use of heavy deep purple velvet drapes at the windows and lamps covered with scarves. It remained at a comfortable temperature, even on the hottest and muggiest days, accomplished by the lack of sunlight and the slow-moving ceiling fans that ran continuously. The healers found that the quiet, calm atmosphere helped their *visitors* to feel relaxed and comfortable before a healing session.

In the middle of the room was a narrow cushioned table and beneath it had been placed several crystal bowls. These were filled with sea salt that had been blessed. Herbs and potions were located nearby in case a visitor needed a *bridge* before the healing took hold. Inconspicuous incense burned throughout the room, giving it a faint earthy smell.

A visitor was never rushed once they entered the healing room. The Miss Rubies performed basically the same ritual regardless of the physical or mental problem that they were asked to heal. Fina was expected to watch from the background and learn, for unlike her sisters she didn't attend public school. Her mother and grandmother were her teachers. They taught her how to read, write, and do math, but more importantly they taught her how to perfect the gifts she possessed and that her sisters did not.

Following entrance into the room the *patient* – for that was what visitors considered themselves to be – was hugged by both women, and then shown to a grouping of well-worn leather chairs in front of a large stone fireplace. With one healer seated on each side, the two women asked questions such as: "What bought you here today?" for a first time visitor, or perhaps "How has your back been since your last session?" for a returning one. It was not unusual for one of them to say, "Tell us about your dreams."

After the questions were asked and answered, the healers and the patient stood and held hands to form a circle. They recited the Lord's Prayer, and then asked Jesus to protect them with His white light as they performed the healing and invoked the Holy Spirit:

"Come Holy Spirit. Fill the hearts of Your faithful. Kindle in them the fire of Your love. Send forth Your spirit and they shall be created, and You shall renew the face of the Earth."

Prayers said, the patient was led to the cushioned table, requested to lay face down, and covered with a light blanket. One woman performed the healing while the other prayed. The women alternated roles from patient to patient, as the healing could be draining. The praying woman stood at the front of the table with her hands gently placed on each side of the patient's head. The healer held her hand at the back of the neck, about an inch above the prone body. Then, as if in a trance, the healer moved her hand slowly over the body.

The ladies believed in the ancient Law of Cure – a law that governs how physical symptoms leave the body – whereby people were cured from the inside out and from the top down. They believed energy centers or 'chakras' were the key to physical health, mental and emotional stability, and spiritual clarity. When a chakra was out of balance the healer felt either a tingling or burning sensation in her hand as she held it over the patient. The healer balanced the chakra by gently massaging the area until it *felt* aligned. They also knew that they weren't the ones doing the healing but that they were being used by the Holy Spirit. They explained this to their patients by saying, "We are the piano; the Holy Spirit is the music."

It was not unusual for a visitor to cry or to laugh after a healing, as the healing process released blocked energy. It was explained that feeling emotional was a sign the healing had started. The ladies always cautioned their patients to get plenty of rest after a healing, explaining that the body needed to regenerate itself.

Fina watched the procedure on a daily basis from the time she was four years old, and by the time she was six her mother and grandmother pronounced her ready. She then began performing healing right along with the Miss Rubies.

To the right of the great entrance hall was a second parlor, similar to but smaller in size and less elaborate in furnishings than the healing parlor. This was used for readings. While the Miss Rubies preferred to perform a healing rather than a reading, they realized that sometimes they had to tune into a visitor on a more emotional level. Fina was expected to attend the sessions in this parlor as well. However, since she had been able to *read* what people were thinking for as long as she could remember, she was usually bored. She found that most of the questions visitors asked during a reading concerned personal relationships rather than spiritual ones.

Once, after several months of readings, Fina's mother decided to educate her daughter on a method to relieve her boredom. She advised her to concentrate not on the person receiving the reading but on the other person in the relationship.

"But how can I read someone who isn't here?" Fina had asked, her interest piqued.

Her mother smiled, knowing she had her daughter's attention, and replied, "Because when someone is in a relationship with another, each partner's energy stays with the other."

This sounded simple enough, so Fina concentrated on perfecting her ability in this area. Sometimes she would get an impression so strong that she would have to interrupt the reading to ask a question or to give an insight. Her elders always welcomed her comments and visitors rarely objected, so soon the little girl, in addition to performing healings, graduated to giving readings on her own. Visitors were usually surprised with the child's accuracy of the reading and often requested her on a subsequent visit.

The gifted child was also able to *see* a visitor's future as well as their past. Her more experienced teachers, however, warned her never to tell a visitor about the future.

"It is okay to look at their past lives to see if they need to rectify a misdeed," they explained, "but never tell anyone what waits for them in the future. It is not your place to decide that they should know. Their future is just that – theirs. By telling them something that has not yet come to pass you could cause them to change the path they are on if they don't like what they hear from you, and that is not always a good thing. There may be karmic reasons to leave their future unchanged."

The ladies also warned Fina that her gift was precious and not to be misused.

"Never discuss what you see with anyone, even the person you're reading unless you have their permission. Sometimes, and you will know when, people don't really want to face their issues even though they have asked you to tell them."

So Fina watched, listened and learned. With each passing session, as her gifts became stronger and more acute, she soon realized that it wasn't always a gift to know someone's past or future. She learned this lesson in the cruelest way.

Fina loved both of her sisters but she particularly adored Monique, a kind, gentle soul who was childishly happy and carefree. She was always ready with offers of help, whether for humans or animals. She was forever bringing home strays: dogs, cats, birds, even people. The Miss Rubies would indulge her and fix what needed to be fixed. Half of the time the old plantation house's many rooms and outbuildings were filled with Monique's finds.

When Fina was eight and Monique was eleven she *saw* that her sister was going to drown before she turned twelve. Frightened by what she saw, she ran crying to her mother, pleading with her to save her favorite sister.

"Oh Mother, you must do something to stop it. I don't want Monique to die."

Young Miss Rubie hugged the child tightly and said, "Let's go find your grandmother. It is time that we had a long talk."

Fina struggled to free herself. "But, Mother, what about Monique? You have to do something." Then, devastated, she dropped to the floor where she stood, overcome with grief. Her mother sat on the floor beside her, once again wrapping the distraught child in her arms.

Soon Old Miss Rubie, hearing the anguished sobs, appeared and knelt down by her daughter and granddaughter. She knew without asking what had happened.

"Hush, hush, sweetheart, let us explain something to you. Come with us."

The two women stood and Fina's mother pulled her gently but firmly to her feet, then ushered her into the healing parlor. With the troubled child in the middle, the three of them sat on the wine-colored brocade settee located just inside the door. The women each put an arm around Fina.

"I know this is hard to understand," the younger Rubie began, "but we can't do anything to prevent Monique's drowning. She herself has chosen to leave this life before her twelfth birthday."

"But why would she do that? I don't understand."

Her grandmother stroked her hair. "Each of us, before we go through the process of rebirth, put together a plan for our new life. We determine what lessons we want to learn, the things we want to experience, deeds we want to rectify, karmic debts to be paid. Sometimes, as in the case of an old soul, past sins have been atoned for so the need to reincarnate is no longer necessary. If a last life is desired, it does not mean it is a hard life or that it will be a long life. In Monique's case, she is indeed a very old soul, and has no need to experience further incarnations. She knew when she chose this life that it was to be her last. She is ready to take the next step in the evolution of her soul, which is to help others from the spiritual realm. Eventually, her soul will reach the ultimate destination: sitting beside the hand of God."

"But I don't want her to die. It isn't fair," Fina sobbed into her mother's chest. "Don't you love her? Why won't you help her?"

"Of course we love her," Fina's mother also wept, for both of her daughters, "but we must not ever try to change the future even when it means we will lose a loved one. We have told you often that the future must not be changed. I know it is hard to accept, especially when it is someone you love, but actually, that is the kindest thing we can do for them."

"And," her grandmother interjected, "we also know that just because we lose someone in this life that doesn't mean we have lost them forever. We will see them again and again, in life after life. In Monique's case, her soul will be able to help us, and when we pass over our soul will know hers."

The eight-year-old Fina wasn't sure she understood everything the women were trying to tell her, but from that day forward she treasured each second, each minute, and each hour of every day...

Chapter 7 – *Fina 1932* – The Stranger

Fina was barely 17 and was on her way to San Francisco to perform a healing for a wealthy woman's grandchild. It was the first time that she had been more that 50 miles from her home in Baton Rouge. The Rubies had sent her sister, Helena, along with her, not because they thought women shouldn't travel unaccompanied but because they thought it would be good for the two young women to have time alone together. The sisters had never been very close; yet they had both been close to Monique, who had drowned on the day before her twelfth birthday, just as Fina had foreseen. After Monique's death, the two remaining sisters did not turn to each other for solace; they each coped in their own way with their grief at the loss of their beloved sister.

Even with the passage of time, as their grief lessened, the sisters did not grow close. They had little in common: Helena's life was about school, teachers, and classmates; Fina's revolved around healings, readings, and visitors. Helena was exceptionally bright and had received a full scholarship to a private boarding school in Baton Rouge. The Marionneaux home was on the opposite side of Baton Rouge, however, so she'd stayed at the school during the week and was only home on weekends, holidays, and summer vacations. She had graduated with honors and was now working at a prestigious law firm in Baton Rouge.

When Miss Ellie, an old family friend, had written that her youngest granddaughter was deathly ill, the Rubies decided they would send Fina to San Francisco; she was as proficient in healing as the Rubies themselves and may be able to help the girl. With the wisdom of age, and a little help from their psychic abilities, it was decided that Helena would accompany her sister. Helena was elated, as she had never traveled outside of Louisiana; Fina was elated because she knew she was destined to meet the man she was to marry – she had been dreaming of him since Monique's death.

As the train departed from Baton Rouge their mother and grandmother waved enthusiastically, blowing kisses and shouting "Don't forget to's" to the young women who waved back from the caboose's platform. Fina and Helena remained on the platform long after the Rubies were out of sight. They reluctantly took their seats only when the conductor beckoned them inside. Taking turns sitting by the window, both young women were fascinated by the world that was whizzing by. And to their mutual surprise, they talked and talked and talked.

Helena, at 21, was a dark-haired beauty with long straight hair. She was petite, had a lovely figure that boasted a small waist, and a wonderfully infectious laugh. Her sky-blue eyes sparkled when she laughed, which was often. Fina was amazed to realize as she listened to her beautiful sister talking about this lawyer or that case that she knew very little about Helena's life. She reached over and lightly touched her older sister's hand and closed her eyes. She was happy to see that her sister was destined to have a satisfying and fulfilling life. Fina didn't share her insights, but it was nice to know that Helena was going to be happy.

Fina's musing was interrupted when she heard, "I've been accepted at the University of Louisiana and Mr. Wilson, my boss, has promised me that once I obtain my law degree I'll have a place in his firm. I'll be the first woman lawyer to ever work there."

Yes, you will, Fina thought to herself, *and you will be the first woman judge in Louisiana.*

Helena continued, "Okay enough about me, tell me about you."

"Well," Fina began, still touching her sister's hand, "unlike most Marionneaux women, I'm going to marry."

Helena squealed with surprise and turned her hand over to grab Fina's. "Who? Who? One of your visitors? I didn't know you were seeing anyone. Do the Rubies know? How long have you known him? Quick, tell me everything."

Fina smiled at her curious sister and answered coyly, "Well, I haven't exactly met him yet," enjoying the confused look on her sister's face, "but I will soon. In fact, I'm going to meet him on this trip, on this very train."

"Okay, you'd better tell me what's going on," Helena demanded, "I know you see things before they happen. What is it that you've seen?"

Fina hesitated. She didn't know his name; she didn't even know exactly what he looked like. She knew he was tall, over 6 feet, and slender. She knew that he always wore white shirts and a custom-made cowboy hat. She knew they would meet on this train and fall madly in love. But beyond that, she didn't see anything else. As she related this information the two sisters became increasingly excited at the prospect of meeting Fina's husband-to-be.

"But if that is all you can see, how will you know it's him? I mean there must be hundreds of men over 6 feet tall, who wear white shirts and cowboy hats," Helena exclaimed. "We are, after all, in cowboy country."

"I can't explain it," Fina sighed, her green eyes sparkling with excitement, "but I know that I'll *feel* it when I see him."

"But what if you're mistaken?" Helena wasn't convinced. "What if you pick the wrong man and then spend the rest of your life with him while your Mr. Right marries someone else?"

Fina just smiled at her sister. The older girl had been sheltered from miracles of the gift, while the Rubies and Fina saw them everyday. Helena had often said she thought the healings and readings weren't really life-changing; they were just something that the Rubies and Fina did. The family didn't sit around the dinner table discussing things like "Isn't it great that Mr. George is walking again?" or "Miss Claire is going to have twins." No, now that she thought about it, Fina wasn't surprised that her sister didn't believe her. She'd just have to wait and see for herself.

"Don't worry, Helena," Fina squeezed her sister's hand, "trust me, I'll know him."

After hours of conversation the sisters were exhausted but happy with their new-found friendship. They fell silent, shoulder to shoulder with their heads leaning back against the train's cushioned seat, as the train gently rocked them to sleep.

The women were startled out of their sleep when the train came to a noisy stop, the brakes screeching on the metal tracks. Fina straightened and looked around her, momentarily disoriented. The train must have arrived at one of its boarding stops. Checking her watch, her first, that was a gift on her 17th birthday, she calculated that they must have reached Houston, Texas.

"Where are we?" Helena yawned, stretching her slender arms and then straightening her dress.

"I think we're in…" Fina stopped and stared. There he was, covered in dust, holding a hat in one hand and running the other through his shoulder-length brown hair, a habit she would grow to love, and would see him do a thousand or more times whenever he entered a room and removed his custom-made dove-gray Stetson.

He was taller than she had envisioned, maybe 6'5 or 6'6". He was wearing a long-sleeved white shirt, its sleeves rolled up to the middle of muscular forearms. His Levis hugged his body in all the right places and came to rest on scuffed but expensive looking black boots. Although she had imagined him many, many times in her dreams, she was unprepared for his beauty *in the flesh.* Unable to speak, she merely nodded when Helena grabbed her hand and whispered loudly, "It's him, isn't it?"

At the sound of Helena's whisper, the object of their attention stopped. He let his eyes adjust to the dimness inside the train car after the glaring Houston sunlight, and stared at Fina for the first time. He barely stopped himself from gasping at the sight that his piercing blue eyes beheld. As if in a trance, unable to move or speak, he blocked the aisle while he drank his fill of Fina's beauty. The spell was broken only when another passenger who was trying to get past him tapped his shoulder.

He found his voice, bowed slightly and said, "Ladies," and moved slowly past their seats, reluctantly dragging his eyes from Fina's face.

"Fina," Helena squeezed her sister's hand again, "tell me that's him."

"Oh that's him alright," Fina said softly, dizzy from the encounter, "that's him." It was all she could do to keep herself from bolting from the seat and throwing herself into his arms. She trembled from head to toe.

"Are you okay?"

"I'm not sure," Fina responded, shaken and breathless, "just give me a minute."

Closing her eyes, she leaned back against the seat, trying to catch her breath, calm her heart. Her whole body tingled and she still felt light-headed. She wasn't sure how long she remained plastered against the seat, eyes closed tightly before she felt the train move, heard its whistle blow.

Slowly she opened her eyes, and there he was again, standing over her, looking at her with those beautiful blues eyes.

"I'm so sorry to bother you ladies," he said smoothly, "and please excuse me for being so forward, but may I sit here?" He pointed at the empty seat that was facing theirs.

Fina loved the sound of his accent, Spanish, she thought, but she was unable to answer him. Noticing this, Helena answered for both of them.

"Of course, please do sit down."

After he had taken the offered seat he extended his arm, taking Fina's hand and bringing it to his lips.

"Let me introduce myself. I am Francisco Luis Luna. And you are?" He looked only at Fina as if she, not Helena, had responded to his request.

"I am Helena Grace Marionneaux and this is my sister, Josephina Grace Marionneaux," Helena offered, looking from the stranger to her sister. She noticed their eyes had remained fixed on each other, and Fina still had not responded to his inquiry.

"Josephina, such a beautiful name, for such a beautiful young woman," Pancho stated, still holding Fina's hand. "It is my honor to make your acquaintance."

Helena watched in amusement as her sister, and apparently her soon-to-be brother-in-law, stared at each other, seemingly unaware of the people or world around them.

At last Fina appeared to come out of her trance enough to remember her manners. She gently removed her hand, still tingling from Pancho's touch, and spoke softly.

"Mr. Luna," she managed, "it's a pleasure to meet you. Where are you heading?"

"Please, call me Pancho. It is a nickname that the people I really care about call me."

"Then Pancho it is," she responded with a smile. "And where are you headed, Pancho?" she repeated.

"Well, my lovely Miss Marionneaux," he boldly addressed her, "I am on my way to my home, which is the Rancho de Luna, in Arizona. It is located near the town of Patagonia. Perhaps you have heard of it? Patagonia, I mean, not Rancho de Luna."

"No, I haven't heard of either," Fina laughed, "and please call me Fina. It is a nickname that the people I care about call me."

Pancho laughed when his own words were repeated back to him. "Then Fina it is, for even though we have just met, I feel I've known you forever," he whispered huskily.

Fina smiled to herself and thought, *And you have, in many previous lifetimes.* She did not voice this; instead she chose to remain silent, but nodded perceptively.

Pancho continued, "And where are you and your sister headed?"

"We're on our way to San Francisco to visit an ailing friend."

Fina knew Pancho wasn't ready to hear about her spiritual healing so she didn't elaborate on the real reason for their trip.

Boldly, Pancho reached again for Fina's hand, and once more bent to kiss it softly. It never occurred to him that she would object, and of course, she did not. The instant his lips touched her hand, however, it was as if a movie began to play in her mind. She closed her eyes, inhaled sharply and laid her other hand over her heart, as emotions flowed through her: love, happiness and sorrow.

She saw their wedding day; they were laughing, dancing, making love. She saw the two of them holding hands and walking in the moonlight. She saw the birth of a baby girl they would call Suzetta. She saw every minute of their wonderful life together. And she saw herself standing over his grave, tears running unchecked down her face.

Chapter 8 – *Sam 1979 - ICU*

In the dimly lit room, surrounded by monitors that were attached to various parts of her body, Sam fought the fog in her mind once more. As she slowly won the battle she became aware of someone sitting in the single chair next to her hospital bed. She could barely open her eyes, but it was enough to see that it was a man. A man who sat with his head bent, holding an open book at an angle to catch the light coming from the curtained door of the ICU room. The way he held it allowed her to barely see the cover of the slim volume in his hands.

Concentrating on the book he was holding, she suddenly felt a jolt. *Oh my God.* It looked like one of her journals; in fact she could now see it was the 1951 journal. The things written in that particular journal were not for anyone else's eyes. She wanted to reach toward the man, to take the book from his hands, but discovered her arms would not move. Frustrated, she could only turn her gaze to his face. She knew that face.

"Poppie?" Her voice was a barely audible whisper.

She had managed to inch her head toward him but that and the one word she had forced from her lips had taken so much effort she was now exhausted. He must have heard her, however, because he looked up, a smile starting to spread over his face.

"Sam, are you awake? Can you see me?"

Her eyes were closing again.

"Sammy, can you hear me? They said they didn't know if you'd ever come out of your coma. Shall I call for the doctor?"

Unable to respond, she started to slip back into the fog. One thought went with her. *Why does Poppie have my journal?* But before she could dwell on it further the blackness overtook her once more.

CHAPTER 9 – *Sam 1957* – The Journal

She was falling, surprised that one minute she could be hanging from the tree and in the next watching the ground coming up to greet her. She stretched out her arms, hoping to soften the impact. But when her arms met the ground there wasn't anything soft about it, and that's when she heard the sickening sound of a bone breaking. Six-year-old Samantha could not keep herself from crying out at the excruciating pain.

Maria, always in the kitchen at this time of the day, heard her screams and came running out the backdoor.

"*Mi Hija*, my poor Sammy, are you okay?" Maria cried, kneeling next to the child who lay sprawled on the ground under the giant tree. It took only a glance at her right arm to know it was broken. It was bent at an unnatural angle.

"I think so, but my arm hurts really bad, Maria," Sam said bravely. She was trying very hard not to show the pain, she did not want to be considered a baby.

"Okay, *Mi Hija*, you just lay still while I go find your Maman and Big Jose," Maria soothed as she stood. "I'll be right back," she called over her shoulder as she rushed toward the stables.

If her arm hadn't hurt so badly, Sam would have laughed watching Maria's large frame running in the direction of the nearby stables. She had never seen Maria move so fast. But the pain in her arm was so horrific she thought she might throw up. She closed her eyes, trying to hold off the nausea.

She must have blacked out while lying on the ground, because the next thing she knew she was waking up in her room. There was no memory of being carried upstairs. She looked down at her arm and saw that it was bandaged from her wrist to her elbow and attached to a board of some kind. Funny, she didn't remember that being done either. Oh well, she mused, at least it doesn't hurt anymore.

Sensing that someone was in her bathroom, she turned her head to face the door and saw Maman standing there. Fina was drying her hands on a towel, and when she noticed her granddaughter watching her she smiled.

"How are you feeling, little one?" There was a look of concern in Maman's eyes, and Sam was sorry that it was there because of her carelessness.

"Almost good as new, Maman," Sam smiled brightly at her grandmother. "How did I get up here? Did you fix my arm?"

"Yes, I fixed your little broken arm," Fina answered while crossing the room to sit on the edge of Sam's bed. She stroked the child's forehead.

"And, yes, Big Jose carried you up. You were in shock. But now you must rest, and your arm will be good as new before you know it." Maman nodded toward her old leather medicine bag. "I've given you something that stopped the pain, and it will make you sleepy."

Sam looked at her arm before asking Maman, "Do Mama and Poppie know that I got hurt?" As always, Sam craved their attention. She was often disappointed and today was no exception.

"Yes, my love, they know. Your Poppie is riding out to the northern division, to get Doc. Tomorrow, Doc and I will put a plaster cast on your arm to hold it in place while it heals, so you won't need this board." Maman sighed before continuing. "And well, your Mother is feeling a little ill today."

Sam looked at her grandmother for a long time before asking, "Maman, can I ask you a question?" Like most six-year-olds, Sam was always asking questions.

"Shoot." Fina squeezed her granddaughter's un-bandaged left hand.

"Maman, how come you can heal everyone except my mother?" Sam, with her too-wise eyes, looked at her grandmother curiously.

Without answering right away, Fina closed her eyes, a habit she had when she was trying to find the right words.

Sam knew that when her grandmother closed her eyes she was thinking about the best way to answer a question; she'd also learned to be patient, and to wait until Maman was ready to speak. She too closed her eyes, curious and maybe a little anxious, to hear what the wise woman would have to say. She was thankful that her grandmother never brushed off her questions. She always found the right words.

At last, opening her eyes and speaking softly, Maman began. "Well," she said slowly.

Upon hearing this, Sam opened her eyes and leaned closer. She did not want to miss a single word.

"I wish, *ma petite*, that I could give you the answer that you would like to hear. I know you want me to tell you your mother will soon be okay, but unfortunately it is not as simple as that. As I have told you many times before, I am not the one doing the healing. It is the Holy Spirit that works through me."

Fina looked around the room trying to find a way to help Sam understand how the healing works. She closed her eyes again and prayed for the right words. When she opened them her eyes were drawn to the lamp on the nightstand. She smiled and thought *yes* while nodding toward the ceiling, having received her inspiration.

Aloud she said, "I am like your lamp," as she touched the lamp lightly, "and the Holy Spirit is like the electricity that makes it work. I am able to heal because the Holy Spirit shines through me, like the electricity lights your lamp. Without the electricity, the lamp is just a lamp, without the Holy Spirit, I am just a woman. But with the help of the electricity the lamp performs the function for which it was made."

Fina touched the tiny broken arm. "With the help of the Holy Spirit, I become a healer." Looking at Sam's sweet face, she asked, "Do you understand now?"

Her grandmother's touch sent a pleasant tingling up her broken arm, all the way to her shoulder.

"I think so," Sam responded, suddenly feeling extremely tired and light-headed. "But that doesn't explain about my mother. Doesn't the Holy Spirit want to help you heal her?" Fighting the desire to sleep, Sam's eyes grew dark with worry over her mother.

"Again, that is not an easy question to answer," Fina tried to explain further. "The Holy Spirit loves your mother, very much. But your mother must want to get better, and right now she likes being the way she is. It's called free will."

"But how can she like being sick all the time?" Sam couldn't believe it, she hated being sick even for a day. Why would her mother choose to be sick?

Reading her mind, Fina answered gently, "Because sometimes being sick is safer than being well. If she were well she would have to face the things she has done in her life, things that maybe she shouldn't have done, things she now regrets. But she's not ready to do that, not just yet, so instead she chooses to stay ill. I know that you are young, and it doesn't make sense to you that someone would choose to be sick, but someday you will understand."

Fina touched the middle of the little girl's forehead. "I promise you, one day your mother will choose to be well again. And when that day comes, she will truly be your mother. Until then, my little butterfly, you are lucky because you have two grandmothers, which is almost as good as having two mothers. Maria and I love you very, very, much." Fina leaned down and kissed her granddaughter's cheek.

Exhausted from her ordeal, from Maman's long explanation, and from the pain medicine, Sam closed her eyes.

"Okay, Maman," she said sleepily, "I'll wait. I'll wait for my mother. I love you, Maman."

"And I love you," Fina whispered before bending down to kiss the forehead of the child who was already asleep. She straightened and tip-toed quietly out of Sam's room, closing the door behind her.

The following day Sam was wide awake and she was restless. Maman and Doc had arrived first thing after breakfast to replace the bandage and board with a plaster cast. They told her that she needed to stay in bed, just for today, to give the cast a chance to harden properly.

She was tired of reading and was bored, needing something or someone to entertain her. Just then, as if summoned, Maria entered the room carrying a tray laden with a plate of Sam's favorites: tacos, and a glass of cold milk.

"So how is my little angel?" Maria asked as she smiled at the little girl and placed the tray on the nightstand. Then she straightened the bedcovers and plumped up the pillows behind Sam's head. Satisfied, she gave the child a quick hug before she reached for the tray, pulled down the tray's short legs, and placed it over Sam's lap.

"I'm bored, Maria," Sam pouted. She didn't usually act this way, but she was still upset from yesterday's events. Since it was not in her nature to complain, however, the pout was soon replaced with a smile.

"Thank you for the food. It looks yummy. I feel better already." She reached out and hugged Maria.

"You are so welcome. Now you eat, okay?" Maria tucked a napkin into the neck of Sam's nightgown. "Your Maman said that she'll be up later to check on you. If all is well you can run around again tomorrow."

"Okay, Maria," Sam said with her mouth full of taco.

Maria frowned and scolded, "Manners, Samantha, don't talk with your full mouth, no?"

Sam swallowed and took a swig of cold milk before responding, "Sorry, but it is soooo good."

"It is okay. Eat. I'll bring you a photo book, *si*? You can look at pictures after you eat."

"Thanks, Maria. Can you also bring up a new journal? I finished the last page in my old one," Sam asked politely.

"Yes, yes. You and your writings. It is a good thing that you are left-handed, like Maman, so you are still able to write."

Maria hugged Sam one more time, then spoke over her shoulder as she started to leave the room, "I'll be back soon for the tray and with the journal and photo book."

After the door closed, Sam pushed the tray away. She had lost her appetite in spite of the fact that Maria's tacos were among her favorite foods. Instead, her mind was recalling what she had been told the previous evening. She still couldn't understand why her mother would choose to be sick, even if she didn't want to face things she had done. *What kind of things could be so bad that she would rather be sick than spend time with her daughter*? She vowed that when she had children, nothing would keep her from being there with them and for them.

Sam was still lost in her thoughts when Maria returned twenty minutes later, carrying a photo album in one hand and a new journal in the other.

"Here you go, *Mi Hija*," she said, then noticed the uneaten food on the tray. "I guess my eyes were bigger than your stomach."

The child laughed, "Yes, something like that. I love you, Maria. Thanks again for lunch and for bringing my journal and the photo album."

"Okay little one, you look at the pictures and write in your book. I'll be back later to see if you need anything."

After Maria left Sam ran her hand over the new journal. She loved writing in her journals and spent a lot of time doing so. Maman had given her 20 of the leather-bound treasures inscribed with her initials, SGLL, for Samantha Grace Luna Lopez. They were a birthday present last Christmas Eve, received with instructions from her grandmother:

"Write down all those dreams and wishes crowding together in your pretty head. When you have five unused journals remaining you must let me know so I can order more."

From that day Sam didn't go anywhere without a journal and a pencil within easy reach. Maman was right, she loved writing. She liked seeing a new blank page and thinking about all the words she could use to fill it up. She wrote about whatever came to mind, it didn't matter what. So far she had used seven journals and she was still surprised at the anticipation she felt each time she started a new one.

Now, confined to her bed, she put the journal down on her bedspread and picked up the photo album. Perhaps she would make up stories about the pictures in the album on her lap. She had always loved pouring over the many family photo albums kept on a special shelf in the ranch's massive library. She knew without opening this particular one that it contained her parents' wedding pictures and pictures of herself as a baby.

Also in this album were some of the last pictures taken of her Papa Pancho. Although he had died before she knew him, she had always felt a special connection with him. He always seemed to be smiling in his photographs. This was especially true when he was standing next to a younger Maman, who was also, more often than not, smiling up at her handsome husband.

When Sam opened the familiar album on this day a strange sensation radiated up her legs and her arms. She thought it felt like when her foot would fall asleep and then waken. It wasn't a bad feeling; in fact she kind of liked it. It reminded her a little of Maman's healing touch. Oh well, she shrugged, ignoring the feeling as she looked at the first picture in the album and touched it gently with her finger tips…

POP! Suddenly she was standing inside a photograph that had been taken on her parents' wedding day. It was a picture of her mother and father standing on the altar of the old church soon after they had exchanged their vows – the picture she had been touching a moment before. Everything around her was in black and white, just like in the photo.

She looked down at her feet. She was definitely here at the wedding, standing in the aisle between the first pew and the altar. She could hear the orchestra playing from the balcony and smell the rose-and-lilac-filled bouquets that decorated each pew and flanked each side of the altar. Carefully and slowly she turned to her left toward the congregation that filled the old church. Sitting in the first row were a younger-looking Maria, Big Jose and Maman. And next to Maman sat Papa Pancho. Her dead grandfather was alive!

Forgetting the strangeness of the situation for a moment, she smiled and waved in greeting. Soon, however, she realized that while she could see them they could not see her. She was disappointed; she would have loved to talk to Papa Pancho, to sit on his lap. As she was pondering this strange occurrence a new sensation was invading her consciousness; she became slowly aware that she was hearing many voices. She could not make out individual words, and they appeared to be inside her head. Her disappointment at not being able to talk to her grandfather was quickly forgotten.

Confused by the voices, unable to sort them out or to make sense of what she was hearing, her eyes locked on Maria. Immediately Maria's thoughts seemed to become clear and the other voices began to fade into the background. In her head Sam could hear the woman's thoughts, as if they had been spoken aloud.

"I still can't believe that my Little Jose is marrying Etta. It is obvious that she loves my son, but I was so sure that he loved Lupita."

Amazed by her discovery, and wanting to see if it would work again, Sam looked at Big Jose. As before, the thoughts in his head appeared in hers, as if he was speaking them.

"Jose looks just like my father. I never really noticed the likeness before."

Sam looked at Maman next and heard, *"Oh, Etta, what have you done?"*

Feeling this was a strange thing for a mother to think about her daughter on her wedding day, Sam turned to look at her parents on the altar. A radiant smile was shining from her mother's face as she looked up at her groom. Her father was smiling too, but the wise child could see that he was smiling with his mouth, not with his eyes, and not in his heart. For the first time since she popped into the picture Sam was afraid. She twirled back around, tearing her eyes away from her parents' faces and faced the congregation.

Will I be able to hear Mama's thoughts too? Do I really want to know what Mama is thinking? Would I then know what she has been hiding from for more than six years? Are the answers here, here on their wedding day? What did Maria mean when she thought Little Jose was in love with Lupita? Who is Lupita? And what could Mama have done that would distress Maman so? The questions raced through her mind like a freight train.

What about Poppie, would I learn why he is always so cold and distant toward me and Mama? And why he seems so sad all the time? More questions. Sam risked another look at her father and suddenly it was as if she was held captive and his thoughts were projecting into her head. Only it was more than just thoughts, it was like she was absorbing a story. At first it seemed that her father was telling the story, but then it was like someone else was telling it. She realized that in this story he was no longer at his wedding. At one point he and her mother were by a river.

It was very confusing: the story would go forward, then backward. She didn't understand a lot of what was being said or what was happening. She hoped she would remember everything so she could write it all down in her journal. Somehow, although much of the story made no sense to her, she knew it would be important to record all that she had experienced and 'heard.'

Eventually Sam's head began to hurt and she was feeling dizzy. She wanted to learn more of her father's story, but she was having trouble focusing. As her head began to pound even harder she reached up to hold it with both hands. It was all so frightening: hearing others' thoughts, not knowing how she got here to this place in a time before she was born, or how to get back to her bedroom where she would feel safe again. As the pain increased she closed her eyes in order to concentrate on what she should do next...

POP! She was instantly back in her bedroom and the wedding was once again just a black and white picture in a family photo album. The pain in her head was gone.

As she sat on her bed with the photo album open on her lap, she began to question whether she had actually been present during her parents' wedding. Her father had been thinking about being with her mother at the river months before the wedding. Had she been there too? Maybe she had imagined it, but if so, why? Even if she had been there, she didn't understand everything that had been said or everything that she had seen. One thing she did know: whether real or not, she felt compelled to write down everything she had experienced before the 'memories' could disappear. After all, what could they be other than memories? She was still sitting in her bedroom, not standing in a church in a black and white photograph.

Regardless, no longer questioning what was real, and determined to get everything down on paper right away, she picked up the new journal and wrote 1951 in the title space on the cover. She knew that was the year her parents were married; the same year she was born. Then she opened the book to the first page and started writing.

The words appeared to flow from her pencil of their own accord, and without any conscious thought from her about what to say or how to say it. Fascinated, she watched her hand move across the page. When she tried to read what had been written down she couldn't make out the words.

Next to appearing at her parents' wedding, this was the strangest thing that had ever happened to her. It never occurred to her to be afraid at what her hand was doing without any effort from her. She felt calm and just knew she was meant to record her experience. She also knew, somehow, that her journal was not to be shown to anyone, at least not for a long time. When the time was right, the person or persons these words were meant for would see them.

After finishing the entry in her journal she put it away on a shelf in her closet. Maybe tomorrow or the next day she would try to return to the wedding and listen to someone else. After all, nothing bad had happened to her, and she knew she was meant to record these things. She didn't necessarily have to understand them now, but maybe when she was older. Maybe when she was ten, or twelve...

CHAPTER 10 – *Jose 1979* – The Phone Call

The insistent ringing of the telephone brought Jose out of his dream, a recurring dream of his beloved Lupita. His arm reached out to turn off the alarm clock before he realized it was the phone that had so rudely awakened him. He glanced at the illuminated face of the clock, and then cursed as he reached for the phone.

"Damn, 12:30 a.m., this can't be good news."

His first thought was that his Aunt Lucy might have passed away. He knew his parents had just returned from a well-deserved vacation, and stopped in Tucson to see his mother's sister before returning home. Aunt Lucy had been having chest pains, and perhaps it had been more serious than they thought. In fact, it must be if his parents or his cousin Humberto was calling him at this hour.

"Humberto!" Jose barked into the phone, assuming his cousin would be the one to call.

"Mr. Lopez?" a female voice answered.

Mentally switching gears when he realized it was not his cousin on the other end of the line, and now fully awake, Jose sat up and swung his legs over the side of the bed. "Yes, this is Jose Lopez. Who's calling at this hour?" he demanded, now more irritated over his interrupted dream than worried about his aunt, since it wasn't Humberto on the phone.

"Mr. Lopez, this is Dr. Lee, Samantha Maxwell's obstetrician. She had this number listed in case of emergency. That's why I'm calling."

"Sam? What's wrong? What's the matter with Samantha?" Jose began to panic at hearing the word 'emergency.'

"Mr. Lopez, you are Mrs. Maxwell's father, is that right?"

"Yes, yes, I'm her father. What is going on? What's happened to my daughter?"

"Your daughter is at St. Vincent's Hospital, here in Los Angeles. Mr. Lopez, I'm afraid I have some bad news. Samantha is in a coma and her prognosis…" Dr. Lee paused, hating having to deliver this kind of news over the phone. "Well, her prognosis is not good," she continued.

"Wait. Wait just a minute. What do you mean, *not good*? Has she been in an accident? Where's Michael, her husband? She's pregnant. Is the baby okay?"

Jose had jumped up at the doctor's news, and was running his hand through his hair as he barked out his questions while pacing back and forth. He was trying to remember his daughter's due date but his mind was drawing a blank. He couldn't think straight.

Understanding Jose's concern and agitation, the doctor answered with a voice that she hoped would calm him a little.

"Mr. Maxwell has been notified of his wife's condition and is on his way."

Before she could continue, Jose, who was anything but calm, grabbed at the word that penetrated his fog.

"Notified of what condition? What's happened to her, for God's sake?"

Please, God, save my daughter, he prayed silently, making the sign of the cross. He was beginning to realize that the prognosis could be more than *not good*, it could be very bad. Slowly he sank back down to sit on the side of the bed.

"Mr. Lopez, Samantha hasn't been in an accident. Her labor stared early and in fact, she has delivered a baby girl. The baby is in the infant ICU here and is…stable."

Dr. Lee had no intention of mentioning anything about the strange birth over the phone. It was something that would need to be explained in person. *Hopefully, by the pediatrician* she thought. While these thoughts were running through her head there was silence on the line.

"Doctor?" Jose, growing impatient, was afraid they may have been disconnected. "Are you still there? Doctor?"

"Yes, Mr. Lopez, I'm still here."

"What about my daughter? Why is she in a coma? Did something happen during the delivery?"

"We don't know what happened, Mr. Lopez Her labor was uneventful, but as soon as the baby was born she lapsed into a coma. We're doing all we can but I suggest that you and your wife come as soon as possible. Since we don't know what caused it I can't tell you when, or even if she'll recover. We're trying to bring her out of it. I'm afraid, though, that there are no guarantees. That's why you need to come right away."

"Oh, my God." The hand with the receiver in it dropped to his lap.

"Mr. Lopez? Mr. Lopez?"

The doctor's distant voice penetrated his thoughts, and Jose moved the receiver back to his ear.

"Okay, we'll be there as fast as we can. Can you give me directions to the hospital from the airport?"

After getting the directions Jose hung up the phone and remained sitting on the side of the bed in the still dark room. "Oh, my God," he whispered again. "What have I done? I might lose my daughter and I don't even know her."

Deciding he needed action, not recriminations, and that nothing was going to keep him from reaching Sam as soon as possible, he reached for the phone and turned on the bedside lamp at the same time. He called Humberto, telling him what little he knew. Humberto immediately promised to have his private plane standing by at the airport in Tucson.

"And Jose, I'll send someone to pick up your mother and father. We'll meet you at the airport," Humberto offered without being asked. "What about Etta? How is she taking this?"

"Shit," Jose swore quietly under his breath. He had forgotten about Etta. Aloud he said, "I'm on my way to tell her now. See you at the airport within the hour."

Hanging up the phone, Jose headed for the hallway and reluctantly approached Etta's bedroom door. He hesitated before knocking. How would he find her, drunk or passed out? Hopefully she will have fallen asleep before she became too far gone to arouse her. He didn't have time to waste trying to sober her up.

Knocking loudly, he shouted, "Etta, wake up. It's Samantha, she needs us. Get up." He opened the door without waiting for a reply.

He fumbled for the light switch in the dark, found it, and winced at the bright light that suddenly flooded the room. The first things he noticed were the smells of old cigarette smoke and expensive whiskey. The room was a mess with discarded clothes everywhere, plus there was half-eaten food, empty bottles, and over-flowing ashtrays covering every dusty surface.

Shaking his head in disgust, he made his way to the bed where Etta lay length-wise on top of the bedspread, snoring, one arm dangling over the side of the bed. The other was buried beneath her. She must have passed out, he figured, because she still wore her clothes rather than her nightgown.

"Etta, Etta," Jose said loudly as he shook her none too gently. "Wake up, Etta."

Etta moaned and rolled over, trying to get away from his rough shaking of her. She showed no sign of waking.

"Damn it," he swore, and strode to the suite's bathroom. Looking around for something to put water in, he spied the wastebasket, grabbed it and up-ended it so the contents fell to the floor. Turning to the sink he filled the now-empty wastebasket from the cold water faucet.

Back in the bedroom, standing over Etta, he unceremoniously dumped the water onto her head. Gasping and sputtering, she sat upright, frantically looking around to find the source of the dousing.

"What the hell are you doing?" she slurred, when her eyes landed on Jose standing over her with the empty wastebasket in his hands. Whether her speech was slurred with sleep or from alcohol, it was hard to tell. Jose had no time to determine which it was. He suspected the latter.

"Get up," he demanded through gritted teeth. At the same time he grabbed both of her hands and pulled her up from the bed. She was standing, but barely. Still not fully aware of what was happening, she stumbled and tried to sit back down again on the bed.

Assuming she was not yet sober, Jose refused to let her sit down. Instead, he picked her up, threw her over his shoulder fireman style, and carried her to the bathroom. Steadying her on his shoulder with one hand, he used the other to turn on the shower. He didn't bother with testing the water temperature; he simply turned it on full, then dumped her onto the shower floor, clothes and all.

Glaring down at her, he said with disgust and barely-controlled fury, "I'm going to pack a few things, and then I'll be back. I strongly suggest you be dressed and ready to go when I return."

"Go where?" Etta cried, trying to focus on his retreating back through the water that filled her eyes and streamed down her face. She was sobering up quickly, yet still fuzzy enough around the edges to be confused rather than angry at the treatment she had received from her husband.

"Just get the hell dressed, Etta," Jose yelled on his way out of her bedroom. "Sam's in trouble."

Since his head was turned toward the bathroom where Etta still sat under the running water, he almost collided with Irene, the housekeeper, when he turned back and practically ran through the bedroom door. Irene had heard the telephone ring and the ensuing commotion and was coming to see if her help was needed. She was modestly clutching her robe closed with both hands and jumped back quickly, to avoid being mowed down by her employer.

"Mr. Jose, I heard noises. Is everything alright? Is it Miss Sam? Are she and her baby okay?"

Surprised by Irene's questions, Jose stopped his headlong rush abruptly and whirled to face her. "What do you mean, Irene? What do you know about Sam and the baby?"

Irene took another step backward, puzzled by the intensity of his question. It was as if he was accusing her of something, but she didn't know what it was.

"I didn't mean anything, Mr. Jose. I was just concerned since I haven't heard anything more since Miss Sam called yesterday afternoon to say she was on her way to the hospital because her labor had started. Has she had the baby yet?"

"What do you mean she called here yesterday? Why didn't you tell anyone?" Jose angrily demanded as he took a step toward the almost-cowering woman.

This unfair accusation gave Irene courage. That, and years of service with the Luna family which entitled her, she felt, to some respect. She stood ramrod straight and became defensive and indignant as she answered the man she'd known since he was a child. She shook a finger at him from a safe distance.

"Now you wait just a minute, Mr. Jose. I informed Miss Etta the minute I hung up the phone with Miss Sam. She was in the library, and I gave her the paper that had the name of the hospital, and the telephone number so you or Miss Etta could call. You were nowhere to be found, as usual, or I would have given it to you." This last was added as a censure for his continual absence from the hacienda, which was legendary.

Taken aback by the older woman's authoritative response, Jose immediately felt contrite and apologetic. "Irene, I'm sorry. I didn't mean to attack you. Etta never said a word, and that phone call was to tell me that Sam is in critical condition. I'm just upset."

Irene grasped her robe even tighter. "I'm so sorry. What can I do?"

"Please go pack a few things for Miss Etta and see that she gets dressed. Again I apologize for my rudeness. As you can imagine, I'm worried and upset."

Irene stepped closer and patted Jose gently on the arm, "It's all my fault. I should not have relied on Miss Etta to tell you," Irene said contritely. "I know how she is most of the time."

"Really, its okay Irene, now please go see to her while I pack my things."

Furious at his wife, Jose stormed into his own room and opened the closet. He stood staring at his clothes before remembering that he didn't own a suitcase. *Shit.* He turned and hurried to Samantha's old bedroom at the other end of the long hallway. Inside, he rushed to the closet and threw open the door, looking around for a suitcase. He knew she'd had several when she still lived at home. When he saw a suitcase sitting on the top shelf of the closet he reached up to pull it down. As he did so a small box was dislodged and came down with the case. It flew open as it fell and the contents spilled onto the floor.

Jose noticed it was one of Sam's journals. He knew she had been writing in journals since she was just a child. He bent down and picked it up, an ache in his heart at the thought that she may never write again. *Oh, Sam*, the thought ran through his head. *I don't want to lose you.*

He took a moment to run his hand over the cover of the journal, fighting not to cry. It was then that he noticed the date written on the cover: 1951. His sorrow was forgotten for a moment as he puzzled over the meaning of the date. Sam was born in 1951. How could she write in the journal in the year that she was born? That was impossible. Curious, his haste all but forgotten, he sat on the floor and opened the book to the first page and began to read, words that were written in a childish cursive:

Today, believe it or not, I visited my parents' wedding...

Confused, Jose flipped through several pages, and then stopped to read more. Stunned, and chilled by what he read, he slammed the journal shut. How could it possibly be that Sam had written those words? My God, it was as if she was inside my head, he thought to himself. *What is going on here?* He was lost in conflicting thoughts, not even realizing that he clutched the journal to his chest.

"Jose?"

It was Etta, standing in the doorway of Sam's closet. She looked puzzled, but her speech and posture were steadier than they had been when he rushed out of her room earlier.

"Irene says Samantha is in trouble. What's wrong with her?"

Hearing Etta's voice brought Jose out of the muddled fog his brain had been wrapped in.

"I'll be ready in a minute, and I'll tell you on the way to the airport," he answered absently.

Then he picked up Sam's suitcase, thrust the journal inside and rushed back to his room to pack. He had no idea what he threw into the suitcase; his mind was still on the journal.

I'll read it on the plane, he told himself, still puzzled by what he had read so far. The thought kept running through his head: *How could a six-year-old write those words?*

CHAPTER 11 – *Jose 1951* – The Wedding

Jose was sitting in Humberto's private plane, flying toward his daughter. He only hoped they'd reach her in time. His worried parents were holding tight to each other, praying together, and Etta had gone back to sleep as soon as she lay down on the leather couch. She was sobering up, but now hung over and trying to sleep it off. He wasn't' sure if he'd gotten through to her just how critical it was to get to Sam as soon as possible. Frankly, he didn't care if she understood or not. If she was sleeping he didn't have to deal with her. Humberto was in the cockpit with the pilot.

Wide awake, and with time on his hands Jose thought about Sam's journal. It was still in the suitcase in which he'd thrown it along with the clothing and toiletries that he didn't remember packing. After retrieving it, and before opening it, he ran his fingers over his daughter's initials that were embossed on the cover. SGLL. After those brief glimpses he'd scanned earlier he was afraid of what he might discover, but was unable to keep himself from slowly opening it. He began to read the first page.

Saturday, May 11, 1957: Today, believe it or not, I visited my parents' wedding. I don't know how I got there, but I could actually hear everyone's thoughts. It was confusing at first, but when I looked directly at one person their thoughts would become clear and separate from all the others'. When I looked at my father it felt like I could see backward and forward at the same time. I don't know how to explain it, but it was as if he was telling a story out loud and at the same time showing me a movie. Everything was happening very fast! I did not understand a lot of the things I saw or felt, or heard, but I will write down everything I can remember. Somehow I think I will understand things when I am older, but for now I need to get everything down. So here goes:

One stupid indiscretion had cost 19-year-old Jose Javier Lopez Jr. the love of his life. The loss of Lupita Carmen Garcia would turn him into a lonely, harsh man. Today he would marry the girl who had brazenly thrown herself at him last spring. In a moment of weakness, born of too much tequila and healthy lust, he had succumbed to her advances. The result was a baby who would be born in seven months. There was never a question about his marrying her; he had been raised to do the honorable thing at all times.

He stood with the priest and his Best Man on the raised altar, waiting for the bridal procession to start, and used the time to search the sea of faces of the wedding guests that were spread out before him. In the same instant that he found and held the eyes of his beloved Lupe he heard, as if in a dream, the first strains of *Here Comes the Bride*. The congregation stood, all heads turning toward the bride coming from the back of the old church. All, that is, except the one person in the congregation who was not smiling, the one whose eyes continued to stare into his above the heads that separated them. In those beautiful black eyes, normally sparkling with good humor, he saw only what he knew was reflected in his own: sadness, disappointment and yearning for what might have been.

Jose knew he should be watching Etta, who was gliding toward him on the arm of her father. He knew she would be breath-taking in her custom-made soft white antique satin and beaded gown that hugged her slim figure. He knew too, that she would be smiling with joy under the lacy veil that covered her face and trailed a full fifteen feet behind her. He doubted that anyone in the smiling throng facing her – other than the two people who had been told – would guess that she was carrying his child. Yes, the kind thing to do would be to watch his wife-to-be.

However, he could not drag his eyes away from the beautiful Lupita, even though by now she too was watching the bride advance. Knowing he was the cause of the sad resignation and hopelessness he'd seen on her face, and that he would never again hold her in his arms, he felt a sharp pain in his heart – the only thing that finally tore his eyes away from hers. The sensation was so keen that he grabbed his chest and his knees started to buckle.

Noticing this movement from the corner of his eye, the Best Man turned quickly and caught Jose under his arms, holding him upright until he was sure he was steady once more. Humberto, who was his cousin as well as his Best Man, assumed Jose was overcome with emotion at seeing his bride coming toward him and may have gotten light-headed.

Since all heads were turned toward the bride nobody else seemed to notice Jose's momentary weakness. By the time Etta and her father reached the altar he was standing erect. He moved forward, down the two steps that separated them, took her hand and walked her back up to the altar. There, in front of more than 200 close friends and family, he woodenly recited his vows, agreeing to be faithful "until death us do part." He would keep that vow, but he would never "love and cherish" his wife. He couldn't love her in the way his father, Big Jose, loved his mother, or the way Pancho obviously cherished Fina. His love belonged to someone else, and always would.

Jose and Etta had known each other their entire lives. They had crawled over each other as infants and along with Humberto had played hide-and-seek and good guys, bad guys as children in the yards of the ranch. Many times, as they grew toward young adulthood, they had all raced their horses through the grasslands surrounding the ranch, down to the Santa Cruz River. They had often left their horses to graze while they climbed ancient cottonwoods near the river, feet dangling high above the ground while they confided to each other their plans for the future.

While Jose loved Etta as he would a sister, and had never envisioned her in a more personal role in his life, he had to admit he suspected she had a crush on him that appeared to grow stronger as they grew from adolescents to maturing teenagers. He pretended he didn't know how she felt, as she had never voiced those feelings to him. He certainly hadn't wanted to encourage her. If only he hadn't let the tequila go to his head last spring when they were alone, he would be standing at the altar now with Lupe instead of Etta. And, along with a wife that he would not have chosen, there was to be a baby as well. He was not ready to be a father. At 19, he knew nothing about babies. *Dios mio. My God, what have I done?* he found himself thinking in panic.

Jose was lost in the private hell in his mind; Etta had to nudge him for the exchange of wedding rings. With her face no longer covered by her veil he could appreciate the fact that, at 18 years old she was absolutely stunning. The glossy shoulder-length brown hair that framed her oval face was filled with gold highlights, nearly matching the flecks in her almond- colored eyes. Her face was almost flawless, with a perfectly shaped chin, full red lips and a small, pert nose that was lightly dusted with freckles. The one and only time they had made love, the color of her skin had reminded him of heavily creamed coffee. She was slim and petite, her head reaching to just under his chin. In contrast to his 6'3" height, she appeared very small indeed. She was a lovely bride, there was no doubt. Lovely, yes; his Lupe, no.

Their vows were said, their first kiss as husband and wife was dutifully completed, and they turned to face their guests. With a forced smile that didn't reach his eyes, Jose scanned the congregation once more for Lupe's face. Twice he rapidly searched the crowd. With an indiscernible sag to his shoulders he accepted what his eyes had already discovered: Lupita was gone.

In the large and elegant dining room of the old ranch house a massive antique table had been placed to one side and decorated for the wedding party. It was covered with an imported silk tablecloth that hung almost to the floor, and set with the finest china and the most exquisite silverware that money could buy. Expensive French champagne had been poured into delicate Waterford crystal flutes, and pure silver Spanish candelabras were placed at either end of the long table. Many smaller tables were scattered about the formal room for the guests.

At the head table Jose sat next to his new wife and glanced around. There were waiters dressed in white jackets bringing in platters of food. The wedding feast was prepared, not by his mother, but by a chef flown in from France for the occasion. However, Jose was not hungry. Continuing to gaze around him, he saw people that were dressed in their finest toasting the newly married couple; and people whose finest did not compare to that of the richer guests, but who were enjoying a rare day without the usual bone-tiring labor that running a ranch this size entailed.

Damn it, it should have been Lupe sitting next to me at this wedding feast, he was thinking. The guests should have been toasting them, not him and Etta. But the deed was done and he prayed to God to help him be a good husband and father. He knew it would not be easy, but he would try.

Etta, holding tightly to her new husband's hand, gave it a gentle squeeze. She noticed that he was quiet and withdrawn; in fact, he looked like his thoughts were either a million miles away, or that he was not feeling well. She smiled at him hesitantly.

"Jose, are you feeling okay? You aren't eating anything. Are you sick?"

This brought him back to the present, and with a strained smile on his face he squeezed her hand and replied, "I'm fine. Just a little tired from my bachelor's party last night."

This seemed to satisfy Etta, so she turned to continue a conversation with Pam, her Maid of Honor and best friend.

"So then on Thursday we'll arrive in Paris, and…."

Jose was only half listening. As with everything else in her life, Etta had planned the itinerary of their two-month-long European honeymoon right down to each minute of each day. She was used to getting her way; it would not have occurred to her that Jose might have plans of his own for their honeymoon. Neither would it have occurred to Jose to try to insert his own desires, had he actually had any that opposed hers. What Etta wanted, Etta got. She was always very decisive about her objectives. In fact, the telephone conversation between them after he found out about the pregnancy was the only time he had ever heard Etta sound anything close to apologetic or submissive.

Suddenly, tuning into her conversation, an ugly thought forced its way into his mind. He pulled free of the hand that was still holding his and picked up his champagne glass. He took a deep drink while glancing at Etta's animated face as she continued confiding 'their' plans to her friend. As unbelievable as he tried to tell himself that it was, and no matter how hard he tried to push the idea away, the thought kept returning as a strong possibility. Was the *accidental* pregnancy not an accident after all?

Growing up together as they had, Jose had often witnessed Etta's ability to scheme and connive to get her way and had usually laughed with her when she was successful. But this? Could she have been devious enough to plan this pregnancy and wedding? To trap him so he couldn't marry Lupe? His head was spinning with questions for which he had no answers.

Starting to feel ill, he set the champagne flute down so quickly that it fell over when he abruptly rose to his feet. He excused himself with a nod and "Ladies," and quickly strode from the room. As he passed through the French doors leading from the Great Room to the porch that wound around the ranch house, he took a deep breath to suppress the nausea that threatened to overtake him. Needing to be alone, he started for the stables before he changed his mind and veered off to head toward the Garden Room.

Almost running by the time he reached his destination, he bounded onto the wide porch and sank into the nearest rocking chair. Bending over and holding his head in his hands, he felt like crying. Why hadn't he thought of this before? Even as a child Etta had never acted impulsively. She usually took days, even weeks to consider and rationalize and plan. The rare times that she was thwarted in pursuance of a goal, she would regroup and come up with a new plan. She always managed to achieve her aims eventually, no matter how impossible they may have seemed.

Could she really have been so scheming, or was he judging her unfairly? Still unwilling to believe irrevocably that Etta would go to such extremes, Jose laid his head back against the rocking chair and began to analyze that fateful weekend in his mind. The weekend that had changed his life forever. *God, please let me be wrong...*

Chapter 12 – *Jose 1951* – The Seduction

Jose put Samantha's journal facedown in his lap, closed his eyes and laid his head back against the airplane seat's headrest. The words in the journal had so clearly captured his wedding day and the doubts that claimed him, that he felt the pain again, as if it were happening now, not 28 years ago. How could Sammy have known? It was months before she was born and yet she recorded every detail, every thought that had run through his mind. Did she even understand what she had written?

He got up and walked around just to stretch his muscles. He hadn't realized how tense he was. Everyone else in the cabin was sleeping, so after a few minutes of pacing the aisle he sat down again. He was almost afraid of what he would read next, yet he was compelled to pick up the journal once more. Sammy had mentioned going back and forth in time. His eyes fell on a passage that captured a time before the wedding picture.

It was April, the weekend before Easter Sunday, and Etta was coming home from medical school for spring break. Jose had promised Maria and Fina that he would pick her up at the train station in Patagonia. As always, he was looking forward to her visit. She was funny and interesting to be around, and he was anxious to tell his childhood confidant about his beloved Lupita and the plans they were making.

When a lovely young woman stepped off the train he would not have recognized her if she hadn't been waving wildly at him and immediately run and wrapped her arms around him.

"Jose, why I do believe you are the handsomest thing this side of the

Mississippi!" she exclaimed in the southern drawl that appeared to come naturally to her after living in Louisiana for the past six years.

Caught off guard, he laughed and held her away from him in order to get a better look at her. It was amazing. She had changed from a skinny, funny-looking kid into this dazzling, grown-up woman. It would never do to let her know she had surprised him, though, he mused. She would lord it over him forever.

"And I do believe," he answered, mocking her accent and lifting her petite body high into the air, "that you are still the biggest brat this side of the Santa Cruz River."

When he set her down he thought he noticed a hurt look pass over her face. He guessed he would have to apologize. Then the look was gone. Was he imagining it? Apparently so, for she was smiling brightly at him and asking where her mother and his were hiding. She glanced around him as if trying to spot the women. Inwardly he gave a sigh of relief. He didn't want to start off her vacation with hurt feelings between them.

"As usual, your mama is out healing someone and my mama is busy cooking all of your favorite foods," he replied as he ruffled her hair. "Sorry, but you're stuck with me."

She shrugged her shoulders, then grabbed his hand and pulled him toward the rear of the train. "Well then, I guess you'll have to do. Let's go get my things; I can't wait to get back to the ranch."

Etta talked non-stop during the hour's drive to the ranch. Taking his interest for granted, she reported on her studies at school, told anecdotes about this professor or that fellow student, hardly taking a breath between sentences. She was one of the few women enrolled in medical studies at the University of Louisiana in New Orleans. The fact that she had earned the honor of having the highest entrance exam test scores on record, and that her father had donated enough money to build a new medical library at the university had assured her acceptance.

She seems almost nervous, Jose thought to himself, but that was so unlike Etta that he quickly pushed the thought from his mind. What puzzled him more was the fact that every time he tried to interrupt her ramblings so he could tell her about Lupita, it was as if he'd never spoken and she launched into another tale of life at university. He soon gave up, figuring she was just excited to be home. He would have plenty of time during the coming week to tell her about Lupe and his decision to marry the dark-eyed beauty.

When they finally arrived at the ranch there was the usual happy confusion of hugs, kisses, and "tell me everything" from the *mothers* – a collective name Jose and Etta had given their mothers, Fina and Maria, from the time they were children. The afternoon rolled into evening and a succession of people wandered in to welcome Etta home so Jose never did have the opportunity to take her aside so he could confide his plans.

Retiring to his room that night after everyone else had gone to bed, Jose lay with his hands behind his head, thinking of the beautiful Lupe, and of the day in January that had changed his life. He smiled to himself as he remembered walking into his mother's kitchen to see Lupe washing dishes and laughing with Maria. He knew he had fallen in love with her instantly.

She was tall for a woman, about 5'8" or 5'9", he'd figured. The sunlight from the windows over the sink had given her long, straight, jet black hair a radiant shine. He had only seen her profile at first; most of her beautiful face was hidden behind a veil of that silky hair. Her body was camouflaged with an apron, but he could tell her figure was full and ripe beneath it. Shapely legs the color of coffee beans appeared to grow longer and more graceful when she stood on tiptoe to put the clean dishes on a high shelf over the serving table. The fact that she was barefoot had seemed both childlike and seductive at the same time. He must have made a sound of appreciation, although he wasn't aware of it, because both women had turned to look at him simultaneously.

It was that first moment when he saw her lovely face and looked into her questioning eyes that would forever be etched in his memory. Her lips were full, naturally red without the need for lipstick, but it was those eyes that held him captive. They were large, and like her hair, soft and black. Where they had asked a silent question at first, now they sparkled with amusement as he stood transfixed and staring. And he had known, just that quickly, that he wanted her for his wife and for all eternity.

His mother hadn't appeared to notice that he had been struck dumb.

"Oh, Little Jose, you startled us. Come, I want you to meet Lupita

Garcia, Hector's daughter. She has just arrived from Sonora and will be helping me in the kitchen."

Turning to Lupe, Maria had then said, "Lupita, this is my son, Little Jose."

Still frozen in place by the beauty before him, Jose had said nothing, only continued to stare.

"Little Jose, what is the matter with you? Where are your manners?" his mother had reprimanded, with both hands fisted on her generous hips.

At last, the amusement Jose saw in Lupita's eyes released him from his spell and he'd stepped forward to take her outstretched hand in his. Ignoring his mother's presence, he had drawn Lupe's hand slowly to his lips, and lightly kissed it.

"It is a pleasure to meet you," he had told her softly, "and please, call me Jose. I am no longer 'little' and so have outgrown the childish name that my mother refuses to give up." He'd said this while looking directly into those gorgeous eyes, and while continuing to hold her hand firmly in his.

Now it was Lupe who stood as if she were a statue while she stared up into Jose's handsome face.

"*El placer es mio,*" she had whispered back. The pleasure is mine. Louder, she had added, "You are right, I do not see anything little about you. And please, call me Lupe." She had then smiled at him and asked, politely, "May I please have my hand back now?"

Jose had laughed, and then reluctantly released her hand. "I am sorry. Will you be staying long?" He did not want this moment to end.

Before Lupe could answer Maria had interrupted, surprised at her son's flirtatious manner. "Little Jose, go away. Lupe and I need to start lunch." She'd shooed him out the door. "We will see you then."

Still awake and still thinking of his Lupita, Jose wondered what she was doing right now. Probably sleeping, as he should be doing as well. Instead, he continued to remember – unaware of the smile that was on his face – how their romance had progressed so quickly.

He would come to meals earlier than anyone else, and stay after the others had gone, often helping Lupe clear the long kitchen table. They had talked and laughed together as they worked, getting to know each other. By the first of February they were secretly meeting in the evenings after they were free from chores, holding hands as they talked about everything and nothing. Then by the first part of March Jose had worked up the courage to kiss her when they parted for the evening.

In April, the night before he was to meet Etta at the train station, Jose had taken the plunge and asked Lupe to be his wife. On bended knee he had told her how much he loved her and how he wanted to spend the rest of his life with her. Pulling him to his feet, she had hugged him tightly, then stepped back so she could look into his eyes before answering him.

"Of course I will marry you. I felt from that very first day in your mother's kitchen that we were meant for each other. I was wondering what was taking you so long to ask," she had laughed up at him. "But we will have to wait until August when my mother and my sisters come from Mexico, *si*?"

Pulling her back into his arms, he had kissed her passionately; all the love that was in his heart for her flowed into that kiss. "I'm not sure I can wait that long," he told her when they broke apart.

Laughing and pulling his head down for another kiss, she'd murmured before their lips met, "You will have to wait, my love, or my father will gladly kill you."

Jose was still smiling as he drifted off to sleep at last.

The next morning, even though it was only 7:00 a.m., as soon as Jose walked into the big kitchen Etta grabbed his arm and rattled off her plans for the day. She sounded as excited and impatient as a child who had been waiting for her parents to wake up on Christmas morning.

"Finally, there you are. I thought you were going to sleep forever. We have the whole day to spend together. After breakfast we're going to ride to the river. Maria's already made up a picnic basket that we'll take with us. Then we're going to…"

Laughing, he unhooked her from his arm and interrupted the recitation of her plans for their day. "Hold on a minute. You may be on vacation but I have a job to do."

While saying this, he was looking around the kitchen for Lupe. It was the perfect opportunity to introduce his two favorite girls. He noticed Lupe was not in the kitchen this morning, but before he could ask his mother where she was, Etta grabbed his arm again.

"Oh no, not today you don't. I've already gotten Big Jose's permission for you to take the whole day off." She smiled brightly, apparently pleased with her own cleverness, and looked up at him for his approval.

Maria, her co-conspirator, nodded her head. "*Si*, you are to spend the day with Etta. She needs some company. Eat, and then you two go and have fun." She pushed him toward a chair.

"Where's your helper this morning?" Jose asked his mother between bites of the enormous breakfast that was put in front of him. Lupe had not joined them the evening before, so he thought he'd ask her to go with them today. That way the girls could get to know each other.

"Her father is very ill so she is still with him. Fina will go over and check on him later in the day. He may not last much longer."

Jose thought about going to the bunkhouse to see her, but Etta was so insistent he finish his breakfast so they could get going, he gave in. He could check with Lupe when they returned to the ranch from their picnic. He decided he would not feel guilty about taking the day off and just relax and have fun with Etta. After all, she hadn't been home in months. They had a lot to talk about. If she couldn't meet Lupe yet, at least he could tell her about the love of his life. He was sure she would be very happy for him.

The horses were already saddled and the picnic provisions loaded when Jose left the ranch house for the stable. Always meticulous about detail, Etta had arranged to have this done so they would not waste any time. Mounting their horses, they headed for their favorite spot on the Santa Cruz River where a swimming hole pooled in a deep part of the river bed.

They rode for awhile in silence, the first time Etta had stopped talking since she got off the train the day before. It didn't last long, for her comments about the changes that had taken place in their surroundings came at a steady pace as they walked the horses and enjoyed the beauty of the grasslands. After ten minutes or so, just when Jose decided this was the perfect time to tell his childhood friend about his newfound love, Etta suddenly shouted, "Let's race!" She caught Jose off guard, and her laugh drifted back to him as she spurred her horse to a fast gallop.

Recovering, and not wanting to be beaten, Jose did the same. It was exhilarating to race over the familiar ground, something they had done often during their childhood and early teen years. Rarely had Etta beaten him to the river, but she had gotten a head start, and he wanted to take no chances. He urged his horse to go faster.

Etta's horse was younger, but Jose's was stronger, and he rode every day. Etta was out of practice because of her time away at university. Catching up to her, and then passing her, Jose reached the riverbank first. He was far enough ahead of her that he quickly dismounted and ran to a giant cottonwood. Reaching it, he sat on the ground and leaned up against it. Then he pulled his hat over his eyes and feigned sleep.

When Etta reached the bank at last and noticed that Jose was pretending to sleep, instead of kicking his boots with hers – their usual winner/loser ritual – she stretched and said casually, "What a beautiful day. I think I'll go for a swim."

Puzzled when he didn't feel the expected kick to his boots, Jose lifted his hat and looked in the direction of her voice. He was unaware that his mouth literally fell open as he stared at the sight that greeted his eyes. Standing directly in his line of vision, turned away from him, was Etta, completely naked. He had a second to appreciate the picture her trim, bare backside presented to him before recovering his senses.

"Suzetta Grace Luna," he shouted, "what in the hell are you doing?" His voice was shaking, and not completely from fury.

They had often been swimming here together but they always wore their swim suits under their clothes. In fact, if the weather had been a little warmer, Jose would probably have had his on under his clothes right now. They had never gone skinny-dipping, never even talked about the possibility of doing it. That was why the sight of Etta's unclothed body had unnerved him. At least that's what he told himself when he began to feel aroused by the sight of her perfectly formed bottom. He struggled to his feet, holding his hat in front of him to hide the unbidden telltale bulge as he walked toward the river. He tried to keep his walk casual, but it was difficult to do with an erection pressing against skin-tight Levis.

"What does it look like I'm doing?" she asked coyly, as she turned slightly toward him. He caught a glimpse of a rose-colored nipple on a pert, upturned breast before she turned back to the river. With a seductive glide she moved to the edge before asking over her shoulder,

"Aren't you going to join me?" Then, not waiting for an answer, she waded into what Jose knew had to be very cold water.

There was no way he was going to join her. And it wasn't just the cold water that was stopping him. Instead, he turned toward the horses to retrieve the blanket he knew she would need when she came out of the freezing water. While he waited he started a fire, and then unloaded the rest of the picnic supplies from the backs of the horses.

As he had anticipated, when Etta realized Jose was not going to join her she swam back to the bank, walked out of the water, and tried to present a confidence he was sure she didn't really feel as she slowly walked toward him. The problem was that she was shivering with cold, so it didn't look quite as seductive as she must have intended. Her smile was more of a grimace than an invitation. If he hadn't been so mesmerized by the sight of her naked body moving toward him he might have laughed.

Jose was quick to bring a warm blanket to cover her nakedness, shocked by her lack of modesty. "Here, cover yourself," he ordered gruffly, trying to pretend that he was unaffected by the sight of her perfect body.

Even covered with the coarse blanket and sitting directly in front of the fire, Etta continued to shiver with the cold. In fact, her lips were an odd shade of blue, not the healthy pink they usually were. In spite of the fact that she was freezing and her shivering hadn't stopped, he could tell by the small smile on her face that she knew he was trying to hide his reaction to her nakedness. He looked away to cover his embarrassment.

After a few minutes Jose went to his horse to retrieve the bottle of tequila he kept in his saddlebag. His father and Pancho always carried one, and told him one never knew when it could come in handy, either for staving off the biting cold out on the range or for doctoring rattlesnake bites. So far, however, he himself had rarely had occasion to uncap the bottle. He brought it back to the fire, uncapping it now and held it out to Etta.

"Take a drink of this, it will help warm you." His gaze was directed somewhere over her right shoulder.

As she reached for the bottle Etta's hand was shaking so violently that it finally brought Jose's eyes to her face. He could see that she was truly chilled to the bone. He brought the bottle to her lips and held it as she took a large swallow and then began to choke and cough as the alcohol burned its way down her throat.

"Easy, easy," Jose coaxed, "just a little sip at a time."

She took another small sip after she had caught her breath, and he then took a long swig from the bottle himself. He hoped it would help steady his nerves, which were finally beginning to calm now that Etta was completely covered by the blanket.

They passed the bottle back and forth between them until that and the heat from the fire began to do the trick and she appeared to feel much better. She was no longer shivering.

"Do you always carry tequila with you?" she questioned. She had never seen Jose take a drink of anything stronger than Maria's homemade cider.

"I keep it for snakebites," he answered, feeling a little light-headed. He was not accustomed to drinking. The picture of Etta's naked body as she'd walked toward him was still etched in his mind. So far the tequila had not erased the image, as he'd hoped it would.

Etta laughed, "So now I'm a snake?" The seductive voice was back. She leaned forward and held out her hand for a turn at the bottle, and as she did so she seemed to have *forgotten* to hold the blanket closed. When she moved the blanket dropped slightly, exposing most of her firm breasts.

"Should I bite you?" she offered, licking her lips.

At the sight of the luscious orbs in front of him Jose's eyes widened just a little and he took another long, fortifying swallow before nervously wiping his mouth and passing the bottle to her. Needing to do something, anything to keep from staring and remembering what else was under that blanket, he jumped up and looked around for more wood to add to the fire.

Etta took another long swig, which emptied the bottle. She put it down and stood up, her eyes never leaving Jose. Softly she called to him.

"Jose. Come here."

Her voice was husky, slurring just a little, and something he heard in it had Jose turning slowly to face her. As if in a trance he stood absolutely still and watched her move toward him. When she reached him she let the blanket fall to the ground.

"Make love to me," she commanded in a seductive whisper.

Then, standing on her toes, she reached up and with gentle hands brought his head down and his lips to hers. She kissed him deeply. He had no will power to pull away from her. Instead, his hands hanging at his sides, he accepted the kiss, wanted more. Pulling slightly away and watching his face, Etta took one hand and placed it over her bare breast.

This brought him out of his trance. Almost.

"Etta, no," Jose cried as he realized what was happening. He yanked his hand back as if her breast had burned him. His attempt to firmly push her away without touching anything but her bare shoulders was hampered by the effects of the tequila he had consumed.

"We can't do this." His voice didn't sound convincing, even to himself.

Standing firm, she moved her hand down to cover the bulge in his Levis. "Don't tell me you don't want me. What I have in my hand says you do." His body was betraying him and he could do nothing to stop it.

He groaned with the pleasure she was creating between his legs. "It's not that." Again he tried to push her away, again not very successfully.

She took his hand from her shoulder and brought it to the moist crevice between her legs. "I want you, Jose. I've always wanted you," her rapid breath whispered seductively in his ear. Her hips were moving with the rhythm of his hand that seemed to have a mind of its own. With her other hand she continued to entice him to a full erection that was straining to be free of the confining Levis.

Jose moaned, all thoughts of Lupe or anyone else for that matter, fleeing from his mind. His only thought now was the need to satisfy the hunger that was raging in him. At this moment he wanted to be inside her more than he had wanted anything in his life. As if in a dream he laid her down on the discarded blanket, then pulled off his boots and struggled to get his tight jeans off without damaging his erection. When at last he was free he hovered over her beckoning body for just a second, and then plunged deeply into the warmth of her sheath.

Her sudden cry of pain was mixed with cries of pleasure as he thrust into her and tore through her maidenhead with his rock-hard shaft. The shock of what he had just encountered made him pause when he heard her sharp cries, and feeling his hesitation she moaned and threw her arms around him.

"No, don't stop. Please don't stop. Not now," she was pleading, even as she tried to capture his mouth with hers.

Overcome with a lust that obliterated any reasoning ability he might have had left, Jose could not have stopped even if someone was holding a gun to his head. He was closing in on the point of no return. His thrusts had quickly brought him such an agonizing pleasure that it was only with the sliver of sanity left to him that he tried to withdraw at the last second before he came. But Etta, anticipating his intent, wrapped her legs tightly around him and would not let him go. He had no choice but to explode with his orgasm while being held captive inside her.

It took him a few moments to remember where he was, what they had just done. Then, still lying exhausted on top of her and still in her, he groaned into her shoulder.

"Oh, Etta, I'm so sorry. I didn't know you were a virgin. Did I hurt you too badly?" Even as he asked her this his eyes closed and Lupe's lovely face swam behind his closed lids. Hating himself, he silently screamed in his mind. What have I done? Damn that tequila!

He noticed Etta's smile when he lifted himself up and rested on his hands. She didn't appear to be upset at all. But before he could gather the strength to pull out of her and try to stand on legs that were still a bit rubbery she slipped her hands under the shirt that he had not bothered to remove. She rubbed the hair that she encountered on his chest.

"Well of course I was, silly; I've been saving myself for you."

Her words were like throwing cold water in his face, causing him to become instantly sober. Disgusted with himself for his weakness, he pulled free, jumped up and hurriedly dressed. He refused to make eye contact with Etta while he pulled on his boots. At the moment he didn't know who he was angrier with, himself or her.

"Get dressed," he ordered, as he stomped over to grab her clothes from where she had let them fall before going into the water. He tossed them in the general direction of where she was now sitting on the blanket. He had yet to look directly at her.

"But what about our picnic?"

Now he did look at her. The contempt he felt for himself showed on his face when he addressed her. "I'm not hungry. Get dressed now, or ride back alone. I'm packing up the horses." He knew he would never drink tequila again.

He turned on his heel to gather their picnic supplies, then took them to the horses and anchored them haphazardly. Once that was done he quickly mounted his own steed and turned in the direction of the ranch.

Etta was dressing quickly.

"Jose," she ventured softly when she had mounted her horse, "I love you." Without answering he spurred his horse and galloped away.

Jose slowed his horse down once he was out of sight of Etta. He just wanted to be alone, to think about what had just happened. He was filled with shame for taking Etta's virginity, but also for being unfaithful to Lupe. He knew that Lupe – like Etta had been – was a virgin. They had spoken frankly of what was going to happen on their wedding night. Jose had told his beloved that he had never been with a virgin before, but that he would be very tender and would do his best not to hurt her. He had also confessed that he had been with two other women before he met the love of his life.

The first had been with a *puta*, a whore, in Nogales, Sonora. Jose was just 14 and Humberto 15 when Carlos, an older cousin, had taken them to a local brothel for their first time. It had not been a pleasant experience, in spite of the climax the whore had given him, and he felt dirty afterward. That was his first and only visit to a brothel.

The second time was when he was 16 and he was helping a young woman who was moving from the ranch to Tucson following the death of her husband, one of the ranch hands, several months earlier. Jose understood that the young widow was lonely and had reached out to him for comfort. She was older than he by 12 years, but he was a good student, and they found mutual satisfaction in each other's arms. It was a brief encounter but one that would always remain in his mind as the turning point between his youth and his adulthood.

He had told all of this to Lupe. He didn't want any secrets between them, and she had listened and understood that often young boys engaged in sexual activities before they reached manhood. It was like a rite of passage.

Thinking about their openness with each other, he felt he had no choice but to tell her that he had been unfaithful to her, and only two days after he had asked her to marry him. He would beg her forgiveness and spend the rest of his life making it up to her. Being drunk on tequila was no excuse, and he hoped he could convince her to forgive this one indiscretion.

Alas, this was not to be his day for redemption. When he reached the ranch house he saw Fina hurrying toward the bunkhouse. She was carrying her medicine bag. He dismounted quickly and ran to catch up to her. He had a feeling he knew who was ill.

"Fina, what is it? Is it Hector? Is it bad?"

Fina stopped when she saw Jose coming toward her. "Jose, I'm so glad you are back. Yes, it's Hector. His time has come," she answered him.

She said this as if they were having an ordinary conversation. For Fina, who knew and had seen many things in her life, death was not a mystery, nor something to be feared. It was simply the end of a life, the beginning of a greater glory. Today she had been hurrying, not to stop death, but to make it more comfortable. She had known it was Hector's day to die; she had known it for weeks now.

As she was explaining this to Jose, she looked directly into his eyes. Now she said, "Jose, don't worry about Etta, she will be fine. And Lupe will forgive you, in time. But you mustn't burden her today. She will be too upset with her father's passing."

The young man reddened with shame and embarrassment. Damn it, he thought. He took Fina's ability to read people and to know their unspoken thoughts for granted. Now that he was the object of her scrutiny he cursed himself for forgetting.

"What's done is done." She turned and started off again toward the bunkhouse, then said over her shoulder, "Don't just stand there, come along. Lupe needs you."

CHAPTER 13 – *Jose 1951* – The Deception

Jose closed the journal and put it in his coat pocket. He was completely exhausted. He couldn't read anymore, at least not now. How could he not have known after all these years that Samantha had inherited Fina's gifts? Why hadn't anyone told him, he wondered. She'd been six years old when she wrote the words he'd been reading. Had she understood even half of them? According to what she wrote at the beginning, she had not. He had never understood how Fina's gifts worked, and he certainly did not understand his daughter's.

Reliving the past through the words of the journal reminded Jose about a conversation he'd had with Fina the night of his wedding to Etta. In fact, it was as he sat on the porch of the Garden Room after leaving his wedding reception. At the time he was thinking back to the day he had allowed himself to be seduced by Etta. He let his mind drift back to the conversation with his mother-in-law that evening 28 years ago.

"Shit," Jose cursed out loud, remembering the day at the river. He was now convinced that Etta had in fact planned the whole seduction, hoping to become pregnant. She would have known that was the only way he would have married her.

"It doesn't have to be as bad as it seems," Fina spoke soothingly as she moved quietly toward him.

He looked up at her when she reached him, then followed her with his eyes as she sat in the rocker next to his and took his hand. He was not surprised to find her at the Garden Room. She often craved time alone and this was the natural place for her to do her best thinking.

"You knew, didn't you, Fina? You knew the day Hector died that it would all come to this. Why didn't you tell me then? You knew what Etta had planned." Angrily he pulled his hand from hers. "Why didn't you warn me in time to stop her?"

Fina, unfazed by Jose's anger or his action, reached for his hand once more. Gently, and with love, she answered him, "*Ma cher*, I don't always know everything, at least not all the details. Sometimes, especially with those closest to me, I only get vague impressions. But even if I see clearly, I cannot change anything. I cannot warn, I cannot tell what I know. It isn't my place to try to change fate. How I wish I could, but I just cannot. I have accepted this, but it is hard for others to understand."

Again Jose extracted his hand from Fina's, more gently this time, and put both hands up to cover his face. His voice was muffled as he said, "Maybe, but then you must know that I love Lupe. And I will never love Etta the way she wants me to. Now that I realize what she did I don't know if I can love her at all. She's robbed me of the life I was planning with Lupita; the life I will never have now."

"I know my dear, I know. But maybe there was a higher purpose all along."

Frustrated, Jose dropped his hands and glared at the woman beside him. "I don't care what the *purpose* was. It was not MY purpose. How can I ever forgive her? How?"

Reaching over to pat his knee, her calm voice in contrast to his anguished one, the wise woman said, "I don't know, Jose. You need to look deep inside yourself for the answer."

Jose had to think more about Etta's deception. He did not understand lies and deceit, and was not sure how to handle it in the woman who was now his wife. He would not confront her tonight, but neither would he lie with her as her husband. There was much to think about. His pain went all the way to his heart.

Fina had said to look deep inside himself for forgiveness. How do you forgive what Etta had done? It would take him a long time, if ever. He knew he would never leave her; he would not dishonor his wife or his family that way. She had hurt him deeply with her schemes and now would suffer the consequences. They would remain married, but in name only. There was more than one way in which to hurt someone.

Jose looked around the plane, as much to ease the ache in his neck as to check on the other passengers. His eyes fell on the sleeping figure that was Etta and on his parents, sleeping shoulder to shoulder, head to head. He wished that he, too, could fall asleep. Only in sleep could he forget. But it was not to be.

Even after all these years Jose knew he still had not forgiven Etta. And he had let the bitterness and anger consume him to the point that he let it override the duty he had to be a good father. In his heart he knew why he wasn't told about Sam's gifts. Why would anyone tell him when it was obvious he would not have been interested? When had he *ever* shown an interest in his daughter? What kind of a man was he? Was he incapable of loving a child born of deception? *Even his own child?*

He was devastated now, knowing he could lose her, when he admitted to himself that he had never even tried to know Samantha. He had stayed in the background and allowed Maria and Fina to raise her. He had never held her in his lap, or told her stories, or soothed her hurts and fears. How had he let that happen? Even Etta had never been there for their child. Her excuse was alcohol. What was his? Jose experienced a new pain, one even stronger than one he'd been carrying around with him all these years. It was the pain of a father who may lose his child.

At last he had the answer to the question he had put to Fina all those years ago. He could forgive Etta by being a father to the child she gave him. He prayed it was not too late. With his eyes closed and tears streaming down his cheeks, he prayed silently to God, something he had not done in many years.

"Please dear God, spare my child. I want to be the kind of parent she deserves, the kind of parent I had, and Etta had. Please give me a chance to know her, to make it up to her, to love her."

CHAPTER 14 – *Sam 1979* – The Apology

"Samantha? Sammy, honey, please wake up," Etta pleaded with her daughter.

She checked her watch. It seemed as if they'd been here for hours, taking turns sitting by the side of Sam's bed, watching their pale, motionless child. She was hooked up to so many machines it was hard to find a place on her hands or arms that wasn't pierced by needles.

Etta pulled her chair closer and gently slid her hand under the one that lay unmoving on the bed. She was careful not to touch any of the needles.

"My poor, poor baby," Etta crooned quietly. "If I could, I would take your place."

As she continued to watch her daughter it slowly dawned on her that it had been hours since she'd had a drink. The amazing thing was, she realized, for the first time in years she wasn't craving alcohol. Bowing her head, she prayed silently: *Dear God, if You let my daughter live, I promise I'll never drink again.*

Aloud, a small sob escaped from Etta.

"Oh, Baby, please forgive me. If I could just go back and do it all again, I know I could be a good mother. If it's not too late I promise from now on that's what I'll be. I'll be a good mother to you…a good mother…a good mother…" she whispered over and over.

Sam could hear her mother's voice but it sounded so far away, as if she was at the end of a long tunnel. She wanted to reassure her mother, wanted to beg her not to cry, to tell her that forgiveness wasn't necessary, but the words wouldn't come. They were only in her head.

She remembered dreaming of her mother's childhood when she was just a child herself; strange dreams that now she was beginning to understand. She mentally smiled as she also remembered many conversations she and Maman had had about Etta.

With an understanding she hadn't possessed as a child, Samantha now knew her mother was the only one who could change what she'd become. And it sounded like she was ready to make that change. If only Sam could tell her she understood, and that forgiveness wasn't necessary.

If only...

Chapter 15 – *Etta 1933 to 1951* – Project Jose

Etta was born without her mother's unique gifts but she had plenty of her own. Besides being adorable, sweet and kind, she was brilliant. She had learned to read by age two. By four, when she wasn't trailing behind her playmate, Little Jose, she was following Dr. Bowman, the ranch's long-time veterinarian, as he made his rounds on the ranch.

"Why are you doing it that way, Doc?" was a question often heard by the old vet. "Have you thought of doing …?" or "I read about a different way of doing that…" would often follow on the heels of the first, always polite, query.

The young girl was full of opinions on how things could be done differently, always trying to improve on the tried and true methods that most vets relied on. Doc had to admit, when he'd let himself be convinced to try her suggestions, she was usually right on the money. She kept him on his toes by challenging him daily, and for this reason he loved having her around.

When she was five, she begged him to let her read his medical textbooks that were kept in the extensive library in the hacienda. He hesitated before giving her his consent, not because he thought that she'd lose or damage his treasured possessions, or even that she was too young to understand the complicated medical terms and theories; he was actually just a little afraid that she'd show him up. He finally relented because he knew that forbidding Etta to have or to do something she had her heart set on rarely stopped her from getting her way. Besides, he had a suspicion that she'd been reading them already, without his permission.

Etta spent hours in the library that doubled as her father's office, often curled up in one of the several horse-hair-stuffed, high-backed leather chairs situated throughout the massive shelf-lined room. She read her way through one shelf at a time, she would say. She had a photographic memory and a keen mind unrivaled by any that Doc had encountered in his 69 years of life. She was a genuine genius, many said, and sometimes she was downright scary.

Pancho's library was like a gold mine. It contained a vast collection of books, all leather-bound, that could put more than one public library to shame. The subjects of the volumes were varied, so the library's shelves were filled with Greek mythology, philosophy, cow husbandry, metallurgy, books of poems, to name just a few. What it did not contain was a single frivolous novel. If one could not find reading material on the first floor, a black wrought-iron spiral staircase led to the second floor, where a railed 15-foot-wide deck surrounded the room. Shelves lined the 10-foot-high second story walls and they contained an extended menu of choices. These shelves were interspersed with strategically placed leaded windows, giving the room a warm glow on sunny days when the fireplace was unlikely to be lit.

Just being in the room itself was a pleasant way to spend an afternoon. As with many of the rooms in the Hacienda de Luna, the library boasted a massive river-rock fireplace. It was built at one end of the long room and provided comforting warmth to anyone who wished to relax with an interesting tome on a winter afternoon. The leather over-stuffed couch and matching chairs arranged in front of the fireplace were perfect for snuggling into their depths while reading.

Pancho's enormous polished writing desk – usually covered with opened books, papers, and ashtrays with remnants of half-smoked Cuban cigars – dominated the center of the room, positioned to take advantage of both the view of the fireplace and of the majestic Santa Rita Mountains, visible through French doors that led to the wrap-around porch of the hacienda.

This room was the site of many important conferences between Pancho and Doc, who had become good friends. Doc no longer had a private practice; he worked exclusively for Pancho. In addition to being the ranch's vet his responsibilities included improving cattle production, lowering calf mortality rates, monitoring herd rotation, and basically anything that was needed to trim costs and to increase the ranch's profit margins. The friends would spend hours in the library bouncing ideas off each other on how to accomplish these goals.

More likely than not Etta would be present during these conversations. She would sit quietly in her favorite leather chair by the fireplace, knowing she wasn't to interrupt the sometimes heated discussions between her two favorite men. However, by the time she was seven it wasn't unusual for Papa or Doc to allow her to offer a suggestion, or even to sometimes vie for her support when faced with a difference of opinion.

During one particular discussion between the men regarding the fact that 'calf dropping' had fallen drastically in the previous couple of years and they might have to increase the size of the herd, the young girl could hold her tongue no longer. She cleared her throat loudly to get their attention.

"You are both wrong. The problem is that the herd sizes are already too big. If we *decreased* the herd size in each division, the heifers would have more to eat and therefore be healthier, which would result in their giving birth to healthier calves. Also, as the calves grow, with more to eat, they would weigh more at weaning time. You can see that the profits would grow, as we would be producing more. Plus, we would have better-tasting beef I might add, per hoof."

Both men stared at the petite seven-year-old, who was almost dwarfed by the large chair. Pancho was the first to speak, voicing what was obvious on his and Doc's faces as they started to smile and nod their heads in agreement with the child's assessment of the situation.

"Damn it, Doc, if that doesn't make perfect sense." Walking to his daughter and scooping her into his arms, he grinned at the solemn face. "Etta, my dear, you are a genius."

"Yes, Papa, I know," she hugged him back, taking the complement as her due.

Doc looked at father and daughter, shook his head, and stood up with both hands flat on the desk.

"Well then, let's give it a go."

Etta had been right. The results were remarkable. After selling off a part of the herd in each division, within the next few years calf production increased from less than 50% to over 90%. The average weight had increased at weaning from around 250 pounds to almost 450 pounds. As the precocious child had predicted, this dramatically increased the ranch's profits; Rancho de Luna became one of the largest and wealthiest ranches in the state of Arizona. Pancho wasn't sure, but they might even rival any cattle ranch in the entire western part of the country, for that matter.

Etta also loved to help her mother, whether it was mixing healing potions in the Garden Room or planting and weeding Fina's herb gardens. Her curiosity was insatiable. She wanted to learn everything there was to know about each plant, from any medicinal properties that aided healing, to which herbs would most enhance Maria's wonderful recipes in the kitchen.

After waiting impatiently one day while her mother searched her files for a particular note on the plant that was being studied, Etta suggested that her mother compile the voluminous notes and drawings into an orderly catalogue. Fina agreed that it was a great idea.

"Maybe that's something you should take on, my dear," she smiled at her daughter.

There was no direct answer, but within a year, in typical Etta fashion, after countless hours of sorting, copying, redrawing and recompiling over many months, she had completed the task. At the age of ten she was the author of one of the most comprehensive encyclopedias of herbal medicine in existence at that time.

Pancho had been so impressed with the finished product that he sent it off to Philadelphia to have 20 volumes printed and bound in the finest leather. When the carton of books arrived he immediately placed a copy in the medical section of the library.

"Here," he said proudly, indicating the book with one hand and resting the other on his daughter's shoulder, "is the first of many books my beautiful and talented daughter will create."

Etta was tutored at home, following the practice of the wealthier families in the area. This was due to the logistics of getting the children to one of the few schools that were scattered around the sparsely populated Santa Cruz Valley. Because of Etta's aptitude for absorbing knowledge like a sponge, her photographic memory, and her goal to read every one of the intriguing books in Papa's library, she soon surpassed in knowledge every tutor hired to teach her. She spoke fluent French and Spanish, her parents' native languages, but she also learned German, Italian, Portuguese, and Latin. Latin was her favorite language because of her love of any and all things medical.

Fina was a healer, not only for the ranch's population, but for surrounding areas. Her pre-teen daughter often accompanied her when it was necessary to visit patients. The inquisitive student asked many questions, but also freely gave advice.

Between working with Doc and with her mother, Etta vacillated between attending veterinary or medical school. Either choice would probably have been ludicrous for the average female in the early years of the 1940's, but for the budding genius in the Luna family a career in medicine – working either with animals or humans – made perfect sense. She ultimately decided on medical school after deciding the field of veterinary medicine was too narrow. Just working with her beloved Doc had her feeling that there was not enough room to grow or to experiment in that field. She knew her father's willingness to endow a school of her choice with a new medical library, as well as the probability of her acing any entrance exam, should ensure her acceptance to any medical school when the time came.

The summer Etta turned 12 it was obvious that she would have to go to boarding school in order to continue her education prior to entry into any college. So, with much discussion, research, and apprehension, a boarding school outside of New Orleans was chosen. Fina was relieved because at least her daughter would be near her maternal grandmother and great-grandmother, the Rubies, relatives Etta had never met, but who still lived in Baton Rouge.

Etta herself was both ecstatic and terrified. Ecstatic because she needed new knowledge as much as she needed food and water to survive, terrified because she'd had very limited exposure to the world beyond the ranch's boundaries. She didn't want to leave her parents or Maria and Big Jose. Then there was Doc, and most of all Little Jose that she would miss.

Somewhere between the ages of 11 and 12 she had realized that she was falling in love with her childhood friend. Unfortunately, it didn't take a genius or a psychic like her mother, to realize that Jose, as she decided to call him from now on, was oblivious to her growing affection. The young girl, however, wasn't worried. She wanted Jose. It was that simple. So, as with anything she had ever wanted, she was convinced she would get him. Going away to school would give her ample opportunity to plan her 'Project Jose' as she called it.

She knew that boarding school was a necessary precursor to college and medical school, yet she doubted that acquiring the knowledge she lacked would be very difficult. Therefore, she would sail through her studies as was expected of her, but the most important goals of the next six to eight years would be to experience life outside the confines of the ranch and to plan her future with Jose.

Etta, who was used to being the center of attention, was in for a big surprise her first week at boarding school. Here she was not catered to by anyone at all; instead, it was as if she had become invisible. Her classmates ignored her because she looked and acted exactly like what she was: a girl straight from a ranch located, of all places, somewhere in Arizona. With her western drawl she sounded like a hick, or so said several girls she had overheard mocking her accent. In the Santa Cruz Valley the Luna name was revered; here it meant nothing. Nobody cared that her father was rich because all the girls who attended this exclusive school came from wealthy families. And among a sea of beautiful faces, hers was not exceptional.

Her teachers barely tolerated her after they found her to be completely confident in her abilities, bordering on arrogant, and realized that in some areas, where life experience was the best teacher, she was more knowledgeable than they were. Basically, she didn't concern herself with the way the professors reacted to her. She knew she was absorbing everything they had to teach her, and she could get straight A's with very little effort

After a few weeks of trying to be accepted by the other students, and being ignored for her efforts, Etta decided on another approach. Using her analytical mind and a scientific approach of observe and record, she put together a long-term plan: she would learn how to be sophisticated; she would cultivate a southern drawl; she would find ways to make her own beauty unique. Actually, her goal was two-fold: to fit in with the other students, and to capture Jose's attention. If Jose saw her as more polished and mature by the time she finished boarding school, he would have to fall in love with her. There was not a doubt in her mind that this was true.

Over the next two years Etta intentionally remained in the background, the better to observe and learn. She eavesdropped whenever she had an opportunity. She learned where the popular students shopped and where they had their hair done.

She always signed up for chaperoned trips to New Orleans when they were planned. During these trips, when the girls were allowed free time, she would visit the best boutiques. Gradually her western garb was replaced with cashmere sweater sets, pencil skirts flared at the hem, the softest, most sophisticated coat to ward off the chilly days in winter. During one of these trips she used most of the allowance she had saved from the monthly checks her father sent her to have her long hair cut into the latest style by the most sought-after hairdresser. It was expensive, but it was worth it.

She worked especially hard to lose her western drawl, practicing in secret. She visited with the Rubies every few weeks and would concentrate on listening to their speech patterns and correct phrasing. She mimicked what she observed from both her relatives and her classmates, and soon she became a clone of every other girl at her school. However, her metamorphosis was so gradual and subtle that her classmates accepted the improved Etta without remembering the western hick that she had formerly been. It was taken for granted that she was one of their own.

She left the acquired southern drawl at school and wore her western clothes for the few times she returned to the ranch during school holidays – she wanted to keep her new, secret persona as a surprise when the time was right. She would have liked to visit her family more often, but it just wasn't feasible since her time was filled with her studies in order to keep to her goal of finishing medical school by the time she was 20.

Genius that she was, Etta finished 'boring school,' as she secretly referred to it, in two years. She then applied to, and was accepted by a college outside of Baton Rouge, where she completed the four-year degree program in two years. After graduation she enrolled in medical school at the age of 16.

Etta wasn't the only one who was changing: by the time he was 16 Jose's voice had changed to a deep, sexy baritone; he had grown at least 6 inches and had the faint shadow of a beard on his chiseled chin by the end of the day. His formerly lean body had become muscular and sculptured as his chores around the ranch became more physically demanding. She thought he was beautiful and her love for him only intensified each time she saw him. She loved him completely with her whole heart, and refused to believe he didn't feel the same way about her.

Now in her second year of med school, Etta was confident that her plan for spending the rest of her life as Jose's wife would be realized after she graduated. She would become a practicing physician in Tucson and they would be happy forever. Then the unthinkable happened.

Maria, who had written to her regularly from the day Etta left home for boarding school, sent a letter in which she mentioned a girl named Lupita. Her letter sounded just like Maria: happy, on top of the world. She couldn't know it brought Etta's world crashing down around her. *You should see Little Jose around Lupita. He is like a puppy and she is like the milk that he wants to lap up*, her letter informed Etta, ignorant of the devastation this news would bring. She apparently assumed her son's childhood playmate would be happy for him.

The 18-year-old Etta was stunned. How could *her* Jose be thinking of someone else like that? Ignoring the fact that they had never spoken of love to each other, she felt betrayed, as if he had been unfaithful to her. She hadn't planned to visit the ranch in the near future, but she made a sudden decision. She hurriedly wrote her mother and Maria and told them she was homesick and had decided to come home for Easter break.

It was time to bring out her secret weapon, the new and improved Etta. We'd see who Jose would want to 'lap up' then.

When she stepped off the train in Patagonia she saw him immediately. He was even more gorgeous than she remembered. She could tell he didn't recognize her because he had looked right at her twice. So far so good, not the little girl anymore, she thought. She waved and called out to him, then ran and threw her arms around him.

"Jose, why I do believe you are the handsomest thing this side of the Mississippi!" This was exclaimed in her best Southern drawl, assuming he would find it sexy. She had expected him to be dazzled by the new and improved Etta, but he merely laughed.

"And I do believe," he said, mocking her accent and lifting her high in the air, "that you are still the biggest brat this side of the Santa Cruz River."

When he set her down she tried to cover the hurt that his remark caused. She glanced behind him and asked, "Where's Mama and Maria?"

He explained that they were at the ranch or something, she really didn't hear or care what he'd said; all she could think about was that he hadn't even noticed how she had changed.

She knew she looked good; she received plenty of attention at school from the opposite sex. And she knew it wasn't just because she was one of only a few women enrolled in medical studies. Why, numerous men had approached her on the long train ride home. They had tried to talk to her, to sit by her; they had offered to get her food or something to drink. Many more had watched with admiring eyes as she walked past them. Yes, plenty of men had noticed her. Why couldn't Jose see how beautiful and sophisticated she had become?

She was determined to talk non-stop all the way home. She wouldn't give him an opportunity to bring up that girl's name. She had never felt so hurt, so uncertain. She couldn't wait to get to the ranch, to see this Lupita, to see her rival. She needed to talk to Maria and her mother to find out just how serious Jose was about this girl. By God, no one, *absolutely no one* was going to take Jose away from her, not now, not ever.

When they finally arrived home Etta was exhausted from trying to act as if nothing was wrong. She wanted to scream but instead she jumped out of the truck as soon as Jose slowed to a stop in front of the ranch house. Of course everyone was outside, waiting to greet her. She hugged them all, said all the right things, while wanting nothing more than to get into the house, into the kitchen and have a good look at Lupita. Finally, she was able to unhook herself from *the mothers.*

"I'm starving. When's dinner?"

Fina laughed, noticing the southern drawl, and ignoring the question. "You look wonderful darling. I love your new look."

Etta glanced toward Jose to see if he was listening but he was busy at the back of the truck unloading her things.

"Why thank you, Mother." Grabbing Maria's hand, she asked, "Maria, did you make tacos?" This would be a sure way to get into the kitchen.

"*Si, si, Mi Hija*, let's go and get you one." Maria squeezed Etta's hand and started toward the open front door.

Fina said, "You two go ahead, I need to first stop by the bunkhouse. I'll be back in a few minutes. Don't start telling Maria anything without me, darlin'." She lapsed into a southern drawl herself.

Maria could not be hurried, so the walk to the kitchen was slow while she updated Etta on the latest doings at the ranch. When they finally reached their destination Etta saw that Lupita was nowhere in sight. She did not have to pretend the disappointment she felt, and let it show on her face. She asked, "Maria, where's Lupita? I thought she would be here, helping you. I was looking forward to meeting her."

Maria's smile faded, "Oh, the poor thing. She is with her father in the bunkhouse. Her father is Hector Garcia. You remember him, no? Anyway, poor Hector is very sick. I told Lupita to take the night off and stay with him. That's why your mama needed to go there." She shook her head as if to rid it of sad thoughts and smiled once more as she grabbed Etta. "Let me get a closer look at you, you are so pretty, so grown-up."

"You sure are," her mother declared, entering the kitchen and hugging her daughter again.

"Mama, Maria says that Lupita's father is ill. Is he going to be okay?" Etta asked, more concerned with Lupita's absence than with Hector's illness.

"I'm afraid not. It's his time; he will not last much longer. But let's talk about that later. Tell me everything," she urged her daughter.

And so it went: continual conversation before, during and after dinner, and still no Lupita. Etta avoided speaking directly to Jose, not wanting to give him a chance to bring up her mysterious rival. However, she watched him covertly all evening. And she didn't like what she saw: the expectant glances as he kept looking at the kitchen door. Etta knew who he was hoping to see walk through the door, and she wished more than anything in the world that he would look at her with that same longing in his eyes.

"Maria, what's going on with Jose and Lupita? In your letter, you said he acted like a puppy around her." Everyone had gone to bed and she was finally alone with Jose's mother.

Maria's face lit up. "Oh, *si*, Lupita is a good girl, a nice girl. I think

Little Jose will ask her to marry him soon. I think she will make him a good wife."

Etta's heart seemed to stop, she felt like she couldn't catch her breath. She was silent for so long that Maria's smile faded to a frown.

"*Mi Hija*? Are you okay?"

Etta feigned a smile, trying to compose herself.

"Yes, I was just thinking that it's been so long since I've had any time to spend with Jose. I was wondering if he could get the day off tomorrow and we could ride to the river, perhaps have a picnic."

"That's a great idea," Big Jose said behind her when he entered the kitchen for his nightly glass of warm milk. "That boy hasn't had a day off in weeks, only Sunday afternoons. You two go, have a nice picnic. Catch up."

"There you go," Maria laughed, hugging her husband. "*El jefe*, the boss, has spoken."

Turning back to Etta she said, "Now you go to bed, you must be tired after your long trip. I'll make a picnic lunch in the morning, and you and Little Jose can go right after breakfast."

Etta went to her room but she didn't sleep. She kept reviewing the day in her mind. Nothing was going according to her plan, nothing. Jose hadn't noticed her hair, her clothes, or her drawl – and even worse, she knew now for sure that Jose was in love with Lupita. What was she going to do? Her whole reason for coming here was to impress Jose with the gorgeous creature she had worked so hard to become.

She felt like a beautiful butterfly that had escaped from its cocoon. She had anticipated the look of love that would shine from his eyes when he noticed the transformation. Instead, she felt as if she was the same ordinary caterpillar who had followed him around all his life. Determined to make him see her as the woman she had become, she vowed to do whatever it took to ensure that he was hers, now and forever – even if it meant postponing her graduation from medical school. She knew she was perfect for him, had always known it, and she would not let him make a mistake by marrying that...that woman who would steal him from her.

And so, lying in her childhood bed, she revised her Project Jose to include a new plan that would ensure Jose was hers forever...

CHAPTER 16 – *Jose 1979 - Reflection*

Jose was alone in the ICU waiting room, pacing back and forth. There was still no sign of Michael, Sam's husband, and Humberto had taken Maria and Big Jose to a nearby hotel. Maria agreed to go only after extracting Jose's promise – several times in fact – that he would call if there was any change in Sam's condition. Etta was sitting with their daughter in her ICU room. They had been taking turns, it seemed for hours, but it was still dark outside so it hadn't been as long as it felt.

As he paced his thoughts centered on his wife. Once she'd sobered up and realized Sam was in grave danger she seemed like her old self, the one he had known and loved when they were growing up together – before her deception had ruined his life. After reliving the past in Sam's journal he'd come to admit that he had wasted the last 28 years of his life. He should have forgiven Etta. So she had made mistakes, who hadn't? They had been so young. He remembered again how he had intentionally hurt her by staying married to her in name only. *There was more than one way in which to hurt someone.* Had he really been that cruel?

He admitted to himself that he had not only hurt Etta by years of unforgiveness, he had hurt their daughter. His aloofness had deprived him and Sam both of the love and affection between a father and child. *I can change* he told himself. *I can forgive Etta and I can ask her to forgive me as well. I know now that I am not without blame, and that all three of us have suffered because of my stubbornness. I will forgive both Etta and myself. And when Sam is better we will ask her forgiveness as well, for being lousy parents.*

All this thinking was exhausting, Jose decided. He wanted to read more of Samantha's journal, convinced he would gain as much insight into Etta as he had into himself. So he settled into one of the uncomfortable chairs in the waiting room and opened the journal. He flipped to the last entry he had read, and was happy to notice that the next entry appeared to be about Etta. This is what he was hoping to find. He was sure it would help him to forgive and move forward.

He began to read…

CHAPTER 17 – *Etta 1951 - Determination*

Sunday, May 12, 1957: This morning I tried to read what I had written yesterday about Poppie and I couldn't understand all the words so I guess that I was right: I'm supposed to write, not to understand.

Last night I had a dream about my mother. I can't remember everything but I'm going to see if my hand will write by itself like it did yesterday. As Maman always says, I think I'm meant to do it…

The handwriting dramatically changed from the childish scrawl of the first two paragraphs. Jose quickly turned back to the previous day's entry; same thing, childish scrawl and then eloquent penmanship. He hadn't noticed this before, but of course he had been worried about Sam and surprised by what he was reading in the journal.

Jose closed his eyes. He felt vastly relieved. As weird as all of this was, he thought, at least Sam didn't know what she had written, not then. He vaguely remembered Fina mentioning something about 'auto writing' when he was younger. Maybe that was what the six-year-old Sam had been trying to explain.

If Jose hadn't been around Fina for all those years, he wouldn't have believed a child of Sam's age – the age at which she wrote her journals – was capable of such things. But he had. He had seen Fina heal, he had heard the stories of her *visitors* and knew that she could *see* the future and the past. She had read his thoughts many, many times. It was clear that Sam had Fina's gift. He opened his eyes, anxious again to read about the past.

Etta was not only unhappy; she was also worried on the train back to New Orleans. She was mentally reconstructing the whole miserable trip in her mind, from the point at which she had alighted from the train in Patagonia, to getting back on it for the return to school a mere three days later. Nothing that had happened during this trip had gone as she'd painstakingly planned. After trying to show Jose that she had become a desirable woman, and shamelessly seducing him at the river, it was downhill from there. No, this was not how she had planned it at all. Unreasonably, she blamed Lupe for the ruined vacation.

If Etta were to be completely honest, and in a generous frame of mind, she could understand what Jose saw in Lupita. The woman would not be considered beautiful, as Etta herself was, but she was definitely pretty. She was also taller than Etta, and her height suited Jose's perfectly.

"How could he fall for someone who is so big?" she grumbled to herself. Big was an adjective that Etta preferred to apply rather than being kind and admitting Lupita was not only tall, she was well-proportioned. However, there was no kindness in her heart toward her rival for Jose's affections.

Lupita's straight hair was long and thick, a shining black waterfall that almost reached her waist. Etta touched her own hair, regretting that she'd had it cut into its stylish shoulder-length bob. She could do nothing about that now, what was done was done. Instead she concentrated on enumerating her own attributes: in addition to being beautiful she was intelligent; she was a published author; her father was one of the richest men in the western United States, which gave her privileges that those who were lesser born would not have; and she, Suzetta Grace Luna, would become a very famous surgeon. Lupita, she assured herself smugly, would always be a housemaid.

Stop it, she told herself. She would gain nothing by comparing herself to that woman. The fact was Jose had always been hers, and he always would be, especially if she was now pregnant with his child. The best woman would win, and there was no doubt in Etta's mind just who the best woman was. She smiled serenely to herself. She had a trump card that Lupita could not compete with. She patted her stomach and spoke aloud to the baby that she was convinced had already been started inside her.

"You are going to help me win your father, aren't you, my little one?"

She leaned back on her seat. If only she could have gotten Jose to make love to her at least one more time. She sighed, and then a sound which resembled a laugh, but was without humor, escaped from her lips. Who was she kidding? She would be lucky if he ever spoke to her again. She closed her eyes while she replayed the past three days in her mind.

She had ridden leisurely back to the ranch after Jose left her in a cloud of dust. Having known him all of her life, she knew that when Jose was upset he always needed time alone. He was definitely upset, that was obvious. She tried to convince herself it was because he had taken her virginity, not because he had been unfaithful to Lupita. They weren't married, after all. Maria said she thought Jose was going to ask Lupita to marry him, and surely his mother would have known if he had already proposed. So that made him fair game. All he needed was time; enough time for him to remember her telling him that she loved him. Then he would come running back to her. She just had to be patient.

She had enjoyed their love-making even if it wasn't exactly what she had been expecting. But then, who really knew what to expect the first time? What she had really enjoyed was the feeling of power that she experienced while watching him succumb to his orgasm. Unfortunately, there had been no lingering afterward in each other's arms the way she had planned. He obviously hadn't been concerned with her welfare, with the fact that she was a little sore as she tried to sit gingerly in the saddle. Jose had ruined the whole experience by storming off in a rage.

As she approached the stables she noticed a gathering in front of the bunkhouse. Several men were standing idly by, when they would normally be working somewhere on the ranch. Maria was hurrying from the bunkhouse to the kitchen at the back of the hacienda. Suddenly, Etta remembered something her mother mentioned the previous day about Lupita's father. But she had been distracted, worrying more about getting Jose alone than what her mother was telling her about one of the hired hands being gravely ill.

Spurring her horse forward, she quickly dismounted by the bunkhouse door and handed the reins to one of the cowboys standing nearby. It was then that she noticed Jose's stallion tied to the hitching post. It was unusual for Jose to leave his horse saddled after a hard ride; he always made sure it was fed, watered, and brushed, as any conscientious horseman would. The fact that he hadn't, told Etta more than any words could that the situation was dire. Absently lifting a hand to smooth her hair, she hurried into the bunkhouse.

Inside, the bunk areas lined both outside walls. They were separated by a wall on either side, to form their own generous cubicle, and were open to a main hallway which ran through the middle of the large building. Each sectioned area was spotless and contained the necessities: a cot or a bunk, a footlocker, a small table and single chair, a nightstand and a lamp. An occasional framed photograph sat on a dresser. Pancho liked to make sure his hands were well paid, well fed, and well housed – unlike most other ranchers, whose bunkhouses contained a cot for sleeping and very little else. He took pride in the fact that Rancho de Luna's bunkhouses offered semi-private quarters for its hands. In addition, Pancho treated his workers fairly and honestly, so he was never short-handed like several other ranches in the area often were.

When Etta entered the bunkhouse she noticed Big Jose, Doc, and her father standing half-way down the corridor in front of one of the bunk areas. It was natural to head in their direction. Noticing her approach, Doc went to meet her, reaching his arms toward her for a hug.

"How's my genius?" he whispered. He had been away yesterday when she arrived, so this was his first glimpse of her.

After returning the welcoming hug she whispered back, "Good, Doc. What's going on in here?"

It was apparent the moment was very grave. She tried to peer around him, but with an arm around her shoulders he turned her to guide her back the way she'd just come. He explained the situation to her, keeping his voice low.

"It's Hector Garcia. He just passed. Your mother and his daughter are in there with him, and Little Jose. Let's give them some privacy, and you can tell me all about school. How are your studies coming along?"

The information that Jose was indeed in there with Lupita caused Etta to whirl away from Doc's arm without answering. Walking quickly back to the bunk area, she stopped outside the open wall of Hector's space. What she saw had her drawing in a breath against the sudden pain in her heart.

Jose was standing at the foot of the bunk. He was holding a woman – Lupita, apparently – in his arms. His head was bent to the dark-haired woman and he was kissing the top of hers, which was buried in his shoulder while she sobbed quietly. He looked up at the sound of Etta's footsteps. He simply stared at her. There was no warmth, no love in his eyes in those few seconds before he lowered his head to Lupita once more, to whisper consolingly in her ear.

Fina was kneeling at the head of the bunk, but Etta did not acknowledge her mother before swallowing back a sob and backing slowly into the corridor. Her heart felt as if it were breaking into small pieces at the sight of Jose holding another woman. How could he? Her body still felt the warmth of his arms around her just a short time before. Needing to escape the scene that was now imprinted in her mind, she turned and ran past Doc and out of the building.

The rest of what was to have been the most important vacation of her school years passed without conscious participation from Etta. Instead, she felt as though she was watching a movie being acted out by others. She was vaguely aware of the funeral preparations being discussed around her, and only she knew how hard it was to force herself to attend the funeral Mass and the reception following. She spoke to no one.

She did not look for Jose during this time. She knew that he would be spending all his time with Lupita, and she did not feel she could handle the rejection she would be sure to see in his eyes. She felt as numb as if it had been a member of her own family who had passed away. The numbness was temporarily holding at bay the despair and the hurt that would come rushing back later, when she was alone.

Lupita's family lived in a small village outside of Hermosillo, Sonora, Mexico, so they were unable to attend the funeral mass which took place the day after Hector's death. His dutiful daughter insisted on taking the body back to their village for the burial. Etta heard from Maria that Jose would be taking her. The numbness had not yet dissipated as she had watched the couple drive off, the old man's body resting in the back of the same truck Jose had used to bring Etta home from the train station two days earlier.

When the dust from the truck had finally evaporated she made the decision to return to school. The mothers voiced their disappointment at her decision; she'd only been there for a couple of days, they said. When she explained that she couldn't enjoy herself after the tragedy of Hector's death, they said they understood. Naturally, she didn't say that it was actually the tragedy of Jose leaving with Lupita that was causing her grief and despair.

Since Pancho and Doc had business in Phoenix, Big Jose took Etta to Patagonia to catch her train. He gave her a gentle hug before guiding her as she stumbled up the steps of the train's passenger car. He assumed her grief over the death of one of the ranch hands was making her less aware of what she was doing.

"Don't look so sad, sweet Etta. You'll come back again when there will be less sorrow. Hector is in a better place now." He waited until she was seated, waved once, and turned to walk back to his truck. Ranch business was waiting.

Once back at school, Etta immersed herself in her studies. If she was pregnant, and she felt sure she was, she would have to leave school early. She could resume her studies later, but now she wanted to get as far ahead in her curriculum as possible. That would just mean fewer credits she would to have to take in order to graduate after the baby was born.

Knowledge came to her so easily that half her mind was free to concentrate on the calendar even as she kept up her studies. Each day she would add another checkmark. One day closer to missing her first period after her tryst with Jose. As each day passed she was more confident that her calculations had been correct. She was so convinced that she was pregnant, that it was with total shock that she awoke two weeks after arriving back at school to feel mild cramps and to see pinkish spots on her underwear.

"Shit," she cursed. "Shit, shit, shit!" Now what was she going to do? She put on a sanitary napkin and fresh underwear, put her soiled pair to soak in cold water and crawled back into bed, then began to cry. She rarely gave in to that particularly useless emotion, as she thought of it, but unable to stop, she indulged herself. It actually felt liberating to give in and let the hysterics come. After all, there was nobody around to witness her weakness.

She had never missed a class, but today she just didn't care. Finally, around two in the afternoon, she decided she was hungry and was definitely tired of crying, so she forced herself to get up and get dressed. She would get something light to eat at a little bistro a block away from her apartment.

She stopped at the row of boxes lining the wall of the foyer of her apartment building and picked up her mail. It was while flipping through the various pieces she found in her mailbox that she came to a letter from Maria. She hadn't heard a thing from anyone at the ranch during the two weeks since she had returned to school. Ripping open the letter, she leaned against the wall and skimmed over Maria's barely legible writing, looking for the words "Little Jose." Toward the end of the letter she found them.

"Little Jose has been so grumpy since he returned from Hermosillo," Maria wrote. "He is so quiet and moody. He refuses to talk to me about Lupita or anything that happened on his trip. But this morning he comes into my kitchen and he lifts me high in the sky. 'Mama,' he says while laughing, 'My Lupita is coming home in a few more weeks.' At last he is smiling again."

Furious, Etta balled up the letter without reading any more. Damn it, damn it. Now what? She leaned her head back against the wall and closed her eyes. More tears threatened, and she fought against breaking down where anyone coming into the building could see her. She was preparing to return to her apartment without eating when an idea began to form, keeping her where she was.

Project Jose still had a chance of working. Nobody would be any the wiser. Why hadn't she thought of it before? It would be even better than sacrificing her trim figure and her looks to have a baby. She'd tell Jose that their indiscretion had resulted in a pregnancy. He was an honorable man and she knew he would marry her. After they were married for a few weeks she would feign a miscarriage. She would be able to convince Jose that she was heartbroken, but that there was no reason they could not try to have another baby. Jose would be hers, and she could even return to school in January. Just until she was pregnant again, she would say to him if he objected. It was perfect.

She nodded, although there was nobody around to see, and then smiled to herself. Yes, Project Jose would be a success after all. With a spring in her step she started for the bistro; she'd work out the details while she ate. Yes, ma'am, the best woman was definitely going to win.

Chapter 18 – *Jose 1979 - Accusation*

"That lying bitch," Jose snarled. He slammed the journal shut just as Etta entered the waiting room from the ICU. Seeing her, he threw the journal down on the coffee table in front of him and jumped up to confront her with fire in his eyes and contempt in his voice.

"And to think I was ashamed of myself for not forgiving you," he sneered.

"Jose?" Etta questioned as she came further into the room. He was obviously upset with her but she didn't know why.

"What's the matter? What are you talking about?"

Stepping around the table, his hands held rigidly at his sides to avoid hitting her, he answered with barely controlled fury.

"I was your *project?* A FUCKING PROJECT? God, you're sick! Well, obviously, it worked. However, if I didn't get you pregnant, then I think I have a right to know *who the hell* did!"

He had never hit a woman, and a lifetime of breeding kept him from doing so now. He did, however, grab the stunned Etta by her shoulders and shook her hard. He didn't raise his voice, but it was clear it took every ounce of his inner strength to keep from screaming in her face. Instead, as his fingers gripped her shoulders so hard she winced and tried to draw away, he put his face just inches from hers and hissed at her, enunciating every word carefully.

"Samantha isn't even my daughter. Who *is* her father, Etta? Tell me! Who?"

It was at this moment that Humberto walked into the waiting room and stopped as he took in the scene before him. His eyes widened and his brows rose in surprise.

"Jose? Etta? What the hell is going on?" he demanded from a few feet away. It was obvious that Jose was furious, and that Etta looked frightened.

Jose yanked his hands away from the now whimpering Etta, releasing her so suddenly she stumbled backward a step before she caught herself. He didn't notice that she was rubbing her shoulders where he had grabbed her. He had turned and was thundering past his confused cousin. As he reached the door he snarled over his shoulder, "Ask her." Then he was gone without another word.

Humberto hurried to Etta and grabbed her shoulders without thinking. When she cried out in pain he dropped his hands quickly. Taking her hand instead, he led her to the couch that Jose had recently abandoned.

"Etta? Are you okay? What was Jose talking about? What did he mean, Sam isn't his daughter?"

When he didn't receive an answer right away he just sat and watched Etta's face. There were tears coursing down her cheeks, which she didn't try to stem. She stared down at her lap and continued to cry. She did not deny her husband's words; it was obvious she knew what he meant. Instead, she put her face in her hands and rocked back and forth. He thought he heard her mumbling to herself. Listening carefully, he heard the words that she was repeating over and over.

"Why now, why now, why now?"

She continued to rock and he continued to sit beside her, not saying a word. He wasn't sure what he should do for her, if anything. Better to let her cry it out. After a few minutes he noticed the journal that had been tossed on the coffee table. He reached for it, wondering what it was. It was clearly not a novel.

It was this movement that had Etta finally removing her hands from her face. She stared at the book in Humberto's hands, thinking it looked vaguely familiar. It was the book Jose had thrown down when she walked into the waiting room. Slowly, she reached out for it. Humberto, noticing her puzzled expression, relinquished the book

"Etta, what is it? Is that yours?"

"No, it's not mine, but it does look familiar."

She turned the book over and gasped, seeing the initials SGLL. No wonder it looked familiar. It was one of Samantha's journals. Why had Jose been reading it? Where did he find it? When she noticed the date on the cover she was even more confused. How could it be dated 1951? The journal fell open, probably at the point that Jose had stopped reading, as the page was slightly crumpled. It looked like he had scrunched it in his hand before throwing the journal down. Curious, she started to read.

"Oh my God, oh my God," she whispered and leaned back against the sofa. The book lay open on her lap. She glanced at Humberto with a disbelieving expression on her face before picking up the journal once again. She slowly shook her head as she read, and didn't even notice when Humberto leaned over and read with her.

Chapter 19 – *Etta 1951* – The Plan

It was time to put her new plan into action. Everything needed to be in place before Lupita returned to the ranch following her father's burial. Etta was determined that her story of an unexpected pregnancy would not fail. There had been a set-back, true, but it was nothing that could not be overcome.

The first step in the revised plan was to call Humberto. He was currently attending law school at the University of Arizona in Tucson, the town in which he and his family lived. She hesitated before picking up the phone to contact him, as she recalled the last time they had seen each other during one of her rare visits home two summers ago.

Etta and Humberto decided to ride to the river. Normally Jose would have been with them, as the three of them always did everything together. However, he was in Nogales on business for Pancho, so it was just the two of them this time. They were looking for relief down by the river because the day was promising to be a scorcher. Upon arriving they dismounted, then left their horses to graze nearby and sat down under one of the old cottonwoods. Neither felt the need to talk, they just enjoyed the feel of the cool breeze coming off the water.

After about ten minutes of companionable silence Humberto cleared his throat, took a deep breath, and told Etta that he was in love with her. He then leaned over and touched his lips to hers. After her initial shock and after she decided the kiss wasn't threatening, she kissed him back. She decided she liked it, how it made her feel. She had never been kissed on the lips before, and it was much more pleasant than she had thought a kiss would be. Kissing him back was probably a mistake, because she soon became aware of hands that were slowly moving toward her breasts.

"No, Humberto," she said as she gently pushed away from him. Laying a hand on his cheek, she explained that it was Jose she loved, but that he, Humberto, would be her friend forever. She could see the disappointment in his eyes and knew that this was not what he wanted to hear. Because he loved them both, however, and because he was above all things a gentleman, he accepted her explanation without an argument and moved away from her.

The outing soon become awkward and no longer relaxing, so they rode back to the ranch in silence. As soon as they reached their destination and returned the horses to the barn to be taken care of Humberto walked to his car without a word and drove off. Knowing he was hurt and embarrassed, Etta did not try to stop him.

Etta had not heard from Humberto since that day. He was in law school and she was in medical school, so it was not unusual for months to go by without communication between them. Two years was longer than it would have normally been, but regardless of how they had parted and how long it had been since she'd heard from him, she was confident that he would be an ally in her plan. After all, they had never stayed angry with each other for long. It never entered her mind that he would not speak to her, so she called and left a message with his mother, asking that he call her as soon as possible. It wasn't until the next day that he returned her call, so she had plenty of time to practice using just the right amount of teary panic in her voice.

"Humberto, I'm so sorry to bother you. But I didn't know who else to turn to."

"What is it Etta? What's wrong?" Humberto's reaction to the sound of her tears brought a smile to Etta's face. She knew she could count on him. Her voice projected only despair, however, as she answered him.

"I don't know what to do. I must talk to Jose about something extremely important, but I don't dare call the ranch because Maria will answer the phone. And if I send him a letter, which I've never done before, everyone will be suspicious. I'm desperate, Humberto, and I need your help."

"Oh." Upon hearing Etta's mention of Jose, Humberto's concern vanished. He had been hoping she had changed her mind about her feelings for him, but as usual it was about Jose. "Well, what do you want me to do?" he asked less than enthusiastically.

She didn't let the change in his voice deter her. "I need to tell him something. I will tell you so you can make him call me, but you can't tell anyone else. If you are truly my friend, you have to promise me," she begged.

His curiosity was peaked so he grudgingly agreed to her request. "Okay, Etta, I swear on my mother, I won't tell anyone. Now what is it you want me to tell Jose?"

Etta's voice lowered just enough that she knew he would have to strain to hear her. "I'm pregnant, Humberto. Jose is the father."

Silence. Had he heard her? Would she have to say it again? Cautiously she asked, "Humberto? Are you still there?"

"Yes, Etta, I'm here. Are you sure?" Disappointment, as well as an acceptance of what now could never be, caused Humberto's reply to sound very tired and defeated, older than his twenty-one years.

Insulted, Etta forgot to maintain the desperation in her voice when she asked, "Are you asking if I'm sure I'm pregnant, or if I'm sure that Jose is the father?"

"No, no, that's not what I meant, I'm just surprised that's all," Humberto said.

"Well, I couldn't believe it either. But it's true. You will tell him for me, won't you?" Etta asked. The edge of panic was back in her voice. She'd almost blown it.

"Yes, I'll tell him. I'll drive down to the ranch tomorrow. I'm sure he will call you right away."

Etta breathed a sigh of relief. "Thank you, Humberto; I knew I could count on you. Remember, please don't tell anyone but Jose."

"Etta have I ever broken a promise to you?" Humberto was now the one insulted.

With the right amount of contriteness in her voice, she apologized. "No, you've always been a good friend. I'll never forget this, Humberto, thank you. I'll talk to you soon." Etta hung up the phone and smiled at herself in the mirror across the room. Step one, check.

On Saturday, the day following his disturbing conversation with

Etta, Humberto drove out to Rancho de Luna. He was upset enough to hurt Jose, he thought, but they were cousins, even more, best friends. He couldn't do that. Or could he?

Instead of parking in one of the visitors' spaces in front of the ranch house, Humberto took the work road that led to the stables. He supposed Jose would be working on his books there, as he did on most Saturdays. Having worked on the ranch every summer since he was ten, Humberto knew the weekly scheduled chores.

Sure enough, Jose was in the tack room located at the back of the huge building. He was sitting at his desk reviewing the stable's ledgers. He heard footsteps and looked up. Seeing Humberto, he smiled and stood, walking around his desk with his arms reaching out to embrace his friend.

"Hey Cuz, what are you doing here?"

Instead of the expected hug and back-pounding, and without any warning, Humberto balled up his fist and punched Jose in the jaw, knocking him to the stable floor. Stunned and in pain, the younger cousin lay where he had fallen and looked up with a puzzled expression on his face.

"Shit. Why the hell did you do that?"

Humberto stood over him, glaring down. His face was red with anger.

"Because, you son-of-a-bitch, Etta tells me she is carrying your baby," he fumed, "and by God, you will do the right thing and marry her, or cousin or not, I'll fuckin' kill you." Having had his say, he turned and started walking toward the stable door.

"Wait," Jose yelled, scrambling to his feet while rubbing his painful jaw. "Humberto, wait up." He hurried after the retreating man. When he caught up to him he lightly touched his shoulder, willing to take another blow if necessary.

"Please, Humberto, it's not what you think. Let me tell you what happened. Please," he begged, bracing himself in case that heavy fist came at him again

Humberto had never heard Jose beg for anything, and because he did love both his cousin and Etta he stopped, turning to face the younger man.

"Talk," he barked out.

Relieved, Jose sank to a bale of hay sitting on the floor just outside of one of the stalls, and began to tell Humberto about that awful day in April. He told him about the picnic, about the tequila, about the seduction.

He talked about his love for Lupita, and that he had asked her to marry him. He even talked about the trip he and Lupita had taken to Hermosillo to bury her father. What he hadn't told his mother he now explained to his cousin: how he had confessed his infidelity, and that Lupita had, with obvious hurt and humiliation, sent him back to the ranch alone. It wasn't until a week later that she had relented and forgiven him, agreeing to marry him in spite of the pain he had caused her.

At some point during Jose's explanation Humberto joined him on the hay bale, and when the young man cried, hanging his head as he talked about his love for Lupita, Humberto laid an arm over his shoulders to comfort him. The story finished, both cousins sat in silence for a long, long time. Finally, Humberto gave Jose's shoulder a squeeze.

"Hey, I'm sorry I hit you."

Jose, rubbing the still painful jaw replied, "Yeah, me too," and he managed a small laugh. Then he brushed his arm across his eyes, drying them on the sleeve of his shirt.

"What am I going to do now, Humberto?" Jose asked, hoping for a solution to the major problem that could forever change his life.

"Jose, you already know what you're going to do. You're going to marry Etta, as soon as possible. I'm sorry but that is the only thing you can do, the honorable thing to do."

"My God, what have I done? How am I going to tell Lupita?" Jose asked.

Humberto was as heart-broken as Jose. Life was so unfair: Jose would marry Etta, whom he himself desperately loved; Jose would lose Lupita and those two were perfect for each other. And as always, for as long as he could remember, Etta would once again get what she wanted.

The next day, across the country, when Etta's phone rang she rushed to pick it up, positive it would be Jose. "Hello," she said, sounding breathless, but trying to stay calm.

"It's me, Jose," she heard. Did he think she wouldn't recognize his voice?

"Oh, Jose, I'm so relieved you called," she answered.

Etta's heart was pounding in her chest. Even though she was positive her plan was going to work, Jose could be very stubborn if he was made to do something he didn't want to do. And she had no backup argument with which to convince him if he chose to balk.

"Listen, I've already told the mothers that we want to get married." Jose almost choked on the word 'want.'

"You did?" Etta wanted to shout with joy, but forced her voice to sound more subdued. She needed to make him think she was as sorry as he that they had to do this. "What did they say?"

"I don't remember their exact words, Etta," Jose answered impatiently. "I told them we wanted a June wedding. If we eloped or tried to set a date any earlier than that they would know something was wrong."

"I agree," Etta responded, still elated, but keeping her voice sympathetic. June was exactly what she had planned. "June will be perfect. School will be out at the end of May and I will be coming back to the ranch then."

"Okay," Jose murmured in resignation. "I'm sure you will be hearing from our mothers soon."

"Oh, Jose, I love you so much. I promise I'll make you a good wife," Etta passionately declared into the phone. But the only answer was a dial tone. She replaced the handset in the cradle, frustrated with his abruptness, but nevertheless smiling to herself. Step two, check.

The short period of time remaining before the June 7 wedding date did not bother Etta. She knew their mothers would come through for them, and that it would be spectacular. During the next few weeks she spoke with at least one of the mothers almost daily, and though it was never voiced aloud, she knew that the details presented to her were already a 'done deal.' Her concurrence was a formality only. Etta would not have presumed to know better than the mothers. Leaving everything up to them was just fine with her. Her plan was to marry Jose – she didn't care about the minor details.

The only thing to mar Etta's happiness at this point was the fact that she suspected her mother would probably know what she was doing: pretending to be pregnant, then to miscarry. She had never been able to fool her mother or to lie to her. How do you lie to someone who can read your mind? It bothered her, but she consoled herself with the belief that her mother loved her enough that she would never betray her. She remembered something her mother told her when she was very young.

Etta was very curious about the mysterious visitors who came to the ranch. She wanted to know why they came to see her mother. She wanted to know what they talked about with her, what she would tell them and what she would read in their minds. Her mother was tolerant of her daughter's questions, but each time she patiently explained that she couldn't answer them.

"Etta, honey, you know I cannot tell you that. Others' thoughts are private. I have no right to share them. I do not always discuss what I see with the person I'm reading, unless they wish me to. Even then I don't tell them everything."

When Etta once begged her mother to tell her if she was going to be a medical doctor or a veterinarian her mother sighed before she said, "Etta, you know that is not for me to tell you."

"But you tell your visitors, don't you?" She was hurt that her mother would not tell her. "Why won't you tell me?"

Fina closed her eyes and thought a moment before answering, wanting to find the right words that a young child would understand. She clearly had a misconception about what transpired between her mother and a visitor. After a moment she opened her eyes and looked at the child.

"Sweetheart, I do not tell a visitor about their future. That is very important. I talk to them about their life now, or discuss their past, when they have lived before. The things that they are doing now or that they have done in one of their past lives may be the answer to what is causing them pain in this one. I will never tell a visitor what I see in their future, because if I did, it could cause their future to change."

Etta thought about what her mother had just said. "I'm not sure I understand, Mama. How could knowing their future change it?"

Fina thought carefully before answering.

"I believe that before we start a new life, referred to as an incarnation, we put together a detailed plan of what we would like to accomplish in the upcoming lifetime. Lessons we want or need to learn, things we need to experience in order to *pay for* the bad things we might have done in the previous life or lives.

"For example, let us say that in a previous life you were a man, a bad man who beat his wife and children. So after you die, when you are a soul between lives and are making your plan for your next incarnation, you decide that you need to be a woman with a mean husband who will beat you. In this way you can experience the pain that you caused others when you were a man. Unfortunately, once you experience rebirth you will forget this plan. You will not consciously remember the lessons you need to learn in the new life.

"Let us say you are now a young woman and you come to me and ask, 'Mother, should I marry this man?' I look at your future, and I see that you will be very sad and unhappy, that this man will not be good to you. So I tell you, 'No. He will make you very unhappy. He is not the right man for you.' If I did this I could cause you to change your future – the future you had chosen for yourself and needed in order to make up for the bad things in a previous life."

Etta's analytical brain tried to absorb her mother's explanation. After a few minutes of thought, and with a frown on her small face, she asked, "But why in the world would I *plan* to marry a mean husband? Why would I do such a stupid thing if I wasn't in the previous life anymore? Wouldn't I want to live a good life this time?"

Fina shook her head. "No, my pet. Because of something called karma. This means the quality of a person's current life is shaped by their behavior in previous lives."

The look of confusion on her daughter's face told Fina she still had not understood what her mother was trying to say. She tried again.

"You planned to be unhappy because your soul needed to experience the pain you had caused others. By experiencing this pain you are being forgiven for what you had done in your previous existence; you are paying for the previous cruelty. You are moving one step closer to having a pure soul, one step closer to being with God."

Fina realized that trying to explain the complexities of karma, even to a genius child, was not easy. She added, "In changing your future you would no longer experience what you needed to in order to be forgiven."

"Well, I'm not so sure I believe in this karma thing. I'll have to read up on it," and she rushed off toward the library.

Later, wondering if her mother was really telling the truth about what she would or would not discuss with a visitor, Etta had tried to eavesdrop when old Mrs. Dominquez was having a reading. She had crouched under a window of the Garden Room, holding her breath, waiting to hear what her mother would say to the old woman. She heard nothing until her mother's voice spoke from behind her, causing her to jump.

"Just what do you think you are doing young lady?"

This was the only time in her short life Etta had seen her mother angry. She was sent her to her room and told she would be dealt with later. Etta lay on her bed for hours, trying to think of what she would say to her mother. She gave up when it dawned on her that she couldn't make up an excuse or lie because her mother would know. So when her mother eventually knocked on her door as she opened it and walked into the room, Etta jumped from her bed and ran to her, throwing her arms around her.

"I'm so sorry, Mama. I promise never to do it again."

Her mother, not angry any longer, held her daughter tightly, "I know you are sorry, Etta. And I already know you will not do it again."

Weeks later, after the incident was almost forgotten by both of them, Etta turned to her mother while they were working in the herb garden.

"Mama? Is there a way someone can keep you from reading their thoughts?"

Fina looked at her daughter sternly before answering, "Why? Is there something you don't want me to know?" Actually, she already knew that Etta was just curious.

Etta, not wanting to make her mother angry again cried, "No Mama. I was just wondering, that's all. Honest."

Fina laughed at this explanation and grabbed her daughter's small hand. "I know, baby, I was just teasing. Now back to your question. Yes, there is a way. If someone doesn't want me to *read* them they merely have to hum or sing inside their head."

Etta's almond-colored eyes grew big with the knowledge.

"Like this?" She started silently singing "Mary Had a Little Lamb" in her head.

Fina hugged her daughter. "Yes, my little lamb, just like that."

CHAPTER 20 – *Etta 1951* – The Professor

Etta was so busy with school and her daily conversations with the mothers about wedding plans that she usually forgot to eat. At last the final exam of the year was over. Not surprisingly, she once again earned the top grade in her class, so she decided to celebrate and treat herself to a fabulous and expensive dinner at La Grandiose Maison. The exclusive French restaurant was located in one of the grand old hotels on Bourbon Street. However, she didn't relish the idea of dining alone, and the truth was she didn't have any close friends at school. Who had time to make friends with all the studying that was necessary?

The only person whose company she would enjoy and feel relaxed with was one of her professors, Dr. Campbell. He was not only the youngest professor at the school, he was the smartest in Etta's opinion. In fact, she found him to be one of the very few people whose intelligence was almost equal to hers. He always made time for her after his Endocrinology class, which happened to be her favorite class.

They had coffee together several times a month, often discussing adenohypophyis, which was a growth hormone she was hoping could be used to increase cattle production. Dr. Campbell was brilliant and pleasant to be with. He was also easy on the eyes, she admitted to herself. He was polished, almost pretty in a thin, blond sort of way. His clear, blue-green eyes that were the color of the Caribbean were graced with thick lashes that most women would covet. Although she preferred taller and more muscular, darker complexioned men, like Jose, she could appreciate Dr. Campbell's looks as well.

Thinking of Jose, Etta frowned. Except for that initial phone call telling her they would be married, she'd had no communication from him. Every time she called him she was told he was not available. After two weeks of silence she had written to him, a long letter in which she'd poured out her heart, begging him to call her so they could talk. Another two weeks had passed since then, and still nothing: no letter, no phone call. She was hurt, of course, but more importantly she was angry. He didn't know that she wasn't actually pregnant. One would think he would be concerned enough to at least find out if she was okay.

Even Humberto had called her. In fact, he called at least twice a week. He was so sweet and considerate, always asking how she was feeling, if she needed anything. And she knew he was as busy wrapping up his year-end studies as she was. She convinced herself Jose would eventually come around, and it was only a couple of weeks until the wedding, so she would just be patient. She would not let her anger and frustration with him cause her to do something foolish that would ruin her careful plans.

After her 'miscarriage' she was planning to convince Jose that the wisest course of action would be to move to New Orleans while she finished med school. She had already applied to, and was all but accepted at, St. Mary's Hospital in Tucson for her residency, so they could move back to the ranch at that time. In the meantime, knowing Jose loved thoroughbred horses, she would talk her father into buying a ranch outside of New Orleans. In that way they could have a couple of horses to keep Jose entertained while she finished school. Being located as far away from Lupita as possible was the incentive for this step in the plan.

Clearing her head of all thoughts of Jose for the present, Etta picked up the phone to call Dr. Campbell. After greeting him she explained that she was going to go out, treat herself to a celebratory meal, and if he was available she would love it if he would join her.

"My treat," she added.

Dr. Campbell assured her that he was indeed available. He sounded both surprised and delighted by the invitation, and insisted on calling for her at her apartment.

As she dressed for the anticipated dinner she thought about

Andrew, as Dr. Campbell had insisted she call him when he accepted her invitation.

"I would be delighted to join you, but there are two conditions. For tonight at least, you must call me Andrew, and I insist on paying for dinner, as a reward for all of your hard work," he had demanded laughingly.

She had drawled her reply, maybe flirting just a little. "Well, if you insist, Andrew, and you must call me Miss Suzetta. That is, after all, my given name."

"Well then, Miss Suzetta, it's a date," he had laughed, a pleasant sound. She had always enjoyed his laugh.

She was wearing a tight-fitting, low-cut black dress, complemented by the pearls her father had given her the year she started college. She'd pulled her hair up into a sophisticated-looking chignon, and smiled at her reflection in the mirror. "Not bad, if I do say so myself," she murmured, then gave herself a small salute as she turned away to answer the doorbell.

She was surprised to realize that she was more than a little excited about their 'date' as Andrew had insisted on calling it. She opened the door with an expectant smile, and wasn't disappointed to see him standing there, handsomely clad in a flattering dark suit with a cobalt blue tie against a dove gray silk shirt.

"Wow," he exclaimed, taking her hand and kissing it lightly, "you look stunning."

Pleased by his compliment, she bowed her head slightly in acceptance.

"May I return the compliment, sir, and say that you fairly take my breath away yourself," she replied, using her best southern belle voice.

She handed him her black lace shawl so he could drape it across her shoulders, then turned, picked up her evening clutch, and put her arm through his. They smiled at each other as they walked out of the apartment.

Once seated at the restaurant he ordered an expensive bottle of *Pouilly-Fume*, a crisp French white wine, one that her father always kept in abundant supply in his well-stocked wine cellar at the ranch, and one of her favorites. It perfectly complemented the meal that began with a half-dozen oysters on the half-shell, followed by *sole meuniere,* a delicate, deliciously prepared Dover sole. In European custom, the salad, fruit and cheese were served after the entrée. They both declined dessert, preferring instead to linger over another bottle of the wonderful white wine.

They had been talking about her studies and her plans for the future in medicine. He was a good listener, and offered suggestions now and then without making them sound like he was the professor talking down to the student. After dinner, however, when Etta would have continued the discussion along the same lines, Andrew reached across the small table and put his finger to her lips.

"No more medical discussions, Etta. I want you to tell me about the personal you, no more of the scholastic you."

Etta was beginning to feel a little giddy by this time as they were well into their second bottle of wine. She enjoyed being seen with a sophisticated, good-looking man, and the more she drank the more attractive he became. Liking the feel of his finger against her lips, she blushed and looked down. She wondered what it would be like to feel his lips on hers, not just his finger.

She had had very little experience in being kissed. Yes, she'd pressured Jose into that one kiss before they made love, but that had been the first and only time he'd kissed her. Actually, she realized, Humberto's kiss had been longer and more passionate than the one kiss she'd received from Jose. She didn't realize that Andrew had been watching her while her thoughts wandered.

"Etta?" Andrew asked at last. "Come back. You look like you're a million miles away. You were going to tell me something about yourself."

His voice brought her back to the present, and realizing what she'd been thinking, especially when she looked at his perfectly-shaped lips, she blushed once more. Then, regaining her composure, she smiled into his handsome face.

"I'm sorry, Andrew. I was just remembering something. It's not important. In fact, I think I'd like another glass of wine, please."

They talked about themselves, not worrying about remaining at the table. In the exclusive and expensive French restaurant the waiters wouldn't dream of trying to hurry them out in order to have the table for new patrons. After the second bottle of wine was empty Etta said she'd love to have a Brandy and coffee. This was fine with Andrew, who was enjoying watching his favorite student in this new light. It was obvious that the alcohol was affecting her, and he was amused. She was far from out of control, but she was definitely much looser, more relaxed than he had ever seen her.

He was enjoying their intimate conversation and he pretended that this was truly a date. Actually he had been secretly enamored with her since she walked into the auditorium for his first lecture of the semester. He could easily let himself fall in love with her, he was thinking. That would not be smart, he cautioned himself, but he could see it happening if he wasn't careful. He remembered the first time he had seen her.

There were only four women in the class of 243 and he had already met the other three, so he knew exactly who she was when she entered the auditorium. This was Suzetta Grace Luna, the highest-scoring student ever to, well, grace the school with her presence. His infatuation had begun when she tripped as she entered his room, dropping her armload of books. It was clear that she was embarrassed, and her poise slipped a little as she picked them up and maneuvered to slide into one of the front row seats.

Genius, rich, and beautiful, Andrew was thinking as they sipped their brandy. She was probably a little spoiled too, he assumed; he knew from her school records that she was an only child. He knew the type well; he already had one of those at home.

His wife, Elaine, was eight months pregnant with their third child. They already had twin eight-year-old boys, Jacob and Joshua. Andrew was pretty sure that Etta didn't know he was married, much less soon to be the father of three. During their conversation after dinner, in which they talked about more personal information, he had left out that small detail.

He had mentioned that he loved medicine, and preferred to teach it rather than practice it. What he failed to include, however, was the fact that he was able to do this due to his wife's substantial trust fund. He thought about his wife and his loveless marriage while Etta talked about her childhood, but he kept an interested look on his face as his thoughts wandered. Occasionally he would nod or murmur, "hmm," as she spoke.

Elaine was an only child, spoiled by her father and her grandfather. She often referred to them collectively as her 'daddies.' In their eyes she could do no wrong, and they rarely denied her anything. In spite of this, Elaine was often unhappy. She could be moody and definitely difficult to please. She pretended to be happy and content with her marriage when she was around her daddies, but in private she didn't even try to hide the fact that she did not find any joy in being a wife or a mother.

Maybe that was one of the reasons Andrew was so attracted to Etta, who always appeared to be in a good mood, even when she was deep into her studies. She may be spoiled, she was certainly beautiful and rich, but more than that, she was serious about medicine, and excited about acquiring as much knowledge as possible. Not that Elaine was ignorant or anything. She had attended a very prestigious all-girl school and had graduated with top honors. She was not a genius, but she was well read and could carry on an interesting conversation on most topics.

Her father and her grandfather were highly respected physicians. In fact, it was her father who had introduced Andrew to Elaine, right after she had graduated from prep school. She was 18 and stunning. However, she had no desire to use her education to pursue a career path. Nor was she interested in continuing with her studies toward obtaining a degree of any sort.

She told Andrew bluntly on their second date that she wanted a husband and children. She was completely candid.

"Even though you aren't wealthy, I think you would make a great husband and father. My daddies approve of you and they have enough money for the both of us. They won't live forever, you know," she laughed lightly, touching his arm.

Andrew had been captivated by her, and fascinated by the lifestyle that she and her daddies lived. He saw nothing wrong with using her family's money; it was offered, after all. Following a brief courtship they were married in grand New Orleans style.

It was on their wedding night that Andrew discovered the Elaine that had been hidden from him. They had just made love on the huge, plush king-sized bed in the $500-a-night Honeymoon Suite at the Grand Pierre Hotel.

He had been pleased to find she was a virgin. However, rather than allowing him to hold her afterward, as soon as their love-making was finished she jumped out of bed, grabbed her nightgown from the floor, and rushed into the bathroom. He could hear water running, then silence after she turned off the faucet. When she emerged from the bathroom she was wearing her gown once more. Climbing into bed beside Andrew, she pulled the sheet up to her chin and lay on her back without looking at him. He thought it was cute that she was so shy and promised himself that he would be gentle with her so she would learn to relax.

"Well that was certainly unpleasant. It was as messy and ridiculous as I expected it to be."

Stunned, Andrew could only stare at her. Then had come the *coup de grace.*

"By the way, now that we are married, I'll let you in on a little secret. I don't like men, I prefer women." She still had not looked in his direction, so she failed to notice that his expression was a shocked disbelief, his mouth gaping.

Impatient with his mute reaction, she had continued, "Oh really, Andrew, don't pretend that you married me for love. We both know you love my trust fund and what it can do for you. Not to worry," she added, "we will have sex. My daddies expect grandchildren, and we're going to give them some. But once I'm pregnant we will not have sex again until it's time for another child." She turned her head now, to look at him, waiting for him to say something.

Still Andrew had remained silent. He felt incapable of speech, even of logical thought. His only reaction was to close his mouth.

The new bride continued to lay out her dictates. "I do have a lover. You've met her; she was my maid of honor at our wedding. You do remember Michelle, don't you? She will live in our house with us, as my personal assistant. You may also have a *special friend* on the side, as long as you're discrete. My daddies would be crushed and disappointed if they ever suspected that ours was not the perfect marriage. You'll find that this will work just fine for both of us."

When he remained mute, still staring at her, she shrugged her shoulders, turned off the lamp on the night stand, rolled over with her back to her new husband, and settled down to sleep.

Andrew had lain awake in the darkened room. Well, he'd thought to himself miserably, she's right; I did marry her for the money. And she's right about not hurting her daddies; they've been good to me. I guess I don't have a choice. I'll have to play it her way. He was not proud of himself, knowing he would fall in with her plan.

So they outwardly put on a show that even the happiest couple would envy. In private, however, it was another story. Michelle and Elaine had their own suite. Elaine visited Andrew's room for sex – he certainly couldn't call it making love – enough times to conceive the twins and later the baby she was now carrying. With three children, he knew she would feel there was no further need for sex in the future. It could be worse, he supposed. At least he was left with plenty of time to do what he loved, teaching medicine. And during the ten years they had been married, he'd discretely enjoyed the company of a *special friend* now and then.

As he tuned back in to Etta talking about her life on the ranch and watching her become more intoxicated and animated with the steady flow of alcohol, his thoughts centered on his sudden desire to make love to her. He had been captivated by her all semester. Was he now falling in love with her? He wanted the chance to find out. And he was hoping that chance would begin with a night of making love to her. He was contemplating how best to find out if she would be receptive to his advances. There's only one way to find out, he decided as he signaled for the waiter to bring the check.

Etta leaned heavily on Andrew's arm as they left the restaurant. He put her in a cab and climbed in after her. He then gave the driver her address. She rested her head on his shoulder and closed her eyes, a little smile on her face.

Andrew decided to test the waters. He placed his hand on her thigh, touching bare skin where her dress had hiked up when she'd stumbled getting into the cab. She hadn't noticed, so had not pulled it down. When she didn't protest he rubbed lightly, then slowly moved his hand a little further up her leg. He watched her as he moved cautiously, and noticed her lips part slightly, although she still had not opened her eyes. She made no move to stop him as his hand inched higher, moving closer to the nest between her legs. "Mmmm," he heard, so he boldly brushed his hand against the silk that was covering her mound. Her hips began to move slightly against his hand.

Taking this as a sign that she welcomed his advances, he slowly inserted a finger underneath the garment and into her moist fold. She began moaning softly now, and the movement of her hips grew more pronounced as he pulled his finger back, then inserted it again…in and out, in and out. While keeping her aroused with the movement of his hand, he leaned over and kissed her, slipping his tongue into her mouth. He moved his other hand around her shoulder, pulling her closer, and covering one breast. When he began to caress the nipple that had grown hard beneath the fabric, she cried out loud into his mouth. It was then that the cab arrived in front of her apartment building.

As Andrew pulled away from Etta with a groan and an ache in his groin, she whimpered, "Don't stop." She still had not opened her eyes.

"Let me take care of the driver, and we can go inside," he placated her as he reached for his wallet.

Throwing the cab driver a twenty, and barking, "Keep the change," he reached a hand to help Etta out of the cab and slammed the door behind her. She had her arms wrapped around him when they reached her door, and didn't seem to realize where they were. He took her small purse, located the key, opened the door and rushed her willingly inside. As soon as he kicked the door shut behind them her mouth attacked his. He gently pulled back. "Where," he asked huskily, "is the bedroom?"

Instead of answering, she tugged him into her room. "More," she begged, "I need more." With her lips pressed greedily to his she began to tear at his clothes.

He firmly pushed her from him and turned her back to him. After unhooking the pearls and setting them on her dresser, he unzipped her dress and pulled it unceremoniously down her trembling body. He picked her up and laid her on the bed, clad only in her lacy bra and panties, and a sexy black garter belt and nylons. He hurriedly removed his own clothes, afraid he might come just looking at the gorgeous body that was moving sinuously on the bed while she waited impatiently for him to join her. With his own clothing out of the way he leaned over and quickly removed the rest of hers.

He lay down next to her and began licking, nipping and kissing her throat before he moved further down her body. At her bare breasts he gently sucked and licked each one, drawing a series of moans from her as she moved her head back and forth on the pillow, her eyes closed once more. Her hips were arching toward his body, so he obligingly moved down to that hidden secret place, pushed her legs open, and ran his tongue over the moist center that was waiting for him there.

"Please, please," she was whimpering as her hips moved up and down and her hands rubbed the nipples that he had abandoned.

He heard her moan loudly, and then cry out, almost in surprise, when she came. It was as if she had not been expecting this feeling that seemed to set off fireworks inside her body. Her reaction had him becoming so rock hard that he hurt; he needed his own release. As she began to come down from the pinnacle, murmuring softly to herself, he moved up to hover over her. As soon as he positioned himself at her entrance he pushed in, hard. My God, he thought, she is so tight, so wet.

He tried to move slowly, to hold back in order to prolong the pleasure for both of them. She moved with him and wrapped her legs around him. He wanted her to come with him to heaven. It had been so long since he had been inside a woman that after a half dozen strokes he could contain himself no longer. He exploded into her, and he need not have worried: with her legs still wrapped tightly around him, she soared with him.

Exhausted, he lay on top of her. After a moment he pulled his head back to smile at her, but her eyes were still closed and he realized she had passed out. The alcohol she had consumed, along with the sex, must have been too much for her. He laughed softly, and then stopped abruptly. Something had been trying to penetrate his consciousness, and it finally broke through. He realized what she had been murmuring after her first climax. It was a name.....Jose.

Etta stopped reading, and reddened with acute embarrassment at the vivid details of her love-making with Andrew. Not only was she embarrassed to think her daughter had written those words, but she was also mortified to be reminded of her deceit. Her anguish deepened when she realized Humberto was reading those same words and would now know how she had not only used him, but had betrayed Jose. She closed the journal slowly and dared to look at Humberto.

"Oh, Humberto, I'm so sorry," she said, taking his hand. "Can you ever forgive me?"

He withdrew his hand from hers and stood, then walked away from her. When he stopped he turned to face her. His voice was soft and his dark eyes were filled with regret and sorrow when he spoke.

"Sorry for what Etta? Sorry you used me to betray Jose, or sorry that we found out about your little plan? No, Etta, I'm the one who's sorry; sorry that I've loved you for as long as I can remember." He turned his back to her, not wanting her to see his effort to hold back tears.

"I'm sorry that I believed your lies, but mostly I'm sorry that I unknowingly helped you and that your scheming kept Jose from the true love of his life." *And me from mine* he thought bitterly. Recovering his composure, he turned back to face Etta again.

At the sight of the sadness that was etched in the face of this good man, Etta felt her heart break. *Oh my God*, she thought, *what have I done to him? He's such an honorable man; he didn't deserve to be a party to my sins. How could I have done that to someone I love? And more, I might be in love with him. My love for Jose died a long time ago, but I've always loved this man standing before me. Why couldn't I see that?* She stood and walked to him. When she reached him she raised her hand to his cheek. She had to restrain herself from wrapping her arms around him.

"Please, Humberto, please forgive me. There is no excuse for my involving you in my plans, but I was so in love with Jose that I wanted to do whatever it took to get him to love me back. I know that it was wrong of me, and I can only tell you how sorry I am. We both know it didn't work."

Lowering her hand from his face, he gently pushed her away. "What about that other man, Etta? That wasn't the act of a woman in love. What can you possibly say that would justify what you did?"

"Nothing, Humberto. It was wrong. Being drunk was no excuse. I can only tell you that nothing like that ever happened again."

Humberto just stood and stared at her, and she stared back. Then, taking the journal that was still in her hand, he asked a question that had occurred to him. "What is this anyway, your diary? But how could you possibly know what I was thinking and feeling? How could you know what happened between me and Jose that day in the barn?"

Etta turned the journal in his hands, showing him the initials SGLL. "It's not mine. I know it sounds crazy but I think Sam wrote this when she was just a little girl."

Confusion and disbelief played across Humberto's face. "But how would that be possible? How could she know all those things?" Remembering what he had read over Etta's shoulder, he blushed, thinking of the details of Etta's drunken love-making.

"I don't know, I just don't know," Etta answered in response to his questions.

Then, recalling Jose's angry words earlier, Humberto was convinced that he had just learned the identity of Samantha's father.

Chapter 21 – *Jose 1979* – The Ultimatum

After leaving the hospital Jose walked the short distance to the St. Vincent's hotel. Humberto had secured a large suite there with several bedrooms so they would not have to worry about a place to rest when their bedside vigils at the hospital became exhausting. It was now dawn, with clouds obscuring the rising sun and rain starting to fall, but he hardly noticed. He was still upset, still furious at Etta because of what he'd read in Sam's journal. She had played him for a fool. It didn't matter that 28 years had passed. The pain was fresh, as was his anger.

Upon reaching the hotel Jose picked up the room key Humberto had left for him at the front desk and took the elevator to the seventh floor. Quietly, in order to keep from disturbing his parents, he put the key on a table in the foyer and pulled out his wallet to lay beside it. All he wanted right now was to get some sleep.

The only light in the room was from a still-lit street lamp that bled through a crack in the heavy drapes that had been pulled together across the room's windows. It allowed him to avoid the furniture as he moved further into the room, trying to determine the direction in which his own room lay.

"Jose, is that you?"

Startled, Jose answered, "Yes, Mama, it's me. What are you doing up? And why are you sitting in the dark?"

Maria sat up and reached for the lamp on the table next to the sofa on which she had been reclining. When she turned it on it was clear she had been praying; she had her rosary clutched to her chest. She was in her night clothes, so she had either gotten up very early or had not gone

144

to bed at all. She blinked against the sudden light, and then focused her eyes on her son's face. What she saw there clearly worried her, for she crossed herself before speaking to him.

"Jose, *Mi Hijo*, has something happened to my poor Sam?"

Jose stiffened at the mention of Sam's name. "No, Mama, there is no change in her condition."

"Then what is wrong? It is the baby?"

"No, Mama the baby is stable." He sank into one of the hotel's plush chairs.

Maria could tell that something was wrong. But if it wasn't Sam or the baby, she was puzzled by the expression on Jose's face. What else could make him look so discouraged, so depressed, she wondered. She rose from the sofa and moved to stand directly in front of her son, laying her rosary on the end table as she stood

"Jose, what is it then?" she demanded, both hands on her hips. "You will tell me now."

A mother always knows, he told himself. Doesn't matter how old you are, a mother always knows. However, he didn't want to talk about his problems right now, so he ignored her question and asked one of his own instead.

"Where's Papa? Is he asleep?"

Maria wasn't fooled by Jose's evasion tactic. "Jose, what it is?" she asked gently, moving her hand to lay it on her son's face. "Please, *Mi Hijo*, tell me what is wrong," she pleaded with him.

Jose took his mother's hands in his and stood, guiding her to the sofa she had just vacated. He sat and pulled her to sit down next to him. It was easier to talk without having her standing over him.

"No, Mama. I don't want to burden you with anything more at a time like this. I will be fine. Please just let it go. Why don't you go back to bed? You look like you could use some more sleep."

Maria watched the young man's face, and refused to give up. She knew him too well. "Jose, I am your mother. Anything that hurts you also hurts me. And I can see that you are hurting, that there is something that is very wrong. I will not sleep until I know what is bothering you."

Knowing he was fighting a losing battle, Jose gave a sigh before answering. "It's Sam, Mama. Sam isn't..." He put his head in his hands.

How could he tell her that Samantha wasn't his daughter, her beloved granddaughter? How?

Maria, thinking that Jose was trying to tell her that Sam wasn't going to come out of the coma, that she would die, took in a sudden breath and put one hand to her heart. Her eyes widened and then she too put her face in both hands, and began to rock back and forth while moaning.

"Oh, no, not my poor baby. Not my Sam. And that poor, motherless child. She will never know what a beautiful mother she has."

Jose quickly realized what his mother was thinking. He put an arm around her and reassured her. "No, Mama, there's no change in Sam's condition. She's still holding her own." He paused, then took a deep breath before he continued. "I found out tonight that Sam isn't…she isn't my daughter."

"What?" Maria cried, dropping her hands to her lap. Disbelief was written all over her face. "Jose, what are you saying?"

Anger was now visible on Jose's face, and was threatening to boil over. Trying not to raise his voice in order to keep from waking his father, he failed. When he looked at his mother sparks nearly flew out of his eyes as he explained, his voice rising with righteous indignation.

"Etta, that bitch that I'm married to, lied to me. I'm not Sam's father. I don't know who her father is."

Maria reacted without the same compunction to keep her voice down. Consequently, it rose an octave. "*Mi Dios,* my God, what are you saying?"

"I'm saying that Sam isn't my daughter. That Etta is a lying bitch and we've all been deceived. All of us except Fina, I'm sure. She always knew everything, there's no way she didn't know this." His voice became a sneer. "Like mother, like daughter. Isn't that how the saying goes?"

Maria immediately jumped up and slapped Jose across the cheek. "You don't say such things about Fina," she yelled at him. "She was like my sister. And you don't say such things about my baby, Sam. She is my *nieta,* my granddaughter."

"What is going on in here?" Big Jose stood at the doorway with only a towel wrapped around him, his hair dripping from his shower. "I could hear you all the way in the bathroom." He looked from his upset wife, who was standing over his son, and then to Jose, who was holding a hand to the side of his face and looking up at his mother in disbelief.

Maria sank back down to the couch as far away from her son as she could get, grabbed her rosary, and nodded toward Jose, her voice now more sad than angry. "He has said awful things about Etta. And about Sam and Fina."

"What things?" Big Jose demanded glaring at his son.

Jose had never seen his father angry. Nor had his mother ever struck him, and now he was ashamed. Before answering his father he rose and knelt in front of his mother. He tried to take her hand, which she refused to give him.

"Mama, please forgive me. I didn't mean to upset you."

Maria did not respond. Instead, she looked away from her son and addressed her husband. "Please, go and get dressed. I don't want you to become sick. When you come back then Little Jose will explain."

Big Jose turned back to the bedroom and returned seconds later wearing a hotel robe. He moved to the couch and sat by his visibly disturbed wife. Their son was now pacing back and forth, obviously agitated.

"Tell me Jose, what have you said to upset your mother so?"

Jose stopped his pacing and stood looking at his parents. How he envied their love. If he had only married Lupe he thought bitterly, they would have had this kind of love. He suddenly felt his old sorrow flooding back and then his new anger surfaced again.

He sat in the chair once more and, running his fingers through his hair as he talked, he told his parents what he had discovered. He didn't want to confuse them so he lied, telling them that he had found Etta's diary. He knew that would be easier for them to understand than the true explanation about finding a journal Sam had written when she was only six. He didn't want them to know she was able, at that age, to see into the past, see through the eyes of others, or to hear their thoughts.

While he was relating what he had learned neither parent spoke. When he finished they remained quiet for a few minutes, digesting what he had revealed. Finally, Big Jose broke the silence.

"Son, for 28 years I've sat back and said nothing about the way you have treated your wife and daughter."

"But…" Jose started to interrupt his father but stopped when Big Jose held up his hand to indicate that he wasn't finished.

"No, Jose, we've heard what you had to say. I'm telling you that for the past 28 years you were not a father to that little girl, even when you thought she was your daughter. And now you think just because your blood doesn't run in her veins you can…what? What Jose? Just walk away? No. You will not walk away. Instead you will do the right thing. As of today, you will become a *real* father to her. You will make up for all the years that you ignored her."

Once more Jose tried to interject, to protest, but Big Jose again held up his hand for silence.

"No, Jose. This is what needs to be done. Sam has always loved you and you have treated her like she was nothing. She, and now her baby, they both deserve more. And you will be there for her as her father, as her baby's grandfather. If you don't, I will no longer have a son. That is all I have to say." Big Jose kissed Maria on her cheek, rose and walked toward the bedroom.

Turning at the doorway he said quietly, "Don't make me choose, Jose, because no matter what, Sam is my granddaughter. Pancho saved your life and your mother's. He was like my brother and Fina was like a sister. Even Etta is more than just a daughter-in-law; she is like a daughter to us. And as much as I love you, I will never forgive you if you hurt Sam any more than you already have. I am telling you: do not turn your back on her and her baby."

Jose stared after his father. He turned and looked at his mother. Her eyes were closed and she was praying, but Jose knew without being told that she too would choose Sam over him. He stood. Straightening his shoulders, he left the suite without saying another word, closing the door quietly behind him.

CHAPTER 22 – *Humberto 1952* – Little Angel

"I need to get back to Sam."

Etta looked at Humberto, her eyes brimming with unshed tears. "I would really like it if you would…" She looked away without finishing what she wanted to say.

How could she even ask him after what they had just read, knowing that he now knew about Andrew and her betrayal to Jose. Surely he must detest her. She knew she had hurt him, thought of no one but herself all those years ago. She wouldn't blame him if he turned and walked out, but he still stood in front of her, waiting to hear what she wanted from him.

When she didn't continue he asked, "What Etta? What would you like me to do?"

His voice was pitched low, with resignation behind the question. He was hurting from the knowledge that she had used him so many years ago and wanted to hate her, but he knew he would do whatever she asked of him. He couldn't turn off his love for her like a light switch. When he looked at her, so small, so tiny, and saw how she was hurting, all he wanted to do was wrap her in his arms and hold her. He wanted to make everything 'all better,' as his Aunt Maria always said.

Etta glanced up to Humberto's face, meeting his dark eyes before lowering hers again. She was so ashamed of all the things she had done, but she had to know if he would still stand by her.

"I know I don't have any right to ask you, but would you stay? I would feel so much better, just knowing you were out here." She turned her head away and continued, her voice so low he had to strain to hear her. "I don't want to be alone if something should happen to... to Sam."

In spite of everything, Humberto knew he would stay because the thought of leaving her here alone was too much for him to bear. Besides, he loved Sam almost as much as he loved Etta.

He knew that Etta had no idea that Sam was and had always been a huge part of his life; she was like his own child. He knew that even when Etta had been sober off and on over the years she had all but ignored Sam. He knew all of this because Sam had told him, had cried on his shoulder, had told him how she had felt like an orphan all those years when her mother and her father had basically abandoned her.

Yes, she was raised by Maria, Fina, and Big Jose, and Sam loved her grandparents immensely. But what child wouldn't feel *discarded* with parents like hers? And of course, he had seen it with his own eyes and he had done nothing.

When Sam was only ten years old she had asked him, "What did I do, Uncle Humberto, to make my parents hate me so much?"

He had tried to comfort her but he knew he hadn't succeeded when she said, "It's okay, really. I don't know what is sadder, that my mother hides either in her room or in a bottle, or that my father hides in plain sight."

Only ten, he thought sadly, *but wiser than both of her parents put together.*

He vowed now, that when Sam was better, he wouldn't allow himself to think of any other alternative. He would sit Etta and Jose down and tell them what a wonderful daughter they had, something he should have done years ago.

With all the bitterness he felt for the way Etta had ignored Sam, he had to admit he still loved her. Even the information that was contained in the journal he read did not kill that love. He knew he would always love her, no matter what happened. He crossed the short distance between them, turned her around to face him, and took her in his arms. With his chin resting on the top of her head he answered, "Yes, Etta, I will stay. I will wait while you are with your daughter. Now go. Go."

Unsure if she had heard him correctly, Etta eased herself back so she could see Humberto's face. What she saw there reassured her, and filled her with gratitude and with love.

"Okay," she whispered, "thank you." She then stood on her toes and brushed her lips lightly across his. "Thank you so much."

She turned and walked toward the door leading out of the waiting room. Before disappearing she paused and glanced back at her friend. In spite of the sadness in her eyes she smiled her thanks before leaving to go to her daughter.

Humberto continued to look at the closed door long after Etta left. Then, sighing, he returned to the sofa.

Oh, Sam, he prayed, *please get well. I need to tell you how much you mean to me, how much I love you.*

He sighed again, thinking about the first time he had seen Samantha.

Humberto was 22, in law school, and home following a year at Harvard. He had accepted a special one-year scholarship after Etta and Jose had married, hoping distance would diminish the love he felt for Etta and the pain at watching her marry someone else. It hadn't worked, and he was now on his way to the ranch after visiting with his mother, anxious for news of the woman he loved. His mother had told him Etta had been sent to Mexico for help with her drinking problem.

Upon arriving at the ranch he went into the kitchen looking for his Aunt Maria. The first sight that caught his eye when he walked into the kitchen was a baby sitting in a highchair, dressed all in pink, with a mass of curls framing her pixie face. She squealed in delight and held her arms up to him as soon as she saw him – and for him it was love at first sight.

"She wants you to free her, *Mi Hijo,* she doesn't like being captured in that chair," Maria informed him even as she hugged him tightly. "I've missed you much. Humberto, this is my Sammy. Go ahead pick her up."

"But I don't know anything about babies," he protested.

"What's to know?" Maria insisted, "She won't break anything except your heart, *Mi Hijo.* Isn't she just a little angel?"

"Yes," Humberto agreed while thinking *an angel, just like her mother.*

Ignoring his fear in favor of wanting to hold Etta's child, he picked up the squirming baby. He noticed immediately how sweet, how fresh she smelled. Sam grabbed at his hair, giggling, and he was head-over-heels in love, just as he had been with her mother for so many years.

The kitchen door slammed and Humberto looked up to see Big Jose entering the kitchen.

"Humberto, son, it is so good to see you. When did you get home?" Big Jose hugged his wife's nephew tightly and reached to take the squirming baby from his arms.

Humberto was reluctant to surrender Sammy to her grandfather as he answered, "Yesterday, Uncle." Out of respect, however, he released her to the older man.

Big Jose sat at the table with his legs crossed at the knee, holding Sam upright on his extended leg. "We are so proud of you, son. Harvard!"

"Thanks, Uncle," Humberto acknowledged the compliment, as he sat down next to Big Jose.

Grandfather and granddaughter began to play a familiar game. Big Jose moved his leg up and down while singing, "This little horsey went to town, this little horsey then fell down." On *down* he dropped his leg almost to the floor while holding the baby's two hands so she wouldn't fall, and Samantha giggled with glee.

Watching the grown man laughing happily with the cheerful baby, it was hard for Humberto to imagine Big Jose as a small child. His mother had told him the story of the man who had to overcome so many obstacles while growing up…

CHAPTER 23 – *Big Jose 1912 to 1931* – | The Orphan

After arriving back in Tucson from Harvard Humberto had dutifully gone to see his mother, knowing she would provide news from the ranch. She didn't disappoint. As soon as she had given him her customary hug and asked him what he wanted to eat, she began reporting the latest.

"Poor Maria and Big Jose. That Etta is drinking again and it's bad – so bad that Big Jose had to take her to Cananea this time to his nuns." His mother's disapproval was thick in her voice.

"Big Jose has nuns?" Humberto asked his mother, clearly confused.

"*Si, si.* Oh maybe you never heard the story of Big Jose's life. Sad, so sad," his mother shook her head as if willing a bad memory to go away. "Sit, sit," his mother commanded. "I'll make you some tacos and tell you the story."

Humberto took a seat at his mother's worn kitchen table.

"Big Jose was the seventh child born to his poor mother – of course, he wasn't called 'Big' Jose then, not until he became a man. Anyway, he was a change of life baby. Do you know what that means?" With barely a pause to take a breath his mother continued without waiting for his answer.

"That is a baby born late in a woman's life. Many times it is very hard on the mother, and this was true for the baby Jose's mother. She died before she could hold her little boy." Lucy crossed herself before continuing her story.

"His mother's death broke his father's heart. In fact, his father, Manuel, actually started to die himself, that very day. I was told this by Theresa, Big Jose's oldest sister, the one who was a nun. Remember, she came to stay with me after I lost your father and I was so sick with grief I wanted to die too.

"Anyway, the father was much older than the mother. I think ten or more years separated them. She was 49 when she died, so he would have been at least 59 or 60.

"Theresa said that her father had always wanted a son but until Jose was born they only had girls, six of them. Then at last, a son was born. But the old man could not be happy because his wife died giving birth to that son. He only felt guilt, not happiness...well, like I said, he started dying the day Jose was born.

"Manuel wanted nothing to do with his new son, and refused to hold him or to feed him. It was left to Jose's poor sisters to raise him. But they were a lot older than Jose and one by one they left to be married and start their own families. Except Theresa. Theresa, she was the oldest sister, and she had already left to become a nun a long time before Jose was born.

"When the young boy was eight years old his youngest sister, the only one still living at home, I don't remember her name, ran off with a soldier. She left her brother and their dying father all alone.

"Did I say that Big Jose was only eight at the time? Anyway, the boy took over the chores, worked the garden, fed the animals, cleaned the house, washed the clothes, he did everything. His older sisters had taught him well – much as I have taught you Humberto, no? You have heard me say, it doesn't hurt a man to know how to take care of himself."

"Mama, please," Humberto begged, knowing his mother was easily distracted, "the story. What happened then?"

"Okay, okay, let me think," she said as she put hamburger into her cast iron skillet. She sprinkled the meat with garlic powder and set the heat at the right temperature to brown it for her tacos.

"Yes, I think it was only two or three months after the last sister ran off that old man Lopez died. Poor Jose, that poor child, found his father dead one morning when he tried to wake him for breakfast. Big Jose told all of this to Theresa and she told it to me, like I said.

"Jose, the brave little man that he was, didn't cry. Instead, he got a shovel and started digging the old man's grave next to his poor mother's. In Mexico it is not unusual to have a family cemetery behind the house...actually in this case it was more of a shack. You are so lucky, Humberto, to have grown up in a nice place like this.

"Anyway, that little boy dug for two days. Theresa said he had blisters on top of blisters, both hands bleeding and wrapped in rags, but he kept digging. Once the hole was big enough, Big Jose tried to carry his father, who he had bundled in a blanket, out to the graveyard. But, Humberto, Jose was just a little boy. And even though his father had wasted away that last year of his life he was too heavy for Jose to lift, much less carry. Plus, this happens, *Mi Hijo*, I know I've seen it, after someone passes, their body gets stiff, like a board."

Humberto smiled at his mother, "Yes, Mama, it's called 'rigor mortis'."

"Well rigor whatever had stiffened that old man and Jose couldn't lift him so he started walking to the nearest village, which was miles away, to get help. Lucky for Big Jose and for his father also, it was winter, or the old man would have been stiff and stinking too, no?

"Don't look at me that way, Humberto," his mother said when her son made a face, "that is what happens, I know this." She stirred the taco meat and started grating cheese.

"Sorry. Mama, let me do that," Humberto offered. He rose and took the grater and cheese from his mother's hands, then returned to sit at the table while he took over the chore.

His mother opened her ice box to look for a head of lettuce. Finding it, she rinsed it off at the sink, returned to the counter next to the stove, stirred the meat again, and started chopping lettuce into long thin pieces.

"Okay, where was I? Oh, yes, Jose was walking to the village. Before he had gotten very far a young priest found him on the side of the road. The poor boy was hungry, dirty, and cold. He told the priest about his father, so the priest lifted the exhausted boy into his carriage, turned around and drove back to the Lopez house.

"Together they buried poor Manuel. The priest knew of Jose's sister, Theresa, and took the now orphaned boy to the little mission were she was performing her service to God – a mission just outside of Cananea.

"I have always thought that you would have been a great priest, Humberto. I think a priest would have been so much better than a…a lawyer." Lucy said it as if the word *lawyer* tasted bad on her tongue.

Humberto kept grating, knowing full well how his mother felt about his chosen profession. He also knew that she couldn't be quiet for very long and would soon have to finish the story. So he continued to silently grate cheese and refrained from reacting to her familiar barbs.

After a minute or two Lucy let out a long, drawn-out sigh and continued as if she had not detoured from Big Jose's story.

"The mission where Theresa was living was a small place, only seven or eight nuns, and one priest. But fortunately for the orphaned child, the old priest had a good heart and agreed to let Jose live there, providing of course that he did chores to help pay for his keep. That wasn't a problem, that little boy had worked hard all of his short life. In fact, Big Jose told me once that it was the 'easiest job' he ever had."

"The nuns, they all adored him. His sisters had never sent him to school so some of the nuns taught him how to read and write. They were amazed at how fast he learned. One of the nuns was from the United States. I think her name was Sister Victoria, and she taught Jose to speak English. That's why he talks so good.

"The old priest taught Big Jose about numbers. And I don't mean just adding and subtracting, but all kinds of things. Your uncle would never brag but Theresa told me the priest said the boy was a natural matha…"

"Mathematician?" Humberto supplied the word for his mother.

"*Si, si*, that was it, a mathematician. Big Jose told me he was very happy at the mission in Cananea. He loved the old priest and the nuns.

"It was at the mission that Big Jose met my sweet little sister Maria. Oh Maria was so beautiful. She still is of course, but back then she could have been a movie star, Humberto. Her hair was long to her waist, and so shiny, so black. She was the real beauty in our family.

"Our mama used to say that Maria got all the good looks in the family. Which I will tell you, Humberto, hurt my feelings a little. But Maria couldn't help it that she was beautiful. Besides she was always such a sweet child that I could never be mad at her for long. Now, your Aunt Pilar, your Cousin Carlos' mother, is another story. That woman is as mean as... Well, never mind. I'll tell you about her later.

"Anyway, Maria was, let me think, only 16 or so when our family moved from Juarez. Our Papa's father had passed and Papa decided to take over his property. It wasn't much, but it was bigger and better than what we had when I was growing up. By this time I had married your father and we were living in Tucson.

"Our youngest brother, Juan, had taken ill on the trip from Juarez, and he wasn't getting better. He was very, very sick. Mama sent Maria to the mission because she had heard that one of the nuns was a nurse. That nun turned out to be Theresa. The Church had sent her to nursing school in Mexico City years before.

"Big Jose was probably around 18 or 19 years old. He was tall and handsome, too skinny for my taste but that did not matter to your aunt. They took one look at each other and that was that. They were married only a month or so after they met.

"They moved back to Big Jose's father's place. It had been empty all those years that Jose lived at the mission. Oh but, Humberto, it was awful, only one room. The leaking roof was the only running water in the place. It started falling apart after Jose's mother died, Maria said. Mama begged them to come and live with them, but with eight or nine kids still at home there wasn't enough room. Besides, they were young and in love and they both worked hard to fix the place up.

"Then Maria got pregnant with Little Jose. That was when Big Jose decided they should move to the United States. They would come to stay with us, and we would help them get a new start. So they packed up everything in Big Jose's old truck and started north.

"They stopped at Cananea to say good bye to Theresa and the others at the mission. And of course they stopped by Mama and Papa's place. Little Juan had gotten sick again and they didn't know if he would make it this time so Maria didn't want to leave him. They ended up staying for several months, until they knew our little brother would be okay. Big Jose helped Papa, and Maria nursed Little Juan. By the time Juan was better, Maria was big with Little Jose. Anyway, I know you know that story.

"Once, Big Jose told me that until he met Maria, he hadn't been able to forgive his father for abandoning him to the care of his sisters. He had prayed and prayed when he lived at the mission, but no forgiveness would come.

"Remember, Humberto, God wants us to forgive. If you don't forgive, the anger or sadness or whatever it is will eat you up inside. Fina told me this also when I was grieving for your father. I was so mad at him for dying and leaving me alone with a small child to raise by myself. I was also very, very sad. I loved your father very much. Fina came to see me. She told me that I needed to forgive your father because my anger and sadness was making me sick. I was sick on the inside and it made me sick on the outside too.

"Did you know that I almost died? Fina told Maria that I needed help – I needed someone to help me pray. She said to Maria, 'Get Big Jose's sister. She will be able to help.' So Theresa came and together we prayed and prayed. She knows how to pray, let me tell you. Anyway, the minute I forgave your father for dying – I know, I know it wasn't his fault, but I blamed him still – I felt the illness leave my body. It was a miracle, Humberto, a miracle."

Humberto smiled at his mother. She was something. She had raised him by taking in ironing and doing light housekeeping for the *gringos*. She never complained or asked for anything. And while he could barely remember his father, or his death, he did remember his mother being very ill. Big Jose and Maria had come and taken him to the ranch. He loved being at the ranch with Jose and Etta, but he had desperately missed his mother.

When he was older and able to understand how hard it was for her not only to raise him by herself but to do all of the other things she did as well – working at the Church, helping out in their community – he had vowed to take care of her as soon as he was able. He had worked hard and gotten straight A's in high school, earning a full scholarship to the University of Arizona, and then one for law school.

His mother's voice brought him back, "Humberto, are you listening? That's enough cheese."

"Sorry, Mama. So what did Big Jose tell you about his father?"

Lucy hugged her son as she placed a plate of tacos in front of him. Then she took some of the cheese he had been grating and sprinkled it on his tacos for him before urging him to eat. No matter how old he got she always treated him like a child when it came to food.

"Okay, where was I? Oh, yes. The old priest told Big Jose that he needed to forgive Manuel. But the child was bitter. His father never told him that he loved him, never held him in his lap, nothing. And after the girls all left Jose had taken on the duties of caring for that old man, like I said. But not once did the old man thank him. After he died, and Jose was living at the mission, all of his bitterness and grief against his father overwhelmed him sometimes. As much as he prayed and tried to forgive him, Big Jose said that he continued to carry his anger in his heart…much like I did for your father.

"Anyway, after Big Jose fell in love with Maria he finally understood his father's heartbreak. He said to me, 'My father must have loved my mother the way I love my Maria, because I know my heart would break in two if something ever happened to her.'

"It was so sweet, Humberto, it made me cry. And you know I never cry."

Humberto was surprised by his mother's admission but he wasn't surprised by Big Jose's or Manuel's love for their women. Yes, he understood all too well, because that was exactly how he felt, had always felt about Etta. It didn't matter whether she was drunk, sober, married, or getting help from the nuns at Cananea.

The sound of the door to the waiting room being opened brought Humberto back to the present. An apparent family member of another ICU patient smiled at him as she took a seat in the waiting room and picked up a magazine. Humberto smiled back as he stood up and stretched.

Noticing Sam's journal still on the coffee table where he had dropped it, he picked it up. It could not be left laying around for a stranger to find and read. He didn't know how it could possibly have been written by Sam, but he decided to see what else might be in the journal anyway. He sat back down on the couch and started to read, almost dreading what else he might discover about the woman he loved…

Chapter 24 – *Etta 1951* – Her Honeymoon

The pounding on the door intensified the pounding in Etta's head. She opened her eyes and then immediately closed them against the light coming in where the drapes did not close completely. She moved her hands to her head to see if holding it would still the throbbing pain. Her throat felt like the Sonora desert but she managed to croak a dry-mouthed, "Yes?"

Maria's cheery voice on the other side of the massive wooden door did nothing to soothe Etta's excruciating headache.

"Wake-up, *Mi Hijos*, you don't want to miss your train."

Etta forced her eyes open again. She glanced around the gigantic bedroom, the room she had grown up in. Like all the bedrooms in the Hacienda de Luna it was a massive suite filled with dark, heavy furniture and complete with a separate sitting area, fireplace, and bathroom. She searched desperately for some sign that Jose had come into the room after she had fallen asleep, might still be there somewhere, but she found none. Double French doors that opened to a second story wrap-around balcony were closed, heavy drapes pulled together over them. She felt her hopes plummet when she realized she was still alone. Her new husband had not come to her on their wedding night.

Maria, now her mother-in-law, continued knocking a little less intently.

"Okay, I'm…we're awake. Thanks, Maria," Etta managed with great effort.

"Good," Maria replied, "I'm making a lunch to take on the train with you. Hurry so you won't be late. That is not how you want to start your honeymoon." Her footfalls echoed down the hallway outside the bedroom.

Etta managed to sit up, and then swung her legs slowly over the side of the bed. But when she tried to stand bile rushed into her throat. Holding her hand over her mouth, she barely made it to the bathroom where she dropped heavily to the floor and retched violently into the toilet. She wasn't sure how long she had been lying on the cold Spanish-tiled bathroom floor when she heard the bedroom door open and close and the muffled sound of footsteps. They crossed the Persian rug, and then stopped at the bathroom doorway. Afraid to move, lest the nausea return, she lay with one arm thrown over her eyes. She knew who it must be.

After hesitating at the door for a moment, Jose walked into the bathroom. At the sight of Etta lying on the floor next to the toilet he assumed she was suffering from morning sickness. The thought that it might be the result of two bottles of expensive wedding champagne never entered his mind. He almost felt sorry for her. Almost, but the feeling didn't last long.

"Etta," he began sternly, not a hint of sympathy in his voice, "I only stopped by to tell you that you are free to do either of two things." He hesitated, to see if she would look at him, but her arm remained over her eyes while she waited to hear what he had to say.

"One, you can get up and get dressed so you can catch your train. I've talked to Pam, and since she was already planning on accompanying us to Boston to visit her aunt, she has agreed to continue on to Europe with you. You and she can enjoy the honeymoon you so meticulously planned. Otherwise, if you prefer, you can continue to lie here on the floor and play the long-suffering abandoned bride. It really doesn't matter to me. I'll be staying with Humberto in Tucson. I'm not sure when, if ever, I'll be back."

Uncovering her eyes at last, Etta looked up at the hard face of her new husband. "Jose," she said in a plaintive voice, "what's the matter? You disappeared from the reception and I waited for you to come to me last night. Where were you? Why didn't you come?" Saying this, she reached out with her hand to grab the boot that was closest to her, but he took a step back.

"Don't," he said, pulling his foot back. He looked down at her with disgust before adding, "Don't even try. I know what you did, Etta, to get me to marry you. And I'm not sure I can ever forgive you." With that he turned and strode purposefully out of the room. She heard the door close behind him.

She tried to get up, to go after him. She was convinced that she could fix the problem if Jose would just listen to her. However, as soon as she stood the nausea returned more violently than before and all she could do was sink back down to the floor and hang on to the toilet while she vomited again and again.

Finally, her stomach emptied of the expensive champagne and food she'd consumed, she was able to pull herself up. She felt completely wrung out and her stomach hurt from the prolonged retching but she moved slowly to the sink to rinse out her mouth and splash cool water on her face. That seemed to help. Holding on to the sink with one hand and reaching for the medicine cabinet where the aspirin was kept with the other, she stopped when her gaze met that of her reflection in the mirror. She barely noticed the gray pallor of the face that was staring back at her, or the mascara that was smeared under her eyes.

Okay, she mentally cautioned herself, don't panic. You need to just let Jose calm down. But how could he possibly know she wasn't really pregnant? She hadn't told anyone...unless her mother...? No, she told herself, dismissing that possibility. Her mother would never say anything; it was totally against Fina's strict sense of honor to betray someone's thoughts. So if not her mother, then who? How could he know her secret?

The longer she continued to stare at her reflection the less she cared what Jose might know. Instead, she began to formulate a plan that would allow her to enjoy Europe with her best friend and at the same time achieve her goal: make Jose miss her and apologize for abandoning her on their wedding night.

"I should be angry with *him*, not the other way around. What kind of man does that?" she asked the image in the mirror, feeling justifiably irritated with the man who had abandoned her.

She splashed more water on her face, used makeup remover to wipe away the traces of the stray mascara, and straightened her hair. The aspirin was forgotten. He will miss me and come crawling back, she told herself as she left the bathroom to get ready for her trip. It will do him good. She didn't want to take the time to try to talk to him now; she didn't want to miss her train.

Although Etta considered Pam her best friend, the feeling was not mutual. It was true that they had known each other all of their lives, but basically they were friends only because their fathers were business associates. Pam's father was one of Pancho's many attorneys, and often went to the Hacienda de Luna for a meeting with his client, then stayed for dinner. When she was younger Pam usually accompanied her father, since she and Etta were the same age.

She was secretly jealous of the more beautiful girl, who seemed to have so much: looks, wealth, and intelligence. It wasn't that she didn't like Etta; she did, basically, so she tried to keep her envy to herself. Besides, Etta didn't seem to have many friends because it was so isolated on the ranch, and she was tutored at home. Pam herself was surrounded by friends, and there were several that she considered *best friends*. She couldn't bring herself to tell Etta that she was not one of them. She preferred to be kind rather than cruel.

Pam had been more than a little surprised when Etta had asked her to be her Maid of Honor. They hadn't seen each other much over the last few years; only on some holidays and once or twice when Etta was home from school. They certainly weren't the kind of friends that wrote once a week and told each other their deepest secrets. She was even more surprised when Jose had asked, actually begged, her to accompany Etta on the honeymoon trip. Her first reaction had been to say no, but she then decided it was a great opportunity to see Europe, and it wouldn't cost her anything. It was none of her business why Etta's husband wasn't going.

So it was Etta and Pam who toured Europe. They stayed at the best hotels, in the honeymoon suites, ignoring the raised eyebrows of the hotel staff that checked them in. They ate the best foods, drank the best wines. From Paris to London to Rome, and all places in between, they laughed, went sight-seeing, and danced with handsome men. There was never a shortage of charming European escorts who were more than willing to let the beautiful American woman buy their drinks and dinner in exchange for their company for an evening with her and her friend.

Etta pretended she did not miss Jose; Pam pretended this was the trip she had always wanted to experience. Jose's name was not mentioned by either woman. It was not that Etta wasn't curious to know what he'd told Pam; she definitely was, but she was determined not to let Pam know how much it mattered to her. Instead, she acted as if spending a glamorous expensive honeymoon with a girlfriend instead of a loving husband wasn't at all unusual.

The original honeymoon itinerary didn't include two stays in London but after a week of hot and humid Rome, Etta suggested they return to London instead of spending the planned additional week in Italy. She was moody and complained that the uncomfortable weather was making her ill. Pam silently believed that Etta's problem was largely due to her over-indulgence of Italian wine, not the weather. Still, when Etta suggested returning to London for the last week of their trip, Pam agreed without hesitation.

She was beginning to worry about Etta. Since they hadn't been close in later years Pam hadn't realized that Etta drank so much. And it wasn't just a glass or two of wine with dinner; she started drinking at lunch and continued to drink late into the night. Concerned, Pam had cautioned her several times to slow down, but Etta would just brush her off.

"Pam, dear, this is my honeymoon. Let me enjoy it," she would say.

During the trip Pam realized that she no longer envied Etta. While she wasn't the beauty or the genius Etta was, she had graduated with honors from the University of Arizona and was planning to attend law school in the fall. Her future looked promising, and she was anxious to return home. No, she was no longer jealous or envious, and she was becoming increasingly tired of the pampered princess, who was so often drunk and had to be helped into bed most nights. She couldn't wait for this never-ending honeymoon to be over.

Back in London, Etta's condition did not improve even though the weather was beautiful. It rained off and on so it was cool, and only a little bit muggy. She continued to feel ill, and when Pam found her vomiting for the third morning in a row she decided to voice the question that had begun to nag at her.

"Etta? Is it possible that you're pregnant?"

Pam had hesitated to ask because she was reasonably sure that Jose and Etta had not spent their wedding night together. What they did before the wedding was none of her business.

Etta, too miserable to be embarrassed at having her friend see her with her head hanging over the toilet, looked up and managed a weak smile.

"Of course not. I'm sure it's just food poisoning or something..."

Then, with the thought planted in her head, she frantically searched her memory for the last time she'd had a period. When it came to her she managed to gasp once before she vomited again. This time it was not because she was nauseated, but because she knew Pam was right. She had to be pregnant. She hadn't had a period since the last one in New Orleans, prior to her evening with Andrew...

CHAPTER 25 – *Humberto 1979* – Possibilities

Humberto closed the journal and sighed. Suddenly he was totally exhausted.

Poor Etta. Poor Jose. Poor Sam. How had everything turned out so fucked up? He rarely cursed but he couldn't think of any other word to describe the awful mess that all of their lives had become.

He thought again of his vow to sit Etta and Jose down and tell them what a wonderful daughter they had. If he had done so years ago would things be different now? Probably not, but at least he could say he tried.

His thoughts centered on Etta and he was amazed to realize that, with all he had read in the journal, he still loved her. He always had and he always would, literally until the day he died.

Humberto knew that if Jose, convinced Sam wasn't his daughter, abandoned Etta and her daughter, well, he would be there to pick up the pieces, just as he always had. And if Etta remained sober, as she was now, maybe he could convince her that he could give her a better life than she'd had with Jose. Anything would be better than the indifference mother and daughter had received from Jose for the past 28 years.

Hell, everyone knew that their marriage was a farce; they hadn't fooled anyone by staying together. They should have divorced years ago. At least then he would have had a chance to step in and be a real husband to Etta and a father to Samantha. Maybe it wasn't too late.

Just thinking about the possibility of a life with Etta excited him.

166

But right now he needed to rest, he was so tired. He would just close his eyes for a minute or two. He needed to be strong when Sam came out of her coma; when he faced Etta and Jose...

Chapter 26 – *Jose 1951* – His Honeymoon

After leaving his parents at the hotel Jose just walked. He didn't know how far or for how long. He simply put one foot in front of the other without thinking about it. And while he walked he thought about those other rambling walks he took so long ago…

After his confrontation with Etta, Jose left the ranch without a word to anyone, even his parents. *Let Etta explain. She's good at lies. She'll think of something*, he bitterly reasoned with himself. He was even too upset to care whether he was leaving Pancho short-handed without any notice.

If Humberto was surprised to see Jose when he showed up at the apartment the day after the wedding, he didn't let on. He simply hugged his cousin and told him he could stay as long as he wanted. Humberto was attending summer school and working part-time for a local law firm, so he was gone most of the day, busy with either work or school. They would not be in each other's way.

At first Jose found it difficult not having to get up early and go to work. He had been working on the ranch for as long as he could remember, and it was natural for his body to come alive at the same time each morning. After the first week, however, a satisfactory routine was established. He still woke up at 4:00 a.m., but instead of getting up he laid in bed dozing and thinking until he heard Humberto's alarm clock go off at 5:30. Then he would climb out of bed and, still wearing the shorts and T-shirt that he slept in, start the coffee and prepare breakfast while Humberto showered and dressed.

The two men enjoyed their coffee and breakfast at the small table and chairs on the apartment's wrought iron balcony. They didn't talk much but it was an easy silence, borne of long companionship and familiarity with each other, so neither felt awkward. Jose never brought up Etta or the honeymoon he was supposed to be on, and Humberto never asked. Instead, they watched the surrounding neighborhood come alive, periodically making comments.

Humberto usually left the apartment around 6:30. He needed an early start, as he rode his bike the two miles to the law firm's offices where he worked each morning before his afternoon classes started. After Humberto left Jose washed the breakfast dishes, cleaned up the kitchen and tidied the small apartment. Next he showered and dressed for outdoors. Then he walked.

Some days he walked all over the University campus, other days he just wandered through unfamiliar neighborhoods, neither noticing nor appreciating the unique character and architecture of the historical Sam Hughes neighborhood that was located west of Humberto's apartment building.

After an hour or so he usually found a bench at the University or in a nearby park and just sat and listened to conversations being carried on around him by others who were relaxing and enjoying being out of doors. Sometimes he went to the University's library and read. It didn't really matter where he went or what he did, all he could think about was Lupe. *Where was she? What was she doing? Did she miss him as much as he missed her?* He rarely let himself think about Etta because when he did, his thoughts were not kind: he wanted to kill her. If she did slip unbidden into his mind, he would then walk to St. Augustine Cathedral to confess his murderous thoughts to Father Miguel.

Between 4:30 and 5:30 p.m. he headed back to the apartment to start dinner. When Humberto came home they dined once more on the small balcony, said little and watched the evening settle in. After dinner Humberto usually had schoolwork and Jose went for an evening walk. He walked until 9:30 or 10:00, hoping to exhaust himself so he could sleep. In spite of his intention, however, he often laid awake until midnight or later, then slept for a few brief hours and woke early to start the same pattern all over again.

In the sixth week of his semi-exile there was a knock on the door.

It was after Humberto had left for the office, and since they rarely had company, especially this early in the day, Jose was surprised to hear it. He opened the door to find Fina standing there, and stepped aside to let her enter the apartment. She immediately wrapped him in her arms. At her touch, he felt all the pain and sadness of the long six weeks grab him, and could not stop the tears that spilled from his eyes. He cried and cried as his mother-in-law held him while slowly rocking back and forth. Neither of them had uttered a word. When he was spent, she gently pulled away and led him to the couch.

"Jose, I know you're still upset but you can't continue with this..," she struggled trying to find the right words, "this depression, and bitterness. Your mother is beside herself with worry. When Etta left for the train alone, and you were nowhere to be found, Maria was on the verge of hysteria. If Big Jose hadn't called Humberto they would not have known where you have been all these weeks. Even knowing, your mother hasn't slept well since you've been gone and she isn't eating."

Fina took Jose's hands in hers as she continued in her soft voice, "You need to come home, back to the ranch. We all need you, not just Maria. Jose? Are you listening to me?" When Jose failed to answer, or to look at her, she tried a different tactic, her voice now becoming stern.

"Okay Jose. I know things aren't as you wish but you need to grow up. Life isn't always fair. You need to think about your mother and father, and…" she hesitated, watching his expression, "and Etta and the baby," she finished.

At the mention of Etta's name he pulled his hands away from Fina's, raised his head and looked directly at her, and almost spat, "Oh yes let's not forget about poor Etta and the baby."

"Yes, Jose, like it or not there is a baby. And that baby is going to need a father. I'm not going to ask you to forgive and forget what Etta has done; it is still too raw a wound. But I will ask you to think about the baby, and about your parents. Even about Pancho, who has always loved you like a son. Jose, it's time to come home. I'm not going to beg you. You need to stand up and do what's right."

"But what about Etta? What happens, Fina, when she comes home also? I can't even stand the thought of seeing her."

"Someday, Jose, you will forgive Etta and believe it or not you will one day be happy again. Until then, you will just have to live one day at a time."

"I'll call my mother. I should have realized that she would be worried and hurting at my abrupt departure. But I can't promise when or if I'll come back. Don't ask me to do something I'm not ready to do yet, Fina."

"Jose," Fina said while patting one of the hands Jose had pulled away. "I know you're thinking about going to Mexico to Lupita. Go if you must, but don't expect Lupe to welcome you with open arms. She is a good woman, an honorable woman. She will not have anything to do with a married man, and certainly not one who is about to become a father. Her honor will win, even over her love for you."

"Damn it! I hate it that you always know what I'm thinking."

"I know how you feel, many things I wish I didn't know. And Jose, I know that you will come back to the ranch eventually. I am leaving now. No one knows I came here. Think about what I've said. I love you, Jose."

She stood and walked to the door. She opened it before turning in the doorway to smile at the young man who continued to sit on the couch.

"Call your mother, *Mi Hijo*," she whispered and then she was gone.

When Humberto came home that evening Jose was still sitting in the same spot.

"Jose?" Humberto asked with concern, seeing his cousin's drawn face. "Are you all right?"

Jose raised his face to look in his cousin's eyes. "No, Humberto, I'm not…and I'm not sure if I ever will be."

CHAPTER 27 – *Jose 1979* – Walking Away

Jose sighed, remembering his six-week stay with Humberto so long ago, and all those long walks he had taken. He came back to the present and realized he had no idea how long he had been walking and thinking. What he did know was that he still hadn't come to a clear decision about Etta...or Sam.

Thinking about Sam, he was now ashamed of himself. He knew his parents were upset with him and he didn't blame them. His father's words still echoed in his head, but he didn't need his father to tell him he had been a rotten father to Sam.

And then there was Etta. He still had to work out within himself how he felt about what she had done. He admitted that not forgiving her for her treachery 28 years ago had ruined not only their marriage but their daughter's childhood. Along with that, the situation had brought grief to his parents and to Fina. Yes, he was angry over what he'd found out this morning, but what was it worth to continue to make all of their lives miserable? His pride?

In six-year-old Sammy's own words, she had been unaware of the meaning of those words written in her journal so long ago. But, did she realize that he wasn't her biological father?

Tired now from lack of sleep, Jose stopped walking and sat down on a bus stop bench. His father's words ran through his mind once more:

"I'm telling you that for the past 28 years you were not a father to that little girl, even when you thought she was your daughter. And now you think just because your blood doesn't run in her veins you can...what? What Jose? Just walk away? No. You will not walk away. Instead you will do the

right thing. As of today, you will become a real father to her. You will make up for all the years that you ignored her."

His father was right; he had walked away from Etta the day they were married. And what was he doing now? He was walking away once again. He had to admit that he was a coward. Yes, he was a coward who wasn't man enough to face anything that he had no control over, or that was just too unpleasant to deal with. How was he going to "make up for all the years" as Big Jose had decreed?

Putting his head in his hands, he heard his father's words continue. They were so clear he almost expected Big Jose to be sitting next to him:

"Don't make me choose, Jose, because no matter what, Sam is my granddaughter. Pancho saved your life and your mother's. He was like my brother..."

Pancho had been like Jose's other father. *If he were here he too would be ashamed of me,* Jose thought, as he remembered the conversation he'd had with his beloved friend the day he returned to the ranch all those many years ago...

CHAPTER 28 – *Jose 1951* – The Whole Story

For another week after Fina's visit Jose delayed returning to the ranch. Then, finally, he admitted there was no valid reason for putting if off, so he thanked Humberto for the use of his apartment and for letting him intrude with no questions asked, and left. He thought about going to Mexico first, to see Lupe, but he knew Fina was right: Lupe may have forgiven him and he was sure she still loved him, but she would never let herself become involved with a married man. She was a devout Catholic and an honorable woman. Reluctantly, he returned to the ranch instead.

He knew there was another week before Etta was due back home. He also knew he still had not thought of a solution to what he considered his problem. He was a strict Catholic and his wife was expecting his baby, so leaving her was out of the question. He did know he had no desire to live with her as man and wife, other than in name only. He supposed he could return to the bunkhouse, but given the closeness of the inhabitants of the ranch he knew that would cause tongues to wag. His mind was in turmoil, so he decided to seek advice from Pancho.

As he knew he would, Jose found Pancho in the library. He was seated at his massive desk, deep in discussion with Doc. The troubled young man stood, unnoticed, in the doorway for a few minutes before clearing his throat to get their attention.

"Jose," Pancho exclaimed, clearly surprised, and happily so, when he lifted his head in reaction to the polite noise from the doorway. He stood and walked around the desk in order to wrap his arms around his son-in-law. He gave him a tight hug before loosening his embrace.

"To what do I owe the pleasure of your company?"

Overcome with emotion in spite of his resolve to be mature and discuss his problem like a man, Jose returned Pancho's hug before pulling back. This man was like a father to him and was loved nearly as much as his own father.

"Hello, Pancho," he answered. His voice was soft, and caught briefly. He cleared his throat and started again. "It's good to see you. I was wondering if you have a few minutes so I can discuss something with you, maybe get your advice. If you're busy now I can come back later."

Pancho sensed there was more to Jose's request than his words revealed. Since the meeting with Doc wasn't crucial he motioned the younger man to a chair near the massive fireplace.

"Now is as good a time as any. Have a seat and I'll be right with you," he said.

Turning to Doc he said quietly, "You don't mind, do you Doc? I think there's something Jose wants to talk about in private. We can continue this later."

Doc rose immediately. He too had sensed Jose was troubled, and agreed to continue their meeting at a later time. "No problem at all. Just holler when you want to get together."

To Jose he waved and said, "It's good to see you, boy. You take care." And he left the room.

"You too, Doc," was the reply that followed the old horse doctor out of the room.

Pancho strode over to the fireplace and seated himself in a chair facing the one that was occupied by Jose. He said nothing, giving the younger man a chance to formulate in his mind what he wanted to say. After a few minutes, while Jose looked everywhere but directly at Pancho, and didn't say a word, he decided to give him an opening.

"You wanted some advice, son?"

"Yes, I...," Jose struggled to find the right words. He brought his eyes forward to meet Pancho's before continuing.

"I think it would be best if I took a different job, one that would keep me away from the hacienda."

This was not what Pancho was expecting to hear. Needing a moment to think, he rose from his chair without commenting. Instead, he walked to his desk and opened a hand-carved mahogany box to take out one of his expensive Cuban cigars. Slowly, still without speaking, he cut off one end with a jeweled cigar cutter and moistened the Cuban with his tongue. He sniffed it and savored the aroma.

Turning back to Jose, "Cigar?" he offered.

"No thanks."

Jose had not interrupted this ritual. He sat with his hands together, hanging down between his knees, and his head bowed. He knew he had taken Pancho by surprise, but wasn't sure how to begin.

Pancho was well aware that Jose had not accompanied his wife to Europe for their honeymoon. He knew too that Jose had spent the past several weeks with Humberto in Tucson. He assumed the young man's statement about staying away from the hacienda had to do with whatever caused him to forego his honeymoon. In Pancho's eyes there was nothing so serious between a husband and wife that couldn't be fixed given enough time and patience. Wanting to live apart, in his opinion, was not the solution.

"Son," Pancho began, then paused to light his cigar and inhale deeply, satisfyingly, before continuing, "these things happen. You and Etta will make up. In fact, I'm sure you'll have many more spats and disagreements in the years to come. All married couples do. There's no need for you to stay away from the ranch."

Jose, realizing that Pancho didn't know the whole story, wasn't surprised at the comment. He felt he needed to explain in detail. Surely then Pancho would understand why it was impossible for him to be near Etta – impossible to live with her as husband and wife. He would not divorce her, but neither could he love her. It would be better if he just stayed as far from her as possible.

"Pancho, I'm not sure how much you know, but Etta tricked me into marrying her. She told me a couple of months ago that she is pregnant. That's the only reason I married her. I don't love her, but I felt it was my duty to give our baby my name. I didn't realize she had planned…"

Surprised, Pancho had stopped listening after hearing the word *pregnant*. It was obvious he was pleased, and interrupted without processing anything else Jose was saying.

"A baby? Why, that's wonderful! Congratulations, son."

"No, Pancho, it isn't wonderful. I realized too late that it had all been planned. Etta knew I was in love with Lupe. She intended to get pregnant all along, and seduced me with that intention in mind. She knew I would marry her once I learned there was to be a baby. She was counting on that, to prevent me from marrying Lupita."

The smile faded from Pancho's face as he listened to what Jose was saying. His daughter had tricked Jose into getting her pregnant? He hadn't married her because he loved her, but because he was going to be a father? Pancho did not want to believe it had happened that way. But he was a fair man and would hear the whole truth before passing judgment. He sat in the chair facing Jose.

"Okay, son, I guess you'd better tell me everything."

CHAPTER 29 – *Etta 1951* – The Promise

Etta and Pam were finally on their way home from the honeymoon trip. Etta was exhausted and completely miserable. She had been in the bathroom of the private Pullman car for almost an hour now. Every time she thought she had brought up everything that was in her stomach, and that the nausea had passed, she would begin again. Even when it was dry heaves the vomiting was violent. Her stomach was very sore and the bumping and swaying of the train wasn't helping.

"Where is Pam?" she groaned into the empty bathroom. She wanted a sip of cool water badly, but was too weak to stand. She didn't know if she'd ever be able to get off the cold floor.

Pregnant. Damn it to hell, she thought as she hung her head over the toilet once again. *At least,* she tried to console herself, *by this time tomorrow I will be home.* She hadn't any idea what to expect once she got there, however. Would Jose have cooled down enough to talk to her? Had he missed her enough to be happy about the marriage after all? Or would he still be angry? She was the one who should be angry, she had convinced herself. After all, he was the one who basically abandoned her, refusing to go on their honeymoon with her. He was a bastard for doing that to her.

After a few more minutes of clinging to the toilet the nausea appeared to have passed at last. She rose shakily to her feet and was able to splash cold water on her face. Holding on to the wash basin she wondered how long her morning, noon, and sometimes night sickness would last. She yearned for home, where she knew her mother and Maria would take care of her.

Where is Pam, damn it? She knows I'm sick, but she sure has managed to make herself scarce. If she wanted to be fair about it, Etta couldn't blame Pam for staying away. Who wanted to hold someone's hand, so to speak, when they were being sick? But she wasn't feeling fair right now, and childishly thought her friend should be with her through her bouts of throwing up.

Shrugging off her pique and feeling a little better now, even hungry, Etta straightened and examined her reflection in the mirror. Not too bad she thought, for someone who had spent the better part of the morning throwing up. She splashed more water on her face, drank some cold water, and smoothed her hair as best she could before leaving the bathroom. She scanned the drawing room to see if Pam had returned from wherever she was, but didn't see her. She sat down on one of the plush divans.

Etta looked around her, admiring the lavish furnishings of the private car. She appreciated her father's thoughtfulness in providing the transportation for a wedding present. By now he would know Jose had not accompanied her on the honeymoon, but not that she was returning a week early. She wasn't sure just why she had not told anyone about her early arrival. There would be no family to meet the train, but that was fine with her. It was embarrassing enough to come home alone without having to endure any fanfare. Besides, she wasn't sure if she was ready to face Jose. Better that he didn't know she was coming.

Etta rested her hands on her stomach. *Damn*, she thought for the thousandth time. She was studying to be a doctor. How could she have let this happen? It was one thing to seduce Jose and try to get pregnant, but it was another to sleep with Andrew and get pregnant by accident. How stupid could she be? Her mother always said there was no such thing as an accident. In fact, Fina believed everything happened for a reason. Thinking of her mother, Etta laid her head back against the back of the divan, closed her eyes and gave in to an overwhelming desire to sleep. She was soon prone on the couch, without ever waking when she lay down.

"Etta, wake-up." Pam gently shook the sleeping woman.

Etta opened her eyes and blinked; she had been dreaming, a dream about Jose making love to her at the river. As she slowly sat up and tried to clear the cobwebs from her brain, a thought suddenly struck her. *Why didn't I think of this before? Jose could definitely be the baby's father.*

She had never had heavy menstrual periods and the only one she'd had since that day at the river was very light. In fact, it had only lasted for three days. There had been some cramping but that wasn't unusual at the early stages of pregnancy, she knew. Could her 'light' period have actually been implantation bleeding?

She closed her eyes. She had a photographic memory; every thing she had ever read was stored verbatim in her brain. The trick was retrieving the information. As a child she had developed an almost foolproof method. She would close her eyes and picture the source of the information; in this case a medical book entitled simply "Pregnancy" by Dr. William H. Crumm.

Within the source she would picture the book's chapters, then the page number where the information was located. From that point it would be as if the book was lying open and her mind was reading what was written there:

Implantation Bleeding: No one knows for sure why but some women may experience a small amount of vaginal bleeding on the onset of their pregnancy, usually around 11 to 12 days after conception or about the time they might notice a missed menses. This bleeding is thought to be caused by the fertilized egg as it burrows itself into the blood-rich lining of the uterus. This process starts just six days after fertilization of the egg. The bleeding is light, usually appearing as red spotting or pink or reddish-brown staining, and lasts only a day or two, at the most three or four days. The spotting can also be accompanied by very mild cramping.

She opened her eyes and made a mental checklist: the timing was right, she remembered it was less than two weeks after their encounter at the river; her period had been very light, more so than usual; the coloration was right; and she had very mild cramping. Yes, Jose certainly could be the father of her baby. Her mood immediately lightened. She realized why she hadn't thought of it earlier. When she was worried or upset – and she had been extremely upset about Jose's behavior after their love-making and after their wedding – her mind didn't always function at 100%.

"Etta? Are you alright?" Pam asked. "You were moaning in your sleep."

Etta sat up even straighter, still lost in thought. *Mama!* She thought suddenly. *Mama will know. She will know for sure who the father is. I've got to make her tell me.*

"Etta?" Pam asked again, worried as she watched Etta's face for signs of illness. "Etta, answer me. You're scaring me. Are you all right?"

Etta laughed for the first time in days, and grabbed Pam's hands with her own. "Yes, Pam. I'm fine. In fact, I'm great. I can't wait to get home."

Pam had planned to spend several weeks in Boston with her aunt after returning from Europe. First, however, she felt she had to make sure Etta got back to the ranch safely, especially in her condition. While still in London she had made the arrangements for a private car to meet them at the train station in Patagonia, and she would ride to the ranch with Etta. *Then,* she told herself, *I can be rid of her and her problems once and for all. Hallelujah!*

As they neared the ranch Etta hugged Pam, thanking her profusely for all she had done. "Pam, I'll never forget how wonderful you've been. I don't know what I would have done without you, honestly. I promise I'll make it up to you somehow."

Pam just smiled, thinking to herself there was nothing Etta could do to make up for the tiresome trip.

For the first time since she realized she was pregnant, Etta was happy. She couldn't wait to talk to her mother. Depending on what she learned, and she just knew it would be good news, she would find Jose and convince him that everything was going to be okay.

When the hired car stopped in front of the hacienda Etta threw money at Pam, leaving her to deal with the driver. Then she climbed from the car and ran to the massive door, barely stopping long enough to push it open.

Once inside she yelled happily, "Mama, Maria, Papa, I'm home!"

When there was no answer she raced toward the library, knowing if her father was at home at this time of the day that's where he'd be. As she neared the library she heard voices. It was Papa and… *Damn it,* she thought, feeling suddenly frightened and unsure of whether she was ready to face Jose, the owner of the other voice.

She slowed, then stopped and stood silent, listening to Jose's voice coming through the closed doors. He was telling her beloved father everything: her not-so-innocent seduction at the river, his original plan to marry Lupe, the surprise pregnancy, and the fact that the baby is the only reason he married her. *Oh my God! How can I face either of them now?*

"I need a drink," she murmured, then turned away from the library doors and, choking back a sob, ran into the parlor, straight to the bar…

Fina was in the Garden Room, replanting tulips, when a familiar voice whispered inside her head.

"Fina, get to the house, now, Etta needs you."

It wasn't often Fina heard her dead sister's voice; when she did, she listened. She removed her work gloves and tossed them on the counter before hurrying out of the Garden Room and running toward the hacienda.

She knew Etta was coming home earlier than planned, as she had dreamt it several days ago. She had also *seen* Jose talking to Pancho and knew he was in the library now. What she hadn't visualized until she heard Monique's voice was Etta standing outside of the library listening to Jose's words. Now, however, when she closed her eyes she saw a humiliated Etta throwing a vase at her reflection in the gilded mirror in the hallway. She knew instantly that her daughter had been drinking, and had locked herself in the bathroom outside of Pancho's billiard room.

Fina had almost reached the kitchen door when she saw Jose storm out of the house, headed in the direction of the stables.

"Jose, wait," she called to his retreating form.

He did not answer. He wasn't being rude, he was just too angry to hear her. He had witnessed Etta's temper tantrum and wanted to be as far away from her as possible.

Fina let him go and rushed into the house and down the main hallway. There she found Pancho, Maria, and Big Jose all huddled in front of the bathroom door. Fina motioned for them to step aside, giving her access to the locked door.

"Etta, sweetheart, open the door. Let me help you."

Fina leaned against the door. Hearing nothing but sobs, she tried a different approach, telling a white lie. "Etta, honey, open the door. Jose wants to talk to you."

She heard Etta's crying stop immediately. After a moment the door slowly opened.

"Jose?" Etta asked timidly, peering around the slightly opened door with red swollen eyes. When she didn't see her husband she tried to close the door, but Pancho stepped in front of Fina and pushed it open.

"Papa?" Etta sobbed and threw herself into her father's arms. "Do you hate me Papa? I couldn't live if I thought you hated me."

It was then that she noticed Big Jose, Maria and her mother. She wailed louder before burying her face in her father's chest. "Oh, God. You all must hate me." She was crying so hard her words were almost incomprehensible.

"Shhh, hush now," Pancho whispered. Then he realized what she had said. "No one hates you, *Mi Hija*. We all love you. Don't we?" He looked to the others for confirmation.

"*Si, si, Mi Hija*," Maria whispered solemnly, patting Etta's shoulder, "we all love you, so very much. We would never hate you."

Fina moved closer to her husband and daughter and touched Pancho's arm. "Pancho, my love, take her upstairs. She needs to sleep."

Nodding his agreement, Pancho lifted his still weeping daughter, cradling her in his strong arms.

Etta looked up at him as if she was seeing him for the first time. "Papa? Do you hate me?" Her voice sound strange.

Pancho looked at Fina, puzzled by Etta's repeated question and by the little-girl quality her voice had taken on. Fina whispered, "It's the whiskey."

Nodding his understanding, Pancho crooned to his daughter as if she were still a child. "It's okay Sweetheart, don't cry. Your Papa is here. I don't hate you, I will always love you. You know you will always be my favorite daughter."

With her eyes closed and feeling safe in her father's arms, Etta smiled when she heard the familiar phrase. It was a game they had played since she was a child. "Yes, Papa, and you will…hic… always be my favorite father."

For the rest of Etta's pregnancy Fina encouraged Pancho and Doc to spend as much time as possible with her, hoping that their presence would help keep her mind off of an obviously absent Jose. For the most part this worked, at least during the day. But at night, alone in her room, grief would wrap her in a blanket of despair, smothering her like a vise until she couldn't breathe. It felt like the walls were closing in. She had to escape.

Her nightly ritual began with a trip to the library – she felt better as soon as she walked through the doorway. She would turn on the lamp by the fireplace, walk over to open the French doors that led to the patio and breathe in the fresh night air. At times she could swear that she smelled Jose's unique scent coming up from the stables. That was where he slept most nights, on the couch in his office instead of sleeping in the bedroom suite next to hers. It was as if having just a wall between them meant he was still too close.

Thinking of his smell often brought back pleasant memories of their childhood together. Like when she would ask him, "Why do you always smell so sweet?" while taking a deep whiff of his hair or arm.

"I guess it's because my mama raised me on milk and honey," he'd tease back. Then, "Did Fina feed you horse manure? Because, Girl, you smell like…"

She'd throw a dirt clod or anything else handy at him in retaliation, and he would laugh. Then she would come back with, "Or, maybe it's because you spend so much time in the stables that you smell like sweet summer hay."

That's what I miss most, Jose, she thought, *I miss the teasing and the laughing with you.* She'd take one last gulp of fresh air before closing the doors, sometimes while tears streamed down her gaunt face.

Next, she might walk to Pancho's bar and turn on the Tiffany lamp that hung over it. She would stare at the bottles filled with amber and clear liquids, longing for just a taste. She'd clutch her hands into fists, willing herself to be strong when all she really wanted was to open a bottle, to bring it to her lips, to drink, to forget.

"No," she'd often yell out loud.

I'll be strong for Papa, for my baby, she'd think. Each night, she would remind herself again and again of the promise she had made to Pancho the day after she had locked herself in the bathroom. She had never broken a promise to him, or he to her. As hard as it was, she just had to be strong.

He had come to her room and sat on the edge of her bed. She'd had a terrible hangover and felt horrible about her behavior the day before. She'd tried to apologize.

"Papa, please, please forgive me…"

But he'd interrupted before she could finish.

"No, Sweetheart, I don't want your apologies." He had taken her small soft hands into his big calloused ones. "Not for yesterday or for anything that happened between you and Jose. What's done is done. What I do want, however, is a promise that you won't drink anymore. Pam told me how much you drank on your…on your trip."

Etta had scowled at hearing this, and started to interrupt but Pancho had put up a hand to stop her. "Don't be angry with her. She called last night. She wanted to make sure you were okay. I made her tell me about the trip, and because she was worried about you she told me about the drinking.

"Sweetheart, I have seen firsthand what alcohol can do to someone who isn't able to hold it. I've never told you about my family, but I think I need to now. It's not easy for me. I had put my past life behind me, but if it will help you then I'm willing to tell you what I experienced while growing up."

He'd taken a deep breath and then continued, maintaining control of his feelings with effort. He knew it would not be easy but he also knew he had to tell Etta if he was going to help her. He would have to tell her things that he had kept pushed deep into the recesses of his mind. The thought of bringing them back made him feel slightly ill, but he would do it for his daughter's sake and her baby's.

Pancho then told Etta about his childhood, about his mother and the monster she was; about her constant drinking and belittlements, not only of him but of anyone who crossed her path. He told how her drinking had helped bring about the ruin of her marriage, that alcohol was more important to her than her husband's love and devotion. He spoke about his beloved father and grandfathers and about the night he had left *Villa de Luna* for the last time. He talked until he was exhausted, both mentally and physically.

Etta had listened to her father without saying a word, periodically wiping her eyes of tears and blowing her nose. When he had finished she hugged him close, hurting for him now that she knew the pain he had endured as a child.

"Oh, Papa, I am so sorry. I don't want to be a monster like your horrible mother. I don't want drinking to ruin my child's life."

Pancho had hugged her back. "Don't cry, baby. I'm not saying that you are a monster. I don't think that at all. What I'm trying to say is if you think alcohol will solve your problems, you are so wrong. Drinking will only make them worse. But, I am asking for your promise that you won't drink anymore. Okay?"

"Okay, Papa, I promise. I'll do it for you and for my baby," Etta said. What she hadn't said was that she was already missing her next drink. Intellectually, she knew it did not solve problems, just as her father said. Emotionally, however, it did seem to ease her pain. She took a deep breath and resolved to try to keep her promise. *For Papa,* she thought, *I will do it.*

Every night, after resolving anew to keep her promise, she would turn off both lamps, throwing the room into almost total darkness. She would then take *her* chair by the massive fireplace – the chair where she had spent so many happy hours as a child, quietly listening to the conversations between Papa and Doc.

In the darkened room she would pull her feet under her and let her thoughts drift to Jose. She would relive happy childhood memories: of her trailing behind him while he did his chores; of the two of them climbing over the rocks on the south pasture on days they accompanied their fathers on rounds of the ranch; of daring each other to wade into the ice-cold creek water in the spring and fall; of laying companionably on soft green grass while pointing out shapes made by fluffy white clouds as they danced across the brilliant blue sky; of swimming and splashing with Humberto in the cool river on hot summer days.

Thoughts of the river reminded her of that fateful day, the day that would be forever etched in her memory. She would usually cry and ask over and over: *Why Jose? Why can't you love me?*

At this stage of Etta's nightly ritual, Fina would wake up, knowing that Etta was weeping in the library. She would quietly get out of bed, not wanting to disturb Pancho, find her robe and make her way downstairs to her daughter.

Kneeling at her daughter's knees she would plead with her, "Etta, sweetheart, you can't keep doing this. It isn't good for you or the baby."

"I know, Mama," Etta would sob. "I try. I try so hard not to cry. But then I think about Jose and ..."

"I know, I know. Come on, Sweetie," she'd say, helping Etta to uncurl and stand. "Let's go to the kitchen and I'll make you a hot coca. And maybe some cinnamon toast too. Okay?"

Another part of the ritual was that every night at some point, whether in the library or in the kitchen, Etta would beg her mother to tell her if Jose was the baby's father. She never mentioned Andrew by name; she was too embarrassed to confirm aloud that there had been someone besides Jose. Her mother knew, of course; there would be no reason to ask otherwise. But every night Fina would just patiently remind her persistent daughter that she couldn't tell her.

"Etta, Sweetheart, you know I can't tell you," Fina repeated for the hundredth time. "The only thing I can say is look into your heart. What does your heart say?" Exasperated, Etta would pull away from her mother.

"My heart? My fucking heart is broken, Mother. Don't you understand? Broken...and the one thing, the only thing that could help it would be knowing, knowing for sure that Jose is my baby's father." She would hug her stomach protectively, as if doing so would convince her mother somehow to tell her.

Etta's stomach grew bigger and bigger with the baby, but the rest of her grew thinner and thinner from not eating enough, and from worry over paternity of her unborn child. At last, seeing how desperate Etta was with each passing day, Fina finally relented. She broke her cardinal rule and told Etta who the baby's father was...

CHAPTER 30 – *Lupe 1958 - Hermosillo*

Time was passing and still Jose hadn't moved from the bus stop bench. He had forgotten to bring his watch when he left the ranch so he had no idea what time it was or how long he had been sitting there. He must have dozed off. Sitting up straight, he tried to recall what thoughts had been going through his mind.

He shook his head briefly, trying to clear his fugue. After a few seconds it came back to him: he had been thinking about his conversation with Pancho that horrible day when he had returned to the ranch. He had just finished telling Pancho of Etta's betrayal and seduction when they'd heard glass breaking and a door slamming nearby in the main hallway.

Stunned by the commotion in a normally quiet household, both men rose and rushed from the library into the hallway. Shattered glass from a massive gilded mirror and pieces of an expensive vase were strewn across the tiled floor. Maria and Big Jose were running in from the direction of the kitchen, alarm on their faces as they met Jose and Pancho in the hallway where the glass lay.

"What has happened?" Maria glanced from Pancho to Jose. "Is anyone hurt?"

Neither man answered, but both appeared to be unharmed, and it was then that it dawned on Maria that her son was standing before her. She stared at him. She hadn't seen him for almost two months. He looked so sad, and older. So many questions were running through her head that she didn't know what to ask first, so she simply said, "Welcome home, son."

She hugged him tightly before bending to pick up the largest pieces of glass. She used her apron to put them in.

Then, turning to her husband Maria said, "Jose, please get a broom, dustpan, and wastebasket from my kitchen."

Big Jose nodded and hugged his son, "It is good to see you, son. We are glad you are finally home." He then turned to his wife, cautioning her, "Be careful, my love, don't cut yourself," and hurried off down the hall toward the kitchen.

Looking up at her son and Pancho Maria asked again, "What has happened?"

Pancho was the one to answer as he bent to help Maria pick up glass. "We don't know what happened. We were in the library when we heard glass shattering."

Big Jose returned from the kitchen and handed the broom to Little Jose. It was then that they heard loud sobbing coming from behind a closed door halfway down the hallway. The four adults looked as one toward the door which led to a bathroom, then at each other, all with puzzling expressions on their faces. It was Maria who spoke first.

"Etta? Is that our Etta?" she asked no one in particular.

The sobs escaladed at the sound of Maria's voice. She stood and dumped the large shards from her apron into the wastebasket held by Big Jose before hurrying to the bathroom door. The three men followed, a little more slowly.

When they reached the door she glared up at her son. "Little Jose, did you bring Etta back with you?"

Before he could answer she admonished, "Why is she crying?"

The bathroom door opened slowly and Etta peered out with puffy red-rimmed eyes. Her glance went immediately to her husband and she reached for him with an unsteady hand, stumbling as she moved toward him. "Jose? Jose, listen to me. Please," she begged in a voice that slurred the words.

"Etta, you're drunk," Jose sneered. "Just stay away from me. I can't stand the sight of you." He turned and headed toward the kitchen, too angry to apologize to those who witnessed the exchange with shocked expressions on their faces.

As he walked away he heard Etta sob even louder than before, then the sound of the bathroom door slamming and the lock turning.

Nearby, a car horn honked, causing Jose to jump. He was actually surprised to find himself sitting on a bench and not at the ranch, so vivid was his recollection of that scene so many years ago. Recalling it, he was ashamed. It was another example of his walking away from unpleasantness and leaving his parents and Pancho to deal with his distraught and inebriated wife.

If he was to be completely honest with himself, and it seemed that today was the day for everyone to be honest, he hadn't really concerned himself with Etta over the years: not her drinking, or the fact that he was probably 98% responsible for her becoming an alcoholic in the first place, or her attempts to reconcile with him and save their marriage. Neither did he concern himself with the raising of his daughter, leaving that to the other adults in her life who obviously loved her. No, his only concern, obsession actually, in the last 28 years had been the loss of his one true love, his Lupe.

He sighed, heavily and slowly, and closed his eyes while leaning back on the bench. *Lupe, oh Lupe.* Everything always seemed to come back to Lupe.

He didn't want to think about her now. He needed to focus on Sam, but try as he might he was once again in the past. His mind relived the day he had decided to find Lupe, to see if she had forgiven him and would be willing to marry him if he divorced Etta. He was tired of the farce of his marriage, and wanted the happiness he felt he deserved.

It was almost seven years since he had seen Lupe. He was in his office that was located in the barn on the ranch, feeling sorry for himself, and was wondering how Lupe would be spending Christmas. At the thought of Christmas, now two days away, he felt a small twinge of guilt. As usual, he hadn't gotten anyone, not even Sam, a Christmas gift. It would also be Sam's birthday tomorrow, on Christmas Eve. He put away the report he had been working on, cleared his desk and stood up. He would drive to Nogales to buy his mother and Sam a present or two. It never occurred to him to tell anyone that he was leaving.

Once in the truck his thoughts again wandered to Lupe and when he reached Nogales he turned left toward the border instead of turning right toward town. *Screw Christmas* he thought bitterly. *I'm going to find Lupe.* He would start looking for her in Hermosillo, the town in Mexico where he had taken her after her father died. He was convinced that if he didn't find Lupe, he would never find peace or happiness.

He devised his plan as he drove. He would explain to Lupe that his marriage to Etta was a mistake. He had given it seven years, and he still did not love her. Never had, in fact, except as a friend. Even that love she had ruined with her deception. He was feeling very self-righteous and justified at offering to throw away his marriage if Lupe would have him.

He would tell Lupe it didn't matter whether he was riding the range, traveling cross-country on business, or driving to town for supplies, all he did was think about her. Night after night, for the past seven years, he had thought of nothing but her and the life they could have had. Could still have, he thought optimistically.

During the long drive to Hermosillo Jose thought about the trip he had taken with Lupe to bring her father's body back to Hermosillo for burial. Lupe had been sitting next to him, looking so sad. And as much has he hated the thought of hurting her even more, he had needed to tell her about Etta and the scene at the river. He didn't want any secrets between them if they were to have a life together.

Of course she had been angry and hurt, finding it hard to believe he could love her and still be unfaithful to her. He apologized profusely, but it didn't seem to make a difference. If he was honest with himself he knew she was justified in her anger and disappointment.

"I love you, Jose, but you have hurt me deeply. I'm not sure if I can ever trust you again. I know you were drinking but that is not an excuse. This time it was your friend Etta. But what if some other woman gets you drunk? Will you make love to her also? I need time, Jose. Time to grieve for my father, and time to think about what I want to do. I will stay in Hermosillo until I know what I will do."

"Okay. I understand you need time," he had said, taking her hand and bringing it to his lips, "but, please can I at least write to you?"

She pulled her hand away from his. "Yes, write if you must. But I can't promise I will answer," Lupe had replied sadly and stubbornly.

Leaving Lupe at her mother's house was one of the hardest things he had ever done and as he drove back to the ranch he'd promised himself that someday he would make it all up to her.

He had written to her every day. And every day he waited impatiently for an answer. In his letters he didn't write about his mistakes; he felt he had already apologized enough for those on the ride to Hermosillo. Instead, he wrote about the life they would have together, the things he wanted to show her, the places he wanted to take her, the children they would have together. He also wrote of his daily chores, telling her that without her he didn't want to get up in the mornings, that he no longer loved doing the things he had always loved because without her each day felt gray and bleak, as if the sun had gone out of his life.

Finally, after the longest week of his life, he found a letter on his bunk. He was afraid to open it - afraid that she was writing that she would not forgive him, would not come back. Sticking the unopened letter in his back pocket he saddled his horse and rode out to his favorite spot on the ranch, high up on the Santa Rita Mountains. The ride took over an hour on horseback and the letter seemed to burn his back side but he was determined to only read it when he reached his destination – the place where he had first told Lupe not so long ago that he loved her.

Lupe had made a picnic lunch that day and they had ridden up the mountain road in Big Jose's old truck. They'd stopped at the edge of the meadow and then walked to the perfect spot. It was one of the few places on the ranch that he hadn't shared with Etta. Lupe had spread out a blanket and started unpacking their lunch. As he watched her he practiced the words he wanted to say over and over again in his head. Finally, when she was finished, he had simply said, "Lupe, I love you. And I want to marry you."

Lupe had smiled and said matter-of-factly, "I know. I love you also, Jose. I have from the very first day in your mother's kitchen. Yes, I will marry you. Now let's eat."

Reaching his destination while still remembering that day, he'd jumped off his horse and tied the reins to a nearby tree. He sat on a fallen log, pulled the letter from his back pocket and slowly opened it. His hands trembled as he read:

Dear Jose,

I have received your many letters and with each one my heart softens.

After much thought and prayer, I have forgiven you. If you will come to get me at the end of the month, I will return to Rancho de Luna and become your wife. But we must wait until next year to marry. My poor mother needs time to mourn the loss of my father and a year should be enough time to save money for our wedding.

Until then,

Your Lupe

He still carried the short letter, folded and tucked inside his wallet. Every night before going to sleep he took it out and it was the last thing he touched. He didn't even have a picture of Lupe but her image was etched in his brain, in his heart. He couldn't wait to see her. *Would she be happy to see him?*

He thought again of the happiness he had felt that day after reading her letter. He had been ecstatic; the long ride back to the ranch had seemed to pass in minutes. He remembered rushing into the kitchen and telling his mother the good news. And then...

And then two days later Humberto had told him that Etta was pregnant. And then he had had to tell Lupe – tell her that he would not be coming for her, not at the end of the month or ever; that he would not be marrying her. That he would be marrying Etta because their indiscretion had resulted in a pregnancy. And if that wasn't bad enough, he admitted to himself now, he hadn't even been man enough to tell her in person. No, instead, like the coward he was, he had written her a letter.

Lupe had not answered his last letter, but she had found a ride back to the ranch, arriving the day before he married Etta. When his mother mentioned that Lupe had returned to pack the rest of her belongings he'd rushed to the little casita where she had been living and tried to talk to her, to tell her how sorry he was. She would not listen. She wouldn't even look at him. Keeping her head down, she ignored him and continued packing her things.

"Please, Lupe," he'd begged, "please look at me. Talk to me."

"Why, Jose? There is nothing left to say. Tomorrow you will marry

Etta and I will return to Mexico." This was said without looking at him.

Jose reached for her but she pushed him away, her head turned aside so she wouldn't have to look at him. "Don't Jose. Please don't. I can't bear it if you touch me. Please leave me to my task. Leave me to my sorrow."

Eventually he left and hadn't seen her again until he was standing at the alter waiting to marry Etta. He had looked out hoping, praying to see her face one last time, and then there she was in the middle of the congregation. She had never looked more beautiful or sadder. He'd carried the sadness that he had seen in her face in his heart for seven long years. And now he was going to see her again – he just knew he would find her...he had to.

Once in Hermosillo he stopped at a cheap motel to clean up. His mistake was lying down on the bed after his shower to think about what he wanted to say when he saw Lupe. He immediately fell into a deep sleep and did not stir until he heard a rooster crowing nearby at dawn the next morning. He was startled awake and couldn't believe the sun was beginning to shine through the curtained window. Cursing under his breath, he jumped up and dressed quickly, not wanting to waste another moment in his quest to find his Lupe. He did not even stop to eat. Food was the last thing on his mind.

Even though it was early, he drove to the modest house on Calle de Vista that he remembered from the trip seven years ago. It never occurred to him that the occupants might still be sleeping. He parked his truck on the opposite side of the street. Gathering his courage, he crossed the street and knocked on the door. After a very long minute the door was opened just a crack. An elderly woman peered out at him but Jose could see it wasn't Lupe's mother.

"Yes?" she asked.

Shaken, he replied, "Excuse me, may I please speak to Mrs. Garcia?"

The woman examined him through the slight opening, assessing him carefully before answering, "I don't know a Mrs. Garcia." Pausing, she asked, "Who are you?"

"Jose Lopez. I am looking for Lupita Garcia. Her mother lived here seven years ago."

"Well maybe she did seven years ago but I've lived here the last four years and I don't know the Garcias," the woman replied before opening the door a few inches wider. He could see she was clutching a robe to her chest.

"I am so sorry to have bothered you," Jose said hopelessly, turning to leave. Her voice stopped him.

"Wait." He turned back.

The woman, feeling sorry for the handsome young man, opened the door even wider. "Try next door. The old lady who lives there has lived on this street forever. And she is a busybody. If anybody knows where to find your Lupita Garcia I'm sure it would be her."

"Thank you," Jose said gratefully, bowing slightly.

Encouraged, he turned away once again and hurried to the house next door. He climbed the three steps to a battered old porch that was in desperate need of paint, and knocked loudly on the door. There was no response, so after a moment he knocked again. He hoped that the old lady was not still sleeping. After a few more minutes, while he tried to decide to leave or knock again, he heard a faint noise, like someone moving around inside.

"Who's there?" a shaky voice questioned from somewhere inside the small house.

Jose cleared his throat. "Hello, my name is Jose Lopez and I was hoping you could tell me where the Garcias who used to live next door are currently living."

When the only answer was a long moment of silence, Jose knocked again.

"Hold your water," the voice yelled weakly, "I'm coming."

The door opened wide and standing before him was the oldest woman Jose had ever seen. *She must be a hundred* he thought in amazement.

The old woman cackled, "No not a hundred, a hundred and one," she said, as if reading his mind. She stepped aside and motioned him in.

"I don't see as good as I used too. Find a seat. Can I get you a drink? Water, perhaps? Or tea?"

"No, no, please sit down yourself," Jose offered his arm. The old woman looked as if she could keel over at any second.

She ignored the arm and walked very slowly to a worn leather chair. It seemed to take her ages to sit down. After she was finally seated, he lowered himself to the edge of an old sofa facing her. He rested his elbows on his knees, folded his hands and waited. Looking over at him, she barked in her shaky voice, "So, you're looking for the Gracias are you?"

"Yes, Lupita Garcia. Do you know where they live now?" he asked loudly.

"Don't shout, young man. I'm old, not deaf. Of course I know where they live. I know everything that goes on in this neighborhood."

Jose waited for her to continue but the old woman seemed to have forgotten he was there. She was just staring into space, her eyes not focused on him or anything else in the room. Suddenly she looked at him, as if noticing him for the first time.

"Can I get you a drink? Water perhaps?" she made a motion to stand.

"No, no please, nothing. Where do they live?"

"Where does who live?" she asked, "Can I get you a drink?"

Before she could say "water perhaps" again, Jose almost shouted, "The Garcias. Where do they live now?"

"The Garcias? Now, let me think." The old woman closed her eyes.

Jose waited some more. Then, thinking she had fallen asleep, he started to stand, deciding she did not have the information he needed anyway. Her sudden voice in the quiet startled him and he quickly sat back down on the sofa.

"Four streets over, three blocks down…a big yellow house with a white fence and flowers. You can't miss it. It's the biggest house on the street," the old lady blurted out. Then she fell quiet again and soon started snoring softly. Jose stood and tiptoed quietly out the door, pulling it shut behind him.

Anxious to find Lupe's house, he started the truck and pulled out into the street. Only then did he realize that the old woman had not told him if the street was four streets to the west or four streets to the east of Calle de Vista– nor did he know if he should then go north or south once he was four streets over. Not wanting to deal with the old woman again, he decided it didn't really matter. He'd just search in all four directions.

He turned west and drove four streets over to a street called Calle de Oro. Then he drove south slowly, looking closely at every house. There was no yellow house with a white fence. At the end of the street he turned around and drove north. Once more, he could see no big yellow house.

He turned around again and this time he drove past Calle de Vista and counted four streets east – Calle de Sol. Sol means sun; maybe it was a sign, as Luna was the moon. Once more he slowly scoured the neighborhood, looking for a big yellow house. He was getting discouraged after driving south and not finding the house, but he wasn't about to give up even if it meant dragging the old woman out of her house and making her help him find it.

However, before resorting to kidnapping, there was one more direction to try. Crossing his fingers he drove north, and sure enough, there it was at last: three blocks north. It was definitely big – not by Hacienda de Luna standards, but compared to the surrounding houses and the other houses he had passed in his search.

He slowed down and passed the house. After turning around at the next block he drove back and parked under the shade of a giant elm across the street and two doors up from the yellow house. He was partially hidden in case anyone was watching.

His heart pounded in his chest while he appraised the house. It was beautiful and graceful, just like his Lupe. It was painted a pale yellow and sat on a large lot surrounded by a white picket fence. Vines laden with bright pink flowers clung to white trellises that graced each side of the four steps leading to a wide front porch that seemed to invite one to sit down and rest.

As he took in all the details of the house he found himself wondering at what he was seeing: *How could Lupe and her mother afford such a place? What had changed so dramatically in the last seven years that they went from living in a small modest house to this one?*

Slowly then, a fear began to take shape in his mind. All this time he had been picturing Lupe single and pining away for him, just as he had been longing for her. What if she had moved on with her life – made a new life that would never include him? The thought terrified him.

Just as he convinced himself that this couldn't be the case, two small, dark-haired children – twins, perhaps, a boy and a girl – stepped out the front door and ran down the steps, squealing loudly as they did so. They were followed by a well-dressed man who appeared to be in his late 30's or early 40's. He chased after them, laughing.

"Come here my little angels. Give Papa a good-bye kiss."

Jose's heart seemed to stop beating. *Please, God, let this be the wrong house.*

He watched as the man grabbed the nearest giggling child, the girl, and lifted her squirming body high into the air before bringing her down and smothering her face with kisses. Not wanting to be left out, the little boy circled his father's legs, yelling up at him, "Kiss me, Papa, kiss me too."

Without putting his daughter down, the man picked up his son as a laughing voice rang out from somewhere on the porch. A beautiful voice, one Jose would recognize anywhere, cautioned gently, "Careful *Mi Hijos* don't get your father dirty or he'll be late for court."

Jose's eyes immediately searched the porch. That couldn't be Lupita, his Lupita. She belonged to him, not to this laughing man, not to those giggling children. However, as she moved away from the shadow of the blossom-covered trellis he recognized the curve of her face and her lovely hair, no longer past her waist as it once had been, but still cascading beautifully past her shoulders in black, shiny waves. Even from this distance he could see the love in her black ebony eyes as she looked at her family. And her lips, the beautiful lips that he remembered so well, held a happy smile as she watched her children being embraced by their father.

Jose watched transfixed as she slowly negotiated the steps. Then he felt as if his heart had literally broken in two, the pain was so sharp in his chest. Lupe was obviously very pregnant. One hand was placed protectively over her swollen belly while the other held onto the banister. Lupe's husband – Jose shuddered at the thought – put the children down carefully and smiled lovingly at his wife.

"A little dirt might be worth a scolding from the judge if it meant that I could spend more time with my children and my beautiful wife."

Jose was filled with a sorrow deeper than any he had felt before, and with regret and jealousy as he watched the man kiss first Lupe's forehead, then her belly. If that wasn't painful enough to watch, the husband finally kissed his wife ardently on her perfect red lips, hugging her tightly. Lupe returned her husband's kiss just as passionately.

Jose's stomach tightened as he felt bile rising into his throat at the sight of the two who were obviously in love. Then he quickly opened the door of his truck, leaned out and vomited onto the street.

Driving the many miles back to the ranch without having made his presence known, Jose was in a daze. He was furious: at Lupe for getting married and having children, and unreasonably, for not waiting for him; and with Etta for all of her lies and deceit that deprived him of his beloved Lupe. But most of all he was furious with himself. His ego had not let himself believe that after seven years Lupe would not be waiting for him. Didn't she know he still loved only her? How could she give herself to another man?

He checked his wristwatch for the time as he finally pulled onto the ranch, and saw that it was already 2:00 p.m. It was now Christmas Eve and he still had not purchased a single gift for anyone. *Hell*, he thought bitterly once again, *Screw Christmas…*

Chapter 31 – *Jose 1958* – The Gifts

The hot sun beat down on Jose. That, and the unhappy memory of that long-ago trip to Hermosillo, had given him a horrible headache. He opened his eyes slowly, sat up straight and looked around. He wondered how long it had been since he walked out of the hotel room following the confrontation with his parents. It seemed like a lifetime ago. He stood and stretched, knowing he needed to return to the hospital. He needed to check on Sam.

The thought of the hospital reminded him he still had to face Etta and his parents. He wasn't sure he was ready for that. There was more in the past that he had to think about – there had to be something there that would help him decide the future with his families. Not only Etta and Sam, but his parents as well.

When his empty stomach chose that moment to growl it sparked another long-forgotten memory that happened the day he returned from Hermosillo. Ignoring the hollow feeling inside he sat back down on the bench and let his thoughts move back in time once more…

After returning from the fateful trip to Hermosillo Jose parked his truck by the barn, stormed into his office, sat down at his desk and mentally beat himself up by reliving the scene with Lupe with her family over and over for the rest of the afternoon. At 6:00, when Maria's dinner bell clanged, announcing dinner would be ready in thirty minutes, his stomach growled fiercely. He realized he couldn't remember when he had eaten last. Food had been the last thing on his mind.

He knew it was unacceptable, unless one was dying, out of town, or too ill to get out of bed, to miss dinner. His mother maintained a strict schedule, even on holidays. It was not worth it to face her wrath because he wasn't in the mood to socialize with his family. He made his way to the main house without encountering anyone, which was fine with him, but with barely enough time to take a quick shower and change into clean clothes befitting a Christmas Eve dinner. Striding from his room he paused at the top of the staircase to look down at the festive decorations adorning the hallway below. He felt a lump in his throat.

The Luna and Lopez families had, over the years, combined each family's traditions into a unique one of their own – from the Christmas Eve Gift to the Christmas Eve dinner menu little had changed since Jose was a small child.

Memories of his childhood joy and anticipation of opening Christmas presents made him feel ashamed once more that he had been selfish in not buying at least his mother and his child Christmas presents. If only he had turned in the opposite direction and driven to Nogales instead of Hermosillo yesterday.

Damn it. I need to stop thinking about Lupe's family and start focusing on my own he chided himself.

His family, he knew, would have celebrated Sam's birthday at the noontime meal. He could picture the disappointment on Sam's small face when she realized that once again her father hadn't gotten her a birthday present or even bothered to show up for her celebration. He tried to push that image from his mind, but it wouldn't let go. *I'll make it up to her next year*, he thought as he descended the stairs and walked toward the formal dining room.

Everyone was already seated at the massive dining room table where Maria, Fina, and even Etta, sober for several months this time, had laid out their traditional Christmas Eve feast. All meals served by Maria were special but holiday dinners were beyond expectation.

The meal, served on the best of the hacienda's china, consisted of everyone's favorites. For Sam it was Maria's mother's recipe for crispy deep fried tacos. Maria's spicy chili con carne and green chile and cheese cornbread had been prepared especially for Big Jose and Etta. Fina's Cajun gumbo, Maria's special request, was served from a huge bowl placed in the middle of the table. For Little Jose there would be his favorite dessert, peach cobbler, to be served only after Christmas

Mass. The cobbler would be served hot, topped with vanilla ice cream that would begin to melt as soon as it touched the fruit cobbler. Jose's mouth watered in anticipation as he took his seat directly across the table from Etta.

No one mentioned his recent absence; he was often away for days without telling anyone where he would be or when he would be back. However, he felt some tension when he was greeted with "Merry Christmas" from everyone, but no one looked at him directly in the eye when they spoke to him. He was sure they were disappointed that he had missed his daughter's birthday party once again, but refrained from saying anything in front of the child. Rather than apologize to Samantha, he said nothing, not knowing just what to say to make her feel better.

After Big Jose had delivered the familiar blessing, and as dishes were being passed up and down the table, Jose felt his daughter's eyes on him. When he looked up she quickly shifted her eyes to her plate. He felt he needed to say something after all.

"Sam," he cleared his throat, "Happy Birthday. How old are you now?"

Her eyes immediately lifted to meet his, brightening when she answered him. "I'm seven, Poppie. As Maria always says, 'Time runs.'"

Everyone laughed, and with this simple exchange between father and daughter the previous tension seemed to dissipate and conversation was lively as the delicious meal was consumed.

After dinner the Christmas Eve custom was for the whole family to participate in clearing and putting away the leftover food, and washing and drying the dishes. As a child this was always one of Jose's favorite things. He had loved being in the kitchen with the family while they joked around and teased each other, and played guessing games about who was getting what for Christmas when the time came to open gifts. This year it reminded him of his lack of gifts for anyone. He would try to sneak away before the presents were opened, he decided.

Once the kitchen was clean and in order the family members grabbed their coats, hats and scarves for the horse and buggy ride to the church. The now traditional custom had been Maria's idea years ago when Etta and Jose were children because she thought it would be fun for the 'kids,' even though there was seldom snow on Christmas Eve, and the family church was not far from the hacienda. It wasn't the weather or the distance that everyone loved, it was sharing the tradition and the season as a family.

Father Miguel conducted the annual Christmas Mass and the church was always packed with the ranch hands and their families. After Mass everyone was invited back to the ranch house to partake of a wide variety of desserts, to sing Christmas carols, and to sing Happy Birthday to Sam.

Around 12:00 a.m., with only the family remaining, now comfortable in lounging clothes instead of church attire, it was time for the Christmas gifts to be separated and doled out to their rightful owners. Jose had decided to stay after all, regardless of the fact that he hadn't contributed any gifts. He was surprised at how much he was enjoying himself this evening, from the great-tasting dinner, the Mass, the guests, to sitting around the fireplace and watching Samantha happily passing out the presents. There were so many he hoped no one would notice his thoughtlessness. *Next year I'll do my shopping in November,* he silently promised himself.

After all the presents had been distributed and before anyone began opening theirs, Big Jose gave his traditional prayer: "Our kind and gracious Heavenly Father, we thank you for our family, our friends, and our wonderful life. Amen."

There were several presents piled in front of Jose. He picked up the smallest one and started to unwrap it, when he heard Sam squeal in happiness. He looked up to see her running to him, and caught her as she jumped into his arms, throwing hers tightly around his neck.

"Oh, thank you Poppie. It's beautiful. Please put it on me." She held out a silver chain with a tiny heart-shaped locket hanging from it.

Jose quickly looked from his mother to Fina, and to Etta, trying to guess which one of them had bought the gift for Sam. He would have to thank whoever it was later. It was wonderful to see the delight in Sam's eyes, excited by receiving a gift from her father.

He took the chain from his daughter's hands and fastened it around her tiny neck.

"Oh, Little Jose, it is beautiful. Thank you *Mi Hijo,*" his mother exclaimed, holding up a chain and locket similar to Sam's.

Well that leaves Fina or Etta Jose decided as he looked at the two women – neither of them indicating that they were the culprit buying gifts and signing his name to the cards.

Jose smiled weakly at his mother and continued unwrapping his smallest present when Etta spoke in a voice so soft he barely could hear her. "Jose, it is lovely. Thank you."

Jose looked up to see Etta fastening a delicate chain around her slim neck. *God she is so beautiful* he thought as he watched her gently caress the silver necklace. Caught off-guard by the thought, Jose realized that he hadn't paid much attention to Etta, had not really noticed her in years. Instead he had been self-righteously ignoring her.

She was even more beautiful – in spite of her off-and-on drinking bouts – than she had been on their wedding day. Of course, she looked older, but the years had enhanced her features. If he was honest with himself she was even more beautiful, breathtakingly so, than Lupe. The thought of Lupe brought back the pain of seeing her with her family, kissing her husband, happy without him. He told himself that he needed to put thoughts of Lupe from his mind and move on with his life also.

"Jose," Fina said, breaking into his musings, "you haven't opened any of your gifts."

Glancing down, he realized she was right. He looked up to meet Fina's eyes. She smiled. Fina, it was Fina. She bought the lockets. He would have to be sure to thank her later, but for now telegraphed his thanks with his eyes.

By the time all the gifts had been opened it was almost 2:00 a.m. and Sam had fallen asleep on the sofa with her head in Fina's lap. Stroking her granddaughter's hair, Fina sighed and looked around her. "I'm exhausted but happily so. Big Jose will you help me get our little butterfly to bed?"

Before Big Jose could reply, Jose volunteered, surprising everyone, "Let me take her up."

"Sure, sure, son," his father acquiesced, and then turned to Maria. "Come my love, I need my sleep." To the rest of the adults he said, "Thank you all for a wonderful dinner and evening."

Jose bent to pick up the sleeping Sam and whispered softly to Fina at the same time, "Thank you for getting the lockets."

Fina smiled at him and mouthed, "You are welcome." Then she patted his arm and whispered before he could straighten up with the child in his arms, "Jose, I'm so sorry about Lupe."

Jose stiffened slightly but answered only to himself, not really surprised after all, *Of course she would know about my trip.*

"I'll help you get her to bed," Etta said at his elbow when he stood erect. He nodded and she followed him up the staircase.

At the landing Etta moved in front of Jose to open Sam's bedroom door. Moving inside ahead of him she turned on the bedside table and pulled back the covers. Close behind her Jose gingerly placed Sam on the bed, and then backed up so Etta could tuck the covers around Sam before kissing her gently on the cheek. She clicked off the light and turned, surprised to find Jose still in the room. He was standing near the doorway, silhouetted by the light from the hallway.

Jose walked to the bed and looked down at their sleeping child. Suddenly overtaken by a strange feeling, he said hoarsely, "She is so beautiful." Without looking at Etta, but knowing she was beside him, he reached for her hand and squeezed it before adding, "Just like her mother."

Jose seemed not to notice that his wife tensed at his touch. Instead, he turned and pulled her into his arms, a move that would have been natural if they had a traditional, loving marriage. For him, however, the move was completely foreign. However, on this Christmas Eve, he put his chin on her head and breathed in deeply. "I've always loved the way your hair smells, like sunshine and strawberries."

When Etta tried to pull back he only tightened his embrace. "Jose, what are you doing?" she asked softly, not wanting to wake Sam, but confused by his strange behavior. She was afraid to hope that he meant anything more than an embrace to celebrate the holiday.

Jose sighed and loosened his grip slightly. He looked down at Etta and remembered the sight of Lupe returning her husband's kiss. Willing the scene to leave his mind, he bent down and murmured before touching his lips roughly to hers, "I'm kissing my wife."

Etta was surprised, but did not pull away. This was what she had always wanted from her husband, and she wasn't going to spoil the moment. She returned his kiss, pressing herself against him. He deepened the kiss and she gave back all that he gave her.

Pulling his lips from hers, Jose picked his wife up and walked out of Sam's bedroom. As he carried her down the hallway to his own room he thought to himself that she hardly weighed much more than their daughter. He wondered briefly why he had never noticed.

It was not a problem to open the door, kick it closed and lock it with one hand before moving to his bed in the dark, all without having to put his wife down. As he reached the bed he carefully deposited his wife on the bedspread and pulled away to undress. He had not turned on a light.

From the bed Etta saw his outline in the semi-dark, now that her eyes were adjusting to the moonlight that was peeking between a slit in the drapes covering the bedroom windows. Afraid of what she would hear, but needing to know, she tentatively asked, "Jose, are you drunk?" *Please, God, don't let him be drunk. Let him mean this.*

"No," he answered bluntly before bending down and claiming her lips once more. In the darkened room he found her hand and guided it to his erection.

Encouraged by his answer, Etta felt herself grow wet at the touch of his member. Her excitement grew when he pushed her dressing gown over her shoulders, pulled up her nightgown and pulled down her panties. She was ready for him when he entered her without any further foreplay.

Jose heard her moan, and wasn't sure if it was from pain or passion… and he didn't care, as he sought to drive all thoughts of Lupe from is mind.

CHAPTER 32 – *Etta 1959* – The Mistake

"Etta," Fina begged as she pounded on Etta's bedroom door, "Sweetheart, please open the door." She was answered with silence.

She looked at Big Jose and Maria, saw the sorrow and concern etched on both of their faces, and then at Doc. Her glance went back to Big Jose and she held up her hand, and then turned back to the door.

"Etta, if you don't open the door, or if you can't, Big Jose is going to break it down."

Fina waited for one full minute. Then, hearing no movement or noise of any kind from inside, she nodded to Big Jose. He was holding a pry bar in his hand, for just this reason. He lifted it to pry the door open but before he could touch iron to wood a sound in the hallway behind them had all four adults turning toward it. There stood seven-year-old Samantha.

The child was standing behind them clad in a long flannel nightgown, her baby blanket clutched in her small hand. Her eyes are wide with fright, noticeable even in the dim hallway light.

"Maman, Maria," Sam said, her voice trembling with fear, "I had a dream. A bad one. It was about Mama."

While Fina and Maria knelt beside their granddaughter Big Jose turned back to the hand-carved door and began to pry at the heavy wood.

"I know, my little butterfly, I had the same dream. It's going to be okay. Your grandfather is going to open her door and then Doc and I are going to take care of your mother." Fina's voice was soft, hoping to calm the frightened child.

Instead of the desired effect, Sam suddenly looked up at her grandfather, her eyes wild, and almost screamed at him. "Hurry, Big Jose, hurry, there is so much blood."

As always, Maria awoke at this point of the nightmare, beads of sweat standing out on her face. She turned on her side, expecting to find Big Jose next to her, but she was alone in the hotel bed. Feeling disoriented by the dream and the strangeness of the room, she sat up. Then she remembered that they were in California, in a fancy hotel room, and their Sam was in the hospital.

Earlier, after their son had left the hotel room, her husband insisted she needed rest before they returned to the hospital. Sam and their new little great-granddaughter weren't going anywhere, at least not right away. He promised to call the hospital to check on them if she would agree to lie down. She didn't think she'd be able to sleep, but agreed to lie down and rest for "a few minutes."

Apparently, she had been more tired than she thought because she had fallen asleep almost instantly and that's when the familiar dream had come. Awake now, she sat on the edge of the bed, still shaken, trying to get the dream out of her head. She hadn't had the nightmare for many years, but suspected it returned because of the things Little Jose had told them earlier.

Contrary to what Little Jose said, Maria didn't believe that Sam was not her son's child. She felt in her heart that Sam was her true granddaughter. Not that she was psychic like Fina, but she just *knew* without a doubt. *I wish you were here, my friend,* she thought to herself. She dearly missed Fina and knew if she were still alive she would have the explanation for what Little Jose had told them.

Calmer now, instead of getting up to look for Big Jose – who was probably in the sitting room, not wanting to disturb her – she sat back on the bed and leaned against the headboard, pulling the blankets up onto her lap. She said a prayer for guidance to understand what was happening, and thought back to the beginning of the problems between Etta and Little Jose. The problems were there from the first weeks, right after they were married.

Maria knew something bad had happened between her son and

daughter-in-law, and she knew that Fina knew what it was. But Fina had told her many times over the years that it wasn't her place to reveal information about others' thoughts or feelings. So she didn't blame Fina for not confiding in her, but it left her frustrated. She and Big Jose both felt the tension and the confusion surrounding the marriage of their son to Etta, but didn't know the reason for it.

Maria and Big Jose had discussed the situation many times. They talked about the urgency of the wedding, how Jose had first professed his love for Lupe, but Lupe had left right after the wedding without even saying good-bye and never returned. And of course, they knew that Little Jose hadn't gone on his honeymoon and they had witnessed Etta's drunkenness on the day she returned from Europe. They had both felt sure that Etta had been pregnant before the wedding. That was the most logical reason for their son to be upset and to marry Etta instead of Lupe. Still, they both hoped and prayed that the newlyweds would make up and have a happy ending.

The situation between Jose and Etta did not seem to get any better, but after they found out Etta was indeed pregnant, Maria still had hope that once the baby was born Jose's heart would melt and everything would be okay. She couldn't know that the day Sam was born and Pancho died – a day that would always be one of the happiest days of her life, and one of the saddest – things would go from bad to much, much worse.

Etta had been devastated when she learned of her father's death. In fact, she was inconsolable. Instead of enjoying her beautiful baby daughter, Etta was plunged into a deep depression by the death of her beloved father…depression and the bottle.

Maria, Big Jose, and Fina had watched helplessly as Etta sank deeper and deeper. Little Jose wasn't much better than Etta. He didn't drink, or at least not that Maria knew of, but he certainly didn't do anything to help Etta, and he never held or played with his new baby. No, he was seldom seen around the hacienda. He took every opportunity to be somewhere on the farthest reaches of the vast ranch or somewhere away from it entirely "on business."

Finally, a decision was made to send Etta to the mission in Cananea. Over the years since Big Jose had lived there the mission had expanded and had become a thriving monastery. Sister Theresa – who had taken over the running of the mission after the old priest had died – assured the family that Etta would be well taken care of. The mission was isolated and peaceful. It would be a good place to dry out.

During the next several years Etta made many visits to the mission. She would return home to the ranch sober and try desperately to fit into her old life by either helping Doc with veterinary duties or Big Jose with the running of the ranch. She could actually be sober for long stretches of time, then something would happen and she'd start drinking again. Maria and Big Jose were never sure what would set her off. Maria suspected that it always had something to do with her son.

Then there was the horrible miscarriage. After Big Jose broke down Etta's door Fina and Doc had rushed into Etta's room. Maria and her husband had taken little Sam downstairs to their rooms. They tried to comfort the child who was almost hysterical, having dreamt of her mother covered in blood. Finally, after drinking hot milk laced with one of Fina's homemade sedatives, she had fallen into a fitful sleep.

Luckily, Fina had had the same dream that Sam did and had called Maria and Big Jose to come and help. It was a good thing because, as Fina told her afterward, Etta would have bled to death if they hadn't gotten to her when they did.

Even before the miscarriage they had all worried about Etta. Having been sober for months, Etta had started drinking again on Christmas Day. Maria tried talking to her to find out what had happened to cause her to take up the bottle again, but Etta had laughed and said, "Why don't you go and ask your precious son?"

So Maria had done just that. Of course, getting Little Jose to talk about anything was like pulling one's hair out, but she had found him in his office and insisted he tell her what was going on between him and his wife.

Jose was surprised to see his mother in the barn, in his office no less. He had been sitting at his desk when she walked in, closed the door and sat down in the old leather chair next to the desk.

"Mama is something wrong?" he asked, concerned by her surprise visit.

"Yes, Jose, something is very wrong but I don't know what it is. I am here so that you can tell me."

"I'm sorry Mama; I don't know what you're talking about."

Maria sighed. "Yes, you do Jose. Why has Etta started drinking again? Why after all of this time? What did you do?"

Jose looked away, but before he did she had seen his cheeks flush red.

"Jose, look at me," she said gently, "you must tell me so I can help Etta."

Now it was Jose who sighed. "It isn't something a man discusses with his mother."

"Well, that is too bad, Jose. You will tell me and you will tell me now. I don't care what it is. I'm not leaving until you have explained yourself."

So with embarrassment and regret, Jose had told her about making love to Etta after taking Sammy up to bed Christmas morning. "And if that wasn't bad enough, we also made love again later in my shower."

Maria looked at her son, confusion apparent on her face. "Jose, why would making love to Etta cause her to start drinking again?"

Jose looked down at his desk before replying, "Because of what happened later."

"Tell me," she demanded.

So Jose told his mother about coming back to his room from the barn and finding Etta...

"Etta, what are you doing?" Jose asked, surprised to see Etta in his closet holding an armful of her clothes.

She dropped the clothes on the floor and ran to him, hugging him tightly.

"I'm moving my things," she said happily, motioning towards the clothes on the floor and the others already hanging on the racks. "You didn't want to move into my room did you? This one is a little bigger and it has a better view of the mountains."

Jose then noticed the opened drawers of the chest and could see her things, folded neatly, resting beside his own in some of them. He pushed her away and she looked up at him, surprise in her eyes. She took a step forward and reached out her hands, as if to hug him again.

"Jose, what it is? What's the matter?" she asked, concern in her voice.

He pushed her hands away, more gently this time. "Oh shit, Etta."

"What, Jose, what is it?"

"Let's go into the bedroom," he said, turning in that direction.

Etta, relieved, giggled. "Again? I'm a little sore...but okay." She grabbed his hand playfully.

He pulled his hand from hers and walked toward one of the two chairs placed in front of the fireplace. Sitting, he nodded to the remaining chair.

"No, Etta, it's not that. Please sit down. We need to talk."

Confused by his actions, but not yet alarmed, she sat with her small hands folded in her lap and waited for him to speak.

"Etta," he started, and then hesitated.

"What, Jose? What is it?" she asked again, a feeling of apprehension at his apparent reluctance to talk starting to prick the back of her neck.

"Etta look," he began again, "this morning was a mistake. I...we...I shouldn't have seduced you." He looked over her head, not wanting to see the surprise and the hurt that was sure to be evident in her eyes. "I'm so sorry. I know you can't forgive me, but..."

Etta sat extremely still for a moment after he trailed off, hardly breathing. Then she stood up, walked the short distance between them and slapped Jose across the face.

"You son of a bitch. *You son of a bitch!* Making love to your wife was a *mistake*? I should *forgive* you for *seducing me*? God, what a fool I am. What was it Jose? A *pity* fuck? You said you weren't drunk, so that can't be the reason. Why, Jose, why now after seven years of going out of your way to avoid me? After seven years of praying you would come to my bed, when at last you do, you sit there and tell me it was a *mistake? I want to know why?"* Furious, she raised her hand to slap him again but he caught it before it could reach its target.

"Etta, I am truly sorry. I never intended to hurt you or to mislead you. I had been to Hermosillo and..."

Etta wrenched her hand from his and laughed bitterly. "Hermosillo. Now I understand. I should have guessed. Your precious Lupe wouldn't fuck you so you came home and fucked me instead? Were you pretending it was her you were fucking? You're disgusting, you pig." She yanked the locket from around her neck, breaking the delicate chain, and flung it at her husband. "Here's your fucking present, you bastard. I want nothing from you. Do you hear me? *Nothing!*"

Still sitting on the hotel bed, remembering, Maria crossed herself and silently thanked God that she had such a wonderful husband. She felt sorry for Etta and for the pain her son had caused her all those years ago. No wonder Etta had started drinking again. It would be three more years before she got sober again.

The year Sam turned ten, for whatever reason, Etta stopped drinking. She went back to school, to the University of New Mexico, and had gotten a degree in Veterinary Medicine. This time it would be for good, they had all thought. She'd never done anything so positive when she was sober any of the previous times. Everything would be fine now.

However, the years of on-and-off drinking had taken their toll and try as she might, Etta had never really bonded with her daughter. Not that Sam was unkind to her mother; she couldn't be unkind if she tried. But after so many years of being ignored, Sam now thought of Maria and Fina as her mothers. Etta was another adult in the household, and Sam was respectful to her, she even called her Mama, but she did not think of her as a mother.

Knowing this, Etta felt left out. Maria had seen the sadness in Etta's eyes every time she looked at Sam, and tried to include her in her daughter's life. In fact, now that she was sober, they all tried to include her in their lives. It was no good; Etta continued to feel like an outsider. So she focused on helping Doc and Big Jose with running the ranch. She stayed as far away from Jose as possible. She had actually remained sober for almost 16 years. Then her mother died two years ago and Etta started drinking again.

Maria's heart ached for the children in her life: for Etta, for Sam, and even for Little Jose. At least Sam had managed to be happy in spite of her parents' indifference. She'd had Fina and Big Jose and Maria herself to love her and care for her.

Oh Fina, Maria thought for the hundredth time in the last 24 hours, *I wish you were here.*

Maria scooted down in the bed, suddenly exhausted, and closed her eyes. Asleep once more, this time she dreamt of her dear friend and the day before she died…

CHAPTER 33 – *Jose 1979* – The Decision

Opening his eyes, Jose cringed when he remembered Etta's slap and that awful scene when he told her that making love to her had been a mistake. She had been right, he was a bastard; he had been horrible to her. And, while not to the same degree, he had to admit that he hadn't been kind to Sam or his parents either.

He had finally come to a decision, and convinced that it was the right course of action he was now anxious to get back to the hospital. There was so much he wanted to tell his daughter. Yes, his father was right: Sam always was and always would be his daughter. He felt the urgent need to tell her that he finally realizes how much he loves her and how sorry he is for his neglect all these years. Even if she is in a coma, it was important for him to talk to her. There were a lot of years to make up for. He wanted to assure her that he will be a loving father to her, and the world's best grandfather to her baby.

Jose was grateful that the journal had helped him come to his senses before it was too late. There was no longer any doubt in his mind that Sam didn't know he was not her biological father: Etta would never have burdened her daughter with that information. And she certainly wouldn't hear it from his lips. She deserved the kind of father Big Jose had been to him and the kind of father that Pancho had been to Etta.

Thinking of Pancho, as he turned in the direction that he thought he remembered leading to the hospital, he whispered to his beloved father-in-law who had now been gone for too many years. *Pancho, if you can hear me, I promise I won't let you down. I'll protect Sam and her baby. I'm so sorry, Pancho, for so many things.* He prayed his father-in-law was listening and would know somehow, just how penitent he was.

CHAPTER 34 – *Etta 1959 to 1979* – Wasted Years

Etta had fallen into a fitful sleep in the uncomfortable hospital chair as she sat by Sam's bedside. Like Maria, she was having a dream about her miscarriage, but unlike Maria her dream didn't stop with Big Jose prying open her bedroom door.

She was laying in a fetal position, her nightgown and bed covered in dark red blood. Her mother and Doc were trying to persuade her to straighten her legs but her pain was so intense that the thought of even moving seemed unbearable. Finally, they had forced her legs apart and then…

…and then she didn't remember anything and hadn't for the next three years.

She struggled to consciousness now, wanting to forget the dream and the pain. Not from the miscarriage, but from the events that had led up to it. As she opened her eyes the pain subsided slightly.

After checking on Sam and finding no change in her condition, Etta stood and walked woodenly to the bathroom. She bent over the sink and splashed cold water on her face. That helped a little. She dried her face on a coarse hospital towel and walked back to Sam's bedside. Once more she sat down wearily in the chair she was coming to hate.

As she watched Sam's motionless, pale form and listened to the beep of the many machines that were monitoring whatever was going on in that precious body, she wondered why she would have that awful dream – why now? She trembled slightly, not wanting to think about the dream, but more specifically she didn't want to revisit the weeks prior to her miscarriage.

It was after reading Sam's journal earlier and seeing things from others' perspectives that had started her remembering. When she was a small child her mother had told her that when you die your whole life flashes before you; but you would see it through the eyes of the people in your life, not through your own.

"But Mama," she had asked at the time, "I don't think I understand. How can that be?"

Her mother had taken her on her lap. "It is like this, Etta. You see how your actions, your deeds were perceived from the other person's point of view. For example, let's say that you hit Jose with a rock – not that I think you would ever do such a mean thing – but let's pretend. Anyway, during your life's review you would see yourself throwing the rock but you would *experience* Jose's pain."

As a child she hadn't quite understood what her mother had been trying to explain, but now it was all starting to make sense. Maybe that's why Sam had written the journal: so they, Jose and herself, could see how their actions had affected each other. So now, even though the memories were so painful, she was going to try to look at them again...

Etta awoke to an empty bed and knew instinctively that it wasn't hers. She looked around and tried to orient herself. Why she was in Jose's room? Then it hit her: it wasn't a dream after all. She sat up in bed and hugged herself, happier than she could remember being for years. Jose had actually made love to her. *Finally,* she thought, *finally we can be a family. We can be happy.*

That thought was still fresh in her mind when an unpleasant one threatened to intrude. *But why now? Why after all of these years? And where is Jose?*

It was then that she heard the shower running and all the bad thoughts vanished. *He's still here.* She picked up his pillow and took a deep breath, trying to capture his essence, his scent. *God how I love him. And now he is finally mine.*

She put down the pillow and leapt from the bed, not wanting to be away from him even a minute more. As she moved she realized she was sore from their love-making the night before. She shrugged it off, and knew that even if she was black and blue she wouldn't care.

Etta hurried into the bathroom, which was full of steam from the shower, and hesitated a moment before opening the shower door to join her husband. She stepped in, thinking, *my husband, my wonderful husband.*

When she wrapped her arms around Jose's torso and kissed his back he turned slowly and took her in his arms. As he kissed her passionately she was surprised to find that her lips were sore too. Relishing the minor pain, she returned his kiss eagerly.

Jose was the first to break their embrace. His fingers trailed a soapy path from her throat to her breast. He was rock hard when she picked up the soap, smiled seductively, and…

Stop she cautioned herself. She didn't want to relive the vivid details of their love-making; it was what happened later that she needed to remember.

Later, after awakening a second time to an empty bed, she knew exactly where she was. She wasn't concerned with Jose's whereabouts; she knew that even on Christmas Day there were chores to be done. She stretched lazily, now more sore between her legs than before. She ignored the pain and climbed out of bed. As she picked up clothes from the floor by the bed she smiled to herself, almost blushing when she recalled the things they had done to each other.

She used the toilet, then dressed and left the bathroom. Reaching the bedroom door, she cautiously opened it and peered into the hallway. Then she laughed softly to herself. She was being silly: they were married, so there was no reason to sneak out of her husband's bedroom. She closed the door behind her and strolled purposely to her own room.

After changing clothes, brushing her hair and then her teeth, she walked to her clothes closet. She decided to surprise Jose and move her things into his room before he returned from his chores. She hummed happily to herself as she moved armful after armful of clothes from her room to his. She was in his closet when she heard him open the bedroom door.

When he appeared in the closet doorway he looked surprised to see her. She dropped the clothes she had been holding and hugged him, but he pushed her away. And not just once, but twice.

Confused by this rejection, she followed him into the bedroom and sat on the chair he indicated. He proceeded to tell her that their love-making was a mistake. He apologized for seducing her, indicating that it was all his fault. She couldn't believe what she was hearing. They had made love, not once but twice, and now he was telling her it was a mistake. She could feel the hurt and the anger replacing the happiness she had been feeling.

Then he told her that he had been to Hermosillo the day before, and she completely lost it…

Now, years later, she couldn't remember most of the things she had said to him. She knew she had slapped him and torn the locket he had given her for Christmas from around her neck and had thrown it at him.

She had stormed out of his room and headed straight for the library, where her father had always kept a bar set-up. She'd needed a drink, badly. But once in her father's favorite room, she remembered her promise to him, so instead of pouring herself a drink she had slumped into a chair next to the fireplace. She let all the hurt and anger run through her, while asking her father to help her keep her promise.

She couldn't remember how long she sat there before she heard loud voices in the hallway. When she'd moved quietly to the library doors, which were slightly ajar, she'd peered out and saw her mother and Jose in the hallway. Jose was yelling.

"Why, Fina? Why did you have to go and buy Etta the stupid locket and sign my name to the card? Didn't you know what would happen? You always know everything. Damn it."

Her mother had sighed and said, "Sit down, Jose."

Jose had sat on the hallway bench and Fina sat down next to him.

"First of all, I don't always know everything. And secondly, I bought the lockets because I knew you wouldn't have any gifts for anyone, once again. And damn it Jose, I'm Etta's mother, Sam's grandmother, and Maria's friend. I wanted them to be happy. I could see the happiness they would feel at having a gift from you. I didn't see anything else.

And I won't apologize for bringing them the happiness that should have come directly from you."

Jose had said nothing, his head hanging, as Fina continued, "And Jose, just for once why don't you take responsibility for your actions instead of trying to put the blame on someone else?"

Etta had been glued to the door, hating herself for being curious enough to eavesdrop. What she had heard both shocked her and made her angrier than she had already been: she hated her mother for buying her a gift and signing Jose's name to it; she hated Jose for being so thoughtless that it was necessary for her mother to step in; and she hated Jose for still loving Lupe instead of her, even after all these years. She had not waited to hear Jose's response. Instead, she'd silently closed the massive doors and walked straight to the bar.

Fuck you, Jose, fuck you, she remembered thinking as she downed a glass of straight whiskey.

Sitting by Sam's bed and remembering, she could almost feel the amber liquid cascading down her throat, feel the familiar burn as it hit her stomach, feel the numbness it always brought before there was no more feeling.

Looking at Sam, Etta thought again of all the years, years she had spent so drunk that she could barely remember them, barely remember Sam growing up. Those years were such a waste. She shuddered, wondering how she could have been so stupid. She had been just as thoughtless as Jose when it came to their daughter.

Taking Sam's limp hand in hers, Etta promised again that things would be different, she would be different...

She had fallen asleep again and woke when a doctor came into the room.

The doctor, a Neurologist, explained that one of the nurses had alerted him to a change in the electroencephalogram that was monitoring Sam's brain wave activity. Etta decided to take a short break while the doctor examined Sam.

Back in the ICU waiting room Etta noticed that Humberto was sleeping on the sofa, so she took a chair opposite him and watched him sleep. She was exhausted, but instead of drifting off her mind focused on all the things she wanted to tell her daughter when, or if, she woke up: how she intended to be a better mother and a perfect grandmother to Sam's little girl, and how she was never going to touch another drop of liquor. She had made this promise to herself and to others many times in the past, but this time she felt she would finally be able to keep that promise. *This time Papa, I know I can do it.* She just hoped it wasn't too late.

The realization that she hadn't had a drop to drink since Jose had pulled her from her drunken sleep and poured her onto Humberto's plane strengthened her resolve that she could stop drinking once and for all. She was so worn out she wasn't even sure how long ago it had been since they had arrived at the hospital. Was it today? Yesterday? Or the day before? Not that it mattered. She couldn't think clearly when she was so tired. What she did know, and what was surprising to her, was that she had no desire for a drink, even now. The oblivion that alcohol brought had always been her way of dealing with life's problems, and certainly there had been many in the past hours: Sam's coma-like state, the baby in intensive care, and most recently, Jose's assumption that he may not be Sam's father after all. She resolved never to rely on that solution to life's problems again.

Several hours had passed since Jose stormed out. She was certain that he would never speak to her again; not that he'd spoken to her all that much during their marriage. The difference was that now she really didn't care. The years of neglect she had received from him had taken their toll. She realized, in her sober state, that she no longer loved Jose. *When did that happen?* she wondered. When no answer was forthcoming she simply shrugged, both mentally and physically, and decided Jose could be as angry at her as he wished – she simply didn't care any longer.

Following this newfound realization, her thoughts turned to Humberto and she found herself smiling as she watched him sleep. Humberto, her friend for many more years than she cared to count, had kept his promise and stayed at the hospital with her. She knew he had continued to love her all these years. Maybe now, realizing that she no longer loved Jose, and how much Humberto meant to her, there might be a chance for them. Certainly, his devotion and his love were worth more than her husband's indifference all these years.

Thinking about a possible future with Humberto jolted Etta's memory: something her mother had told her years ago, before Sam was even born. Upon returning from Europe and facing the fact that she was pregnant after all, she had asked Fina to break her rule of not telling anyone what was in their future. Knowing she was pregnant, she wanted her mother to confirm that the father was Jose. After much begging and pleading Fina relented, and told her that Jose was definitely the baby's father.

This had made Etta very happy, until her mother explained further that even though the baby was started on that fateful day she had seduced Jose by the river, theirs would not be a happy family. They had many years of sorrow and bitterness ahead of them. Etta had tried to brush this off, to assure Fina that she would make sure they were happy, the three of them. Fina simply smiled, albeit sadly, and said that some day Etta would be happy and would be in love, but it was not to happen for many years yet. Etta had dismissed this; after all, she was happy and in love now. She was determined to bring Jose around, so she had put any other consideration out of her head. She had not thought of that conversation again, until just now.

If she had only listened to her mother back then or had kept her promise to her father those many years ago, things could have been so different. In her sober state, her mind not foggy with alcohol, Etta felt an ache in her heart when she thought of her parents. She missed them terribly, and wished she could see them and talk to them just once more. She longed for the comfort of their arms, especially now when she herself could not comfort her own child.

At least her mother had had the opportunity to know and love Sam. Fina and Maria, after all, were the ones who had raised her daughter, Etta herself being drunk most of the child's formative years. *Oh Sam*, Etta cried silently, again promising her daughter, *I will be a good grandmother to your baby, like your Maman and Maria were to you.*

Thinking of Sam's baby made Etta wonder if the journal, which was still lying on the coffee table across the room, contained anything about the day Samantha herself was born…another fateful day in the lives of the Luna family.

Chapter 35 – *Pancho and Fina 1951 –* Birth and Death

Fina lay awake watching her husband sleep. Their bed was dimly lit by the flickering light from the fire, providing a perfect picture of his chiseled face. He is even more handsome now she thought, than the first time I saw him on the train. *God how I love you, Pancho.* She watched the gentle rise and fall of his chest until he turned over to his side. Then she snuggled up to him, spoon-style, and put her arm around him. *Oh, Pancho, my love, what am I going to do without you?* she thought for the thousandth time. Then she wept softly, quietly, against her husband's back.

The night passed much too quickly and when light began to creep through the French doors Pancho awoke to find Fina staring at him.

"Christmas Eve Gift," he shouted happily, beating Fina to the punch for the first time in all the years they had been married.

Christmas Eve Gift was a Marionneaux family tradition – the first person to shout "Christmas Eve Gift" on Christmas Eve morning was awarded one gift from the loser. Fina had explained the tradition to Pancho when they married and he agreed they would continue it. In the years since, everyone, from Big Jose to Maria, and from Little Jose to Etta, could be heard shouting "Christmas Eve Gift!" upon waking the morning before Christmas. Maria usually won one from Big Jose – Fina knew that Big Jose liked to let her win. Fina herself always beat Pancho – for the same reason and of course because she could read his mind. When they were children, it was one of Etta's and Little Jose's favorite rivalries.

Fina laughed with Pancho now, although it didn't reach her eyes.

"Yes, my love, you have finally won. I owe you a gift. I'll give it to you now," she said seductively, as she reached under the covers to discover he was more than ready.

"Oh, I do like winning," he purred, as he gathered her into his arms.

They made slow, sweet love – the way couples who have been together for many years do – knowing exactly where to touch, to kiss, to caress. It was so sweet it made Fina cry, knowing that it would be… *Stop*, she told herself. Just stop thinking and enjoy this precious time with your husband.

All too soon the alarm clock rang and the sun was now streaming through the French doors. Even holidays couldn't stop the ranch's chores. Today Pancho was going to finish delivering the bonus checks and Christmas baskets that Fina and Maria had put together for every family on the Luna payroll. Most had been delivered yesterday, only the families living furthest away remained and Pancho insisted that it was his job, his pleasure, to show his employees and their families how much the Luna family appreciated their hard work. It was his favorite time of the year.

Fina watched her husband dress before climbing out of bed and donning her robe.

"Stay in bed for a little longer," he suggested, wrapping his arms around her.

"No, my love, I want to see you off. I want to make sure you don't forget your lunch. Maria has packed a feast, as usual. Also, I want to give you your real Christmas Eve Gift."

"Are you kidding? I love the one you just gave me. Do you want to give it to me again?" he teased.

"Always, but I know you have to go," her voice cracked, and tears gathered in her eyes, threatening to spill over. She clung to him fiercely.

Surprised, Pancho pulled back to look at her. "Are you crying, my love? That's not like you. Don't worry I'll be back before you know it."

"I'm sorry, I just feel a little weepy this morning. Come, let's get your lunch and gift."

Pancho headed for the kitchen while Fina went into the living room for his gift. It was a small box wrapped in silver foil and tied with a bright red bow. She had tucked it into one of the lower branches of the floor-to-ceiling Christmas tree – a gigantic blue spruce, decorated with antique ornaments.

Pancho was eating his breakfast and chatting with Maria and Big Jose at one end of the long table when Fina entered the room. Immediately, Maria shouted, "Christmas Eve Gift, Fina. I beat you, Pancho, and Big Jose. I'm sweeping up this year."

Fina chuckled half-heartedly. "That's cleaning up, and you certainly are. I'll get your gift after I see Pancho off," she promised her friend.

Maria looked closer at Fina. "Are you okay? Your color is not so good. You are not getting sick are you? You never get sick."

She squeezed Maria's hand and reassured her friend, "I'm okay, Maria. I'll be right back."

Finishing the last drop of coffee in his cup, Pancho rose from his seat and grabbed his lunch pail from the counter top. He then kissed a happy Maria good-bye, clapped Big Jose on the shoulder, and walked out of the kitchen hand-in-hand with his wife. His truck had already been brought to the back door of the kitchen. The bed of the truck was packed with the remaining baskets and covered with a tarp, as snow had been predicted for later in the day.

When they kissed good-bye Fina wrapped her arms tightly around his waist. "Pancho, I love you so much. Please know that."

He hugged her back, just as tight. "I know, my love. And I love you more than life itself. You are my reason for living."

After a moment he gently loosened her grip. "Sweetheart, you need to let me go. I want to beat the snow." He kissed the top of her head.

"Pancho…" She tried to say the right words but she couldn't find her voice as tears flowed down her face.

"Fina, honey, please don't cry. What's wrong with you today? I've never seen you so sad. Are you sure you're okay?"

"I'm sorry, sweetheart. It's nothing. I just love you so much." She hugged him one more time, tucked the little gift into his shirt pocket and stepped back.

"Don't open this until you're on your way home, okay?" she asked, patting the pocket.

"Okay. I love you." He kissed her one last time and climbed into his truck's cab. "I'll be back before you know it."

Fina watched as he drove away. She would have collapsed with the agonizing pain that was in her heart if she hadn't felt the spirits of her mother and grandmother holding her up, one on each of her arms.

Her mother whispered gently in her ear, *"You have to let him go Fina. Now go to your daughter, she needs you."*

Her grandmother added in her other ear, *"You'll see him again."*

Pancho was driving home on the back roads of the ranch, high in the Santa Rita Mountains. He was singing Christmas carols, loudly and happily. He loved this time of year. He loved giving his employees the gift baskets and their bonus checks. He loved shaking their hands and thanking them for helping to make Rancho de Luna such a success.

Yes, he thought, *I am a lucky man.* He looked at the sky that was dark and ominous, thick with black clouds laden with snow, and then at his watch. It read 11:50, so it was almost noon. It definitely was going to snow. Good, he thought, we'll have a white Christmas.

He felt a slight pain in his chest. Taking it for a hunger pang, he pulled to the side of the road. He couldn't help but admire the expansive majestic view. He stepped out of the truck to take it all in – from this vantage point he could see miles and miles of beautiful countryside with its rolling grass-covered hills, sprinkled with Southern Live Oak trees and ancient giant Mesquites. It was all his, all a part of Rancho de Luna. He reached for the binoculars under the front seat of the truck, and putting them to his eyes he looked southeast. He could just make out the top of the hacienda, smoke rising from its many chimneys. Joy tightened around his heart at the thought of his family and friends waiting there for his return. *Yes*, he thought again for the second time, *I am a lucky man.*

When his stomach growled slightly he laughed and climbed back into the cab, noticing the time was now 11:55. Another growl made itself heard as he opened his lunch pail in anticipation. Mmmm, Maria had packed a carne *asada* burrito, an apple *torta*, and a thermos of coffee. He opened the thermos first and poured steaming liquid into its cap.

He took a sip - hot, strong, and black. Out loud he said, "Oh, Maria, you are definitely a saint."

Thinking of Maria reminded him of her excitement this morning at having won three Christmas Eve Gifts. That, in turn, reminded him of Fina's gift that was still tucked inside his shirt pocket. He set the cup of hot coffee on the dashboard before reaching into the pocket.

He retrieved the small box and shook it once, but heard nothing. He smiled to himself. Fina always got him the best gifts. He, on the other hand, could never surprise her. He laughed, thinking of all the times he tried to fool her. It was pretty hard to do when your wife was able to read your mind. When he opened the box he found a hand-crafted medallion of the Holy Spirit strung on a long sterling silver chain. He lifted it to put it around his neck and was surprised to find a sheet of purple stationary folded under the gift. He immediately recognized Fina's neat handwriting:

Pancho, my dear, dear, love, as you read this know that I have always loved you. And even though I know that you haven't always believed in my psychic gifts or understood some of the things I've told you over the years, please know this – I have loved you in many, many lifetimes and I will love you in many, many more. This is not the end. I will see you in my dreams until we are together again.

"*She's right of course,*" a soft voice next to him said knowingly.

Startled, Pancho dropped the note.

He turned slowly to his right and there sitting next to him was his father who had died many years before.

"Papa?"

The pain hit again and Pancho clutched his chest and fell forward against the steering wheel. The clock on the dash read 12:00.

"Fina, Fina, come quick," Maria yelled from the kitchen door. Fina was still standing outside the back door, watching the direction in which Pancho had driven away. His truck was no longer in sight.

"It's Etta. The baby is coming. The water has broken."

For the next few hours Fina and Maria coached Etta thru her labor. They took turns wiping her brow, encouraging her to breathe deeply, telling her not to push yet. Now, at 11:50, they agreed that it was time to push. Maria helped Etta into a sitting position and Fina situated herself at her daughter's feet.

Between contractions both women praised an exhausted Etta. At 11:59, the baby crowned. "One more, Etta, bear down, only one more," Fina promised her daughter.

As the antique grandfather clock in the hallway chimed 12:00 noon, Samantha Grace Luna Lopez slid into the world and into her grandmother's waiting hands. Fina cut the umbilical cord and wrapped the baby in a warmed blanket before holding her up for Etta to see.

"You have a beautiful daughter."

Then she said to Maria, and to Pancho who had just materialized at the head of the bed, next to his daughter. "We have a granddaughter."

Maria closed her eyes in prayer, "Thank you, Blessed Mother."

Pancho wordlessly told Fina, *"I love you all, my favorite girls."* He kissed a weary Etta's forehead, a joyful Maria's cheek, his new granddaughter's nose and his beautiful wife's lips before he faded away…

Chapter 36 – *Etta 1979* – The Kiss

Etta closed her daughter's journal and put it back on the coffee table in front of her. Reading about the day of Samantha's birth and her father's death caused her to begin to shake. It also brought back a memory, a puzzlement long forgotten, but now made clear.

Exhausted after the last final push that brought Sam into the world, Etta had closed her eyes. She desperately needed to rest for a moment. That was when she felt her father's kiss on her forehead. Surprised that she hadn't heard him enter the room, she opened her eyes to smile at him. However, he wasn't there. She saw only her mother, Maria and the baby.

She had convinced herself that she must have imagined the kiss from her father. In fact, that moment was one of the last clear memories she had of that day...and every day thereafter for almost two years. Everything else was hazy, dulled either by too much pain or too much tequila.

Sam's journal confirmed that indeed her father had been there that day. Etta smiled, happy for the first time to think that her father had seen his granddaughter after all.

Thoughts of her father brought with them an old pain that clawed its way back up from the dark place where it had been kept hidden and now lodged itself in her heart. But instead of wanting a drink – her solution to pushing the pain back again for so many years – she wanted to remember. She wanted to remember how much she loved him and how much he loved her. And she wanted to forgive and to be forgiven. He had promised never to leave her; she had promised to stop drinking.

They had both broken their promises and needed to be forgiven. *I forgive you, Papa, and I forgive me too. With your help I won't break my promise ever again.*

She felt something on her cheek, soft, almost like a light kiss. Brushing her cheek with her hand she brought away a small white fluffy feather. *Oh my God,* she thought as her heart swelled with love. *Could it really be?*

Chapter 37 – *Etta 1956* – The Feathers

Sam was five and Etta was sober. She had been sober for 365 days this time. She thought to herself, *one year, Papa, one year.*

It was Christmas Eve and, as Maria always said, a good day and a sad day. It was a good day because it was Sam's birthday and it was almost Christmas, and a sad day because it was also the anniversary of Pancho's death. For Etta it was also a bench mark for how many days she had been sober…or not.

After giving birth to Sam five years ago and then learning of her father's death the same day, Etta had vacillated between being drunk to the point of passing out or stone cold sober. She didn't do either halfway. The worst thing was that she could not decide in which state she despised herself the most.

The family was gathered in the kitchen now, to celebrate Sam's fifth birthday. The gaily decorated birthday cake held 6 candles, five plus one to grow on. Her daughter's gorgeous face was angelic as she closed her eyes to make a wish before blowing out the lit birthday candles.

"Oh, *Mi Hija*, look your wish will come true," Maria cried happily, "all the fires are out."

"Yes, all of them," Fina laughed.

Humberto ruffled Sam's hair. "I for one am not surprised. I always knew you were full of hot air."

Sam scrunched up her face at her uncle. She was used to his teasing and gave back as good as she got.

"And this from *the lawyer*?" Sam said mimicking her great Aunt Lucy's voice.

They all laughed.

"What did you wish for, *Mi Hija?*" Big Jose asked, kissing the top of his granddaughter's wild hair.

"Now, Big Jose, you know I can't tell you or it won't come true."

Sam admonished him playfully, putting her hands on her narrow hips in perfect imitation of Maria's notorious stance. Her grandparents and uncle laughed again, watching the little girl's performance.

To herself she was thinking: *It's already come true because my parents are here.*

Etta watched her family's interchange with envy. *They are so easy, so happy together* she thought wistfully. She felt excluded, although she knew her family would be surprised to learn she felt that way. She just didn't know what to do or what to say to fit in. She glanced at Jose and could tell by the look on his face that he felt as she did, like a stranger watching the happy family scene.

Fina sensed that Etta and Jose felt awkward and did her best to bring them into the camaraderie of the celebration. "Etta, do you remember your tenth birthday? Jose wrapped up a live frog and when you opened the box, it jumped out and right into the middle of your birthday cake."

"No way," Sam squealed in delighted surprise. "Did Maria scream and run around like she did that time when a mouse ran under her apron in the barn?" She looked from one parent to the other.

Etta looked at Jose, waiting to see if he was going to answer or if she should. He was smiling and looking at his daughter, but said nothing. So she tried to find the right words, something funny to make Sam laugh – she loved to hear her laugh – but felt frustrated when nothing came to her.

Maria, noticing their hesitation, replied for them. "Yes, I screamed. Then I got mad and tried to catch him. That frog was tracking frosting all over my clean kitchen. Your mother was trying to catch him with me."

Big Jose joined in. "I thought Pancho was going to bust a gut, he was laughing so hard. Remember Fina? He said, 'If I know my Etta, once she's caught him, she'll dissect him.' And she would have, too, if someone hadn't come in the kitchen just then. That frog saw his chance and jumped right out the door."

At the mention of her father's name, Etta paled. *Oh God, I need a drink* was her immediate thought. As usual her mother knew what she was thinking and changed the subject.

"Look, Sam, see what I found today." She held out a bright red feather.

"A cardinal's feather in the middle of winter?" Humberto asked, surprise crossing his face.

"Yes," Fina said giving the feather to Sam. "Close your eyes and think about the feather," she instructed the child.

Sam shut her eyes as the adults watched.

"What are you seeing?" Fina coached, "Do you see more feathers?"

"Oh, Maman, I do. I do see them. They are so beautiful. They are falling from the sky. There are all kinds and colors. I see white ones, brown, black, and blue, and red."

"That's good Sam, really good. Now look even closer. Do you see anything else?" Fina encouraged her granddaughter.

Sam was silent, eyes still tightly shut. "Yes, Maman, I see two ladies." More silence. Then, "They look like you Maman, pretty with curly red hair. They are smiling. They are so happy."

Sam shut her eyes even tighter, her forehead wrinkled in concentration. "I see rubies, like the one in your ring, Maman, red and shining."

"Good, good, now open your eyes slowly." Fina and the others watched as Sam very slowly opened her green eyes. They were wide with awe and wonder.

"I know who they are Maman, the ladies. They are the Rubies, your mother and grandmother."

"Yes, my little butterfly, you are correct. And whenever I'm having a bad day, or feeling sorry for myself, or even just sad, one of them sends me a feather. It is their way of saying, *'Hi, Fina. Don't worry. We're here, always looking out for you.'*"

"And you keep them in your feather jar!" Sam said excitedly, thinking about the big jar full of feathers sitting on the counter in the Garden Room.

"Yes, I do," Fina said, smiling.

She then turned to Etta and held out a small white fluffy feather.

"Here's a feather for you, Etta. I found it today also. I knew it wasn't for me, it is for you, from…"

"Pancho," Maria interjected with a whisper.

"Yes, Papa Pancho," Sam shouted happily, agreeing with her other grandmother. "I saw him too, with the Rubies."

"Yes," Fina answered Samantha softly, while still looking at her daughter and still holding out the feather. "It's from Papa Pancho."

In the ICU waiting room Etta looked down at the feather she held in her hand and, with a single tear running down her cheek, said, "Hi, Papa…I know you forgive me…for everything."

As she clutched the feather other memories began flooding her mind. Things from long ago that she had pushed away or buried with alcohol. There was something Maria had told her many years ago, and something else she had totally forgotten – until just now…

CHAPTER 38 – *Maria 1951* – The Funeral

It was the day before Christmas Eve. Etta and Maria were in the kitchen wrapping Christmas presents. Sam was having a tea party on the little table and chairs set that Big Jose had made for her first birthday. She would be two years old tomorrow. What should have been a happy time, this time spent with her daughter, actually made Etta feel overwhelmingly sad.

She had been sober for 57 days this time. Instead of being proud of herself for her accomplishment, though, she was sad because of all of the missed time with Samantha. *What kind of a woman am I?* she thought bitterly. *What kind of a mother?*

Maria noticed the sadness on Etta's face. She might not be psychic like Fina, but she was very intuitive and knew Etta was troubled. Knowing how hard it was for the young mother to remain sober, she felt she knew the reason for the sadness she was witnessing. She decided to do what she always did when someone was troubled and needed to get their mind off things: she started telling one of her stories.

"*Mi Hija*, I think I need to tell you about something that happened at your father's funeral," Maria stated. "Do you see the tape anywhere?"

Etta located the tape and smiled at the older woman. She loved Maria almost as much as she loved her own mother.

"Here you are," she said, handing over the tape. Then, after a brief hesitation, she continued, "Maria, I'm not sure I want to relive Papa's funeral. I don't remember much about it or about anything else that happened that week." *Or the next year and a half* she added mentally, looking over at her daughter. The golden head was bent over her tiny table, laughing and carrying on an animated conversation with her dolls as she poured tea into tiny teacups.

"You are right, *Mi Hija*. Let me start on the day your sainted Papa died."

Etta sighed, quietly. She knew that once Maria had her mind set on telling a story it was hard to detour her. So she decided that since she could only remember bits and pieces of that horrible week she may as well listen.

"After making sure you and the baby were taken care of," Maria began while wrapping a small package for Big Jose, "your mother told me and my Jose that we needed to go downstairs and wait for her in your father's library.

"My Jose didn't want to go downstairs; he had just come *upstairs* to check on you and our new granddaughter." Maria looked over at Sam and smiled at the beloved child before continuing with her story.

"But your mama insisted. You know how she can be at times," Maria lowered her voice, "you know, a little bossy. Anyway, so downstairs we went and sat on the big couch in the library waiting for her. After a few minutes she joined us. She sat down next to me and took my hand in hers.

"'Maria, Big Jose, I am so sorry to have to tell you this...'

"Oh, Etta, when she said those words I thought I was going to faint. I knew there was something wrong," she looked at Sam again and whispered, "with the baby. I started praying *Please, Blessed Mother, let our baby be all right. I can't lose another baby.*

"Of course, your mother read my mind like she always does and said, 'No, no, Maria, the baby is fine, she is wonderful in fact.'

"I was relieved to hear this, but still very worried, so I asked her, 'Then what is the matter?' I will tell you, *Mi Hija*, I was very frightened.

"Your mother continued, 'I know how much the two of you adore Pancho, but...' When she looked at us her eyes were big and full of tears.

"Suddenly My Jose jumped up from the couch, surprising both of us. Well, surprising me at least. I'm sure your mother already knew he would do this. My Jose stood there, looking scared. Then he demanded in his loud voice, 'What, Fina? What about Pancho? I didn't hear his truck.' He sounded really mad but I knew he was just frightened. He sounds mad when he is nervous or afraid, as he was now. So he almost yelled at Fina, 'Where is he? When did he get back?'

"'Well,' your mother continued in her soft voice, 'that's just the thing. He won't be…he isn't…' It was so hard for her to say. But she took a deep breath and said it very fast. 'Pancho died this afternoon, at the very moment the baby was born. He died of a heart attack. I'm sorry to have to tell you both this – I know how much you loved him.'

"Oh, Etta, I knew if your mother said something was so, then it was so. I had no doubt that our Pancho was gone. I couldn't speak. And My Jose, well, he just stood there looking down on Fina like she was crazy.

"Your poor mother just shook her head and said, 'I'm not crazy, Big Jose. Pancho is gone. I need you to go get Doc and Little Jose.'

"My Jose sat back down. And, *Mi Hija*, he started crying and shaking. Fina wrapped him in her arms. We should have been…what's the word?"

"Consoling?" Etta offered.

"*Si*, that's it. We should have been consoling your mother but no, instead she was calming us." Maria wiped a tear from her eye.

"I don't know how long we all sat there but finally My Jose got up and said, 'I'll go get Doc and Little Jose.' I tried to stand also but my legs wouldn't work. My husband had to help me up. Oh how I cried. I loved your father, Etta, so much. He was so much more than just a dear friend.

"I looked at your mother. She was so…what's the word? Composed, almost business-like. And she stayed like that the whole time while she took care of the details for your father's funeral and memorial service. It was a good thing too, because I was totally worthless. All I could do was cry.

"Your father was a wonderful friend. And from that very first day, after he delivered Little Jose, he made our family a part of his. He was so much more than a friend, or even an older brother, he was our… savior, a gift from the Blessed Mother, an answer to my prayers in so many ways."

By this time tears were running freely down Maria's cheeks. She wiped them away with one of her ever-present hankies and blew her nose loudly.

At this point Sam came running over to her weeping grandmother, her tea party forgotten. She leaned against Maria's lap and begged, "Don't cry, Maria, it's okay." She then moved back from her grandmother and said, "Papa Pancho doesn't like it when you cry. He says 'Don't cry for me, Maria. You know I don't like it when one of my girls cries.'"

Hearing her daughter's words, Etta felt a chill run up her back. Her father always said those exact words when any of the females in the household cried: "You know I don't like it when one of my girls cries." And if that wasn't startling enough, hearing those words spoken by a two-year-old, the child's posture had changed with the message. She stood with her feet apart and head tilted to one side, just like Pancho had always stood.

Then, shocked and confused, and not knowing why she did so, Etta yelled at her daughter, "Sam, don't call your grandmother Maria. Call her Nana."

Sam's ever-changing eyes went from bright green to a vivid blue and filled with tears at her mother's angry words. Maria intervened.

"It's okay, Etta, if she calls me Maria." She lifted the child to her lap. "Ssssh, *Mi Hija*, don't cry. You can call us Maria and Big Jose if you want. Whatever makes you happy. Okay?"

"Okay, Maria," Sam answered, her head buried in her grandmother's bosom.

To a still-shaken Etta, Maria explained. "Really, Etta, it's okay. I love the way she says *Maria*. She says it just like Pancho always said it."

Etta felt awful. The last thing she wanted to do was upset Sam. It seemed that no matter how hard she tried, she just couldn't *connect* with her daughter. She always said or did the wrong thing, was always making the little girl cry. Maria again sensed her distress and decided the best thing to do was to return to her story.

"*Mi Hija*, your babies are missing their mommy. Go, sweetheart, go back to your tea party." Maria gently hugged Sam before putting her down.

"Okay, Maria. I love you, sooo much," Sam bubbled, wiping her eyes, now green again. Then she smiled weakly at Etta. "I love you too, Mommy."

Etta felt better until the child walked back to the table, holding her hand out as if it were being held by someone else's hand. Her little two-year-old voice was clearly heard to say, "Of course silly, I love you too, Papa Pancho."

In the ICU waiting room Etta closed her eyes, puzzling over the thought that, as far back as when her daughter was a small child, her father might have been watching over her. And as she sat there her body began to tingle, as it used to when her mother would balance her chakras…and the perfumed smell of roses was everywhere. She opened her eyes and looked around the room for the source of the aroma, but saw nothing. Then, softly, she heard a voice, as if it were inside her mind: *Yes, my dear, Papa was there, holding Sam's hand.*

Etta sat up straighter. *Think; think what else did Maria say that day?* Etta wrinkled her brow in concentration, closed her eyes again, and willed the memory of that conversation back.

"Where was I? Oh yes, we were still in the library. Your mother didn't want to tell you yet. You had just given birth and were exhausted, and she knew you would take your father's death hard. She decided to wait until the next morning to tell you. It was more important to bring Pancho back to the ranch first."

Maria stroked Etta's arm. "Sweetheart, I know how much you loved your father. I also know this is hard for you to hear, but please trust me, someday you'll be glad to know this." A small sob threatened to escape from her lips, so Etta nodded and motioned for Maria to continue.

"Your mother gave My Jose directions, just like she had been there with him. 'You'll find him and his truck up on the ridge, about halfway up. I'll get you some blankets. Please wrap him up tightly.'

"Turning to me she said, 'Maria, I know this is a lot to ask of you, but you're going to have to take care of our new baby. Etta won't be able to do it and I need to make Pancho's funeral arrangements. We'll have the service the day after tomorrow.'

"She told My Jose where he would find Doc and the foreman, and Little Jose. She wanted him to tell our son about the baby, to tell him to go and see you and his daughter, and then tell him about Pancho. She was very efficient, even though it was obvious that her heart was breaking."

At this point Etta remembered, barely, what it had been like sitting in the chapel for the funeral. It was overflowing with mourners. There were even more people in attendance than had been at her wedding less than nine months earlier. They spilled out of the church, standing or sitting on rough benches that had been constructed at the last minute.

Although it was very cold, the sky was a cloudless deep blue – the very color of her father's eyes, more than one person had mentioned. The snow that had fallen on Christmas Eve was still on the ground, but Big Jose had managed to get four huge fire pits dug into the half-frozen earth. Several ranch hands kept the fires stoked to keep the mourners who had to sit or stand outside as warm as possible.

Inside the chapel, with the doors wide open it was almost as cold as it was outside. However, those lucky enough to be inside huddled together on the church's hard pews and that helped to keep them a little warmer than the late-comers. Somehow Fina had managed to fill the chapel with fresh yellow roses, Pancho's favorites, and their smell was so robust that even the outside mourners were privy to their sweet fragrance.

The family sat together in the front pew on the left, which was always reserved for the Luna and Lopez families. Fina had insisted on keeping an empty space on her left side, next to the outside aisle. Etta remembered sitting on her mother's right side, unable to contain her sobs. On her own right Maria sat with the baby, who had been wrapped in several blankets to keep her warm. Big Jose sat next to his wife, and occasionally wiped tears from his eyes with a balled-up white handkerchief. Doc was next, openly crying at the loss of his long-time friend, and the last figure in the family pew, sitting on the main aisle, was a dry-eyed Jose. Etta was convinced he purposely sat at the opposite end of the pew, as far from her as possible without causing tongues to wag.

The casket rested at the front of the chapel. Father Miguel had concluded the service with his closing prayers after several people, including Doc and Big Jose, had eulogized the beloved man. Her mind was not clear beyond this point.

"Tell me about the funeral. I don't remember very much," she urged Maria.

Maria nodded and began. "I didn't want to look into the casket. I knew it wasn't really Pancho in there but…still. I handed the baby to

Fina when we all rose to take our communion. She stayed in the pew while the rest of us said goodbye to Pancho. Oh, Etta, you could barely stand and My Jose and Doc had to hold you up as they walked you to the casket. Looking down at your father, you became hysterical and cried, 'Why, Papa, why? You promised you would always be here for me. You promised.' They had to pull you away and carry you outside.

"What happened next," Maria crossed herself, "was a miracle.

"I leaned down and kissed Pancho's cold cheek, and whispered *Adios*. On my way back to the pew I looked up and sitting next to Fina, on her left side, was your father. He looked like he did 26 years ago when he came riding up from out of nowhere to save me and Little Jose. He was holding Fina's hand and looking lovingly at the baby in Fina's arms. And if that wasn't enough, standing next to Pancho in the aisle was a giant angel at least seven feet tall. He had the most beautiful face, and his wings! Oh, Etta, his wings were folded and gave off this white glow. As I stared at him the angel smiled down at me. At the same time Fina and Pancho looked at me and also smiled.

"*Mi Hija*, I'm telling you that I would have collapsed if My Jose was not right behind me with his hand on my back. I was too shocked to even cross myself. I grabbed at my husband's other hand, trying to steady myself, and whispered loudly, 'Do you see him, Jose? Do you see Pancho?'

"But he misunderstood my question and answered, 'Yes, my love, I saw him. He looked very peaceful.'

"I realized his mistake and turned toward him. 'No, not in the casket, there, there by Fina.' But when I turned back toward the pew I saw only Fina and the baby. There was no Pancho, no angel. There was only your mother who continued to smile sweetly at me, like she knew what I had seen. Her face was so peaceful and so beautiful. I turned back to My Jose and said, 'I need a drink.'"

Maria laughed then, remembering the surprised and confused look on her husband's face.

"'A drink of water, my love?' he asked me. I know he was concerned by my strange behavior.

"'No,' I answered, so loud, Etta, that I know the people in the back of the chapel heard me. 'Tequila,' I said, 'I need tequila.'

"I heard your mother laugh, also loudly.

"My Jose just shook his head, clearly confused. Then he took my arm and we walked to the family cemetery. After the graveside service had ended your mother walked over to me. I was kneeling in front of my babies' four little graves. I had brought a small bouquet of roses for each. I remember thinking: *So many babies, so many lost babies.*

"Oh, Etta, back then that was the only thing I truly regretted about my life, the fact that I had not been able to give My Jose more children. But after having two stillborn babies and two late-term miscarriages your mother told us that Little Jose was to be our only child. She also told me that Pancho had wondered with each miscarriage or stillbirth if something he had done or hadn't done at Little Jose's delivery was the cause. And no matter how many times Fina or I told him it wasn't his fault, he was not totally convinced.

"Anyway, I was kneeling in front of those four little crosses and Fina knelt down beside me, taking the last spray of roses and placing it on the last grave. Then she took my hand and said, 'Maria, Pancho wanted me to tell you that he's now with your babies. They are all looking down on you. He also said to tell you *'they were made with love so everyone loves them.'* He said you would know what that means.'

"I couldn't speak. Tears were running down both of my cheeks. But Etta, the second miracle happened then. As we sat there thinking of Pancho, and of my little babies, four tiny white feathers floated down from the sky and landed one by one on the four wooden crosses.

"Sweetheart, to really understand how important those words were to me I have to tell you about that first day when your father brought us back here after delivering Little Jose. The day he gave us those wonderful rooms for our own and made us feel so welcome, like family."

CHAPTER 39 – *Maria 1932* – Made With Love

Once again Etta found herself in the present, still holding the white feather. She glanced at Humberto, who was still asleep, then rose quietly and went out to the vending machine in the hall. She wasn't really hungry, but it had been so long since she'd eaten anything she decided to force herself to get something down. She bought a small packet of cookies and a cup of coffee, then returned to the ICU waiting room.

While she ate the cookies and drank the coffee she thought back to what Maria had told her about the day of her father's funeral. How could she have forgotten about the feathers? *Alcohol fries your brain,* she thought to herself, and vowed anew to refrain from ever drinking again.

She thought about the servants' quarters at the hacienda. They were down the hall from the kitchen and consisted of four rooms: a sitting room which boasted a river rock stone fireplace positioned between two large windows, two bedrooms, and a bathroom with a shower and bathtub. Maria and Big Jose lived there to this day.

Feeling better with something in her stomach, Etta laid her head back, closed her eyes and tried to remember the rest of Maria's story so many years ago.

Maria's eyes were shining when she described her first look at their new living quarters.

"Oh, Etta, when your father showed us our new home that included a bathroom with a shower and a tub, I was *fascinado,* I mean, fascinated by what I saw. I had never lived in a house that had an inside toilet, much less a shower and a bathtub. I couldn't wait to take a bath in that giant tub and I wasn't sure what a shower did, but I liked the sound of it.

"I was so young and so naive. I asked Pancho where I could heat water for the bath. He laughed and said, 'The water is already hot.' Then he showed us how to work the faucets, the shower and the toilet.

"I pinched My Jose. You should have seen him jump. 'Ouch, why did you do that?' he asked me, rubbing his arm."

Maria laughed, thinking about her husband's reaction. "I smiled up at him and said, 'I was just making sure we have not died and gone to heaven. Hot water, Jose, not just water inside the house, but hot water.'

"And, *Mi Hija*, the place was so big. The house where we were living in Mexico was so tiny that it could have fit inside our bedroom here. I remember thinking *the quarters,* as Pancho called them, was a house within a house. Later, after I visited my sister Lucy in Tucson, I realized that our rooms were much bigger than Lucy's entire house."

Etta pictured Maria and Big Jose's quarters. It had been years since she had visited them, not since she and Little Jose had played there as children. She remembered the rooms as warm and cozy. The sitting room furniture, while worn, was in good condition. There was a leather couch and two big over-stuffed leather chairs that sat on a handmade light brown and red hooked rug. It made the hand-hewn oak floors feel homey. There were other pieces of furniture placed here and there, all contributing to a feeling of welcome.

As if reading her mind, Maria continued. "All the furnishings were nicer than anything we had ever seen, even nicer than the old priest's furniture in the mission that we both thought was grand.

"Your father told us, 'This is now your home, for as long as you want to stay.' Then he asked My Jose if he wanted a job as a ranch hand.

"'Of course,' my husband said, 'I can start now.'

"Oh, how your father laughed, that special laugh of his. You know the one, the one that made you laugh too, just hearing it.

"Then he said, 'No, Jose, today you will rest and enjoy your beautiful new son. Tomorrow you'll unload your things and get your family settled into your new home. You can start your new job the day after next.'

"Since the quarters were *sin una cocina,* he told us to use the big kitchen as if it was our own, to use any supplies in the pantry that we needed – can you imagine how we felt? Even My Jose thought we had gone to heaven.

"The next morning, when Pancho came downstairs, I was cooking breakfast: chorizo and eggs, and of course my flour tortillas. Little Jose was wrapped tightly in a blanket and fast asleep in a huge pot sitting in the middle of the center table – you know that big old pot? I kept Sammy in it when she was just a baby also.

"Anyway, My Jose was up on a ladder fixing a cabinet door that had been crooked since the kitchen was remodeled, something that had bothered Pancho every time he looked at it he told us later. He said he had been meaning to have someone fix it but he never got around to it, so he was happy to see it was being taken care of.

"I turned from the stove when I heard your father come into the kitchen and asked him if he wanted some breakfast. He nodded, but asked if I was doing too much after just having a baby.

"'You men, My Jose said the same thing,' I told him. 'Senor Pancho, I've seen my mother have a baby one day then work in the fields the next. I'll rest after you have eaten and I've cleaned up the dishes.'

"Your father then looked at Little Jose and laughed loudly, 'That's the first *potted* baby I've ever seen. And please, I'm just Pancho.'

"I poured him a cup of coffee. I knew he'd take it black with one sugar cube. I don't know how I knew but something just told me. Hey, maybe I am psycho like your mother."

Etta laughed, "I think you mean psychic. But Maria, what does all of this have to do with the feathers?"

Maria grinned and said, "I'm getting to that. Let an old woman remember a happy time, *si?*"

"Anyway, just when I put a plate of chorizo and eggs and a cup of coffee in front of your father a man came into the kitchen. It was Don, who was the cook back then. He was surprised to see me at the stove.

"'What the hell...oh sorry, miss,' he said when he saw me. Then, 'I mean, what is that wonderful smell?'

"My Jose translated Don's words for me, leaving out the part about 'what the hell' but *Mi Hija,* I knew enough English to know those words.

"Pancho stared at my husband, surprised to learn that he could speak English. My Jose explained that after he was orphaned at eight years old he was sent to live with his sister who was one of the nuns at a small mission outside of Cananea, and he learned English there. 'And that's where I met my beautiful Maria,' he added proudly.

"Then your father stared at me. 'You were a nun?' he asked unbelievably, in Spanish. How we laughed, seeing Pancho's expression.

"We told him no, of course, and that we'd explain the whole story at dinner if he liked. Then I asked him if he liked tacos, and told him I would be happy to make some for him using my mother's famous recipe.

"Before Pancho could answer, Don cleared his throat. We had forgotten all about him. I handed him a plate of eggs and a cup of coffee and told him to sit down and eat. It was while he was eating that he said, 'These are the best eggs I've ever eaten.' Pancho had not yet started to eat, so he also took a bite. That was when he smiled and told Don he had been replaced in the kitchen. He, Don that is, was happy to let me take over.

"Pancho took a tiny sip of the coffee. You know how he loved his coffee. He always said it was one of his few vices and he liked it just so. He closed his eyes, enjoying the taste, and then said, 'Maria, this is the best coffee I've ever tasted. You might not be a nun but I swear you are an angel. What's your secret?'

"'Love,' I answered, laughing at him. 'My mama always says if you make something with love, then everyone will love it.'

"Your mama said those same words to me that day at the graveside when I was kneeling in front of my babies' graves: 'Pancho also said to tell you *they were made with love so everyone loves them*. He said you would know what that means.' And I did know, and I was comforted."

Maria then took a locket from around her neck and gave it to Etta. "Here, *Mi Hija*, I want you to keep this. Someday you will know why."

CHAPTER 40 – *Fina 1977 - Reunion*

Sitting in the ICU waiting room, Etta dug out the locket from inside her blouse – the one Maria had given her that day in the kitchen so many years ago. She always wore it around her neck, next to the Holy Spirit medallion that her mother had given her father as his Christmas Eve gift the day he died. After his death her mother gave it to her. She had not taken it off since that day.

Opening the locket from Maria now, she looked at the four tiny feathers contained inside. She knew now why Maria had told her that story and had given her the locket. She was supposed to remember the feathers, to remember that she was never alone. She added the tiny feather in her hand to the others and closed the locket. She felt better than she had in years, maybe ever.

The door to the waiting room opened and Maria and Big Jose came into the room quietly. As one, their eyes went from Etta to Humberto, still fast asleep on the couch, and back to Etta sitting next to him. Their daughter-in-law smiled at them, looking happier than they had seen her look since before marrying their son.

"So, have you heard any more news about our Sammy?" Maria asked. "The nurses would not let us see her," she added.

"No, there's no change that we know of. The Neurologist is in with her now," Etta answered her mother-in-law.

Looking around the room for any sign of Jose and finding none, Maria tentatively asked Etta, "Where is Little Jose? I thought maybe he was here." She chose not to mention the conversation with their son at the hotel.

Etta dropped her eyes. "I...I haven't seen Jose in several hours. He was angry with me when he left earlier. I think I need to explain some things to you both. Could you sit down, please?"

Maria and Big Jose looked at each other, then chose two chairs together and sat.

Wanting to spare the younger woman any embarrassment, Maria spoke first, before Etta could begin. She took Big Jose's hand in hers and said, "Etta, *Mi Hija*, you don't need to explain any things to us. Does she, Jose?"

Big Jose smiled at his wife and then at his daughter-in-law. "No, you don't. Etta, we love you and Sam. And nothing will ever change that...nothing."

Etta looked at them and knew then that Jose had told them about Andrew, or at least that he was convinced that he was not Sam's father. She stood and walked over to them, then knelt and put her head in Maria's lap.

"I love you both so much. I know I haven't always been the best daughter-in-law or mother to Sam, but I promise you I'm going to change. I can't promise that I'll still be your daughter-in-law but I will always be your daughter. I don't know what I would have done without you. Please forgive me."

She looked up with tears in her eyes and covered their hands with her own. "I want you to know that no matter what Jose thinks, he is Sam's father and you are her grandparents. Don't ever doubt that."

Maria whispered, "We know, Etta. And sweetheart, there is nothing to forgive. If your dear mother was here she would tell us that things happen for a reason. Let us all forget about the past and just look at the future, okay?"

"Okay, Maria." Etta dried her eyes and pulled the locket from inside her blouse. Opening it, she took out the newest little white feather. "Look what I found today, here in the waiting room."

Maria laughed and pulled an identical feather out of her pocket. "I found this one this morning in the bedroom at the hotel. Your father is telling us that he is here with us. I think everything is going to be okay. He's saying that our Sam and her little baby will be fine."

Etta rose, hugged each of her in-laws, and went back to her seat next to the still sleeping Humberto.

"Yes," Etta said, looking toward the ICU doorway, "I think that's exactly what Papa is telling us. Now all we have to do is wait."

Maria picked up a magazine that she knew she wouldn't read and let her mind wander. Regardless of her brave words to Etta, she was still worried. *What will become of our son and his family now? Will Little Jose stay with Etta and Sam, or will he choose to shut them out of his life, even more than he has done already?*

She looked at Etta sitting next to Humberto. Etta was gently caressing his arm. Suddenly, it dawned on her that Etta was in love with Humberto. *Why haven't I noticed before?*

She knew, in fact everyone in the family knew, maybe with the exception of Jose and Etta herself, that Humberto had been in love with Etta for years. Maybe she hadn't noticed Etta's feelings before because Etta was just now realizing herself that she loved Humberto. Jose must have killed the love she had for him a long time ago. Didn't she just tell them that she couldn't promise she'd be their daughter-in-law, but she'd always be their daughter?

Maria looked again at Etta and the sleeping Humberto. She loved Humberto like a son, and he had been a much better father to Sam than Little Jose was. As much as she loved her son she wasn't entirely blind to his many faults, but like Big Jose had said this morning, she sometimes looked the other way when it came to Little Jose – she was guilty of pretending things were alright when they were horribly wrong.

She sighed. She had so many questions about the future but they were questions she could not ask – at least not yet. She would just have to wait and see what happened when Sam was well. There was no doubt in Maria's mind that mother and baby would be okay. God answered prayers, and hadn't she prayed all through the night? Hadn't Pancho told them so by sending them feathers? She had found hers on the nightstand after she woke up the second time that morning, after dreaming of Fina. She had held the feather in her hand and had prayed that Fina was watching over Sam and the baby.

Her thoughts turned again to Fina. If only Fina was still alive so they could talk together. She missed the companionship and the love of the woman she'd thought of as a sister for 45 years. How they would both have showered love upon their shared great-granddaughter. But even more, maybe she could have reassured Maria that all would be well with Jose and Etta whether they stayed together or not.

Maria put the magazine down, then leaned back in the chair and laid her head on Big Jose's shoulder. She closed her eyes, thinking of the dream she had of Fina this morning before coming to the hospital…

Maria was sitting in the kitchen, savoring a well-deserved cup of coffee. It was the time she looked forward to every morning, the time between the breakfast cleanup and lunch preparation; one of the few times during the day she could actually sit down for more than a few minutes. She had been missing her grown-up granddaughter, wondering how Sam was doing in California. *I'll call her later today* she was thinking.

Fina walked in from her garden, took off her gloves and gardening hat, and poured herself a cup of coffee. She sat down across the table from Maria.

"Good morning," Fina said as she reached for the sugar bowl.

Maria looked up, scrutinizing her friend's face. Fina looked tired. This concerned her, as Fina was never sick.

"Fina, are you feeling okay?"

Without answering the question directly, Fina reached across the table and took Maria's hands in hers.

"Maria, my dear, dear friend. I have made a decision."

"What, Fina? What is wrong with you? You are frightening me."

Fina laughed tiredly, "I'm sorry, my friend. That was not my intention."

She sat back and tucked a red curl laced with gray back behind her ear before she continued. "Maria, it has been almost 26 years since Pancho passed and everyday I miss him more and more."

"*Si, si,* I miss him also," Maria replied hastily. Then, impatiently, "but what does that have to do with anything?"

Fina laughed, and then leaned forward once more and covered Maria's hands with her own again. "Actually, it has a lot to do with my decision. It is time; I have decided to join him."

Maria stared at her friend, confused, and then realized what Fina was saying. She abruptly pulled her hands from Fina's and stood up. Maria, who rarely was angry, looked angry now.

"What are you saying, Fina?"

Fina stood also and walked around the table to embrace her friend. "I'm saying that tonight I plan to join my husband. We've been separated too long. Sam is a grown woman now, and Etta will be fine. So, Maria, my dearest, I will die tonight."

Maria pushed Fina away and crossed herself. Her anger was gone, replaced by a soothing voice. The sun must have gotten to Fina.

"Fina, sit down. Let me get you a cool drink. I think you are sun-baked. You are not making sense. You cannot just tell me you are going to die." She hurried to the cupboard and took out a tall glass, then moved to the sink and started filing it with cold tap water.

Fina followed Maria to the sink, took the glass and placed it on the counter and turned off the water.

"Maria, come, sit back down with me. Please, please try to understand. Imagine what it would be like not to be with your Jose... for 26 years."

Maria refused to sit; she started pulling things out of the refrigerator and tossing them on the counter.

"Fina, I know it has been hard on you. But," she crossed herself again, "you can't just say you are going to die. It does not work that way."

She stopped her frantic movements and turned to look more closely at Fina. "Are you sick? Are you trying to tell me you are sick?"

"Maria, please stop. Sit, please." This time she took Maria by the hand and led her to the table.

"Okay, I'll sit. I'll listen," Maria said. Fear of what Fina would say was written on her pleasant face.

Seated once more, Fina took Maria's hands in hers. "My friend, I know you have seen many things over the years and sometimes you haven't wanted to believe everything you have seen. I also know that you know I love you like my sister; even more so in many ways. So what I'm telling you, you must believe. I *can* choose to die even if I'm not sick. And I assure you I am not."

Maria pulled her hands from Fina's once again and folded them on the table before bending her head. She could not stop the tears. "But why, Fina, why would you do this?"

Fina sighed and patiently tried to make Maria understand.

"Because I want to be with Pancho all the time, not just now and again. I know that you've seen Pancho with me from time to time — you've even remarked on how young he looks. That happens when we die, Maria. We are young — we're at our prime, like we were when we were thirty — and we're ageless, not the age we are when we die. But I'm getting off the track. It isn't enough to have him with me from time to time. I want to be with him every minute and the only way I can do that is to die. I hate that word *die* because you know we don't really die, we pass — we pass to the other side."

Maria raised her head and looked at her friend, wiping the tears from her eyes with her hankie.

"Yes, I have seen Pancho with you several times. And many more times I have heard you talking to him. Oh, Fina, isn't that enough? What am I going to do without you? What about Sam and Etta? They will be so upset."

"Maria, Maria, just as Pancho comes to me at times, I'll come to you and even if you can't see me, you'll know I'm here with you. And you can always talk to me, just like I talk to Pancho. I'll hear you, I promise. As far as Sam and Etta go, they have their own lives now. I'll be watching over them too. But Maria, I need to be with Pancho. I want to be with him all the time." She stood and put her arms around Maria's unresponsive shoulders.

"Maria, please don't make this harder for me. I don't want to leave you but I miss Pancho too much to go on without him." Then she, too, started to cry.

It broke Maria's heart to see Fina cry; she never cried. This, more than any of her words, convinced Maria that she had to let her friend go.

"Okay, Fina. I promise I will be brave. Please, please don't cry."

Fina smiled through her tears and took Maria's face in her hands. "Oh, how I love you, my dear, dear friend. Thank you. Thank you for understanding. Thank you for being my friend and my sister for all these years."

Maria hugged Fina back. "I'll never forget you; you'll always be in my heart."

Fina patted her friend's back. "And you in mine...you in mine."

Remembering, missing her friend, Maria pulled out her hankie and wiped her eyes. Suddenly, she heard a soft rustle nearby, like that of angel's wings. When she looked at the others in the room nobody else seemed to notice. Then she looked at the doorway, and smiled. Standing there were Pancho and Fina, their arms around each other, and looking as they did when she first met them. They smiled at her, then turned and walked toward Sam's room...

CHAPTER 41 – *Jose 1979* – The Cafe

Jose was exhausted. He should be getting close to the hospital by now, he thought, but after looking around he began to think he might be lost. His feet were killing him; cowboy boots were great for riding horses but not so great for walking long distances. In fact, he hurt from head to toe; his head was throbbing almost as much as his feet. He was in desperate need of a cup of hot coffee but after checking his back pocket he realized he had left his wallet at the hotel. He left in such a hurry after the argument with his parents that he'd forgotten to take it. He reached in his side pockets and came up with only 32 cents in change.

Damn it he thought bitterly. *Can this day get any worse?*

Although he had made a decision about Sam, his feelings still fluctuated between anger, shame and all elements in between. He spied another bus stop bench a few yards away and limped slightly as he walked wearily toward it. Grateful to sit again, he didn't even mind the cold hard metal. Leaning back on the bench, he took a better look at his surroundings. He was surprised to realize that the sun was hanging low in what he assumed was the western sky and a cold breeze had picked up. It looked like he wasn't exactly in the best part of town, but which town he had no idea.

He was too tired to really care. Maybe he'd get lucky and get mugged for his 32 cents, killed in the process and put out of his misery. His left foot was aching painfully. Using his right foot, he kicked off his left boot to inspect the damage.

"Shit," he moaned loudly as he gingerly touched a large blister on his heel.

"You look like a man in desperate need of a cup of hot coffee," a voice said from beside him.

Jose looked up, startled, not only by the voice but because those were almost the exact words he had thought to himself just minutes earlier. He didn't remember noticing anyone on the street when he was looking around to assess his whereabouts after he'd sat down.

"Mind if I join you?" the stranger asked, "or better yet, I know a warm café just up the street. They make a great cup of coffee. Come on, friend, my treat."

Without waiting for Jose to reply the man turned back the way Jose had just come.

Funny, Jose thought as he pulled his boot back on and limped after the stranger. He didn't remember passing a café, but then again he hadn't really been watching where he was going or he probably wouldn't have ended up on this shabby-looking street.

Jose didn't know how he could have missed the café. There was a welcoming neon sign in the window that proclaimed home cooking just above the OPEN sign. Inside, the café was warm, cozy actually, and the aroma of coffee and pastries caused Jose's stomach to growl with hunger. He hadn't eaten since *When? Yesterday or the day before?*

The stranger laughed at the sound of Jose's stomach and he took a seat in a well-worn booth. "Guess maybe you're also in need of something to eat."

Jose nodded, taking the seat across from the man. He realized he hadn't introduced himself to his savior from imminent starvation.

"My mother would be embarrassed by my lack of manners," Jose said, holding out his hand to the man. "I'm Jose. Jose Lopez."

"Ahh, your mother," the man laughed again, his blue eyes crinkling in his handsome face as he took Jose's hand in his. "It's nice to meet you, Jose Lopez. You can call me Frank."

Jose studied the man's face in the dimly lit café. He was young, younger than Jose himself, certainly. "You look so familiar. Have we met?"

The man smiled pleasantly. "You know, I get that a lot. People are always mistaking me for someone they know or some celebrity." He laughed once more and Jose laughed with him.

Glancing around the café Jose realized that they were the only two customers in the place. Just then an attractive woman appeared from somewhere at the back of the café, the kitchen he assumed.

"Evenin', Frank," the woman said in a pleasant voice as she took a notepad from her crisp apron's pocket. "Who's your friend?"

Before Frank or Jose could reply, Jo, as her name tag declared, continued. "Let me guess, two coffees, black, one sugar for yours and two sugars for your friend. And two slices of my mother's peach cobbler," she added, smiling brightly down at the two men.

Jose looked up at the waitress with a surprised grin. "Peach cobbler, that is my favorite."

"So I guessed," she winked at Frank and headed back toward the kitchen.

After watching her walk away with the hint of a puzzled expression on his face, Jose shrugged and turned back to Frank. "I can't thank you enough for your kindness and generosity."

"Well, friend, sometimes you need to let people help you," Frank responded while he peered intently at Jose. "You also need to be willing to forgive yourself so you can forgive the other people in your life."

Somehow this odd statement didn't surprise Jose but before he could respond Jo returned carrying a tray laden with full cups of coffee and two bowls of peach cobbler. She set one bowl of the warm cobbler, topped with vanilla ice cream, in front of Jose; the other in front of Frank.

"I thought you'd like yours with ice cream," she said as she set his coffee next to the bowl.

"Scoot over, Frank," she teased in a slight southern-sounding drawl, "I'll be joining ya'll."

Jose looked up from his cobbler, his spoon almost to his mouth, noticing as he had before that the waitress also reminded him of someone. She was young too, younger than Frank, and had curly red hair that was pulled back into a pony-tail, laughing green eyes, and a sing-song southern voice. He couldn't place her and finally decided that he was just tired and his eyes were playing tricks on him. The café was so dimly lit he really couldn't make out hers or Frank's features very clearly.

Frank smiled at Jo and then nodded at Jose's food. "You need to eat your cobbler before it gets cold." He hadn't touched his own.

"Mmm, this is wonderful," Jose moaned, closing his eyes, as he savored the sweetness of the delicious pie.

"As I was saying," Frank continued, stirring his coffee, "before I was interrupted by the lovely Jo, you need to forgive yourself, Jose."

"Yes," Jo nodded in agreement, her soft voice gentle as she admonished Jose, "once you forgive your own mistakes it is so much easier to forgive others for theirs."

Suddenly Jose was so sleepy it was all he could do to keep his eyes open. He let them close, lulled by Jo's gentle voice. *So tired* he thought, *I'll just rest for a minute.* The cobbler was forgotten as he leaned back in the booth and immediately fell asleep.

"Excuse me, sir."

Someone was nudging his shoulder.

"Sir, you can't sleep here. You have to move along."

Jose managed to open one eye. It was night, but he didn't know how late it was. Disoriented, Jose opened his other eye to see a young-looking police officer standing over him.

Blinking into the flashlight that the policeman was shining on his face, Jose pulled himself into a sitting position. Ouch, he hurt everywhere, especially his left foot. He looked around; he was sitting on a bus stop bench, the one where he'd met Frank. Confusion filled his face. How did he get back here?

"Sir, have you been drinking?" the officer asked, his voice harsher than previously.

Without answering the question Jose straightened even further, realizing that his left boot was off. In the moonlight he could see it lying on the ground in front of the bench. Reaching down to recover it, he pulled it on over his blistered heel and winced in pain. Now that he had both boots on he stood and finally answered the police officer.

"Uh, no I haven't been drinking. I was walking and I'm afraid I got lost. My daughter…my daughter is at St. Vincent's Hospital. I need to get back there. Can you point me in the right direction?"

Hearing this, the young officer frowned.

"Sir, you must be mistaken. St. Vincent's Hospital is at least 20 miles from here. I'll need to see some identification."

20 miles? How could I have possibly walked 20 miles? Ignoring the officer's request Jose unceremoniously sat back down on the hard bench. He put his head in his hands, wondering how he was going to get back to the hospital. He could call over there and ask Humberto to come and get him, he decided. He should still have 32 cents. He stood and checked his front pocket. There was nothing there.

"Sir, do you have any identification?"

Jose stared at the officer, still not responding to the request to identify himself. He thought of asking him for a dime so he could call Humberto, but decided instead to return to the café. Jo had seemed so nice and he hadn't even thanked Frank for his generosity. At least he didn't think he had. He looked around, unsure of which direction to take.

The officer waited, becoming impatient for him to produce his identification.

"Which way to the..," Jose began, and then hesitated as he tried to remember the name of the café. He closed his eyes, concentrating, and he remembered seeing a sign above the door. There was a small picture of a rose. *Rose Garden Café,* that was it! "…Rose Garden Café," he finished, happy that he remembered.

The officer shook his head. "The Rose Garden Café?" he asked incredulously. "Why in the world would you want directions to the Rose Garden Café? Sir, are you sure you haven't been drinking?" He stared intently at Jose.

Jose was becoming frustrated. "Look, I really need to get back to the hospital. If you could just point me in the direction of the café, I have friends there and they'll help me."

Now the officer laughed. "You have friends at the café, do you?"

"Yes, I have friends at the café. I was just there earlier this evening. And I don't drink. Now, please just tell me which way to go."

"Well you may not be drunk but you are delusional. That café's been closed for at least 4 years."

Shocked, Jose was the one now doing the staring.

"Just tell where it is, please," Jose begged. "I know I was just there." *Am I losing my mind?* He wondered, beginning to worry that he just may be. *What is happening to me?*

The officer sighed and shook his head, then pointed to his left. Jose turned without another word and started walking, limping from the pain in his left foot. He reached the café in 15 long, slow minutes. It was indeed closed and appeared as if it had been for quite some time. There was no neon sign and boards partially covered grimy windows. Unconvinced of what he was seeing, he tried to pull the door open; it was locked. In despair, he sank down to the sidewalk in front of the door, exhausted and confused.

As he leaned back against the door he noticed a pale lilac envelope partially sticking out from under it. Curious, he pulled it out all the way. He couldn't believe it when he saw his name written across the front in an eloquent handwriting.

Cautiously, he tore open the envelope and peered inside. There was a note written on lilac-colored stationery, a twenty dollar bill and a tiny, white fluffy feather. He left the twenty and the feather in the envelope but pulled out the note. Opening it, he read:

Our dearest Jose,

We thought you would need money for a cab ride back to St. Vincent's. As for the feather...well it is just a small keepsake of our visit.

Tell Sam, your parents, Etta, and Humberto that we're thinking of them, that we are always with them and of course with you, dear Jose.

Kiss your new granddaughter for us.

Love as always,
F & J

F & J. Frank and Jo? Suddenly it came to him: Francisco and Josephine. Frank and Jo were Pancho and Fina!

Jose wasn't a very religious man but after he folded the note and placed it back in the envelope he crossed himself. He was putting it in his shirt pocket when a yellow cab pulled to the curb. The driver rolled down his window and leaned in Jose's direction.

"Hey, mister. You the guy who needs a ride to St. Vincent's? It's gonna cost ya twenty bucks."

Jose looked up at the sky, shot a salute, then stood and limped toward the taxi. He was laughing when he replied, "Yep, that would be me."

CHAPTER 42 – *ICU Waiting Room 1979 –* The Miracle

Jose was barely limping when he burst excitedly into the ICU waiting room carrying a huge stuffed Teddy Bear and a bouquet of red roses, Sam's favorite. He'd had the cab driver drop him at the hotel first, where he'd showered and changed clothes, bandaged his blistered foot, then picked up his wallet. He was feeling ten times better than when he'd been awakened by the police officer earlier that evening. He couldn't wait to relay the messages written in the note in his pocket, but first he had some apologizing to do.

Looking around the room, he was happy to see that Etta, Humberto and his parents were all there. He had so much to tell them. Setting the bear and flowers on the table in front of his mother, he pulled her into a standing position.

"Mama, I am so sorry that I upset you this morning. Please forgive me. I promise I'll never hurt you again."

Maria hugged her son, surprised to see him in such a good mood. "It is okay, *Mi Hijo*, we're all under a lot of tense." Knowing what she meant, Jose laughed and kissed the top of her head before releasing her.

Next he turned to face his father, who was now standing next to his mother.

"Papa, please forgive me. And thank you for telling me all of those things. You were right. I promise I won't disappoint you again."

Big Jose took his son in his arms. "You're welcome son. I believe you, and I forgive you."

He hugged his father back. "I just hope I can be the kind of grandfather you have always been to Sam."

Jose turned and looked at Etta and Humberto, who were sitting side-by-side on the sofa, and who were watching him with stunned looks on their faces. He glanced at Sam's journal that was still sitting on the coffee table. He needed to try to forget what he had read in that journal, but if he couldn't he knew that nothing she had written mattered now. He walked over and stopped in front of Etta, looking down at her.

"I'm sorry I stormed out, Etta," Jose began quietly. "I am sorry for so many things. I know I've blamed you for everything that went wrong in the past 28 years or so, and I want to tell you I don't blame you any longer. I can't tell you I'm in love with you; I never have been, but you've known that. That's why I realize that your drinking problem is as much my fault as yours. You've stayed all those years, while I went about my own business and never gave any attention or affection. Not to you or to Sam. I want to change that. I know Sam will live, and I will be a good father to her. She'll never hear from me that I'm not her biological father."

When Etta tried to speak he held up a hand to stop her. "As I said, I can't tell you I will love you; I think it's too late for that. But I can say I will treat you with more compassion and consideration than I have in the past. And I will be the kind of father to Sam that I should have been while she was growing up. I will also be a good grandfather. Etta, I'm asking you to try to find it in your heart to forgive me for being such an ass."

Jose glanced guiltily at his mother. "Sorry, Mama for the language."

Maria waved her hand at her son dismissively, "*Mi Hijo*, it is okay. You *were* an ass."

Everyone laughed.

Jose turned to Humberto. "Humberto, will you forgive me also? You are a good man and have been a better father to Sam than I have been."

Humberto stood, grabbing his cousin in a tight bear hug. "Sure, man. I forgive you. But if you ever hurt Sam or Etta again, I'll beat the shit out of you." Then, realizing what he had said in mixed company, he stood back, embarrassed, and looked from Etta to his Aunt Maria and shrugged, adding, "Sorry, Tia."

Maria smiled, "Again, no problem. But you will have to stand in line because I will beat the shit out of him first."

Etta jumped up and grabbed Jose's arm. "You never gave me a chance to tell you before you rushed out, but you need to know that Sam *is* your biological daughter. Yes, I was with another man before we got married, but he is not Sam's father. You are. You must believe me. My mother assured me of this before Sam was even born." She glanced at Humberto, to make sure he had heard her too.

Relief, not the denial she expected to see, washed over Jose's face. "Thank God. Thank you for telling me. I can't wait to see her, to let her know how much I love her. When can I see her? Has there been any change?"

"No, there's no change that we know of. The Neurologist is in with her now," Etta answered tiredly.

It was at that moment that the Neurologist entered the waiting room. "I have good news, folks. It looks like our new mother is going to be fine. She awoke from her coma, is completely coherent and aware of where she is. We can't tell you why she lapsed into the coma in the first place, but she appears to be none the worse for wear. You can't all go in at once, but two at a time can go in to see her, for no more than five minutes at a time. It seems ridiculous to say she needs her rest, but after what she's been through, that's exactly what she needs right now more than anything else.

I thought I'd let you know too, that the baby is going to be just fine. The pediatrician was in talking to Samantha while I was in there and she was saying that the baby was born with a veil covering her face but it is nothing to worry about. Apparently Samantha's mother-in-law fainted when she saw it, but trust me it was not harmful and has been removed. The baby is as good as new. There is an old wives' tale that says a baby born with a veil, or caul, as it's called, will have psychic powers, but as I said that's just an old wives' tale.

At this the adults in the room all turned and smiled at each other, but none enlightened the doctor as to why this made them smile.

The doctor continued, "While I'm spreading good news, I'll tell you that the strangest thing happened. If I hadn't been there myself I wouldn't have believed it. The minute Samantha came out of her coma hundreds of tiny white feathers fell from the ceiling over her bed. They completely covered the bed, then slowly faded away and disappeared... except for this one."

He held out his hand: in it was a tiny white feather, identical to those that were in Etta's locket, Maria's purse, and Jose's pocket...

About the Authors

Rhonda Feltman and Linda Brown have been friends for over 30 years. They always talked about writing a book together, so after they both retired they realized their wish.

The Journal is the first Rhonda Brown book in a trilogy about the Luna family. Watch for *In Her Eyes* and *Just Call Me Sara*, the second and third books, when they become available in the near future.

TheJournalbyRhondaBrown@gmail.com

Secrets of Scarlett Hall

Whispers of Light

Echoes of the Heart

Voices of Shadows Past

Silent Dreams

Songs of Yesterday

Vows of Honor

Ballad of the Innocents

Harmony of the Soul

Cry of the Baroness

Prologue

Scarlett Hall, 5ᵗʰ of June 1805

Scarlett Hall had been the home to the Lambert family for over a century and a half with its jutting parapets and grand towers. It represented a vast fortune and a noble place in society since its inception when the First Baron Lambert gained his title and had the house requisitioned. Yet, Lady Eleanor Lambert, the current mistress of the household, feared it would not endure another year.

Oh, it would remain standing, for it was a formidable manor with strong walls and tiled roofs. Whether or not its deed would remain in the hands of a Lambert was what was in question.

The debt collector had called not an hour earlier, the man offering no mercy as she pleaded for his goodwill. He had left with her promise to pay the debt owed in two months' time – with interest, of course, which came to no surprise to Eleanor. What had frightened her the most was the promise he made that, when he returned and she did not have the required money, the manor would be taken as payment and the family thrown out on its ear.

1

Every part of her being wanted to scream, to cry out to the heavens and perhaps even hide in hopes that it would make the troubles disappear. Yet Eleanor was no child; she was the mother to three young ladies and a younger heir, and their future depended upon the actions she took in these next two months.

Tracing her hand over the desk that belonged to her husband, she thought back to another time when these worries were not for her to endure. Times when she could focus on her family and not concern herself with matters of business. Those days where now gone now, and she had no other choice than to set matters straight.

The sounds of laughter had her moving to the window, where she watched her youngest daughter Juliet, walking down the garden path with her cousin Annabel, daughter of Lord Lambert's brother, at her side. They would be up to some sort of mischief, Eleanor was certain but had not time to deal with their antics.

As the two moved out of sight, Eleanor's eyes moved to her middle daughter, Hannah, who sat beneath a tree with a book in her hand, as was as commonplace as a cookstove in the kitchen.

It was her eldest daughter, Isabel, for whom she was searching, and she found her at the farthest gate of the garden gazing out over the rolling green hills as she was oftentimes prone to do. Although it was not cold outside, Isabel stood with her arms crossed over her stomach and her wrap falling around her elbows.

"Forgive me, Charles," Eleanor whispered as she allowed a single tear to spring forth. There was much she needed to tell her husband, and therefore, she returned to the desk. Readying the parchment and quill, she considered what she would say. How would she tell him what she needed to share?

Her eyes fell to a letter written two days prior, ready to be sent, and she knew what had to be told.

Dipping the quill in the inkwell, she began to write, allowing her heart to guide her words.

2

Dear Charles,

There is much to say, although I will keep this letter short, as I know you prefer it so. The truth of the matter is that Scarlett Hall is in near ruins, and I am afraid acts of desperation will be needed in order to save it. You often boasted of the strength, wealth, and wit of your family who built such a majestic home; that those elements are what bound it together.

I realize now that the secrets within its walls will soon tear it apart if I do not find a way to save it. There is enough money to secure us for only a few months. The debt collectors are not pleased, nor should they be, for they only wish what was promised them. It was in that fear and desperation that I made a promise to them, but I cannot lie to you any more than I can to myself.

I knew this day was drawing nigh, and I have prepared a letter in anticipation for the worst. The words contained within are not for you but for the man whose eyes I have seen settle upon our eldest daughter, Isabel. Our daughter who walks in heartache and despair. Soon, I will ask her to do the unthinkable, to take upon a burden that is not hers in order to save our beloved Scarlett Hall.

The secrets that threaten to destroy our home shall, and always will, remain hidden. I carry them alone; not for the sake of integrity, but for our children. I do wish you were still alive to see how they have grown, but that age has passed, and another has come. A new era threatens to unravel the very heart of our family. And destroy it. I will do everything in my power to stop that from happening.

I have made my decision. I will send the letter at once.

Your Wife,
Eleanor

Eleanor leaned back in the chair, the burden upon her shoulders heavy. Guilt and worry knotted her stomach as she placed her hand on the already prepared letter. She did not want to send it, yet she knew in her heart she had no choice.

A single knock on the door had her turn. "Come."

The door opened, and Forbes, the family butler, entered. "Lady Lambert," he said with a diffident bow, "you asked to see me?"

Eleanor rose, the sealed letter in her hand. "I did," she said as she approached the man. "See that this is delivered immediately."

Forbes looked at the name of the recipient. "I will see it sent now." Then, without another word, the man left, closing the door behind him.

Returning to the window, Eleanor's heart went out to Isabel. Although her eldest daughter had no idea of what was to come, Eleanor did, and therefore, she managed to whisper but a few words.

"I am sorry."

Chapter One

Mrs. Isabel Barnet, formerly Miss Isabel Lambert, had not always been sorrowful. In fact, she had been quite happy for the majority of her life. She had grown up in Scarlett Hall, a place she loved. She had married her beloved Arthur during her first season, and the world had been theirs to conquer.

That was not meant to be, and now, three years after their wedding and one after his death, she was alone. Not alone as in the sense there were no others around her, for she had her family. No, this was a sense of a constant fog enveloping her mind, which made thinking clearly difficult and constricted her vision. The only thing on which she could focus was how her life was now forfeit.

Sheep dotted the rolling green hills behind the gardens of Scarlett Hall. The sun hung over the horizon, continuing to warm the air, and yet she felt chilled. It was the cold that had sunk in not long after her vows were completed, and the chill had only worsened the day she learned Arthur had died, as did a part of her. Her hopes and dreams were gone at a moment's notice, replaced with despair in the next breath.

Her mother had welcomed her back to Scarlett Hall with open arms. Her sisters, although troublesome at times, did their best to console her. Yet the pain, the heartache inside, could not be healed. And although it might be possible to find new love, she found it difficult to hope for such fortuity.

For love was sweet whispers of promises never kept. It was given and not received, and above all, it destroyed one's soul. Of course, these were not words written in the poetry she once read, nor was it the advice of a sage of wisdom. Rather, it was the understanding that comes from experiencing the life she had lived thus far.

Indeed, she had experienced many things, most of which she had kept secret. For her burden of shame and guilt was a heavy weight to bear, and she wished not to burden another with that which was for her alone. To do so would be an unfair action indeed.

Hurried whispers came to her ear, and she turned to see her youngest sister, Juliet, aged seventeen, and their cousin Annabel, aged sixteen, walking down the path, their heads close together. Juliet's hair, which was as dark as the eyes of a fox – an appropriate analogy if one knew of her antics – flowed behind her, and the grin she displayed told much. She wore the blue muslin dress usually reserved for special occasions, and Isabel knew that something was amiss.

The truth of the matter was, Juliet was prone to flights of fancy and getting into mischief, and Isabel feared that one day the girl's behavior would get her into trouble. That is, more trouble than she had already gotten herself into thus far in her life; the type of trouble from which she would not be able to extract herself. Then, as was typical, it would be left up to Isabel to see her returned to safety.

Sighing, she went in search of where Juliet had gone only to encounter Hannah sitting beneath a tree, her customary book opened in her lap. Hannah was nineteen and had proclaimed her life would be spent reading and writing poetry. In her mind, marriage was old fashioned, meant to keep women under the thumb of men. In a way, Isabel could not help but agree, but it was the way of things, and Hannah would see firsthand how difficult it was for a woman to not marry.

Hannah's first London season had come and gone, yet she had been unable to attend due to a sudden illness, one of which Doctor Comerford was unable to explain. Isabel suspected her sister had fabricated the entire illness in order to remain home rather than attend the season. At least, she would not put it past the girl.

"It seems our sister has disappeared," Isabel said when she came to a stop beside where Hannah sat.

Hannah sighed and closed her book, her finger marking her place. Her hair was much like that of Isabel, the color of wheat, a stark contrast to their scheming sister. Also quite different from Juliet, she wore a more appropriate morning dress, yellow in color with white daisies embroidered on the bodice. "Do you not care that she may find trouble?" Hannah asked as she squinted up at Isabel.

Isabel gave a derisive sniff. "It is not a matter of caring but rather a matter of whether or not my words will do any good if I was to warn her. Juliet will do whatever she desires, and no amount of scolding or harsh words will change that." She gave a heavy exhale of breath. She loved her sisters dearly, but being the eldest, she had to take their burdens upon herself, something she found tiresome the older she became. Hannah was old enough to take over watching their sister, but she refused to be of any aid whatsoever.

"You wish me to help." It was a statement, not a question. Did the girl know how to read Isabel's thoughts? Hannah shook her head and stood, clutching the book to her chest. "One day you will see that our sister is beyond help."

"Do not say such things," Isabel said as the two began to walk down the stone path their sister and cousin had taken. "There is no one who is beyond help, and more so our sister. We cannot simply ignore what she does."

"You should allow Mother to handle her," Hannah replied with a huff. "It is her duty, not ours."

Anger flared in Isabel, and she reached out to grab her sister's arm. "Do not say that about her," she admonished. "Mother deserves our respect, not insolence. You have no idea what it is like to be a widow and be forced to change everything in your life."

"I am sorry," Hannah whispered, making Isabel's heart ache. "But Mother never joins us anymore. It is as if she has become a recluse." Then, the quietest of the sisters added, "And I miss her."

Isabel wished to weep. To weep for the hurt she, herself, suffered, but also for that of her sisters. Yet, releasing tears would only compound the sadness they all endured; therefore, she held them back.

Instead, she embraced Hannah. "I understand," she whispered. "I miss her, as well. Perhaps, like many of us, she is having a season of sadness over father. It has only been two years since his passing, and you know how close they were."

"That could be," Hannah said as their embrace broke. "You believe it is because she misses Father that she hides away?"

Isabel nodded. "Indeed, I believe it is."

As the words left her lips, Isabel was not so sure. The entire family had grieved, their mother right there beside her children. It was only in the last month or so that she had withdrawn from them all, and her once beautiful face, which had always been full of smiles, was now gaunt.

"Come," Isabel said with a forced smile. "Let us go in search of Juliet before trouble finds her."

"Or she it," Hannah said with a laugh.

***

They had circled the garden twice, checking behind every bush and hedge, and Isabel grew frustrated with each breath.

"One does not simply disappear," she said. "Where has she gone?" Her eyes searched about once more before she turned to Hannah at her side. The woman held her head low, and Isabel sighed. "Tell me what you know."

Hannah shook her head. "She threatened me."

Isabel wished her mother was there to handle the situation, but she was not. As usual. Although sadness consumed her, Isabel placed a hand on her sister's shoulder and offered the woman a smile. "Her threats are merely that; there is nothing she can do. You should know this by now. Therefore, tell me. What do you know?"

Hannah gave a heavy sigh. "Very well. Earlier this morning, Juliet spoke to Annabel about Daniel."

"The stable boy?" Isabel asked in confusion.

"Yes. Although I do not believe what Juliet said, I do wonder…"

Isabel tightened her hand on her sister's shoulder without thought. "Come now. Tell me. What is she planning?"

Hannah looked up at Isabel. "To kiss him!" she blurted. "She told Annabel that every day she finds him and he kisses her. She wished to prove to our cousin that her story is true."

Isabel stifled a groan and took her sister's hand in hers. "Thank you for telling me. Let us go in search of her. And not a word of this to Mother. Understood?"

Hannah nodded, and the two hurried through the garden – several of the gardeners offering them bright smiles, which Isabel returned despite her urgent errand. She had always felt it necessary to be kind to those employed by her and her family, for they worked hard to make her life comfortable, and therefore were deserving of at least a smile if she could not offer them anything else.

They moved around the house to the stables, which were hidden behind a copse of trees.

"Do not tell her I told you," Hannah said. "The rumor will hurt me."

Isabel came to a stop and turned to her sister. "What did she threaten?"

Hannah sighed and worried her lower lip. "That she will inform everyone of the *ton* that I faked my illness last season."

Isabel arched a single eyebrow. "And did you?"

Hannah dropped her eyes to the ground. "Yes."

"I suspected as much," Isabel replied as they returned to their trek. "I will deal with that, as well. But for now, we have bigger fish to fry."

As they neared the stables, Isabel prayed that her youngest sister was not indeed kissing the stable hand. He was a good and kind worker, and she doubted the boy of nineteen...boy? He was of the same age as Hannah! Regardless, he would not do such a thing. Or at least she hoped he would not.

The stables were large with one long center passageway with doors that opened to the many stalls. Not all the stalls contained horses, but each daughter had a horse, as did their brother Nathan and their mother. They also owned four carriage horses, which were used more often than the riding horses, for few took time to go riding these days. Isabel wondered why they even bothered to keep the riding horses.

Upon entering through the large double doors, Isabel placed a finger to her lips to signal to Hannah she was to remain quiet. Halfway down the passageway, Juliet and Annabel stood talking with Daniel.

"Mother is terribly upset with the condition of the stables," Juliet was saying as she produced a handkerchief and covered her mouth as if to fight off a stench. "So much so that she has become bedridden."

Daniel lowered his head. "I've tried my best, Miss Juliet. I work hard to keep the stalls clean and the horses well taken care of."

Juliet placed her hand to her breast. "I am afraid that your best is not good enough." The man sighed, but then what happened next made Isabel widen her eyes in shock, for Juliet dropped her handkerchief and said, "Now I have dropped my favorite handkerchief. Please, fetch it for me."

When the boy went to one knee in order to retrieve it, Isabel felt an anger erupt in her as Juliet reached out and petted him on the top of his head! Poor Daniel said nothing; although, his face turned a bright crimson and his eyes grew as large as saucers.

"Very good," Juliet praised.

Isabel had seen enough, and she stalked out into the open, doing her best to keep her rage in a tight rein. As she drew nearer, she realized how difficult it would be. "What are you doing here?" she demanded of her youngest sister.

"I am showing Annabel the stables," Juliet said without hesitation, as if lying was second nature to her. She reached out and patted the head of the still kneeling stable boy again. "Daniel was kind enough to retrieve…"

No, Isabel would not be able to keep her anger controlled. "Enough!" she said, her voice loud enough to startle the horses nearby. "Annabel, we will meet you in the sitting room. Juliet, wait outside."

Juliet raised her chin in clear defiance. "I believe…"

"Now!" Isabel said, this time her tone a low threat that she reserved only for the most heinous of offenses.

Juliet spun around with her typical dramatics, her skirts swishing around her ankles, and the two girls walked away. That is, Annabel walked away; Juliet stalked.

Isabel walked over to the stable boy, who rose from his kneeling position, his eyes still on the stable floor. "I am sorry she has treated you so horribly," Isabel said kindly. "Our mother is not bedridden as Juliet said, and I assure you there is no issue with your work."

"Thank you," Daniel replied, his eyes still cast to the ground. "I'll be sure to keep the standards high."

Isabel took a step forward and placed a calming hand on the boy's arm. "I am sorry for Juliet's actions," she said.

Daniel looked up at her. "I appreciate your saying so, Miss...that is, My Lady."

"Now, off you go."

The boy gave an awkward bow and rushed away.

Now it was time to deal with Juliet, something Isabel looked forward to even less than speaking to Daniel. She hoped her sister had heeded her command and remained waiting outside rather than returning to the house with Annabel. She would not put it past the girl to do just that, if only to defy Isabel's authority.

To her surprise, Juliet was waiting just as Isabel had asked. Thank goodness. "Now, I will ask you a question, and you will answer it truthfully."

"I always do," Juliet said with a sniff; although her eyes twinkled. Juliet was beautiful, a fact of which she was well aware, and she used that knowledge to get her way. Coupled with the sweet words she expertly contrived, it typically achieved the effect she wanted.

Isabel knew her sister all too well and, therefore, did not fall for her lies. "Have you allowed that boy to kiss you?"

Juliet gaped. "I would never," she whispered in a hurt tone. "How could you think such a thing of me?"

"For the simple fact that you told Annabel you committed such acts," Isabel replied firmly. When Juliet shot a glare at Hannah, Isabel added, "And if you share even one secret from this household to anyone, especially one belonging to Hannah, so help me, you will be sorry." She despised using threats to make a point, but if that was what it took to get her sister to keep silent, it had to be done. The time for games had long passed. Juliet was mean-spirited and spoiled, and her disrespectful attitude needed to be put to rest once and for all.

Where had the sweet child she once had been gone?

"Fine, then," the younger sister replied. "I shall leave Hannah alone as well as the stable boy. He is just a servant, anyway. No one over which to be upset."

"He is a person with feelings," Isabel retorted. "Do not think yourself better than he."

Juliet rolled her eyes. "You sound like Mother," she said. "But you are not her. If anyone is to correct me, it should be she."

"Mother has been..."

"Hiding," Juliet snapped. "Yes, I know. As much as you do. You believe that because your husband died, it has placed you in charge of us all. But you are not!"

The words stung Isabel's heart, and Juliet looked down at the ground. "I am sorry. I did not mean it."

"Go inside," Isabel whispered.

Her sister turned and hurried away, and Isabel walked over to a large tree and leaned against it. Many years ago, she had stood in this same spot and thought about her wedding that was approaching. How happy she had been! Now, a few years later, she wondered what the future would hold. Not only for her, but for her mother and siblings, as well. Thus far, it did not hold much promise.

The sound of a carriage coming up the lane made her stand and looked toward the tall columns that flanked the drive. A beautifully crafted white carriage ambled toward the house and came to a stop in front of the front door.

That was strange, for Isabel had not heard they would be expecting guests. Curious, she walked toward the circular drive, and the door of the carriage opened to a man Isabel recognized immediately, one Laurence Redbrook, Duke of Ludlow. He lived several miles from Scarlett Hall, and Isabel did not know him well, at least not recently.

The Duke walked – or rather limped, for he had been injured in his younger years – toward the front door of the house.

Although she did not know why the duke was at their home, she could not help but wonder why her mother had not informed them the man would be calling.

Chapter Two

L aurence Redbrook, Duke of Ludlow, studied the invitation in his hand. Lord Rayment had invited him to a party that was to take place in just a week's time, and although Laurence found the gesture kind, he would not go. One week was not enough time to make a place in his busy schedule, for one reason.

That was more an excuse than a true reason. What kept him from accepting this invitation, and others like it, was the fact that the *ton* took it upon themselves to stare and whisper behind fans and hands whenever he entered a room. Or rather when he stumbled into a room.

He had grown accustomed to his limp, but those of the peerage felt sorry for him. Either that or they gave him looks of disgust. And who could blame them? He was but half a man, destined with the curse of lameness for the remainder of his life.

Not only was it a curse, but it was also a reminder of how he had failed.

Reaching across his desk, he grabbed the glass of brandy and gulped it, the fiery liquid burning his throat. It was not that he wished to drink, but as he rarely left his home, he often found himself doing what dukes were wont to do: to drink and at times engage in a game of cards with his butler, Weber. More important matters had come to light, one of which was to find a wife in order to produce an heir.

He laughed at the notion before taking another drink, a sip this time, of his brandy. No woman, especially one of the *ton*, would wish to be seen with the likes of him.

Duke or not, his limp would bring ridicule to a lady, and no woman should be forced to bear such shame. It was his burden alone to carry, the secret of the cause of his limp belonging only to him.

That did not mean he did not dream of having a woman at his side. She would be a woman of beauty and intelligence, one who could see past his shortcomings and see that he was a decent man underneath. Someone with whom such a woman might enjoy laughter and conversation.

He sighed as he placed the now empty glass on the table. No such woman could be found, and he had to resign himself to that fate. Yes, there were plenty of eligible women who would jump at the chance at marrying a duke, yet marrying a young lady who saw only what she would gain from him financially was not appealing at all. Furthermore, spending the remainder of his years listening to the droll conversations of those women held even less appeal.

He glanced down at the invitation once more. A part of him dared him to accept and make a rare appearance. It would be good for his business to meet other men in a casual setting; men with whom he could converse and perhaps with whom he could arrange meetings.

The truth of the matter was he knew himself all too well. In the end he would be left in shambles. It was the reason he no longer accepted invitations to gatherings.

There was always a woman who piqued his interest, but the same thing occurred whenever he approached her. Any conversation halted and, oftentimes, the woman to whom he wished to speak would pretend interest in anything except him. As if he were of no more importance than the servants serving the drinks.

Once they realized he was a duke, they would applaud his every word with false smiles and cloying words, for a duke had title and wealth, something any young woman coveted. Yet, when he walked away, the whispers would follow. And he knew what they were whispering, even if he could not hear the words. They had to be speaking of the duke who was not a full man. The duke who was lacking. The cripple who was not worthy of the love of a woman.

The door opened, and Weber entered. The butler had seemed to age much in the last few years. His once dark hair was now gray, and he had lines around his eyes that were much less pronounced than they had been in the past. Suddenly, it occurred to Laurence that he, too, was growing old, and one day he would be like Weber. Alone. The thought brought terror to his heart for a moment before passing as Weber approached with a silver tray that held a letter.

"Your Grace," Weber said with a bow to his head as he extended the tray to Laurence. "This arrived a moment ago. The messenger said the matter was urgent."

"Thank you." Laurence took the letter, broke the seal, and read it silently to himself.

My Lord Duke,

Although it has been some time since we last met, I am afraid I must appeal to your goodwill concerning the matter of which we last spoke. Your presence is needed at Scarlett Hall, and although I do not hazard to impress a time on you, I do ask – no, I beg – that you come quickly.

Sincerely,
Eleanor Lambert

Laurence read over the short letter once more. About what matter could Lady Lambert possibly wish to speak to him? It had been a year since the passing of Mr. Barnet, and he had not seen Lady Lambert since. He had no recollection of any previous conversation beyond those typical at a wake. He had been present at the funeral of both the woman's husband as well as her son-in-law, which had taken place within a year of one another. Had he said something out of the ordinary at the latter?

Yet, no. He could not recall anything specific beyond the usual words of condolences and the offer of aid if either she or her daughter were in need of it. Perhaps that was the reason for the letter; she was in need of his aid. As it was, he had not spoken those words lightly;

he never did.

"Your Grace?" Weber, who had not yet left the room, asked. "Is everything all right?"

"I am uncertain," Laurence said as he rose from the chair. "Tell the messenger that I will go to Scarlett Hall at once. Have my carriage ready immediately."

The butler bowed and then hurried from the room as Laurence tidied his desk. Many years before, Lady Lambert had consoled Laurence after the loss of his parents. Her words of kindness and wisdom had always remained with him, and he hoped that, somehow, he could return the favor. It appeared that time had come.

Weber was waiting at the door with his coat and hat. Outside, the sun shone, the birds sang, and the grounds on which he resided were meticulous. Although everything appeared perfect on the surface, it was all an illusion, for he felt as if it were all crumbling down around him.

He had no time to worry about such things, for the carriage trundled around the corner of the house and came to a stop before him. As he rode away, Laurence knew that, although he would not attend parties, he would leave the house to honor a promise. And whatever Lady Lambert asked of him, he would comply.

***

The carriage came to a stop before the front doors of Scarlett Hall, and Laurence found himself filled with curiosity as he alighted from the vehicle. The house was renowned for its grand architecture with its dark gray bricks and large windows peeking through ivy that covered its facade. Built several generations earlier, Scarlett Hall was easily double that of Camellia Estates, the large home Laurence had inherited upon his father's death. Yet, even if his home was considered stately, it lacked the large fountain that was encircled by the drive and the grand turrets of the corner towers of the house. The gardens had always been immaculate with carefully trimmed hedges and a variety of flowerbeds that rivaled those of the Royal Palace.

A movement to his right made him turn his head, and his eyes fell upon Mrs. Isabel Barnet as she emerged from a gate flanked by large hedges.

Mrs. Barnet was beautiful, far more so than that about which poets could write. Golden curls framed her face and blue eyes expressed the strength she carried. The woman had endured much in her one and twenty years, and although he had only seen her a few times over the years, he had always admired her for that strength.

His smile faded as the woman slowed her steps, seeming surprised to see him. Had she expected someone else? He felt foolish that he had believed for a moment that her steady gait had been for him, and he sighed as he looked down at the ground. Well, he had business to conduct; time could not be wasted on what he could not have.

When he looked up again, the woman was leaning against a large tree, and she seemed to be studying him. It was on rare occasions when anyone gazed at him openly without a grimace upon his or her face.

Well, he was not here to speak with Mrs. Barnet, even if he wished it were the case. Lady Lambert would be awaiting his arrival inside. Therefore, he made his way up the steps, and although making such a trek could oftentimes be a burden, today it caused him no pain.

The door opened before he was able to knock, the butler giving him a deep bow.

"Your Grace. It is an honor to see you again. Please, come in."

Laurence gave the man a smile. "And it is good to see you again, Forbes." He looked around the foyer. Above him hung a massive chandelier, and a wide oak staircase with crimson carpeting led up to a landing that branched out in either direction to another set of stairs that led to the next floor. "I received a message from Lady Lambert to call."

Forbes swallowed visibly. "She is in the sitting room, Your Grace. If you will follow me."

Something was definitely amiss. It was not like the man to show any indication of concern. Politeness, yes. Gladness, indeed. Concern? Not unless what was causing such apprehension was of the gravest importance.

17

"Thank you," Laurence said. He followed Forbes past the staircase and down a short hallway with various paintings of former Barons Lambert hanging from the walls, a vase placed between each, although they stood empty of any flowers.

A few doors down, they stopped, and Forbes knocked before opening the door. "Lady Lambert," he said with a diffident bow, "His Grace the Duke of Ludlow."

Laurence stepped into the room decorated with furniture covered in gold fabric and the walls displaying large tapestries of garden settings. Lady Lambert stood beside the window in a yellow dress, and when she turned, Laurence felt a pang in his heart. The woman he had known always wore a smile, but today she bore a look of sadness, and he worried something terrible had happened.

"Your Grace," she said with a deep curtsy. "I appreciate you responding so quickly on such short notice. I apologize for the urgency."

"I was happy to come. It is good to see you."

"Please, have a seat. Would you like a brandy? Wine? Tea?"

He took the chair she offered. "No, thank you."

She sat on the sofa across from him and wrung her fingers in her lap. "I am unsure where to begin. I have come to a place where I must ask a very big favor of you."

"Are you and your children in good health?" he asked, uneasiness filling him.

"Oh, yes, we are all well." She glanced toward the large window that looked out to the gardens. "We are well enough."

Laurence sighed with relief. "Then how is it I can aid you?" When she did not answer right away, he added, "Lady Lambert, when I was a child, you consoled me in my hour of grief. You are a friend, and there is nothing you can ask of me that can change that. Nor will anything you request offend me. Therefore, speak freely."

"I appreciate you saying so," she said, and she relaxed somewhat. "When Charles died, everything changed. Responsibilities that I had never known were now mine. I say this not in complaint but rather in order to make you understand the position in which I find myself at the moment.

One day, Nathaniel will inherit Scarlett Hall and all of the business holdings once owned by his father. Although that day is far off, for the boy is but thirteen years of age."

"Did you need advice on your holdings?" Laurence asked in an attempt to understand her request to speak with him. "I have the finest accountants who can also be of service."

She shook her head. "No, it is nothing like that." She looked down at her hands once more. When she spoke again, she did not look up at him. "I seek your aid in saving Scarlett Hall."

Laurence leaned back in his chair in shock. Scarlett Hall was in trouble? How could that be? From what he understood, the house, the lands, all of it had been dutifully maintained. As far as he knew, none of Lord Lambert's holdings had fallen into ruin, or at least he had not heard any rumors of such hardships. None of this made sense.

"We, that is I, am in debt. In two months, if I do not pay a particular sum, I will lose our home."

"This sum," he asked with caution, "how much is it?" To ask such a question was outright rude, but he had to know if he was to help her. His coffers were hefty, but if the amount owed was too much, he worried he could be of little help.

"Seventeen thousand pounds." Her whispered reply was choked. "Although I am not asking to borrow money from you."

Confused, and yet intrigued, Laurence leaned forward. "What is it you ask of me then?"

She looked up at him, her eyes rimmed with tears. "That you marry my Isabel," she replied. "To provide her with a life I cannot. And in exchange, I would ask that you ease the debt that is owed." The woman hung her head, and Laurence could feel the shame she carried. The amount of debt was large and would take some time if he were to help her. But marriage? Despite the fact that he found her daughter quite handsome, how could he expect such a woman to be interested in him? It did not matter that many marriages were based on similar circumstances, but he did not wish to be in such a predicament.

"Lady Eleanor, to produce that much cash in a short amount of time will be difficult, but I may be able to procure it through various avenues. But, as to marrying your daughter…"

"She is a good woman," Lady Lambert insisted.

Laurence raised a hand and the women went quiet. "All your daughters are women of integrity, and I would never speak an ill word against them. It is not Mrs. Barnet who is the problem, but rather it is I." He pursed his lips. How much should he share with this woman? She was only an acquaintance, and he had no obligation to her or to her daughters. What she was asking was a great step; one he was certain he did not wish to take. "Not even two hours ago, I contemplated my life and how lonely I am."

This made her brighten. "Isabel is lonely, as well. Not only would a marriage to her save our home, but it would also bring about happiness to you both."

He shook his head at the woman's words. "I have no desire to wed." He cocked his head. "And Mrs. Barnet? What does she think of this arrangement?" Lady Lambert stood and walked to the window, confirming his suspicions. "I see," he said, stifling a sigh. "She is a widow and far too old to offer her hand in the traditional sense. I have a feeling that if she were asked, she would not wish to marry me."

"I believe that she would," the baroness replied. "Her spirit has been crushed, and I know you are the man she needs to break the curse that has fallen upon her."

"Curse?" Laurence asked in astonishment. "What curse?"

"The curse of this home," she replied. Then she motioned him to the window.

He stood beside her and peered through the glass. There he recognized Miss Hannah and Miss Juliet speaking to one another near a large tree.

"Hannah has yet to find a suitor, and Juliet is not yet of age. Isabel has already completed the customary mourning period and is already well-acquainted with the expectations of running a household. Granted, she did not marry a titled man, but he was the younger son of an earl, so she also understands what it takes to manage servants and to host parties. Nathaniel will eventually finish his schooling and therefore be able to take over the running of Scarlett Hall. Yet, until then? To lose our home, our wealth, I fear for his future as well as the future of my daughters."

She turned toward him, and he had to stop himself from taking a step back. "I know this is sudden, and I do not expect you to make a decision today. I would make one request before you decide."

"Very well."

"In two nights' time, be our honored guest for dinner. After we have eaten, spend time with Isabel in the drawing room. If at that time you still do not wish to marry her, I shall never speak of it again." Although her words were clipped, they reeked of her desperation.

Laurence turned his gaze back out to the garden, and he found he could not stop the smile that formed on his lips as Mrs. Barnet walked toward them up the path.

Although she was some distance away, he could not help but wish to be at her side, for her smile and composure were things for which he longed in himself.

"You say she is sad," he said. "Yet I see a woman who stands with her head held high and a smile upon her face. I would say she has a strength about her."

"She is much like this house," Lady Lambert replied with a small smile. "By all appearances, it is magnificent;, yet inside it is falling apart."

"Then I shall come to dinner in two nights," he said. Something inside him was drawn to the young widow with the secretive smile and the power to carry the world on her shoulders.

Chapter Three

Something was amiss at Scarlett Hall, although Isabel had not yet figured out what that something was. It had begun with the arrival of Laurence Redbrook two days earlier, and he had been sequestered with her mother for more than two hours. When the man left, her mother informed her that the duke would be joining them for dinner this night, yet when Isabel had pressed for the reason why, her mother had said it was of no importance.

Now, Isabel sat before her dressing mirror as her mother restyled her hair. She had styled it earlier in the day, yet Isabel's mother had insisted on changing it despite the fact the duke would be arriving at any moment.

"I remember doing this many times when you were a child," her mother said in that same thoughtful tone she had used on Isabel's wedding day. "You were not like the others, who complained and yelped like urchins whenever I pulled the brush through their hair." Then she sniffed amusedly. "Well, not too much."

Isabel laughed. "Well, I am an adult; far past the age to complain."

Her mother smiled as she placed the brush on the stand and rested her hands on Isabel's shoulders. "That you are," she said to Isabel's reflection. "You have grown into a strong and understanding woman."

Isabel gave her mother a look of suspicion. She could always tell when her mother had ulterior motives, and this was one of those times. For one thing, her mother had insisted Isabel wear one of her gowns typically reserved for attending balls – a satin garment overlapped in lace trimmed with tiny intricate flowers and short puffed sleeves – rather than a less formal, although still appropriate, dress meant for dinner.

Isabel had never been one to challenge her mother in any way, and she would not begin now. Her mother would tell her what was going on when she was ready and not a moment sooner.

"Tonight shall be entertaining," her mother said as she picked up the white gloves. "We have not spoken to the duke in some time."

Isabel nodded. "It has been at least a year." She remembered the friendly man coming to their home when first her father and then later her husband had died. Although Isabel remembered very little of either time, her grief was so great, she had not forgotten the kind words he had shared with her.

"And he is very handsome."

Isabel turned to her mother. What was her mother up to? Despite her rule of not questioning her mother, she could not keep her curiosity under wraps any longer. "Why did he come the other day?" she demanded.

"It is simple. The duke is a man of business, and he has helped me in matters of the estate." Although Isabel knew her mother would never tell an outright lie, she felt an underlying current of untruth to her words. "Now, stand and allow me to look at you."

Isabel did as her mother bade, and her mother smiled her approval. It was wonderful to see her mother smile again, for she had not done so for a long time.

"You are such a beautiful woman," her mother said as she ran a finger down her cheek. "We must be careful lest the duke whisk you away from here."

Isabel laughed. "That will not happen, I assure you. He is a kind man, yes, but I have no interest in him in any romantic sense. Or any man for that matter."

"Is it because of his leg?"

"His leg?" Isabel asked, taken aback that her mother would think so little of her. "Of course not. I would not care if his leg was missing, or even an arm."

"Then why?"

Isabel sighed. "I was once married, and I do not wish to travel down that path again."

Perhaps it was her imagination, but her mother seemed troubled by her words. Of course, it was understandable; a mother wished her daughter to be happy. At one time Isabel had been happy, but that was when she was young and naive and thought that vows of marriage were sacred.

"Do not worry about me, Mother. I am content to be here at Scarlett Hall. Let us enjoy our evening rather than wasting time talking about a duke who rarely leaves his home."

"You are right," her mother said and then took both of Isabel's hands in hers. "I do have one favor to ask of you before the duke arrives."

"Yes, of course," Isabel replied. "Anything."

"The duke, as you said, hides himself away. Whatever he speaks of tonight, please feign a great interest. I believe it may help the man. Can you do that?"

"And why would I do that?" Isabel asked.

"The duke accepts few invitations, from what I understand," her mother explained. "I do not see why he should feel unwelcome in our home. And because he rarely is in the company of anyone other than his sister or his servants, I thought it would be a nice gesture on our part to make him feel comfortable here at Scarlett Hall."

Although the request seemed odd, Isabel agreed. "Yes, Mother. I believe I can do that." It was not that she was prone to being rude to callers. She wondered if the woman had already had this same discussion with Juliet.

"Good," her mother said with finality. "Come. We should be in the foyer when the duke arrives."

Isabel followed her mother downstairs, but she could not help but feel a bit of resentment. Her mother's wish was yet another burden placed on her shoulders, and although Isabel was not one to complain, she wished the woman would take back the responsibility of her sisters and other matters that should have been her mother's in the first place.

As they walked down the first flight of steps, Isabel glanced at her mother. Sorrow filled her heart. The woman had aged as of late – silver streaked her hair, and tiny wrinkles creased the corners of her eyes. Her smile and the sparkle in her eyes had become a rarity, and if engaging with the duke or minding after her sisters aided in their return, then Isabel would do as her mother requested.

The duke was just entering the foyer when Isabel and her mother came down the last flight of stairs, and she gave him a warm smile. He was a handsome man in his impeccable dark coat and carefully tied cravat, and Isabel recalled Hannah and Juliet whispering about him with low giggles. A curious dark wave of hair fell over his forehead, and he brushed it back as he returned her smile.

A warm sensation in the pit of her stomach almost made her stop short. No, she had no inclination of allowing this man to induce those feelings that had once left her breathless. Not just this man but any man, for she had not lied when she told her mother she had no interest in marrying again.

She stifled a laugh. She had yet to speak to the duke and she had thoughts about him asking for her hand? Being kind did not lead to such actions.

She and her mother dropped to a deep curtsy when they reached the bottom of the stairs. "Your Grace," her mother said. "My apologies for keeping you waiting."

"No apology is needed," the duke said as he returned the greeting with a nod of his head. "In my excitement to dine again in Scarlett Hall, I believe I may have arrived too soon."

Her mother gave a strange loud laugh, and Isabel scrunched her brow at the woman. Why was she acting so strangely?

"You could never arrive too soon," her mother replied.

The man smiled and then his gaze turned to Isabel. "Mrs. Barnet, it is a pleasure to see you again."

Remembering what her mother had asked of her, Isabel returned the smile. "And it is a pleasure to see you, as well,

Your Grace," she said. "I have been looking forward to this evening and dining with you once again. It has been much too long since you have come calling."

The man gave her a surprised look. "Indeed, it has."

"Please," her mother interrupted, "let us go to the dining room. It has been redecorated since you were last here."

She took the duke's offered arm, and Isabel followed behind them, her mind spinning as she wondered if the duke was there for dinner or business, or was it something else altogether? Something to do with her mother and the duke perhaps?

***

Dinner had been pleasant enough, with polite conversation as they dined on roast partridge and yams. The duke had been patient with Juliet and her barrage of questions, which was typical of her when they had the rare occasion to entertain a guest. Hannah ate in silence, also very common for the middle sister, for she had more interest in reading about people and their lives than speaking to them.

Once dinner was finished, Hannah and Juliet were sent off to bed, much to their chagrin, and now, Isabel sat with her mother and the duke in the drawing room partaking in after-dinner drinks.

Isabel took a sip of her sherry, and as her mother and the duke conversed, her mind traveled back to a time when Arthur had reclined in the very chair the duke now sat. They had returned from their honeymoon in Scotland and shared stories with family until late into the night. Her mother and sisters had been thoroughly entertained, for Arthur had a marvelous sense of humor back then; so much so, he could have made a stone laugh. Suddenly, Isabel missed that man – the man with whom she had fallen in love – dearly.

"Isabel," her mother whispered, interrupting her thoughts, "His Grace asked you a question."

With heated cheeks, Isabel placed her glass on the table and turned her attention to the man. "My Apologies. Would you please repeat the question?"

The duke smiled. "I was curious about your current horsemanship.

I recall when we were younger, you once mentioned that you often took your horses out. Do you still ride?"

Isabel shook her head. "No, I am afraid I do not." Riding, like many pastimes she had once enjoyed, had long been forgotten. Her mother gave her an encouraging nod, and Isabel remembered the promise she had made. "And you, Your Grace? Do you ride?"

"Much like you, not as often as when I was younger. Although, I do find myself riding from time to time despite my injury." He placed his glass on his knee.

Isabel had completely forgotten about the man's leg, although she had followed him into the drawing room. It was strange what a person noticed. She took notice of how his eyes crinkled when he laughed or how his grin was slightly crooked, but not once did she note his limp. If she did, it was of little consequence to her.

"When we were young, do you recall when you demonstrated how you were able to jump the hedge near Blandton Pond?"

Isabel smiled. It had been many years since she thought about Blandton Pond, but the memory was as vivid as if it had happened yesterday, for it had been a rare occasion when the former duke and his family had come to Scarlett Hall for an early dinner. "I do, admittedly. I had never received such applause before."

She was surprised he had remembered, for that single incident was the only exchange that she could recall the two of them ever truly having. His sister had refused to accompany them to the pond, and Juliet had outshone them all with her horsewoman skills – even though she was only ten years of age at the time and had shockingly rode astride, something about which Isabel had never told her mother.

"Now I find myself buried in ledgers," he said with a sigh. "Managing business, numbers...all those joys one has when they become of age and must become responsible."

"Well, your lands are certainly large enough," Isabel offered. "You should spend some time away from your work and take pleasure in them." Her father had been notorious for shutting himself away in his study, and she suspected the duke did the same.

"I realize this is sudden," he said, "but would you like to go riding on Saturday? I believe it would be nice to leave my work behind for even a short time, and there is little joy in riding alone."

Isabel was unsure how to respond. The invitation was kind, but she had no interest in spending time with anyone. One glance at the stern countenance of her mother told her how she would reply. "That would be lovely. I look forward to it."

"Childhood friends," her mother said with what Isabel suspiciously thought sounded like wistfulness. It was not as if she and the duke had spent any significant amount of time together as children to have even the tiniest amount of nostalgia! "It has been an honor watching you grow into the adults you have become."

The duke finished off the remainder of his brandy and rose from his chair. Isabel and her mother followed suit.

"This evening of speaking of old friends has been pleasant," he said.

Isabel had to fight herself from shying away as his gaze remained on her. And to keep herself from laughing at the absurdity of speaking of them as 'old friends'. Yet that steady gaze was more than a bit unnerving.

"I must be on my way," he continued. "Mrs. Barnet, I look forward to our outing." He took her hand and kissed her knuckles, his eyes never leaving hers.

"As do I," Isabel replied, wondering if she was lying or telling the truth. In all honesty, she was unsure.

"Allow me to walk you to the door," her mother said. "Isabel, will you refill our glasses?"

Isabel nodded, although she found the request odd. She did not want more sherry, and her mother never had more than one after dinner. Regardless, she gathered their glasses and walked over to the liquor cart, the events of the evening playing in her mind.

Her mother had seemed excited at the prospect of Isabel and the duke spending the afternoon together. The reason for his presence this evening had never been clarified, but surely dinner had not been planned simply to arrange an outing?

No, that made no sense, for the invitation came only because of their talk of a single incident that the duke found reminiscent of his youth. She could not blame him for that; everyone had special memories others might be less likely to recall, for that same event might not have been as impressive to them.

Returning to the sofa, Isabel placed the glasses on the table, her frustration over this evening growing. Something was amiss, but she struggled to see it, so she considered what she did know. For one, the duke was a kind man. Perhaps he was lonely and in need of a friend.

She closed her eyes and recalled a time not long after the passing of her father. The duke had arrived, and despite the fact she had said little, he had offered her words of comfort.

"Never feel alone," he had said, "for if you are in need of a friend, Camellia Estates is but three miles from Scarlett Hall. If you need anything, and if I am able to give aid, simply ask."

Letting out a sigh, Isabel opened her eyes. According to rumor, the duke rarely left his house. He was a proud man; therefore, he would not say so openly, but it was clear he was in search of a companion. Her mother knew her desire to remain unattached now that Arthur was gone, and the woman would never force her into something more with a man for whom she did not have a great affection. Well, she would return the kindness he had shown her.

"What a wonderful evening," her mother said when she returned to the drawing room. "His Grace is certainly not the young boy he once was."

"No, he is not," Isabel replied as she gave her mother the sherry she had poured for her. "I hope my actions and words tonight pleased you."

Her mother sipped at the sherry before responding. "Yes, my dear," she said. "It went even better than expected." Although she tried to hide the small smile behind her glass, Isabel noticed it, and more questions arose in her mind.

"Mother," she said as she returned the untouched glass to the table, "you said that the reason the duke had come to dinner was for matters pertaining to business, correct?" She had never had a head for numbers, and during her two years of marriage, Arthur never expected her to worry herself with matters of business.

"I did."

Isabel felt a stab of annoyance at the lack of details in the reply her mother gave. "What matters, if I might ask?"

Her mother heaved a heavy sigh. "Isabel, these things are always complicated. All I ask is that you enjoy any time you spend with the duke and be sure the man remains happy."

"But I do not…"

Her mother raised her hand to forestall her, and Isabel fell silent. "We have nothing more to discuss," she said with that tone of finality that said the conversation was over. "Let us enjoy our sherry."

Isabel nodded but left her glass untouched. She could not help but wonder about the strange actions of her mother. The woman had grown impatient with her questions, something that she rarely did in the past. It was as if she were hiding something. Yet, that seemed unlikely, for what could she possibly be hiding?

Oh, how she wished this wretched fogginess would leave her head! Then at least she could think straight.

She glanced at the sherry – her third this evening. She, like her mother, rarely had more than one. Perhaps that was what was causing her to be suspicious. She was an adult now, already widowed; there was no reason for her mother to hide anything from her.

Relieved that she had found the culprit for her own strange behavior, her mind turned to the duke and their plans for horseback riding. Granted, she preferred to spend her days inside or walking the gardens alone with her thoughts, but she had to admit that an excursion did sound pleasant. Even if it meant going with the duke rather than being able to do so alone.

Chapter Four

The sun shone as Isabel and Hannah waited for the carriage to be brought around. Isabel had asked Daniel to ready the horses just as Juliet disappeared once again. Not that Isabel minded; not with how often the girl could be such a handful.

"Thank you for coming with me today," she said to her sister. Her mother had insisted Isabel have a chaperon for this outing with Laurence, which was idiotic in this stage of Isabel's life as far as she was concerned. Her mother was never one to see another's argument, and therefore Isabel had reluctantly agreed. Well, perhaps not all that reluctantly. At least she would not be forced to be alone with the duke.

Hannah shrugged. "It will give me time to read," she said as she clutched the book to her breast. "You are unlike Juliet, so I will not need to worry."

Isabel let out a small laugh. "No, you will not have to worry. Besides, Laurence is a gentleman, and beyond that, a duke."

Hannah seemed to consider this for a moment. "You are right, although I do find it odd that the man has suddenly appeared for the first time in a year."

"It was a matter of business," Isabel explained. "One of which I am privileged to know." Isabel smiled at her sister's reaction. They might be grown women, but Isabel could not help but tease Hannah like she had when they were younger. She fought down the sadness that tried to take over; today was to be great fun, something she had not experienced for some time.

"Please tell me," Hannah begged, her eyes bright with curiosity. "What business is it?"

"I cannot say," Isabel said as she pulled at her glove although it was already on her hand. "I have been sworn to secrecy." She glanced at Hannah and stifled a giggle. "Well, perhaps I can trust you." Then she sighed. This was the most fun she had had in a long time! "No, it is not worth the risk."

"Oh, please! I beg of you, tell me!"

Before Isabel could respond, Juliet charged from behind a nearby hedge, a wicked grin on her face. She placed a hand on Hannah's arm. "I shall tell you, dear sister," she said with her typical enthusiasm when she had a secret to tell. She leaned in and lowered her voice. "Many years ago, our sister kissed the duke, promising him her undying love!"

"Juliet!" Isabel gasped wondering how her sister could tell such tales.

"It was the type of love one might find in a book," Juliet continued as she walked over and leaned against a pillar. "Therefore, the business mother and the duke are conducting is quite simple."

"And what is that?" Hannah asked, her excited curiosity clear in her tone.

"You cannot kiss a man and expect him to forget. He is now wanting more. Men are like that, you see, even to the point of taking women away in the middle of the night."

Hannah's eyes widened.

"That is enough," Isabel chastised. "Tell Hannah you are only teasing."

Ever the dramatic one, Juliet placed her hand on her breast. "Oh, Isabel is correct," she said with a sigh that could have been deemed appropriate for the stage. "I was only teasing about the duke."

Hannah gave a relieved sigh. "Oh, that is good."

"I was not teasing about the men who have been known to take away women after they have kissed or ones they desire and cannot have," Juliet said. "Do make sure you lock your window at night." With a flourish, and before Isabel could force her to take back her words, Juliet turned and walked away.

32

"Pay her no mind," Isabel said as the carriage pulled up, two saddled horses tied to the back. "She is only telling tales again."

"I know," Hannah said with a shake to her head. "I would not worry even if it were true. I do not plan on ever marrying."

"No?" Isabel asked as the carriage stopped before them and the driver retrieved the steps. "And why is that?"

"Because I love my books more than I could ever love a man," Hannah replied as she thrust her book out before her. "Men are mere barbarians, and they do not appreciate the finer things in life."

"And what are these 'finer things in life'?"

Hannah gave her an indignant glare. "Why, art, reading, writing, and the theater, of course."

The driver opened the carriage door, and Isabel allowed Hannah to get in first. When they were both settled, she looked at her sister. She was a pretty woman who could marry any man of her own choosing, and yet she was so absorbed by books and make-believe, she could not see it for herself.

It was a pity Hannah chose to wear dresses of the blandest colors, much like the brown riding dress with its high collar and loose sleeves. Her straw hat displayed not a single piece of lace or accessory, and her gloves, what could be seen of them, although white, had no buttons or lace! The word 'Wallflower' came to Isabel's mind, and she was shocked to realize that it was the exact word to describe this particular sister.

"Perhaps one day," Isabel said, "you will meet a man who likes the same things you do. Then perhaps you will change your mind."

Hannah seemed to consider this idea for a moment before speaking. "Then I would have to allow him to court me, then marry me, and finally I would be forced to have his children. Then, as he enjoyed his life, I would have less time to enjoy mine."

"It appears you have given this some thought," Isabel said.

"I have." Hannah placed the book on the seat beside her and leaned in toward Isabel. "I must share a secret with you, and you must swear you will never tell."

The carriage jostled as it moved forward, and Isabel considered telling her sister that she could not do that.

How could she be expected to keep one more secret? She could not find it in her heart to be so cruel. "I promise. You may tell me." So often she missed the camaraderie she and Hannah had oftentimes shared when they were younger. Before Isabel married. Before she left Scarlett Hall.

"Mother has always spoken of the season with such wonderment," her sister said, her voice just above a whisper as if someone outside the carriage might overhear. "And I know I cannot fake another illness."

"No, you cannot. It would only make Mother worry."

"That is why I shall hire a man to court me!"

Isabel could not help but stare at her sister. "I expect such things from Juliet, but certainly not from you!" she said in shock.

"Who do you think gave me the idea?" Hannah asked. "It was she who advised me in this area. And although our youngest sister lacks discretion in most areas, she is right about this. If I pay a man in secret to appear as if we are courting, I will not have to go to London, and therefore, Mother will not have to be concerned I will become a spinster."

"But that is exactly what you will become!"

Hannah chuckled. "Yes, but Mother does not need to know that. By the time I am a spinster, I will be old enough to make my own decisions."

Isabel could not believe this young woman would stoop to such levels. "You cannot pretend to be interested in a man for the approval of others."

"Oh?" Hannah asked, the corners of her mouth turning upwards in a tiny smile. "Is that not why you are going riding with the duke?"

The words rang true, and Isabel had no answer to give. Her sister was correct, but her situation was much different from that of Hannah. Explaining as much to her sister would be difficult, so instead, she handled it as her mother had just three nights prior.

"Enough of this talk," Isabel snapped. "We are almost there."

Hannah gave her a knowing smile, and Isabel could not help but return it, for she knew her sister had certain ideas about this outing that Isabel refused to address.

***

Laurence considered, not for the first time, how numerous events had shaped his life from the prestigious schools he attended, living with an uncle when his parents died, and then later returning to Camellia Estates when he was old enough to take over the responsibilities of the dukedom. All of them had a significant influence on the man he was today.

His family home was quiet on most occasions, minus the typical sounds of servants going about their duties. Today it would entertain new voices, and one of those voices had been heard only once before – that of Mrs. Isabel Barnet.

In just under an hour, Mrs. Barnet would join him to go riding and, he hoped, to have meaningful conversation. He had not yet decided in regards to the request made by Lady Lambert, but after speaking with the daughter in their drawing room, he found the idea more intriguing. If they were to marry, they would save the Lambert ancestral home, for which he would be glad. The place could never belong to any other family.

Although he did not know Mrs. Barnet well, especially now that she was an adult, he did find her interesting. And beautiful. Over time, they would learn to love one another, and that thought excited him. The manner in which she showed interest in their conversation during the evening of the dinner in Scarlett Hall only reinforced the idea that they might have a shared attraction for one another.

A slight pain engulfed his leg, and he massaged the damaged muscle, a movement that had become habit, for it did little to ease the pain. It was not an unusual incident, but it did cause him to reconsider marriage.

Although Mrs. Barnet never made mention of his leg, nor had she looked at him in disgust, he could not help but ask that one question that always came to his mind in moments such as this: Would she wish to be seen in the company of one who was only half a man?

He could walk, true, but he could only do so for short treks before his leg pained him. He also could ride, but he would be required to tie one of his legs into the stirrup. If only he had been injured in battle like other self-respecting gentlemen! Then he would have no reason to feel shame.

What was I thinking by asking her to go riding with me? he asked himself as a surge of anger coursed through him. Now she would be able to see what little he could do and therefore be repulsed by him as much as he was for himself. Well, it was too late to cancel now. And, if he were honest with himself, he would not have canceled even if he could have.

With a sigh, he walked over to the desk and picked up the invitation to the party he had not attended the previous night. Then, the thought of attending such a party with Mrs. Barnet made him smile. The people would look on in wonder at the beauty on his arm, and then, perhaps, they would look at him differently. They would no longer see the lame duke but rather the man married to such a beautiful creature. He could almost hear their words:

"He must have more to give than we previously believed."

"Such a lovely woman would never agree to wed a man who could not care for her. He is not a complete loss."

"Perhaps we were wrong; he is a whole man after all."

It was not that he had heard such statements from any of his peers, but the words echoed in his mind for so long, at times he wondered if they had not originated from whispers he had overheard somewhere. Regardless, he would be seen as an equal to those of his station, and the more he thought on the possibility of marriage to Mrs. Barnet, the more the idea appealed to him. She would be able to make him happy, and he could do the same for her. No expense would be spared; she could have anything and everything she desired.

Sighing, he pushed the card away and dropped his head into his hands. He was never one to make a decision in haste. He had told Lady Lambert he would give his decision after careful consideration, and allowing his imagination to run wild was not being careful. He had to look at this with a logical mind and not allow his heart to run amok.

"Your Grace?"

Laurence looked up to find Weber standing beside his desk, and his heart skipped a beat. "How is it you are able to enter a room so silently?" he asked the man, still attempting to calm his racing heart. "I wonder if your feet ever touch the ground."

"My apologies," the butler said with a bow. "A quiet butler is an employed butler."

Laurence chuckled. "I suppose you are correct," he said. "What is it you need?"

Weber produced a small tray carrying a letter. "For you, from your sister."

Laurence grimaced as he picked up the folded paper from the tray. "Thank you, Weber. Is the basket ready?"

"It is. Would you like me to bring it here?"

"No. Leave it by the front door."

The butler bowed again. "As you wish, Your Grace." Then he was gone.

Laurence walked over to one of the wing-backed chairs that sat in front of the empty fireplace. There, he opened the letter.

My Dearest Laurence,

I find it troublesome to my soul that you do not write to me as often as I write to you. Nevertheless, I shall continue to pen letters although it is a burden.

Laurence shook his head. Harriet had always been spoiled and overly dramatic. It was no wonder they did not get along. Why she bothered to write to him at all was beyond him, but perhaps she was simply bored and had no one else to whom she could correspond. With a shrug, he continued reading.

Ambrose is leaving for business, as he is often prone to do. Since you never bother to reply to my letters, I shall come and see you. Expect me in three weeks' time.

With love,
Harriet

37

Laurence groaned as he set the letter aside. In truth, he wished the woman would stay away, for she was unkind in her words and manners. Not only toward him but to any who had the unfortunate luck to encounter her. She was family, and he could not bring himself to deny her request.

He laughed. She had made no request but rather had stated a fact.

Returning to his chair at the desk, he penned a reply. The words were brief, and he conveyed that he looked forward to her visit; although it was a lie. Yet, nothing would be gained by speaking one's mind in a letter.

When he finished, he sealed the letter and glanced up at the clock. Mrs. Barnet would be arriving at any moment, and the dread the letter his sister had sent was replaced with pleasant expectation.

Standing, he took a step and then groaned as pain shot up his leg and into his hip. He prayed that it would not seize up today, for the embarrassment would not only be great for him but for Mrs. Barnet, as well. Therefore, he willed the pain away and then headed to the front of the house where Weber stood waiting, the basket of food and drink on a table in the middle of the round foyer.

"Thank you, Weber," Laurence said. "I believe I shall wait outside for Mrs. Barnet so I can greet her when she arrives."

"Excellent decision, Your Grace," the butler said. "Women appreciate such gestures from a gentleman."

Laurence took the basket and stepped outside. He took a seat on the stone bench that had been placed to the left of the door, the basket on his lap. Moments later, the Lambert carriage came up the drive, and when Laurence looked down at the basket he held, an overwhelming sense of foolishness flooded through him. Only a child waited outside for a guest; certainly not a duke. He would appear too eager and scare off the poor woman in the process.

He jumped up from the bench, but worry seized his feet, rooting him in place. No matter how hard he tried, he could not get them to do his bidding, and in the end, gave up, resigning himself to standing there like a fool with a basket clutched in his hands.

The carriage came to a stop in front of him, and the driver jumped down from his seat to give Laurence a quick bow. Then he placed the step and opened the door, bowing again as he reached a hand out to lend aid to the occupants.

When Mrs. Barnet alighted, everything else around Laurence disappeared as he focused on the woman. She wore a celadon riding dress with tiny white flowers embroidered on the lapels and white lace at the cuffs. A black hat with a yellow ribbon that matched her dress shaded her features, and Laurence thought no other woman could have been lovelier than she.

"Your Grace," she said as she dipped a curtsy to him.

Another young woman followed from the carriage. He blinked in surprise as Miss Hannah Lambert came to stand beside her sister. It never occurred to him she would come with a chaperon.

He bowed to the two women, wondering why his tongue was so tied in knots. When Mrs. Barnet smiled, his worry dissipated, and his tongue unraveled. "Mrs. Barnet. Miss Hannah. Shall we go inside? Or perhaps we should head to the stables first?" Then he glanced at the horses tied to the carriage. "Oh, I see you have brought your own mounts."

"We did," Mrs. Barnet replied. "With little time for riding, I thought bringing our own horses would be best. You know how temperamental horses can be with unfamiliar riders."

Laurence chuckled. "Indeed." He turned to Weber. "Would you see my horse brought about?"

"Yes, Your Grace," the butler replied before snapping his fingers at a nearby footman, who rushed off to do Laurence's bidding.

When Laurence returned his gaze to Mrs. Barnet, he saw she was eying the basket in his hands. "Some food and drink for us all," he said, and then felt relief as Mrs. Barnet smiled again. If Lady Lambert asked him in that moment if he would accept her offer to marry this woman, he knew what the answer would be.

Chapter Five

As she waited for the duke's horse to be brought from the stables, Isabel wondered at the odd addition of the picnic basket the man held in his hands. It was not that the gesture was unkind, but she hoped the duke did not have any romantic notions about this outing. When she glanced over at Hannah, she was panicked to see her sister peering from the basket to Isabel and back again, as if she had the same thought as Isabel. Which only worried her that much more.

The duke seemed to be surprised that Hannah had accompanied her, and Isabel could not help but feel a sense of relief that she was not the only one looking at her need for a chaperon as an absurdity. After her quick appraisal of how he wore his dark riding coat and buff breeches made her a bit breathless, she realized that perhaps her mother had been in the right in sending Hannah. The insufferable woman!

As the duke untied the horses from the back of the carriage, Hannah leaned in and whispered, "Does he intend to get you drunk on wine?"

Isabel felt her cheeks heat. "Hush!" she hissed back. "What nonsense you speak. Now, stop teasing."

Hannah gave a derisive sniff. "It is what men are prone to do, or at least that is what I have heard."

With a glare, Isabel replied, "It is simply an act of kindness and nothing more. Now, enough of your balderdash." She punctuated her words with a firm nod in order to keep her sister quiet as a stable hand joined them, a dark and tall thoroughbred in tow.

The duke brought over Isabel and Hannah's horses, a broad smile on his lips. Isabel had never seen the man smile so, and she had to remind herself that he had few friends, if any. The picnic basket, much like the riding invitation, was meant as a gesture of goodwill and nothing more. She would do as her mother counseled and simply enjoy the time and do what she could to make the man happy, for it was the right thing to do.

"Allow me to aid you," the duke said as Isabel placed a foot on the step the stable hand placed beside her horse, Winterfall.

All white, the mare had been a gift for her sixteenth birthday, and the horse had gone with her when she married; a familiarity in a place that was new to her. When she returned to Scarlett Hall, Winterfall also came with her. She was glad for this outing, for she had neglected the poor animal as of late.

The duke helped her mount the horse, not an easy task in a sidesaddle. Not that she had ever ridden astride; no lady with an ounce of respect ever rode astride. Unless she was a rebellious Juliet, of course.

"Miss Lambert?" the duke asked Hannah, who had attempted to mount her horse, Teardrop, without aid, much to Isabel's angst, and with little success.

"Hannah," Isabel said, attempting to keep her voice even, "allow His Grace to aid you." What had come over her sister? Isabel prayed the girl would not take up behaving like Juliet. As luck would have it, Hannah accepted the duke's help and was soon mounted upon her horse and riding over beside Isabel.

Despite whatever issues the man had with his leg, he mounted his horse with little trouble – and with the aid of the step she and Hannah had used. Once he was upon his horse, he groaned, a grimace on his face as his hand went to his leg. Her heart went out to the man, for she could see the pain he endured, but rather than embarrass him, she fiddled with her reins as if she took no notice of his discomfort.

He had seen she had noticed, for he said, "I apologize." His cheeks reddened considerably, as well.

She shifted in her seat as if to find a more comfortable position. "Sometimes I wish I did not have to deal with all these skirts," she said with a smile. Then she turned to the duke. "I am sorry, Your Grace. Did you say something?"

"No," the duke replied, and his sigh of relief did not escape her notice.

The stablehand tied the basket to the cantle of his saddle and then looked up expectantly at the duke, who waved him away.

Soon, they were riding down the drive side by side. "It is a pleasure having you here as my guests," the duke said.

"We are honored," Isabel replied. Hannah echoed her words. "The weather is ideal. You selected the perfect day for an outing."

"Perhaps luck is with me," the duke said with a light laugh. "Or is it that you and your sister have brought luck with you this day?"

Isabel offered a polite smile and then turned right on the main road, leaving the house and stables behind them. Although she had reservations about coming out today, she was glad she did. For the first time in a long time, her mind was at peace.

"Miss Hannah," the duke said, "are you looking forward to the upcoming season?"

Of all the questions the man could ask, Isabel had hoped it would not be this one. Although she trusted Hannah to watch her tongue, she did not wish to risk it and therefore spoke for her.

"She is quite excited, Your Grace. It is all about which she and her friends speak. The way they carry on, I worry she will leave for London early just so she is able to spend more time there."

Hannah frowned, but the duke let out a laugh. "My sister Harriet loved the London season," he said. Then his smile faltered. "No matter. We are not here to discuss her."

Isabel recalled the former Miss Redbrook. She was a disagreeable woman who preferred rudeness not only toward her peers but to her family, as well. Although Isabel suspected the duke had the same dislike for his sister, it would never be appropriate to speak ill of one's sister in his presence. She could not help but be curious, nonetheless.

The conversation lagged as they crested a hill, and Isabel gazed over a magnificent sight. Stretching before them was a large valley with a spattering of small cottages surrounded by green spotted with yellow flowers and white sheep.

"I have never seen such a view," Isabel said with a sigh. "This is truly marvelous. Hannah, do you not agree?"

"Yes," her sister replied. "It is like the scenes about which the poets write."

"That tree down there?" the duke said. "The large one surrounded by the others?"

Isabel narrowed her eyes and followed where he pointed. Indeed, one tree rose above a dozen or so clustered around it. "Yes, I see it."

"Let us ride there, and then we will rest."

Although Isabel had come on this outing as a way to appease her mother, she found she was enjoying it much more than she had expected. To have a day that took her mind off Arthur was a blessing in itself. Therefore, as she followed the duke down the other side of the hill, she closed her eyes and inhaled a deep breath. Yes, today was a blessing, indeed.

***

The duke flicked the blanket and placed it on the ground in a shaded glen beneath the trees he had pointed out at the top of the hill. He had chosen a place with trees on three sides and the expanse of the valley floor on the other. It made for a wonderful view, as if they were seated in the front row of the theater.

After placing the basket on the blanket, he glanced around. "Your sister?" he asked in confusion.

Isabel felt her cheeks heat. Why was she blushing so much? "She has gone off on her own, I am afraid," she replied, pointing to where Hannah leaned against a tree, her nose already in a book. Despite Isabel's insistence that she remain, her sister had no interest in conversation with Isabel or the duke.

"I came to read," Hannah had whispered while the duke was readying the picnic. "I cannot do that if I must listen to the two of you prattle on about the weather." Then, much to Isabel's chagrin, she had turned and with a sinister grin added, "Just keep control of your lust for the man."

If the duke had not been so close at hand, she would have given the girl a great tongue-lashing! She expected such behavior from Juliet, but not from her quiet, sensible sister!

"I thought this spot would be perfect," the duke said, breaking Isabel from her thoughts. "Do you like it?"

"Oh, yes, Your Grace," Isabel replied with honesty as she sat on the blanket, spreading her skirts around her. "It is lovely."

The duke sat across from her with his legs outstretched. As if absently, he massaged his bad leg. "Would you mind very much addressing me as Laurence?" he asked.

The question caught her off-guard. How could he expect her to be so intimate as to address him by his Christian name?

"We are friends, are we not?" he asked. "We have known each other since we were children."

Isabel shot a glance toward Hannah, but the woman's attention was on her book. She and the duke might have been acquainted as children, but friends? Perhaps it was a sign of how few friends the man had. "Well, yes, I suppose we have," Isabel replied.

He gave her a wide grin, much like a young boy who has gotten his way. "Then I believe friends should be able to speak freely with each other." He opened the basket and produced a bottle of wine. Another surprise. "Furthermore, I do not hear my Christian name anymore and I am quite fond of it." He gave her a wink, and Isabel let out a genuine laugh.

"Very well, Laurence," Isabel said, finding the ability to laugh strangely freeing. "You may address me as Isabel then, since we are such close friends." She could not have put away the grin she wore if she tried.

As Laurence poured the wine, Isabel took in their surroundings. Cool air brought in by a light breeze made tiny strands of hair tickle the edges of her face under her hat. Birds chirped in nearby trees creating a symphony of song. The sun peeked through the boughs overhead to warm her back. She recalled a time when Arthur had taken her to a similar place just two months after they were married, and she had thought her love for him at the time was endless.

"There you are," Laurence said as he held out a wine glass toward her. "Would your sister like a glass?"

"No, thank you," Hannah called from her perch beside her tree. So, she wanted to only give the illusion of giving them privacy. Fool girl. As foolish as their mother believing she needed a chaperon in the first place!

"Would you like a scone? Or perhaps a roll?" He motioned to the basket, and Isabel could not help but smile. Although the man was a duke, he was as hospitable as a vicar.

"No, thank you."

Laurence glanced again in Hannah's direction. "She does love to read," he said. "I remember the girl always had a book clutched in her hand the few times I was at Scarlett Hall." Isabel was surprised how much he remembered from his visits to Scarlett Hall, for she recalled very little.

She gave a small laugh. "It is true. Although, I would rather she cling to her books than behave in the manner of Juliet." When she realized that she had said the thought aloud, she scolded herself inwardly. "Forgive me. I did not mean to complain or speak ill of my sisters."

"Please," Laurence said. "If you feel you must share, I will be happy to listen."

Isabel considered his offer for a moment. How could she share such personal information about her family with a man she barely knew? The need to unburden herself was too strong, and she let out a heavy sigh. "You see," she said in a lowered voice so Hannah could not hear, "Juliet finds trouble at every turn. I am surprised my hair has not turned gray with the number of times each day I must chastise her." She looked down at the untouched glass of wine in her hand. "Please understand that I do not mind looking after her, but I do have my own matters to which I must attend."

"The burden of the family oftentimes falls on the eldest child,"

Laurence said with a sympathetic nod. "Although I can see it wears on you, your strength remains."

Isabel smiled at the compliment. "Thank you," she said. "I do it for my mother. She does not have the strength to handle much at the moment." She clamped her jaw shut. Now she had said too much. If Laurence and her mother were to enter into a business agreement, the words may make him reconsider. "Not that Mother does not have a sharp mind, of course. She is still formidable with any task, large or small."

Laurence chuckled. "I have no doubt in the woman's capabilities. Her daughters are a testament to that."

Isabel smiled at his words, and any concern about being too open with her thoughts disappeared. He was much different than she expected; not that she had many expectations when he came to mind. He was a duke, and most men in his position tended to be overbearing and haughty, did they not? Yet, here he sat beside her to show her that her assumptions had been wrong.

"What do you see for your future?"

"My future?" Isabel asked. This man had a way of catching her off-guard all too often. And yet, it did not make her uncomfortable. "I suppose I have not thought about it all that much, to be honest."

"Well, do you plan on traveling? Or do you wish to remain at Scarlett Hall forever?"

The last stung her heart, for she suspected they rang true. She had no desire to leave her family home, and she hoped to remain living within its walls until her death.

"I have waded in areas that are none of my concern," he said in a quiet voice. "Please forget I asked."

Isabel sighed as she moved her gaze to the surrounding trees. "Your question is not without merit," she replied. Then she looked at the duke. "I do not have any desire to leave Scarlett Hall. It is my home, and I cannot imagine anywhere else I would rather be."

Laurence seemed to consider this for a moment. "I understand. When my parents died…"

His words trailed off, and Isabel could see the pain in his eyes. Her heart went out to him, and instinctively she reached out and placed a comforting hand over his.

He stared at her hand for a moment, and she almost removed it. Something told her to keep it there.

"I had thought there was nothing left for me in this world," he continued. "Of course, there was the dukedom, the estate, but I speak of deeper things. Somehow, I believe you understand my thoughts."

Her heart ached as the memories of the deaths of her father and husband washed over her. "I do," she whispered. "The loss of the conversations once had, the smiles, the embraces. Nothing can replace what was lost."

Laurence nodded. "Like you, I do not wish to leave my home." He let out a small laugh and tapped his leg. "This is one of the most prevalent reasons." He shook his head as if to clear it. "I have another question, if you do not mind."

"Not at all. Please ask."

"What is it that prevents you from leaving your home? Or rather, why do you wish to remain?"

The question bore into her like an arrow from a hunter's bow. Isabel felt an uncomfortable racing of her heart and mind. She did not wish to continue this conversation, and a need to change the topic forced her to set her still untouched glass of wine on the blanket and stand.

Laurence hurried to do the same, a confused look on his face. Yet, he did not ask his question again.

"The homes across the horizon," Isabel said, motioning toward the opposite side of the valley, "do you see them?"

"I do."

"Who do you believe resides in them?"

It was quiet for a moment, and then he spoke. "I imagine families live there. Men who work fields or own their own shops. Women tending children. Indeed, families who are happy at the end of the day." He turned to her. "What do you see?"

The hurt inside her threatened to escape in the form of tears, and Isabel held them back as she had learned to do so well in the past few years. "I see families, as well," she whispered. "Yet they do not know the hurt that is to come in the future. Wives will weep for their husbands. Children for a father who will never return."

She then turned to Laurence. "That pain cannot overtake me in Scarlett Hall. In its walls, I am safe from the suffering I had when I was gone. When I lost my father, so had my sisters and mother, and therefore, we carried our mourning together. Then my husband died, and I returned home once again. Those walls are much like the caring arms of a loved one, for they offer me safety and warmth."

Isabel had never shared these thoughts with anyone before, and she was not quite certain why she did now. Yet Laurence did not judge or argue with her.

"Thank you for sharing," he replied. He studied her for a moment. "Would you like to return to the house?"

Unable to form words, Isabel simply nodded, and Laurence began to pack up the untouched meal. As he worked, she returned her gaze to the cottages once more. There had been a time when she would have wondered what it would have been like to be like those who lived in such humble settings. Now she knew how great the pain was to be in a place that never felt like home, and therefore, she would never risk her heart again.

Chapter Six

After a night of careful consideration, Laurence returned to Scarlett Hall, a ready response to the request Lady Eleanor had made of him on his tongue. The decision was not all that difficult, to be honest, for he had enjoyed his time with Isabel at the picnic. She was a kind soul who was an easy conversationalist; although he could not ignore the obvious beauty she bore.

"Lady Lambert is upstairs, but I will inform her you are here," the butler said. "Would you like to wait in the drawing room?"

"Yes, please," Laurence replied, and he followed the man down the hall.

"Might I get you a drink, Your Grace?" Forbes asked.

Laurence shook his head. "No, thank you."

The butler bowed and left the room, leaving Laurence alone. Laurence browsed the titles of several books on a shelf as he waited, then the sound of light laughter came to his ear. He walked over to the window, which looked over the gardens, and saw the three sisters standing in a tight circle beneath the shade of a large oak. Each wore a smile, but of the three, Isabel wore the largest, and he could not help but hope that smile was for him.

"Your Grace."

He turned to find Lady Lambert enter the room. "Lady Lambert," he said with a bow.

She offered him a curtsy and joined him at the window. "It seems just yesterday they were but small children," she said and then turned to him. "Even you were so young when we first knew you and your family. Now you have all grown into adults."

"Nathaniel is still young," Laurence replied, speaking of the youngest of the Lambert family, and also the heir.

"Indeed," she said with a smile. "And when he returns for the summer from boarding school, his sisters will spoil him with attention, as they always have." She moved from the window. "Would you care to take a seat?" she asked.

"Thank you," he said.

When they were seated – Laurence in a high-back chair before the empty fireplace and Lady Lambert across from him on the sofa – Lady Lambert took no time to get to the point of their meeting.

"Isabel had a wonderful afternoon with you," she said. "It was a kind gesture on your behalf. Did you enjoy the outing, as well?"

"I did. She spoke the truth when she said I do not leave my house often enough." He paused. Would speaking his concerns for the young widow be appropriate? Yet, if he was to follow through on their agreement, he had to speak his mind. "I learned that Isabel does not leave Scarlett Hall all that often, either."

The door opened, and Forbes entered with a silver tray. Laurence and the baroness remained silent as the man served the tea, and then with a bow of his head, the butler left the room, closing the door behind him once again.

"There are certain things you, should understand about Isabel," Lady Lambert said. "When Arthur died, she was distraught, which would be expected of any woman in that situation. She returned to Scarlett Hall immediately after, for Arthur's brother inherited everything, and Isabel and Arthur had yet to have children. The man, Albinus by name – he is the second eldest – was not unkind, but he has his own family, you see. I thought that, if Isabel was in her old home and amongst family, she would have an easier time during her mourning period. Then, as the days passed, she did not want to leave the house. Invitations were ignored or refused without excuse, and I feared she would remain in Scarlett Hall forever."

She glanced over toward the window, and Laurence could see the lines of worry around her eyes. "My Isabel is strong, but I fear the burden, the hurt, she carries is great."

"I see a sadness about her," Laurence replied. "And what you say is understandable, for grief can be a difficult condition to overcome. I have given your proposal the greatest of consideration, and I have come to a decision. I must be honest with you; it was not an easy one to come by."

"I understand," Lady Lambert said with a sigh. "Such matters are never easy."

"No, they are not," Laurence said. "The woman is unhappy, and you are struggling to keep your home. The truth of the matter is, I do not wish to witness either of these situations. As you mentioned, Isabel has fortitude within her, and speaking with her during our outing forced me to see a side of her I did not realize existed. Therefore, I believe we are compatible."

In all honesty, most men would have jumped at the chance to wed the woman simply for her beauty and grace, but Laurence saw something in her, a strength of character and an integrity lacking in many women of the *ton* these days, and he believed those attributes would benefit him as much as they did her. He did not verbalize what he was thinking, for even he could see the selfishness in the thoughts.

"I believe the same," the baroness replied. "I saw a sort of camaraderie between the two of you when you returned from your outing yesterday. Thank you for accompanying my daughters and seeing them safely returned home."

"Of course," Laurence replied. "It was getting late and I did not feel comfortable with them traveling alone. And as to our agreement, if Isabel agrees, I believe we can build a marriage on the foundation of that compatibility."

The woman's shaking hands was the only outward sign of how distraught she was over her current situation, and Laurence could not help but feel pity for her. To be forced to arrange a marriage for her widowed daughter had to be difficult, to say the least.

"If Isabel does this of her own free will," Laurence continued, "I will marry her. In exchange, I will pay off the debt owed, and if you would allow, I would like to review your business accounts. That way you do not fall into debt once again."

"Thank you, Your Grace," Lady Lambert said. "That would be most welcome."

Although Laurence did not think ill of the woman, for she more than likely had little to do with any business matters left by her husband, but he admired her for what she had attempted to do on her own. Women had little training in such things, and he could not fault her for where she found herself today.

"So?" he asked. "Do we have an agreement?"

Her reply came as a whisper. "Yes, we do."

"Very well. I will return in five nights' time to speak with Isabel, so I can hear her answer from her own lips." He stood. "I do not believe it wise to have a grand wedding, so I shall order a special license and contact the vicar in order to hasten the ceremony. If you do not mind, of course."

"Not at all." The baroness rose from her seat. "Then the wedding will take place soon?"

Laurence nodded. "Indeed. I believe a fortnight will be appropriate, three weeks at the latest. She has had her year of mourning, and I have no need for pomp and spectacle. I will also begin the paperwork to clear your debts."

The woman looked down at the floor, clear shame on her features, and Laurence's heart went out to her. "You seem to carry a burden that is heavy," he said in a kind tone. "I do not know if it matters, but I admire your strength and your willingness to correct any error you may have made. There is no shame in righting such wrongs."

"Thank you," she replied, although her cheeks reddened all the more. "I will speak to Isabel this evening."

Laurence offered the baroness a smile. "And I will be on my way. There is much to do."

As he walked out to the waiting carriage, he paused and turned to look back at Scarlett Hall. He could not help but feel sorry for Lady Lambert.

How difficult it had to be for her to admit she had been unable to continue her husband's business arrangements with the same ability as he. He was glad that he would be able to help. He would save their home and, in the process, find happiness for himself with Isabel.

***

Although Isabel laughed with her sisters, an uneasiness remained inside her with the arrival of Laurence. She had no explanation for what it was that bothered her exactly, but she could not help but wonder what matters of business the man found so important that he had returned to Scarlett Hall once again.

"There is no cause to lie," Juliet teased. "Have you fallen in love with the man? Did he seduce you with words as you drank wine together in order to get you to kiss him?"

Isabel glared at her sister. "Your obsession with people kissing is becoming quite redundant. Surely there are other things that are worthy of comment?"

Juliet sighed as she clasped her hands behind her back. "It was only a question," she said with a pout. "And it is with merit. For the man I speak of is gazing at you this very moment from the drawing room window."

Isabel turned, ready to chastise her sister for lying, but her words failed when she saw that, indeed, Laurence was peering out the window.

"You see," Juliet said, the typical haughtiness in her tone, "I do have justification in my suspicions."

Isabel forced a smile and then turned back to her sisters. "Allow me to explain a few things that I believe would benefit you both." She ignored Juliet's raised brow but was pleased Hannah nodded. "Men and women becoming friends is not unheard of. Friends enjoy speaking to one another, and even participating in activities such as riding together."

Hannah nodded in agreement, but Juliet, the ever stubborn one, refused to let the matter go. "Picnic lunches?" Juliet asked. "Do friends also participate in those, as well?"

"Yes, they do," she replied, although she doubted few friends enjoyed such an activity on their own. She was not going to admit as much to Juliet, not if she could help it.

"And conversation?" Juliet said, the haughtiness replaced by thoughtfulness. "Is it appropriate for a woman to speak to a man as one would a friend?"

Isabel nodded. Thank goodness the girl was finally seeing reason. "Yes. It is quite appropriate."

"Good," Juliet replied with a finality that made the hairs at the nape of Isabel's neck rise. "Then I shall have the stable boy prepare me a picnic lunch so we can enjoy a nice conversation together."

Anger flashed through Isabel. "You are twisting my words!" she said. Juliet's laugh made her anger deepen. "One cannot simply do such activities without a chaperon unless they are married." She turned to Hannah. "Is that not correct?"

Hannah nodded, but Juliet gave an unladylike snort. "She is a wallflower. What does she know of men? I am certain I know more than she, and therefore her opinion is invalid."

Isabel had had enough. "You will apologize to your sister at once! She is not a wallflower, and her opinion is just as important as yours."

Juliet sighed. "My apologies," she said, although Isabel did not believe her sincerity. "Please, dear sister, tell us your opinion of men."

Hannah looked up, her cheeks crimson. "Men, that is gentlemen, act in the ways of their fathers. If the father is boorish and uncouth, so will be the son. The same goes for the fathers who act with dignity and elegance. One may have to search carefully, but she might find a few of the latter amongst the multitude of the former."

Isabel was surprised at her sister's response, for the woman had always believed men brutish – all men. Perhaps she had changed her mind. Isabel certainly hoped so.

"Then there are women such as yourself," Hannah continued, a tiny smile playing at the corner of her lips.

"And what does that mean?" Juliet demanded.

"You know the kind," Hannah replied, her words filled with malevolence. "Those who seek pleasure from kisses." Her voice rose as she continued. "Your name will be ruined by the time the season begins, and the only men who will approach you are those who desire a woman who lacks moral value. And that is what you are!"

"Why you…!" Juliet shouted.

As they threw insults at one another, Isabel could only stare at her sisters in shock. How could these two girls be her sisters? They certainly were not dignified enough to be considered ladies! "Quiet!" Isabel snapped, but her words went unnoticed. She looked back and forth between the two and found that all she wished to do was run away.

Yet this was her home, a place meant for refuge from the hurt that resided outside. Somehow, that hurt had found its way in. "Both of you!" she shouted to be heard above the two girls. "That is quite enough!" This gained their attention, and they fell silent. "You two fight like enemies, and I for one am tired of it."

"I am sorry," they said in unison.

Isabel's rage was so great, she did not stop. "I returned to Scarlett Hall for peace, and instead I find more troubles than I can bear." She turned to Juliet. "Kiss the stable boy if you so desire, but remember that you must live with the consequences of such behavior. I do not care." This brought about wide-eyed surprise from the younger of her sisters.

Then she turned to Hannah. "And you. You are smarter than to fall for her words, and yet you do every time. If you choose to have a conversation with Juliet, then you must accept the person she is. Spouting hateful words will not make her suddenly change into someone she is not."

"I was only teasing about the duke," Juliet said in a quiet voice. "I did not mean to upset you."

"I agree," Hannah added. "We will do our best to not hurt you anymore. We love you too much." Juliet nodded in emphatic agreement.

Tears filled Isabel's eyes. "I love you both very much. We mustn't fight. We must support one another always."

Soon, tears were rolling down their cheeks, and Isabel pulled her sisters in for a tight embrace. "We are sisters, and if we do not look after one another, no one else will. I want only the very best for you, but in return, I must have your help."

Juliet pulled away and dabbed at her eyes with a kerchief. "What can I do?"

Isabel took a hand of each of her sisters. "Come on now, join hands." Hannah and Juliet did as Isabel bade, and the three stood in a circle, each holding a hand of another.

The breeze picked up around them, tousling their hair, but no one released her hold to move the wisps from her face.

"I do not know what business mother speaks of concerning the duke, and whatever it is, it does not matter. She is our mother, and we will support whatever decision she makes. I know you miss her doing things with us as she once did."

This brought about a new bout of tears, for they had spoken of the nostalgia of the days before the passing of their father. "But we will do our best to make her days easier. That means no sneaking out to the stables to cause trouble." She shot a glare at Juliet. "And you must honor her request if a gentleman sends a card." This glare was for Hannah. "And likely the most important of all, we must look after one another. That will be the best way we can help Mother. If she is not worried about us, then we have lessened her burden significantly."

"And Nathaniel?" Juliet asked.

"Yes, we will also help more with him." She smiled. "Although, we must not spoil him as we have in the past." This brought on a bout of laughter that was refreshing after the tears. "Today, I ask you to swear that all we have said of supporting one another is true. Do I have your word?"

"You have my word," Juliet replied eagerly. "I may argue with Hannah on many occasions, but I will always be there for her."

Hannah gave a small smile. "Yes, you have my word. Although I may not understand Juliet at times, I do love her and will support her always."

"Then I shall do the same for the two of you," Isabel said.

The three remained holding hands, and each spoke from her heart. Isabel listened carefully, responding to their questions concerning gentlemen, marriage, their mother, and their lives ahead.

Later, when they returned to the house, Isabel felt confident that life in Scarlett Hall would only improve for them all.

Now all she had to concern her was what her mother was planning with Laurence.

Chapter Seven

Dinner that evening had been one of the most pleasant Isabel had enjoyed with her family in some time. She had found peace in her sisters, who were – for now – getting along. A heaviness seemed to have lifted from the home, but their mother remained quiet as she had for the past few months. Something was worrying the woman, but asking brought about little to no response; therefore, Isabel had given up asking long ago. When her mother was ready to share, she would and not a moment earlier.

Once dinner was completed, the family went to the drawing room, as they were wont to do. Each had her favorite activity – Hannah, of course, reading in the corner, her legs drawn beneath the blue skirts of her dress as Isabel and Juliet played a game of whist at the table that sat at the back of the room. Their mother stood at the window and gazed outside, the ribbons of her ivory dress shimmering in the candlelight. She had said very little during dinner and even less after, and Isabel was surprised when the woman requested to speak to her alone.

Juliet and Hannah exchanged quick glances, but neither argued as they retired for the evening. Isabel knew both girls would be asking for a detailed explanation in a private audience once she retired for the night.

"When your father died," her mother said from where she continued to stare out the window. It was doubtful she could see much, as the sun had set not an hour earlier, but Isabel did not ask. "I had made a promise to keep Scarlett Hall in order until the day Nathaniel came of age." She shook her head, the light reflecting off the silver pins she wore in her hair. "In many ways, I succeeded, and in many I failed."

"You have done well, Mother," Isabel said. She stood and walked over to stand beside her mother. "We are all healthy and happy, and you had no control over the death of Arthur."

Her mother gave a brief smile. "You are not happy, are you?"

The question caught Isabel off-guard. Her mother was a widow herself; why would she ask such a thing? She of all people should know the grief of a widow.

"I will be honest with you, Isabel, for I know you can handle the truth."

"Mother?" Isabel asked as worry coursed through her. Something terrible had to be happening for her mother to include her in her worries. "You may share anything with me, and I promise I will not disclose what you tell me to anyone."

"I know that, my child," her mother whispered. "It is why I must tell you that I am unhappy, as well."

Isabel nodded. It was as she had expected all along. "It is why you have been withdrawn as of late. I spoke to Hannah and Juliet today. They have vowed to stop their bickering. If that is the cause, you have no need to worry, for it will end. Or at least they will make a better attempt to get along."

Her mother did not respond right away but instead continued her vigil out the window. Isabel followed her mother's gaze. She could barely make out the light of the stars and moon overhead, but otherwise all she could see was the reflection of the room behind them.

"When I first came to Scarlett Hall," her mother said after a moment of silence, "I was taken by its beauty and size. There is truly no other place like it."

"I agree," Isabel said, wondering where this line of discussion was headed. "Our friends who have traveled all over the world have said the same."

"Your father's family built this home through hard work and honor."

Isabel could hear the choked tone, and she placed a hand on the woman's arm. "Mother?" she asked, worried there was more to her mother's sentiment. "Honor is still here within these walls. It is what has held it together, and it shall remain so for centuries to come."

Her mother spun so quickly to face Isabel that Isabel took a step back in startlement. "No," she said. "Scarlett Hall may soon be lost."

Isabel stared at the woman. Had she heard correctly? "L-lost?" she managed to stutter. "I do not understand. How would it be lost?"

Her mother sighed. "Since your father's passing, debts have increased..."

Isabel forestalled her mother. "Then we shall use our allowances to help pay this debt," she said, certain it would be more than enough. She and her sisters received a very nice monthly allowance, and Isabel also received a small stipend from her husband's estate as a part of his will. "I imagine that the small expenditures that my sisters and I forsake will help tremendously."

Much to Isabel's shock, her mother shook her head. "The debt is great. A sum not worth speaking, for it frightens me to utter the amount aloud. We have only two months in which to pay it or we lose our home."

"This does not make sense," Isabel said. "How long have you known of this debt?"

"For a few years now. I thought I could pay it off without seeking the aid of anyone, but I was wrong."

It was as if the air around her had been removed and the room began to spin. How could this have happened? They could not lose Scarlett Hall; not now, nor in the future.

"No matter what attempts I have made to rectify the problems, they have only worsened."

Isabel did not miss the despondency in her mother's voice, and although she sympathized with the woman, she could not stop the frustration that rose in her. "You have known about this for all this time, and now, with only two months remaining, you thought to mention it? I am not a child, Mother. I have been married, so I understand something about running a household. I could have helped in some way. I am certain Arthur would have offered…"

"Yes, I know," her mother interrupted. "I did everything I could to save our home, but you were a newly married couple and had your own family to worry about. Now, I have no choice but to ask you for your help."

Isabel heaved a sigh of relief. Finally, her mother was asking for someone else to carry the burden, and she was more than happy to do what she could to help. As she mentioned to her mother, the allowances would be of great assistance, she was certain, and if there was anything else she could do, she would agree. She imagined that if she sold most of her jewelry and a few of the heirlooms she had been allowed to take with her when she returned to Scarlett Hall, perhaps that would be enough to cover the debt.

"Of course," Isabel said with a smile. "What is it I can do?"

"His Grace has offered…no, I will restate that. I have asked His Grace to help us."

"Laurence?" Isabel asked in surprise. She had not considered asking anyone outside of the family for help. Yet, what did that have to do with her?

"Yes. He will take care of the debt and also lend his resources and knowledge in handling your father's businesses to get them back into order."

Isabel smiled. "What a marvelous man he is," she said. "And what aid can I give? Does he wish me to go with him on another outing? Or perhaps I am to join him for dinner?"

"You will accept his hand in marriage."

Although the words were spoken softly, they had a firmness behind them that brooked no argument. Yet, Isabel could only stare at her mother in shock. "Marriage?"

"It is the only way to save our home."

Tears of anger overwhelmed Isabel. How dare her mother do this to her! "I am to marry him?" she asked in utter astonishment. "I am to marry a man I do not love? I have not even a slight affection for him!"

"I am sorry, my dear," her mother began, but Isabel cut her words short.

"Sorry?" she demanded. "You know my heart is broken and that I do not wish to ever fall in love or marry again!"

"I have no choice," her mother pleaded as she made an attempt to take Isabel's hand in hers.

Isabel took another step back, wishing to put space between her and the woman who asked too much from her. "Once again I must take responsibility," she said as she fought back the tears that welled in her eyes. "For the happiness of my siblings. While our mother runs our estate into near ruin and hides away, only to appear long enough to ask me to marry a man for whom I do not care." She glared at her mother and refused to allow the woman's pain to break through the wall she built around herself.

Then the truth fell on her like a grand oak toppling to the ground. The proposal might make her angry, it might make her furious, but in the end, she knew she would agree. Therefore, she straightened her back and pursed her lips. "Very well. If I accept his offer, my sisters will be cared for and Nathaniel will have a home to return to when he is of age, am I correct in saying so?"

Her mother nodded.

"If I do not, all that I care about is lost, and the lives of those I love will be destroyed."

"I did not mean for it to come to this," her mother said, a tear sliding down her cheek. "I had no other choice."

"You could have sought help sooner," Isabel said, not caring that her tone carried accusation. "You could have taken control of the spending. There is so much we would have been willing to give up in order to ease the burden, but you never informed us. Instead, you offer a plate of your troubles to me."

"Oh, my Isabel," her mother said in the fawning tone Isabel recognized when the woman wanted something from her. Oh, how she wished she could deny her!

"No," Isabel seethed. "You will not find mercy from me. Not after what you have done. My plan was to grow old in this house, and now, whatever choice I make, it is I who will be thrown out of Scarlett Hall. If I say no, we lose the house and we all must find a new home. If I agree, I marry Laurence and am still forced to leave.

That is my reward for my decision. Either decision sees me removed from the home I love so dearly."

Her mother remained silent, and Isabel was glad she did, for if the woman made any other arguments, or tried to convince Isabel that the decision was some sort of wondrous sacrifice, Isabel worried she would say something she would regret later, her anger was that great.

"When does Laurence expect an answer?"

"In five nights' time," her mother whispered.

"I will give him my answer then," Isabel said and then turned to head toward the door.

As she reached for the handle, her mother called out to her. "I am sorry," she said. "I did not mean to place this burden upon your shoulders. I simply had no choice."

Isabel did not turn when she replied. "Whether or not you meant to, the burden is now mine to bear." She stepped through the door and closed it behind her. She stood there for a moment before what had happened came crashing down around her. Yet she would not weep here in the open. She was no longer a child to throw a tantrum in the hallways as might have happened when she was younger and knew little of life. She would wait until she returned to the privacy of her rooms.

Hurrying up the stairs, she made her way to her bedroom, but when she opened the door, she halted, for there upon her bed sat her sisters in their dressing gowns.

"So?" Hannah asked with excitement. "What did Mother wish to discuss with you?"

Isabel took a deep breath. How she loved her sisters so, and because of her love for them, she could not bring herself to burden them with what had been settled upon her. "Everything is better than fine," she replied with a forced smile. "In fact, it is nearly perfect. Now, tell me what matters are you two discussing in my bedroom?"

She joined her sisters on the bed, and they formed a circle, their legs crossed beneath them. And as they laughed and giggled and shared with one another, Isabel found her mind returning to the request her mother made of her. She struggled between being overwhelmed and being angry with the woman for putting her in such a predicament.

As her sisters laughed and carried on, she pushed those feelings into the back of her mind, for she would rather hear their laughter and bickering than the sounds of misery that threatened to echo within the walls of Scarlett Hall.

Chapter Eight

The day arrived when Isabel was to give her answer to Laurence, and as she stood before the large standing mirror in her bedroom, she thought about the life this unobtrusive piece of furniture had seen over the years of the woman who stood before it. At one time, this mirror had reflected the laughter of a young girl. Then the smile of a woman as she anticipated her wedding.

Now, the person who stared back at her wore a mask of sorrow. If one were to observe her, they would believe it was her reluctance for the upcoming nuptials that made her sad. Her sorrows began well before her return to Scarlett Hall.

Her hand went to a small ornate jewelry box on the table. She hesitated as she stared at the ring on her finger, the ring Arthur had given her on their wedding day three years earlier. Soon, another ring would rest on that finger, a symbol of love to the casual observer. Yet she did not love Laurence, and she never would. How could she love a man who wed her under such circumstances? Any notion of love was impossible in such a situation.

Yet, she would marry the man for the sake of her sisters and her brother Nathaniel. It was their future that was important, and if that meant she was to be without love, then she would do so with a smile. Not to please her new husband, nor her mother, but for her siblings. For they were the future of Scarlett Hall.

It was imperative no one learned the reason behind her marriage to Laurence, especially Hannah, for if she knew, her perception of marriage would only be solidified. The girl might believe she had no interest in love, but Isabel knew her too well; if she became a spinster, she would live to regret it eventually. Hannah might hide behind her books, but she had a passion within her that even she did not realize she carried.

Juliet, on the other hand, would search for a man of wealth rather than marry for love. The younger of her sisters also had passion, but she did not hide it as Hannah did. All too often it got her into trouble, and if she was unable to express it properly – meaning if she did not marry a man she loved – who knew what would happen to her?

No, they could not learn the sacrifice Isabel was making for the afore mentioned reasons, but also because they would do all they could to impede the wedding. If that were to happen, Scarlett Hall would be lost to them forever.

Therefore, Isabel removed the ring that represented her former marriage, placed it in a box, and hid it away, along with her secret.

With a sigh, Isabel walked to the door. She had heard a carriage arrive several minutes earlier, so now it was time to speak to Laurence about their upcoming marriage.

Marriage. Just the thought of the word had her mind racing and made her stomach knot. Yet, she pushed aside the dread and forced her mind to consider not herself, but everyone who would benefit from this arrangement.

She did wonder what benefit Laurence would receive. Was he concerned about heirs? Or, as she had considered before, was he simply lonely? Had he had an interest in marrying her all along? If so, for how long? Certainly, he had not found a sudden infatuation with her. And was the picnic and the words he spoke the day of their outing both means to win her over? Or had he been speaking the truth? So many questions, none of which she was likely to ask – or for which she would receive any answers if she was inclined to do so.

She paused on the landing to look out over the foyer. Sunlight from the setting sun streamed in through the large window above the front door, creating a crisscross pattern of yellowish orange across the ceiling.

How many times had she seen that pattern throughout her life?

How often had she entered through that door as a child? And later as a woman? Soon, she would leave through that door for good, perhaps only to return a few times a year. Yet, had she not had these same thoughts the first time she was wed?

With a sigh, she continued her journey to the drawing room. No amount of recollection would stop the moment from arriving, so there was no need to search for ways in which to forestall it. She halted at the sound of voices belonging to her mother and Laurence coming to her ear. Memories assaulted her senses, catching her breath in her throat. How smooth Arthur had been in his words to her mother – and to Isabel's heart. What she had learned was that behind the sweetness of Arthur's tongue lay bitter lies that would one day sour her soul.

Attempting her best to push the thoughts aside, Isabel regained her steps. In the drawing room, she found her mother seated upon the sofa, Laurence in one of the sets of two chairs across from it. When she entered, her mother smiled, but Isabel did not return it. She might be forced to show contentment to her siblings, but she refused to give her mother the satisfaction; it was her fault they were in this mess in the first place.

Laurence stood and bowed, and she dropped into a flawless curtsy. Would he read the mocking in it? She hoped not, but she also could not help herself.

"It is good to see you," Laurence said as he waited for her to sit.

"Thank you, Your Grace," she replied in formal tones. If he expected her to be friendly, he was sadly mistaken. As he returned to his seat, she could not help but recall how charming he had been during their outing together, and she wondered if that kindness would transfer to their marriage. Or had it been his way of donning sheep's clothing?

"Now that Isabel is here," her mother said as she rose from her seat, "I will leave you two alone to speak. Can I send anything in for you to drink? I can have a tea tray sent up, or Forbes can pour some drinks?"

"No, thank you," Laurence replied. "Unless Isabel wishes something?"

The question rang inside Isabel's head. Did she wish for something? Indeed, she wished for this marriage to not take place. She wished her mother had not squandered their family's fortune to leave Scarlett Hall in ruins.

She wished her father were there to ease the burden; he would have known what to do, and that would not have included marrying her off to some duke she did not love.

"No," she said instead. What good would come about by speaking her thoughts? They would only complicate matters, and in the end, she would marry the duke anyway.

Isabel's mother nodded and left the room, closing the door behind her. A silence that seemed to last an eternity remained, and Isabel considered that perhaps the man was just as nervous as she. Yet, that made no sense; he was a duke, not some young boy who knew nothing of the world.

"Have you considered my offer?" Laurence asked, breaking the silence. "That is…our marriage?"

"I have," Isabel replied.

Before she could continue, Laurence spoke again. "I would like to explain several things before you answer. Do you mind?"

She shook her head. "No, I do not mind." She wondered if he would explain his expectations for her. Perhaps that was a good idea. No one wanted to enter a marriage without knowing what he or she was getting into.

"If you agree to this marriage, which I hope you will, I promise I will do everything I can to make you happy." He sighed as he placed his hands on his knees. He was nervous! "I do not believe that money can bring joy, but it does make life less miserable."

"That is true," Isabel replied. "For without it, well…" She allowed her words to hang in the air.

"I realize we are not marrying for love, but I do not believe that in itself is horrible. I am open to exploring it when the time comes."

What she wanted to tell this man was that she could never love him. That she had tried love before and would not take that chance again. Instead, she offered what she thought would appease him. "I believe we are compatible in many ways. I look forward to that."

Her words clearly placated him, for his face beamed with a large smile and, although she did not feel it, she returned the gesture. She was well-practiced at pretending to be happy, a lesson she learned not longer after taking her vows. An angry man was a dangerous one, and it was better to pretend all was well when it was not than to later face his wrath.

"That is wonderful," he said. "I believe the same. In fact, I believe this marriage will be a blessing to us both." Isabel went to ask why he would believe such a thing, but he barreled past her with his words. "I have longed to be happy, and together, we can explore this new relationship. You will bring the happiness I need, and, perhaps, I can do the same for you."

His words were thoughtful but not realistic. What did this man know of heartache and the destruction of one's soul?

Then it occurred to Isabel that Laurence might not love her, but he did care for her, which was more than she would have if her mother had arranged for her to marry some old baron or a rogue simply because he was willing to pay off the debt she had acquired. Her life could have been so much worse.

"I agree."

Laurence gave her a wide smile. "You will be a duchess; have you considered that fact?"

"No, I have not," Isabel replied. In truth, she had not thought or cared if she received a title. Such things were unimportant in life as far as she was concerned, yet it was expected. As the eldest daughter, the fact she had married a man of the Gentry rather than of the peerage had been enough to wag a few tongues. "It is an honor, and I promise to bring no shame to your family or the title."

"I never expected you would. That is why I am honored to be marrying you." He paused. "The wedding will take place in two weeks. Is there anything I can do for you before then?"

Isabel rose from her seat. "No. I believe we have it well at hand. A short engagement requires a short wedding and, therefore, less planning."

Laurence walked over to her and took her hand in his. "I realize this may not be what you wanted, but, as I said before, I will do everything in my power to make you happy. If you want to explore foreign lands, spend your days reading, whatever you wish to do, you may."

"You are kind," Isabel replied. "Thank you." He was indeed kind. Many men were not so generous. Oh, a man might allow his wife to make lavish purchases, but Laurence spoke beyond what she could buy with his money. He spoke of accepting what brought her joy. She was not an avid reader like Hannah, and she did not wish to explore foreign lands, but she would find a pastime that allowed her some breath of happiness.

"Then I will begin the arrangements," he said as he stepped toward the door. He paused for a moment as he faced the door, his hand on his leg. Was he in pain? Yet, before Isabel could inquire, he was walking again, so rather than bring attention to his impairment, she remained quiet as she followed him to the front door.

When he was gone, Isabel's mother joined her in the foyer. "What was your decision?" she inquired without looking at Isabel.

"Is there a need to ask?" Isabel replied curtly. "Do you believe me so cruel that I would have my sisters suffer? To have Nathaniel return to find his home is no longer his?"

"No," her mother said. "I know you are not a woman who would do such a thing." Isabel made to move past her mother, but the woman placed a hand on her arm to forestall her. "I know you are angry with me. I wish you knew how much this pains me."

Isabel pursed her lips and then replied, "If you knew how much this pains me, you would never have made the request."

Her mother released her arm, and Isabel moved to the stairs. Being angry with her mother did not bring her enjoyment, and it grieved Isabel to speak such hateful words to her. Yet, the woman had brought her family to near ruin, a sin for which Isabel was forced to pay. Therefore, she had every right to voice her opinion, even if the words she spoke stung.

When she reached the top of the stairs, Isabel glanced down at the woman she had once thought strong. Although she still loved her mother, Isabel also understood the strength she once possessed was now gone. And for that, she could not offer forgiveness, for, in two weeks from today, she would be forced to marry, and the remainder of her life would be set for her.

Chapter Nine

W hen Laurence returned home, he realized that, for the first time in a very long time, he was happy. Not only had Isabel accepted his offer of marriage, but it was also clear she shared his optimism. It had been his worry that she would accept but with reservation, and, although he was not ignorant to the fact reservations were expected, her seemingly positive attitude pleased him.

"Good evening, Your Grace," Weber said as he removed the coat Laurence wore, draped it over an arm, and took his hat from him. "All went well, I assume?"

"Not only well; it was perfect." Laurence gave Weber a friendly slap on the back. He knew showing the man such intimacy made the poor butler uncomfortable, but Laurence had few, if any, friends, so the old butler was stuck being as close a friend as Laurence had. "Soon, we shall have a new member of our household."

Weber smiled. "Excellent, Your Grace. Might I ask who this guest will be?"

"She will not be a guest, my good man," Laurence said. "She will be the new mistress of the house!"

"That is good news, Your Grace. And who is this woman?"

Laurence laughed. In his excitement, he had forgotten to mention her name! "Isabel Lambert, or rather Mrs. Barnet. We are to be wed in a fortnight."

"Congratulations, Your Grace. Mrs. Barnet is a sterling example of a lady. I have no doubt the new duchess will fill her role well."

"Indeed. She has a strength; unlike anyone I have ever known. These halls will no longer be empty, for her presence will fill it with happiness unlike any we have seen in a very long time!" Then a thought occurred to him. "Weber, do you believe Mother and Father would approve of her?"

The old butler smiled. "The years I spent serving your parents were some of the finest times of my life. I have no doubt they would be pleased, for they only ever wanted you to be happy."

"Thank you," Laurence replied. "I will retire to the drawing room. Have a bottle of red brought up."

Weber cleared his throat. "You have a guest waiting in the drawing room."

"A guest?" Laurence asked. "I was not expecting anyone, especially at this hour."

"Have you forgotten me already?"

Laurence turned to find his sister Harriet approaching from the hall that led to the drawing room. Her red hair glinted with gold hairpins, as did the jewels on her neck and ears, and her emerald-green gown was of the finest silks covered in the most delicate lace with ornate patterns throughout. Clearly, her spending had not decreased since he had last seen her. He would be surprised if the woman's husband had any money left in his coffers.

"I did not expect you for some time," Laurence said as he leaned in to kiss her cheek. "What are you doing here?"

Harriet snorted. "Do you understand the troubles I have had my whole life, Weber?" she asked of the butler. "My own brother does not welcome me into his home with open arms." She sniffed as the man left without replying. "The old fool never spoke to me anyway."

Laurence took a steadying breath. Old Weber knew who paid his wages. "What brings you here, Harriet?" he asked.

"I needed time away from Ambrose. You there," she called to a passing maid, "get that mangy old butler to bring me some wine to the drawing room."

The maid bobbed a quick curtsy and scurried off to do the woman's bidding, and Harriet threaded her arm through that of Laurence. "Come. Let us go and relax. My journey here was more than taxing."

What Laurence wanted was time alone in order to think and enjoy his contentedness in the prospect of marriage. Nevertheless, he allowed Harriet to lead him to the drawing room.

His sister was disagreeable enough without being denied such a simple request. She could stack requests as quickly as a beaver creates a dam, and the possible disaster left in her wake could be as terrible as the flooding left by the clever rodent. Furthermore, it would not be long before she became bored and returned to her husband in Malmsbury, a half-day's carriage ride from Camellia Estates.

"You need more candles in here," she declared as she took a seat on the sofa. "I have told you before; when one uses few candles, it gives the appearance that one is struggling with money."

"I recall your wise counsel," Laurence said as he went to a cart and poured himself a brandy. With Harriet visiting, the stronger the spirits the better. "There have been more pressing matters with which to deal."

Harriet laughed just as Weber entered the room. The butler poured her a glass of wine and handed it to her with a bow.

"Thank you, Servant," she said in her haughty tone and a dismissive wave of her hand. "That is all."

The man gave an acknowledging nod and turned to Laurence. "Is there anything else you need, Your Grace?"

Laurence waved a hand to indicate he did not, and Weber placed the wine bottle on the table and left the room. It was not the butler who rankled him.

When the man was gone, Laurence turned to his sister. "Weber has been with our family for years. If you wish to call him anything, at least call him by his name."

Harriet rolled her eyes. "You always have treated the servants as if they had any significance. If it were not for me, you would have them wearing clothing like ours rather than the livery they should be wearing."

Ignoring her rude remarks, Laurence walked over to stand behind one of the blue high-backed chairs. "I imagine you are wanting to visit old friends," he said hopefully as he leaned with his forearms on the back of the chair.

"Oh, yes," she replied. "Do not worry, I will keep out of your way." Then she gave him a secretive smile that made him stifle a sigh. "You recall my friend Miss Margaret Portsmouth, do you not?"

"I do," Laurence replied. "Will you be spending time with her?"

"Of course. She is looking for a suitor. You should speak to her. She is much like you in that she rarely leaves her home most days. Although, guilt is not the cause of her monkish behavior." Laurence tensed, and she smiled at him over the rim of her wine glass. "I only speak the truth, and you know it."

He had hoped his sister would leave before he had the chance to inform her of his upcoming nuptials, but it appeared that was not to be. Therefore, with reluctance, he said, "There will be no need for me to meet her, for I am marrying in a fortnight."

Harriet coughed and set the glass on the table. "You are what?" she asked as she dabbed at her chin with a kerchief. "Marrying? To whom? I certainly am eager to know what woman would consign herself to be imprisoned within these walls with the likes of you."

Although anger raged inside him, Laurence tempered it. Too many years had been wasted arguing with this woman, and he had no desire to start that up again. "Isabel Barnet will be my new duchess."

Harriet gaped at him. "Baron Lambert's daughter?" she asked in astonishment. "Has she not already been married?"

Laurence downed the brandy and poured himself another. "She was, and her husband was an honorable man who met his death far too young."

To his surprise, Harriet laughed. Bold the woman was with the servants, but to be so disrespectful of a deceased man who had been of the *ton* was more than unexpected. "You speak as if this man was a friend." She shook her head. "I am sure his wife will find comfort in your coffers."

"Isabel is not after my wealth!" Laurence snapped. "She is not like that."

Harriet stood and pointed at his injured limb. "We both know that your leg is quite the cause for embarrassment for you and those around you. What other reason would she have for agreeing to marry you but to get to your money?"

What he wished to say was that the reason was for their happiness as well as to save a family home. He had learned long ago that any argument thrown at his sister would only be used against him in some heinous way. He had been happy not ten minutes earlier, but now, the old worries crept over him. Instinctively, his hand went to his leg as Harriet came up and placed a hand on his shoulder.

"I know my words seem cruel," she said. "And I know that you secretly hate me."

"I do not hate you," he murmured. And the words were true. Did he find her distasteful? Yes. Worthy of pity? Most definitely. He did not hate her. She was his sister after all and the only remaining member of his family left.

She ignored his protest, perhaps because it came out more as a whisper. "It is only because I care for you. I have always looked after you, especially after the death of our parents."

The statement was silly, Laurence knew, for he had been raised by his mother's brother. Harriet had been but ten when their parents were killed, and their great-aunt Francine had taken her in. She was raised with the best tutors money could buy, and she was for want of nothing. Aunt Francine, a widow by the age of forty, died a wealthy woman at seventy-eight and had left her entire fortune to Harriet.

Laurence chose not to argue with his sister if it was something he did not have to do. What good would come from it? She paid little heed to anything he said unless it affected her in some way.

"It was I," she continued as she took the glass from his hand, "who defended your name when accusations came against you concerning the death of our parents. It cost me dearly, but I would do it again."

What price did Harriet have to pay? he wondered. Yet, as he considered that question, he realized she had paid much. She had lost her parents. "I am not responsible," he said, choking on the words even as he spoke them.

Harriet shook her head. "Let us speak of happier times, not of your past." She took a drink from his glass. Was that a smile that played on her lips behind the rim? No, she was mean-spirited, but she was not cruel. "I plan to leave tomorrow to call on Margaret, but I must admit my funds are low. Do you have a pittance to give your sister?" She pushed her bottom lip forward. "Must a sister beg her brother for a show of kindness?"

He sighed. "No." He reached into his coat pocket and produced a handful of notes. Without waiting, Harriet took them from his hand.

"Thank you," she said in a gay tone. "I am happy for you and Mrs. Barnet. You deserve a woman who will take care of and serve you." Laurence was shocked that she would take time to congratulate him, even on his announcement of marriage. "I shall retire to bed now. I look forward to spending time with you and your betrothed."

Laurence wished his sister a good night, and when she was gone, he poured himself another glass of brandy. What he hoped was that the woman would finish whatever business she had and return home immediately after. Knowing his sister, she would remain simply to drive him mad.

A jolt of pain shot through his leg, and memories returned of how the leg had been damaged and the deaths surrounding it. He downed the entire glass of brandy in one go, hoping the fire it caused in his throat would take his mind from the pain in his leg – and in his heart. Hopefully, Isabel would see past his shortcomings and perhaps one day even Harriet would forgive him his trespasses.

He had learned that one cannot know the future. No, he is forced to wait until it arrives.

Chapter Ten

The days passed by quickly, and on the eve of Isabel's wedding, she felt neither excited nor worried. In fact, she felt nothing but an overwhelming numbness that consumed her heart and soul. As she rolled the wedding ring in her fingers, she wondered at how different her life could have been. If Arthur had not joined his friends in hunting, she would not be a widow today. If her mother had sought help with her finances rather than believing she could manage them herself, Isabel would not be forced to marry a man she did not love.

It was time to put such thoughts aside, for it did nothing to change what would soon take place. She returned the ring to the box and closed the lid, and a knock came to the door. When she opened it, she was surprised to find her sisters standing in the hall.

"What are you doing?" Isabel demanded. "And both of you in your nightgown? You should be in bed!"

Juliet smiled and whispered, "We have a surprise for you. Come. It is the last night before you are married." She giggled and added, "Again."

Isabel went to interject, but Hannah grabbed her by the hand and pulled her from the room. The glow of the single candle Juliet held created a ball of light around them and combined with their intimate knowledge of the house, they hurried through the corridors until they got to the top of the main staircase.

"Where are we going?" Isabel demanded, ignoring her sisters' hushing. "We are acting as thieves."

"I am better than a thief," Juliet replied with a grin. "For I am your sister, and I will not have you leave this home like the last time you were married – without a proper farewell." She shook her head. "If I knew then what I know now…Enough of that. Come on!"

Before Isabel could respond, she was led down the steps of the eerily quiet house. Hannah opened the door and the trio went outside. The moon was full, allowing enough light to see the drive, and Juliet blew out the candle and placed it on the ground beside a large bush.

"Quick, this way," Juliet said in a hushed tone. "It is just past those trees."

Although Isabel was now a grown woman, she could not temper the giddiness that bubbled inside her. It was as though she were a child sneaking away into the night to explore, an act she was certain Juliet did not find foreign. "Hannah, did you plan this escape with Juliet, or did she do it on her own?"

"I did," Hannah replied with a grin. "You spoke of us looking after one another, and it was my planning that will ensure this night will be without incident."

Isabel chuckled, but when she caught sight of an object at the end of the drive, her eyes narrowed. "A carriage?"

"Oh, yes," Juliet replied. "Cousin Annabel wished to take part in tonight's activities."

Isabel shook her head. What were these girls thinking? The truth of the matter was, they were not thinking. Yet she could not see it in her heart to deny them this adventure. At least she would be present to keep them out of trouble.

"Isabel!" Annabel said, hurrying over and pulling her in for an embrace. "I am so happy for you." She, too, wore her nightdress with a dressing gown covering it, and her hair, which was so much like that of Isabel and Hannah, hung down her back in long blond waves. It was no wonder people believed her to be one of Isabel's sisters.

"What are you doing here?" Isabel demanded.

"You have not told her?" Annabel asked, glancing at the other two girls.

"Well, it does not matter." She gave a theatrical bow and added, "Your carriage awaits."

"I appreciate this gesture, I truly do, but I cannot be responsible for your actions this night." She pointed a finger at Annabel. "Your parents will be angry if they learn about this." Then she turned the finger on her sisters. "And Mother will be furious."

Juliet waved away Isabel's concerns. "Annabel's parents are away, so they will never know. And as to Hannah and me? We do not care what punishment we receive. This is our last night with our sister, and we mean to make the most of it!"

Isabel's heart softened as she looked at the three girls who stood before her. No, they were not girls any longer; they were young women. Poor Annabel was left alone often, her parents off on one adventure or another, so she had become more a sister than a cousin. And although Juliet was prone to mischief, Isabel loved her vivaciousness. Hannah, typically the quiet one of them all, wore such a wide grin, she could do nothing but agree to their mad plans, whatever they were.

"Oh, very well," she said to a chorus of cheers. "But we cannot be out late. I am getting married in the morning, after all."

They traveled no more than fifteen minutes before coming to a stop. "Come on!" Juliet said as she jumped from the carriage. "It is over here."

Isabel followed the trio down a path that led to a wide glen where a small campfire crackled inside a ring of stones. Beside it stood a lone figure she could not make out.

"Who is that?" Isabel asked. "And what are we doing here in such a remote place?"

"That is Daniel, the stable boy," Juliet replied in a sing-song voice. "I asked him to arrive early and prepare the campfire for us."

"He is not your personal servant to do your bidding," Isabel chastised. "Perhaps the man needs to rest after a hard day's work in the stables." She could not see Juliet's face in the darkness, but Isabel was certain the concept eluded the girl.

As they approached the fire, Daniel bowed. "Miss Juliet," he said, "I did what you asked me to. Is the fire acceptable?"

Juliet gave the man a smile. "Very good. You have done me proud."
Isabel rolled her eyes.

"Now, I ask but one more favor of you," Juliet continued.

"Yes," came his ready reply. "Whatever you wish."

"Stand guard close by, for while we enjoy ourselves, we would not wish to have unscrupulous highwaymen stumble across our campfire and find we are women of high society. Who knows what they would do to us!" She did not sound one whit concerned that those four women would be found in their nightclothes!

"That I will, Miss," Daniel replied and then moved to the outside of the glow of the fire, facing outward and peering into the near darkness.

Four blankets sat around the fire, and rather than unrolling them, they used them as cushions, for, although the sun had set several hours earlier, it was late summer, so the air was warm enough to not require more covering. This thought made Isabel want to laugh; their state of undress most certainly called for covering!

Annabel pulled a bottle from her bag and held it up for all to see. "This is the finest brandy in all of England. Tonight, we share in it as a token of our love for Isabel."

Isabel looked on in astonishment. Rather than removing glasses from her bag as Isabel would have expected, the girl simply removed the cork and took a drink straight from the bottle! She coughed into her arm before passing the bottle to Juliet. When Juliet drank, Isabel could not help but notice that her sister did not cough, a clear sign that this was not her first experience with drinking brandy. Nor her second, for that matter.

When Juliet passed the bottle to Hannah, the poor girl gave it a concerned look.

"Go on," Juliet said. "I shall make sure the man behind you does not put his hands on you in a disgraceful manner."

Hannah gasped and looked over her shoulder, and Isabel could not help but join in the laughter. With a glare, Hannah took a drink and then grimaced as she handed the bottle to Isabel.

For a moment, Isabel simply stared at the bottle. Although she had not received such attention before her first marriage, she would never be able to express how much this night meant to her.

Therefore, she held up the bottle and said, "We are drinking like thieves in the night. Or perhaps this is what pirates do? Either way, we drink to our future – all our futures!" She smiled and put the bottle to her lips. The liquid burned her throat, but it warmed her chilled limbs and sent a pleasant tingling through her body.

She passed the bottle back to Juliet. "Thank you for this," she said. "I am already enjoying our time together."

"Think nothing of it," Juliet replied. "It is my pleasure...all of ours...to plan this."

Isabel laughed. "We certainly are not acting like ladies tonight, are we? If we are caught, the shame will be great." This made them all laugh.

"Isabel?" Annabel said. "May I ask you something? About your marriage, that is."

Isabel nodded. She wondered if the subject would arise. In all reality, she had expected it, but she had hoped it would not come. She was still steadfast in her decision to not have them learn the truth behind her impending marriage, no matter the cost. And especially not while they had gone to such lengths to celebrate.

"Do you plan to have lots of children?"

"Yes," Hannah said, leaning forward with interest. "I am curious about this, as well. Juliet believes you will bear the man at least a dozen, but I believe four is more to your liking."

Relieved, Isabel smiled as she looked at the curious faces. As much as Juliet believed she was knowledgeable about the ways of the world, she was not, and she had a hard reality awaiting her. "When the time comes," she replied, "Laurence and I shall decide how many children we will have. However," she turned her attention to Juliet, "I can assure you that it will not be a dozen."

This seemed to appease Annabel, but then Hannah asked, "I have a question. Juliet said you kissed Laurence when you were younger, and that is why he has come back for your hand. Is that true?"

Juliet giggled, and Isabel could not help but grin. "No. It was not for that reason."

"Then why?" Hannah demanded. "I thought you would never marry again."

The words stung, and Isabel had to stay her tongue. "The notion of love," she said as she took the bottle from Juliet, "is certainly worthy conversation, but around a campfire on a night such as tonight? No, we have more interesting topics to discuss."

"I agree," Juliet said. "Such as kissing. May I ask...what is it like?"

Hannah gaped at her sister. "You have not been kissed yet?"

"No, silly," came Juliet's reply. "And certainly not by a simple stable boy. My kisses are reserved for a man so handsome that his mere presence will cause women to fall over in envy."

"Isabel?" Annabel asked, "what is a kiss like?"

Isabel laughed. "It is something that is not to be taken frivolously. Only those in love – and married," she added with a glare for Juliet, "but as to the feeling..." Her words trailed off as she recalled the first kiss she received from Arthur. What an amazing experience that had been. "Well, it is wonderful."

The questions continued, and the girls soon talked of men, marriage, and the upcoming season. Through it all, Isabel answered when she could, and sought to give them advice that they needed, while at the same time reserving the most intimate of details to herself.

The night grew long, and as she took another drink from the bottle, she was thankful for the excursion her sisters had planned, as crude as it was around a campfire and brandy straight from the bottle. But it had been done in love, and that meant everything to Isabel. Soon, these three young ladies would fall in love, marry, and eventually leave Scarlett Hall, and she could not imagine spending these last few days in any other way.

Chapter Eleven

Promises. Isabel had made many in her life. She had made promises to be on her best behavior. Given her word to keep a particular secret. Pledged to complete a task asked of her.

Now, she stood in the gardens of Camellia Estates to make a vow to obey, serve, honor, love, and keep until death as she had done when she married Arthur, and her mother and sisters were once again in attendance to bear witness. The numbness had returned, but with her family offering her the grandest of smiles, she at least could force her lips to speak the required words.

One attendee did not offer a smile. Lady Harriet Darlington, Marchioness of Gattlingstone, might have been sister to Laurence, but the two were as different from one another as cats are to dogs. She made it quite clear that she was bored, evident by the tapping of her foot on the cobblestone. She made no comment beyond several sighs. Other than the marchioness and Hannah's family, no others were in attendance, for which Isabel was glad.

The truth of the matter was it was difficult enough to put on the appearance of joy for the few who witnessed the ceremony. Knowing the *ton* and their propensity to gossip, the peerage would wonder at the reason for such a quick wedding, and she did not have the strength to lie. Not at that moment and about such a complex situation. Certainly, she could speak an oath she did not feel, but that was different from skirting around the truth and making it believable with people she barely knew.

The old vicar raised a hand as gnarled as the trees that surrounded them as he recited one of the many prayers. Love would guide their footsteps. A bright future lay before them. The words were meant for Isabel and Laurence, but Isabel hoped her sisters would listen, as well.

Hannah and Juliet – and even Annabel – had been spared the disgrace of a rushed wedding, and although they were not aware of the true reasons behind this decision, she prayed they would capitalize on the time that remained before they were also married. The time as children had come to an end, and now they were women; she prayed they would act as such. How they spent the remainder of their unwed lives was what was important.

"Isabel?" Laurence whispered.

She turned her gaze to him. His wavy hair had been neatly combed back, and he wore a kind smile.

"We are finished."

"Oh," she said, stifling her gasp. "I am sorry. The excitement…"

The vicar offered a polite smile, and Laurence turned to address their families. "It has been an honor to have you here today; to witness our exchanging of vows. I suggest we return to the dining hall where breakfast will be served."

Lady Darlington rolled her eyes, acting less a lady than even Juliet. She might be sister to Laurence, but Isabel hoped the woman would be returning to her own home soon.

"Laurence," the woman said in her haughty tone, "I must speak with you."

"I will meet you inside," Laurence whispered. When Isabel nodded, he walked over to his sister and Isabel joined her family.

Her mother wrapped her arms around her, her eyes brimming with tears. "I am so pleased."

I am sure you are, Isabel thought; although she said nothing, for that blessed numbness stayed her tongue.

"You are a duchess now," Hannah said. "I would never have thought you would receive such a title!" Then she hung her head. "Not that you are unworthy of such a title."

Isabel laughed. "I understand your meaning." She waited out the other embraces and showers of congratulations before saying,

"Shall we go eat?"

"I am hungry," Juliet said. "And tired." She displayed a wide grin, and Isabel could not help but return it. They had returned to Scarlett Hall well past midnight, and it had taken Isabel several hours to fall asleep despite the effects of the brandy.

Laurence approached and said, "May I have a word for a moment?"

Isabel nodded and turned to her family. "I will meet you inside."

"I hope there are scones," Juliet said as she followed Hannah, Annabel, and their mother inside. "I will waste away to nothing if I do not eat soon."

"You are going to become as large as a house if you are not careful," Annabel said with a giggle.

Soon, they were out of sight.

"Is everything all right?" Isabel asked when her family had gone.

"Indeed," Laurence replied. "All is wonderful, in fact. It is Harriet; she wishes to speak to you alone."

Isabel glanced over at the woman in her delicate blue dress and wide-brimmed hat. "Oh?" she asked, attempting to hide her suspicion.

"I believe she wishes to welcome you to the family."

Isabel studied the marchioness for a moment and doubted highly what he said was the case. Rather than argue the fact, she said, "Then I shall speak to her." She forced a smile that Laurence seemed to accept without fault.

She walked over to Lady Darlington, who waited in the shade of a large tree, fanning herself with vigor. "You wished to speak to me?" Isabel asked, pleased that her voice remained calm.

"It must be exciting to be a duchess," the woman said in an overly sweet tone. "Do you not believe so?"

"I am pleased to be married to Laurence, if that is what you ask," Isabel replied. "Whether he has a title or not is of no concern to me."

Lady Darlington looked past Isabel as if she had not spoken. "Laurence," she called, "you have guests inside. Do not keep them waiting."

Isabel was shocked enough at the manner in which this woman spoke to her brother, but when he complied without thought, she was flabbergasted.

"My brother is not the brightest of dukes," Lady Darlington said with a dismissive hand. "Like a dog, he must be trained."

Whatever numbness that had settled on Isabel disappeared, replaced by annoyance. "I believe he is acceptable the way he is," she said in retort, not caring if her tone had a bite to it. If this woman was not careful, she would bite her!

"Oh?" Lady Darlington replied. "Does that include his leg?"

Isabel was taken aback. "Of course. Why would it not?"

The marchioness sniffed. "Most women find the sight of his limp revolting. Like a serving of haggis. It is spoken about in wonder, but it scares anyone away."

"I assure you, his leg – and his title – are of no importance to me," Isabel said, finding it difficult to remain in the woman's company for too much longer. If she did, she might just slap the ninny! "Now, if you will excuse me, I have guests waiting."

As Isabel turned to leave, Lady Darlington caught her by the wrist. "I do not know what game you are playing, Mrs. Barnet, but rest assured, I shall be keeping my eye on you."

"You believe my marriage to Laurence contrived?"

"I believe so, yes," the marchioness replied with a quick nod. She released Isabel and gave her the sweetest of smiles as footsteps approached. "But we shall see," she said, her dulcet tones returned. "I believe that, in the end, we will become good friends. Like sisters."

Laurence walked up to them, but Isabel could do nothing but stare at the woman.

"Sisters?" Laurence said with a laugh. "I had hoped you two would become fast friends, but this is better than I could have hoped."

"We shall do everything together," Lady Darlington said with a smile. "That is, if the new duchess would be so kind as to allow me to be near her?"

Isabel clutched the skirts of her gown to keep from striking the woman. She wanted to call out this woman as a liar, but she could not. Not yet. Therefore, she replied, "Indeed. That would be lovely."

"Brilliant!" Laurence said. "Come. The food is ready, and we have our marriage to celebrate."

As they walked inside, Isabel's stomach began to knot once more. Not only had she gained a new husband to please, but it also appeared she had acquired a sinister sister-in-law, as well.

***

Isabel gathered with her sisters as they waited for the carriage to be brought around. They had enjoyed a lovely breakfast banquet that consisted of pickled herring, honey cakes, a variety of tarts, and lovely rolls dripping with butter.

Now, her family was to leave, and Isabel was shocked when Juliet threw her arms around her crying and clinging as if she did not want to leave.

"I will miss you," Juliet cried. "Will we see each other again?"

Isabel kissed her head and laughed. "Of course we will. We are not but three miles apart. I will be at Scarlett Hall so often, you will wish me to leave!"

"Never," Juliet said as she wiped at her eyes. Then she kissed Isabel's cheek and moved to allow Hannah to fawn over Isabel.

"If I need you," Hannah said as she grasped Isabel's hands so tightly, Isabel thought the bones would break, "may I call over?"

"The silly questions I have received today!" Isabel said with a light laugh. "One would believe I have never been married and away from Scarlett Hall before. Of course, you may call over whenever you wish." She took Annabel's hand. "All of you are welcome." Her words seemed to calm them, and they were less reluctant to leave when the carriage arrived.

As the girls stepped into the vehicle, Isabel turned to face her mother. She did not wish to be angry with the woman any longer, but she could not help the feelings that remained.

"I know you are angry with me," her mother said as if she could read Isabel's thoughts. "And I will not attempt to convince you otherwise." She gave a heavy sigh. "Since the day you were born, I have wanted the best for you. I hope that, one day, you will understand that."

Without so much as an embrace or a kiss on the cheek, the woman left Isabel and stepped into the carriage, leaving Isabel to stare after her. It did not matter, for words failed her. The anger remained, but it lessened somehow. Her mother was right; she only wanted what was best for her. And for her family.

As the carriage drove away, Isabel sighed. Her sisters were returning to Scarlett Hall, and she prayed they would find happiness.

Then the curtain moved, and Juliet pressed her face against the window with her tongue sticking out. The melancholy that had befallen Isabel washed away, and she laughed until the carriage was out of view. Juliet had always been one to change her moods. Sometimes she could frustrate her, but at other times, such as this, she brought her joy.

As she turned, she nearly jumped out of her slippers when she found Laurence standing directly behind her.

"It has been an exhausting day," he said. "Although it is not yet noon, I am tired."

Isabel nodded and then stifled a yawn. "Forgive me. And yes, I am exhausted, as well."

The two stood staring at each other. The awkwardness was palpable, and Isabel wondered what they would do next.

She did not have long to wait, for the door opened, and Lady Darlington walked out. "I am going to call on Margaret," she said, her nose in the air. "Do not expect me for dinner, for I shall be dining with her this evening."

"Give Margaret my best," Laurence called after her.

She waved a hand in reply without turning and then stepped into the carriage that had pulled up in front of the house. Soon, that carriage followed the route toward the main road her family's had.

Once inside, Laurence closed the door, the sound echoing in the foyer – and through Isabel's body. Suddenly, panic overtook her. She was alone in a new home with a man to whom she was married. And although she had considered it a few times, his next words confirmed her worst fears.

"Allow me to show you to your bedroom," he said and then motioned to the stairs.

Isabel found it difficult to breathe. She gave him a nod and followed him up the stairs.

"You will find the pillows filled with the softest down."

"Lovely," Isabel whispered. The man seemed to waste no time in wanting to consummate their marriage. Why had she not considered he would? Even after all the questions her sisters had asked the night before, she had rarely thought about it.

They passed a line of portraits of previous dukes and duchesses, and they stared down at her with accusation in their eyes. Was she worthy to be where they had once stood? A woman once married, and to a man of the Gentry at that? She had been lucky when her mother had agreed to her marriage to Arthur, but now she wondered how that had come about. Perhaps being forced to marry Laurence had been her retribution for being allowed to marry for love the first time around.

"Here," Laurence said as they came to a stop at the top of the stairs, "is where our portraits will hang." He smiled down at her. "I am certain there will be no argument that yours will be the most beautiful."

Isabel could not calm her racing heart, and her "Thank you" came as a choked mumble. He did not notice, for he gave her a wide grin before continuing to the next floor.

Almost at the end of the long hallway, he stopped before the last door and opened it. He allowed her to enter first, and she glanced around her. A dressing table sat between two tall windows, and a wardrobe twice the size of hers back home sat against a far wall. It was the massive four-poster bed with white and pink striped drapes and matching cover that stayed her breath.

Try as she might, no excuse would come to mind to put off the inevitable. She had to be resigned to her fate.

"Isabel?" Laurence said, concern marring his otherwise handsome face. "Are you all right?"

"It-it is lovely," she said, her eyes falling to the bed once more. "I-I will prepare myself." She swallowed hard, hoping her breakfast would not make a sudden return.

Memories returned of her wedding night to Arthur. What she had hoped would be a celebration of love, and instead her fears had been ignored. She had a duty as a woman, or so proclaimed her new husband, and those words haunted her the entirety of their marriage.

Laurence placed a hand on her shoulder, making her start. "No," he whispered. "This is your bedroom, not mine."

Confusion ran through her. "I-I do not understand. If this is my bedroom, where is yours?"

"Next door, at the end the hall," he said with an amused smile playing on his lips. "I understand this marriage was not planned. I know we were not married because of love, that is, love of lovers." He sighed. Was he as nervous as she felt? "We have our whole lives ahead of us, and I will never make any demands on you. Whatever we do, it should be done in love."

A single tear rolled down her cheek. For the first time in several years, someone had taken consideration of her feelings.

"Rest and we shall talk later."

He turned and she placed a hand on his arm. "Laurence," she said, "thank you. You have extended much kindness to my family. And to me."

"You are most certainly welcome," he replied and then left the room.

Isabel sat on the long chest at the end of the bed and looked around her new room. Although she was angry and saddened by her circumstances, she was also aware of the fact that Laurence continued to treat her with the utmost respect. She had thought the man wished to take her to his bed, but instead he had sought to comfort her. And, although she did not love him, it was in that moment that she realized that she did hold a small affection for him. Perhaps it was just the seed that was needed to grow a love they could share together.

Chapter Twelve

Isabel opened her eyes after falling into an exhausted nap, and for a moment, she forgot she was no longer in Scarlett Hall. Memories of the day's events flooded her mind, accompanied by a sadness at how much her life had changed and a curiosity at what her life would be like from this day forward.

She rose, glad to see the sun still high over the horizon, and she was thankful she had not slept the day away. Then again, what would she do now that she was in a new home? With a new husband?

Sighing, she splashed cool water from the pitcher on her face, and the sleepiness dissipated. Reinvigorated, she dressed, arranged her hair, and then left the room. The house was eerily quiet as she made her way down the shadowy hallway, and she stopped before one of the portraits. The former Duchess of Ludlow had been a beautiful woman, and Isabel remembered the few times she had spoken to her. Not only was she lovely, but she was also kind to those around her, and her wit had been entertaining. Laurence, she realized, was very like his mother in those ways.

"Do you remember her?" Laurence asked, causing Isabel to start. "It has been so long, I sometimes forget what she looks like until I see this painting."

"I remember her quite well," Isabel replied. "I was just thinking what a kind woman she had been."

Laurence nodded. "My father would say that she held her title so well that no other should be allowed to be called Duchess." He smiled and shook his head. "At the time, I did not understand what he meant. Now, I do." He turned to Isabel, the smile remaining. "I believe you will fill the role perfectly."

"I will try," Isabel said, her cheeks aflame.

"Now that we have rested, I believe it is only proper to introduce you to your new home."

Isabel smiled. "Thank you. That would be nice." And she was surprised when she realized that it was true.

She followed Laurence to the first door. "This is the room I had when I was young, but I had it redecorated when I moved into the suite down the hall. Now, I call it the Blue Room, and it is reserved for guests." He sighed. "Not that any guests have used it, for there have not been any in quite a while." He frowned, shook his head, and then opened the door.

Isabel peered into the room. Indeed, it was a blue room. The striped wallpaper, carpet, bedding, and window trimmings were one shade of blue or another. It was a lovely room, in all honesty. "Is this where your sister sleeps when she visits?" she asked.

"No. Her room is in another part of the house. She claims this is too small for her, although her room when she was younger was of the same size as this."

"She does not stay in her childhood room?" Isabel asked in astonishment. "I would never give up my bedroom at Scarlett Hall to be used as a guest room. Where would I stay when I go to visit?"

He chuckled. "If she had it her way, she would appropriate my room for herself. But no, she insists on being as far away from me as she can manage, so she confiscated the largest in the west wing."

He shook his head as he closed the door behind them and continued down the hallway. Three more rooms, all named for the color that dominated the room, followed. At the end of the hall were a set of double doors, and he swept them open. "This is my room."

If her bedroom was large, his was massive and had a clear masculine taste in the décor. The large bed had deep brown drapes that hung to the floor. A large dresser held a flawless mirror and a pair of wardrobes lined one wall. On the floor was a round rug with splashes of orange and rust mixed with the brown.

"Is this the brown room?" she asked teasingly.

He laughed. "No, but perhaps we should name it as such."

Along one wall was a large window and another set of double doors. "A balcony?" she asked in shock.

"Oh, yes. One of my favorite places."

"May I?" she asked as she indicated the door. She imagined what she could see from such a wonderful location would be lovely.

"Isabel," he said with a warm smile, "this is your home now, too. Never ask where you may tread, for it is all yours as well as mine."

Smiling, she opened the doors and stepped out onto a wide balcony that held an ornate wrought iron table and a set of matching chairs. "What a marvelous view," she gasped as she walked over to the iron baluster.

"I could not agree more. I often find myself staring off from here for hours."

"And no wonder," she replied. "I could do the same myself."

"Then join me whenever you please."

She gave him a smile. How kind this man was! He did not force himself upon her, nor did he set expectations, and for that, she felt great relief.

With reluctance, she followed him from the room and down the main staircase to the drawing room. "Of course, you have been here," he said.

She nodded. "I have. It is a lovely room."

They visited a study that he clearly used as an office and a library filled with books on all sorts of subject. It was the ballroom that left her in awe.

"Oh, Laurence, it is magnificent!" she said as she walked out to the middle of the room. It had tall white pillars and gold walls trimmed in white. Wall sconces lined both sides of the room and two grand chandeliers hung from the ceiling.

The wooden floor had been waxed to a bright sheen, and she could easily envision herself spinning in such a lovely place. Then she turned to him. "Your home...our home is beautiful."

"I am glad you believe so," he said with a chuckle. Then he glanced around as if in search of eavesdroppers. "May I share a secret with you?"

Isabel could not help but giggle. "Of course," she replied, lowering her voice, as well.

"You must not tell Harriet," he said, his face solemn. "She would not understand, and I do not wish to explain myself to anyone, but especially not to her."

Isabel thought the comment odd. He was the duke. Why would he have to explain himself to anyone, including his sister? "I promise."

"This way, then," he said.

They walked to the far corner of the room, and Laurence placed his hands on one of the panels. With a wink, he lifted it, and to Isabel's surprise, it swung into the wall.

"A secret passage?" Isabel gasped.

"It is," Laurence replied and then stepped inside.

Isabel paused. "It is very dark in there," she said, doing her best to search out Laurence and seeing only the vague outline of his body and the white of his cravat and the lace on the cuffs of his coat.

"Do not be afraid. I may not be able to chase after any ghosts, but I will do my best to fight them."

Isabel could not help but laugh, and she took the hand that he thrust through the opening. Once inside, Laurence closed the panel. With her hand still in his, he led her a dozen or so steps forward in complete darkness. Then she heard a scratching noise, and a door opened, light streaming into the passageway. She had to squint against the sudden light that came from a large window.

"This is my secret room," he said. "Only you and a few trusted servants know about it."

Isabel looked around as Laurence opened the drapes. The window looked out into the garden. It was not the view that caught her attention but rather numerous canvases that dotted the room. Two easels sat in different places, one facing the window and one away.

And leaning against every space along the walls were various paintings of landscapes, animals, houses, parks, everything imaginable.

She walked over to a painting of a horse in a field. "You painted these?"

"You speak as though I have committed some offense," he said with a laugh.

"Oh, not at all!" she said as her eyes soaked in the artwork. "These are quite good."

"Thank you," he replied. "It would not bode well for people to know my secret, but it is something I enjoy doing quite often."

Isabel turned and smiled at him. "Well, your secret is safe with me. You are a talented artist."

"You are too kind." He paused. "Do you paint?"

"I?" she asked with a laugh. "No. I have no artistic abilities whatsoever. My father brought in a tutor once when I was young to teach me to play the pianoforte and they both gave up after a month when I still could not play the scales."

He chuckled. "I will keep that in mind in case I ever think of asking you to play." He gazed at her. "If you would like, I can teach you how to paint. I promise you will learn at least the basics in much less than a month."

His offer was kind, but Isabel had no interest in taking up any activities, least of all painting. The idea was even less appealing than playing the pianoforte had been. It all seemed so...intricate. Yet he appeared so beseeching, she could not get herself to turn down his offer right away. "May I think on it?" she asked. "I still feel overwhelmed by the day's activities."

"Of course." He looked down at her and smiled. "It feels as if you have been here for years."

Isabel said nothing. What could she say? 'Actually, I want to return home to my mother'? No, she could not hurt him in such a manner.

"Well, we will need to dress for dinner soon," he said, returning to close the drapes once again.

Isabel followed him down the dark passage and the brightness of the ballroom. She was glad for the tour, for it helped her take the first steps in seeing Camellia Estates as her home. She was also glad dinner would be served soon, for she found for the first time since yesterday that she was hungry.

Although the morning reception after the quick ceremony had offered a fabulous array of choices, she had been much too nervous to eat a bite.

As she dressed for dinner, she considered his offer to teach her, although she found it kind, she decided she would leave him to enjoy his favorite pastime alone. It was not that she did not enjoy his company, but spending too much time together might bring about false feelings that would only end in heartache.

This was something she had learned firsthand.

***

Laurence closed the book on which he was unable to focus and placed it on the table beside him. His hand went to his leg of its own accord, and he rubbed at the ache that was a constant part of his life as he thought on the day's events. He had not been surprised when Isabel retired once everyone had left Camellia Estates after the wedding breakfast, but he was disappointed when she refused to join him for a drink in the drawing room after dinner.

He took a sip of his brandy as he thought of the other disappointment he had endured after dinner. Isabel had refused his offer to teach her to paint, and he found that refusal to be more devastating than the other. Sharing his pastime with her had been a difficult decision, but she was now his wife, and it would be unfair of him to keep any secrets from her.

Painting was the one activity that he could enjoy because of his leg – so many others required either physical strength or a prowess he did not possess. It also gave him the opportunity to transfer all his emotions from his heart to the canvas.

"This is only the first day," he mumbled into his glass. There were more days to come, and therefore, he would remain patient. Her reaction to learning of how he amused himself had been genuine, he was certain, and that led him to believe there could be hope she would change her mind in the future. As long as she was happy in her new life, that was what mattered to him the most.

The door opened, and Harriet entered the room, her skirts swirling around her ankles. "Margaret is such a bore," she said in exasperation. She already had a glass of wine in her hand.

Laurence recognized the look on her face all too well; she was about to unleash her disdain for her friend.

And indeed, she did. "Even her husband is a bore. All he enjoys doing is reading." She glanced at his book with disgust. "Much like you."

"There is nothing wrong with reading," Laurence said. "It is exciting to go on adventures and not even leave the house. You can also learn all sorts of new things. For example, there are new animals discovered in foreign lands..."

Harriet waved him off with annoyance. "I do not really care, if you must know." She glanced around the room. "Where is your new wife? She has not left you already, has she?" She threw her head back and laughed as if her words held great humor. "I was only teasing. But the question remains; where is she?"

"She has retired early. Preparing for the wedding and then the day's events have left her overtaxed."

Harriet clicked her tongue. "I still do not understand why you did not leave for a honeymoon." Then she glanced down. "Is it because of your leg?"

Laurence downed the remainder of his drink. He hated to admit, especially to Harriet, that part of the reason he rarely made an appearance in public was because of his leg, and that included going on a honeymoon. The other reason they remained home rather than traveled was because he did not wish to put Isabel in a situation that was unnecessary. "We will take a honeymoon at a later date," he replied. His sister did not need to know every intimate detail of his and his wife's plans.

This seemed to appease her, for she leaned back into the sofa. "It is a shame she is in bed already. I did wish to see her again." She sighed. "I suppose there is tomorrow."

"There is," Laurence replied. He picked up his book once again and opened it at the page he had been reading earlier, hoping Harriet would take it as a signal that he wished to be alone.

His ever-selfish sister ignored the gesture. "Have you arranged for her to buy new dresses yet? Or jewelry?" Laurence glanced up from his book but did not speak. "I can see by your look you have not considered it."

"I have not. If she wishes to buy a new dress or jewelry, I do not care. But she has not made any mention of it."

Harriet stood and walked over to the liquor cart. "Laurence?" she asked as she poured herself a healthy measure of sherry. "Do you remember our mother?"

Laurence heaved a heavy sigh and closed his book "Of course I do. What about her?"

"Do you recall her wearing dresses of the finest fabrics?"

He nodded. What point was she trying to make?

"How about her fingers or her neck? Were they bare?"

"No," he replied, not hiding his impatience. He did remember that their father never spared the smallest expense when it came to their mother, but what did that have to do with Isabel? "What does all this mean?" he demanded.

She handed him a new glass of brandy. "You are fortunate I am willing to take the time to look after you," she said as she returned to her seat. "If you were left to your own devices, you would destroy our family name within six months of this wedding."

"Speak plainly," Laurence said, tired of her beating around the bush. "What is it you are wanting Isabel to do?"

His sister took her time to reply, swirling the sherry around in her glass before giving a dramatic sigh. "You cannot have Isabel as your wife and duchess walking around without jewelry and fine gowns. That is, unless you do not care for her as Father did for Mother."

"I do want the best for my wife," he argued. He thought again about how his father acted toward his mother. The truth of the matter was, his father allowed his mother free rein to buy anything she wanted. He sighed. "I will send Isabel to town tomorrow. There she can buy whatever she pleases."

Harriet groaned. "You are such a fool," she said. "Her father might have been a baron, but that does not mean that she had access to the kind of money a duchess has. How will she know which gowns to buy or the best jewelry to match? Then there are the hats, gloves..."

"All right," Laurence interrupted. "But you know I prefer not to go into town. Would you be willing to accompany her?

That is, if she is willing to go shopping."

After several moments of what appeared to be careful consideration, Harriet replied, "I did promise Margaret I would call on her again tomorrow, but Isabel is now my sister-in-law; I would like to see her succeed." She still appeared to be contemplating her decision.

Laurence nodded. "Please," he said, hoping he would sway her decision.

"Oh, do not beg," Harriet replied. "You have done enough damage to our family already. It appears it will be up to me to save the day once again." She downed the last of her sherry and placed the empty glass beside her empty wine glass on the table. "Then I am off to bed, for we will have an early day tomorrow."

"I appreciate you offering to accompany Isabel," Laurence said. "Being newly married cannot be easy for her."

"By the way," she said, stopping at the door, "my funds are low, and it will be difficult for a woman to help another and suffer the embarrassment of being unable to buy a dress for herself."

"You may put it on my account," Laurence said with a sigh.

"Thank you," she said with a wide smile. "Perhaps there is hope for you yet. Goodnight, Laurence."

When she was gone, he opened his book once more, but his mind kept returning to the words Harriet spoke. His sister could be, and had been, cruel on many occasions, more so since his parents died. Yet, although he wanted to rebuke her often, she had those moments when he appreciated her candor.

Then his thoughts turned to the times when she was not as helpful, and he knew her accusations were true. It was his fault his parents were dead, and he had his disfigured leg as a constant reminder of that fact. He had destroyed their family, and he hoped one day Harriet would forgive him. For now, he cared only for Isabel and what she thought, for if she was able to look past his sin, then perhaps, in that, he would find forgiveness.

Chapter Thirteen

Isabel had planned to spend her first full day at Camellia Estates walking its corridors and acclimating herself to her new home. She had already written letters, one each to her sisters, brother, and mother, and strolled through the garden, and planned to begin exploring after having a few bits of breakfast. Laurence met her at the bottom of the main staircase as she made her way to the dining room, a wide grin on his face.

"Good morning," he said. He hesitated and then leaned forward to kiss her on the cheek. "I hope you slept well."

She had to stop herself from raising a hand to the place where he had kissed her, for her traitorous body found the intimate display pleasing. Luckily, her mind had more influence over her sensibilities.

"I did," she said in response to his question. She looked past him and was surprised to see his sister leaning against the door jamb of the dining room tearing a piece from a buttered roll, a small smile playing on her lips. "Good morning, Lady Darlington."

"Indeed, it is a good morning," the woman replied before popping the tiny morsel into her mouth, that smile remaining. There was a smugness to it, and Isabel could not help but wonder what the woman was up to.

"You seem pleased this morning," Isabel said as she walked past the siblings and into the dining room.

"I am," Laurence replied. "Harriet made a suggestion yesterday, and I thought it a marvelous idea. Today, you and she shall go into town and visit as many shops as you please. If you find something you want, feel free to put it on my account. If I do not have an account at a particular shop, set one up in my name."

"Shops? I need nothing."

"Oh, my dear Isabel," Lady Darlington cooed, "you do not care if I address you by your Christian name, do you? I mean, we are sisters now, are we not? I must admit I have always wanted a sister." She shot Laurence a look of disdain. "Unfortunately, all I was burdened with was him."

What Isabel wanted was for the woman to leave her alone, but it was clear that was not to be. As uncomfortable as it was to have the woman address her so intimately, perhaps it would ease the tension that clearly existed between them. Therefore, she gave a nod to her head.

"Wonderful," the woman said dramatically. "And you will call me Harriet. Now, what my brother was trying to say was that, as a duchess, you must continue in the role our mother played."

"I have promised I would," Isabel said, uncertain the point the woman was attempting to make. "Have I upset you in some way?" she asked Laurence.

"Not at all," he replied quickly. "It is just that..."

"Allow me," Harriet interrupted. "You are a man and can never understand the ways of women." She turned to Isabel. "My mother was the duchess of all duchesses. Her beauty, her elegance, her style, were admired by all. Laurence only wishes to continue her legacy, and that can only be accomplished by assuring you have the best of everything."

Isabel glanced at Laurence, who nodded emphatically. She did not wish to go into town, and certainly not with Harriet, but if she did so, perhaps she would be given some time alone either in town or when they returned.

"An outing does sound pleasant," Isabel lied. "Will you be joining us?"

Laurence shook his head, but his sister answered for him. "He is much too busy with work." She walked over to Isabel and took her by the hand.

"Come. We can leave now. I have already asked that the carriage be brought around."

"But, I have yet to break my fast," Isabel said in astonishment. This woman was by far the most intrusive woman she had ever met! "Nor am I properly dressed for an outing."

Harriet clicked her tongue. "I imagine we will find a tea house or inn where we can sit and share in a pastry or some other food. And as for your dress, you may be right. We have so much to do today, we should be going as soon as possible, and therefore, it will have to do." Soon she was dragging Isabel toward the front door.

"Please, enjoy yourself," Laurence said as he followed behind. "And spare no expense. If you see anything that piques your fancy, have the proprietor send me the bill."

Before she could refuse, her wrap was thrown around her shoulders and a hat placed upon her head, and Harriet was dragging her to the waiting carriage.

"Our first outing as a family," Harriet said with a smile as the vehicle made its way down the long drive. "I must admit that I enjoy a day of shopping." She tilted her head and furrowed her brow. "You seem distressed."

Of course, she was distressed! She was practically trussed up and thrown into a carriage against her will with a woman who had threatened her the previous day. What did this woman expect?

"I realize we got off on a bad start," Harriet said with a sigh as if hearing Isabel's thoughts. "You must understand my position. My only brother, the heir to a great fortune, marries a woman he barely knows..."

"We have known each other since we were children," Isabel argued, although she should have admitted that Harriet was correct in her assessment of the situation. Something about this woman did not sit well with Isabel, and therefore, she refused to give the woman any advantage, for the truth was, she did not trust her.

"Those few times my parents called on yours?" Harriet asked with a sniff. Then she waved her hand. "But that is not of any importance now. I can see that my brother has an affection for you, and many marriages have been built on less. That is why I suggested this outing.

We are now family, and it is my duty to see you welcomed with open arms. And to see that you are put on the right path to fill Mother's shoes." She said the last as if it was a great burden, and Isabel could not stop the feeling of unease it brought her.

Yet, she did not know the role of a duchess. As a baroness, her mother had her expectations, but a duchess was a much more important position in society. Perhaps Harriet was right; Isabel did lack knowledge in this area.

"I appreciate you taking the time to help me," Isabel said finally.

Harriet smiled. "Think nothing of it," she replied as if what she was doing was of no consequence. "I will be honest with you. Laurence asked me to be here to help you make the transition. I did not particularly wish to leave my home in Malmsbury, but if Laurence asks for my aid, as his sister, I suppose I should come."

Isabel studied her new sister-in-law for a moment. If she – Isabel – had been summoned by one of her siblings for a particular task, would she not go running? Indeed, she would. Furthermore, if one of her sisters married a man of lesser means without a period of courting, she would be as suspicious of the man's intention as Harriet was of Isabel's. For the first time since meeting this woman, Isabel felt a connection with her.

"I appreciate your honesty," she said with a smile that, for the first time since meeting Harriet, was genuine.

"I always try to be honest," Harriet said with a small smile. "And we are family." She took Isabel's hand in hers. "We live and die together."

Isabel could not stop the small shiver that ran down her spine, but she pushed aside the remaining reservations and returned the woman's smile. Laurence wanted Isabel to be happy and had sent his sister to attempt to do just that. It was not his fault that Isabel could never be happy no matter how many dresses or hats she owned.

***

After a hectic day of shopping – Harriet had insisted they visit every dress shop, millinery, cobbler, and haberdasher the town had to offer – Isabel returned to Camellia Estates pleasantly exhausted. She had been poked and prodded, dressed and undressed, and run off her feet for hours.

They had visited three dressmakers before Harriet was satisfied with the selection of fabrics and quality of work, where two separate women took her measurements – Harriet insisted the first were incorrect – and they spent more than an hour scouring the plates of just one book of drawings. It was not long before Isabel became lightheaded – she had been dragged from the house before she was able to eat a bite, after all. Luckily, the proprietress sent one of her girls to a nearby bakery to have a selection of tarts brought in, and Isabel felt much better after eating one with apples accompanied by a cup of tea.

The dressmaker was followed by a visit to both jewelers, where Harriet insisted Isabel purchase two rings – one with a large diamond surrounded by sapphires and another with the largest ruby Isabel had ever seen – two gold necklaces, a variety of pendants, and a brooch in the shape of a butterfly, three emeralds for its body and spun gold for the wings.

As they entered the house, Harriet sighed as if she, too, shared Isabel's fatigue. "I believe I will go upstairs and freshen up." She turned to the butler – Weber, if Isabel remembered correctly – and shoved her hat into his hands and waved at the boxes a liveried servant set on a nearby table. "Have that brought to my room."

"As you wish," Weber said with a bow.

Isabel stared at the woman. The manner in which she treated this poor butler was despicable, and she offered the man a small smile, for which she received the smallest upturn of his lips in return. That was enough to tell Isabel that he appreciated her kindness. Then he was off to do Harriet's bidding.

Laurence walked up to Isabel. "Tell me about your day," he said with a wide grin before leaning in to kiss her cheek. Once again, that warmness ran through her, and she had to force it away in order to reply.

"It was an adventure," she said with a laugh. Then she removed a package that contained several small boxes tied together with a ribbon. "Harriet insisted I get these, but I believe them to be too much."

He opened one of the boxes, which contained most of the jewelry she had purchased. "They are beautiful," he said when he had seen them all. "And your dresses? Were you able to find any you liked?"

"Yes, thank you," Isabel replied. Her feet hurt, and all she wanted was a bit of time alone. "Would you mind if I take some time before dressing for dinner to rest in the garden?"

He chuckled. "Of course. It is your garden, as well. Might I bring you a glass of wine?"

"That would be nice," she said with a smile.

Laurence nodded and walked away, and Isabel made her way to the drawing room, for it had a door that led to the gardens. The quiet of the place was a welcome relief after the hustle and bustle of the day. No, of the last two days. The thought of spending another moment with Harriet made her stomach churn, for the woman talked incessantly, typically laden with complaints.

What confused Isabel more was how the woman had accused her only yesterday of marrying Laurence for his money, and then today, she forced her to spend an exorbitant amount on things she did not need. And all the while, she pretended they were the best of friends.

"There we are," Laurence said as he took a seat beside her on the bench she had chosen beside a lovely lilac, its fragrant scent calming. "That wine is one of my favorite vintages that I keep in stock."

"Thank you," Isabel said, and she took a sip to please him. "Very nice," she said with honesty.

"I am glad you like it," he replied.

They fell silent for several moments, that awkward silence two people who have just become acquainted endure.

"Did Harriet make any purchases?" he asked.

"She did," Isabel replied, although she did not quantify her response, nor did she make mention of the many rings the woman had stored away in her pockets.

Laurence glanced over his shoulder toward the house. "I told her she could make purchases today." Isabel was unsure if he was simply telling her this or if he was asking her permission. "Her funds are short at the moment. I thought it would be a kind gesture on my part." He paused and took a drink of his wine.

Was he nervous somehow? And why did he deem it necessary to share with her the current financial situation of his sister?

"Did you enjoy her company?"

The last question was asked with concern, and Isabel knew she could not tell him the truth outright. "I must admit, Harriet is…sociable." She could not think of a better word, and she certainly could not use exasperating, although it was much more accurate a term. "I admit that it has been a while since I have experienced such a day."

Laurence let out a sigh. "Good. I have to admit that I was concerned."

A question came to Isabel. "How long will she be staying with us?"

Laurence rubbed his chin. "I am not certain, but I believe only a few more days. You do not mind, do you? Did you want her to leave sooner?"

"Not at all," Isabel lied. If having his sister nearby pleased him, she would do what she could to make the most of the woman's visit. "It is just that I am missing her already. I want to cherish every moment I can with her." Although the lie burned her tongue, it was worth the reaction she received.

"I am pleased," he replied with a wide grin.

As they sat together on the bench, an easy silence fell around them. She did not mind being in his company. He was so unlike his sister – quiet where Harriet was boisterous, thoughtful where his sister would speak whatever was on her mind without deliberation, and selfless where Harriet thought only of herself.

Laurence placed his hands on his knees. "I must go dress; dinner will be ready soon. Braised lamb with a complementary wine sauce."

"That sounds lovely," Isabel replied as she stood. "I believe that sounds nice enough to send me rushing to dress for dinner."

He offered her his elbow, and she threaded her arm through his. They walked into the house without speaking, as if there was no need for words.

At the bottom of the main staircase, he stopped and said, "I have a few things to finish before I dress. I will see you at dinner."

She paused before continuing. "Thank you again for today," she said.

He gazed down at her, and for the first time in his company, her heartbeat quickened. "Of course," he replied, a huskiness to his voice.

She hurried to her room and closed the door behind her, leaning breathlessly against it. With her hand on her breast, she willed her heart to return to its normal pace. It had been several years since she had experienced such a reaction to a man's closeness, but she pushed it aside. She could not allow her heart to be caught in that web again.

She forced her thoughts from that all too familiar warmth of being in the company of Laurence to her outing with Harriet. If she could manage to endure one more week in the presence of his sister, the woman would be gone, and Isabel looked forward to the peace that would be returned to her.

Or at least the semblance of peace.

Chapter Fourteen

A week passed, and contrary to the prediction Laurence had made, Harriet still had not returned to her home in Malmsbury, and there was no indication she would be leaving anytime soon. If what the woman was saying at the moment was true, her stay might turn into another month.

Isabel had yet to spend any time to herself, for every waking moment was spent doing whatever Harriet desired. They had returned to town three more times, making more purchases neither needed, and then visited Harriet's friend Margaret before returning home. Margaret was the exact opposite of Harriet – quiet and unobtrusive – and Isabel wondered how they could have been such good friends.

Isabel was more than happy to suffer through it all in order to please Laurence, but it was the manner in which Harriet spoke to her brother that ruffled her feathers. Even a blind man could have seen how she used him for his money without so much as a lick of respect for his station. Laurence lacked confidence, and it would never build with his sister's constant ridicule.

"You know," Harriet was saying, "I was thinking that the ballroom needs redecorating. The styles are changing rather quickly, Laurence, and its current state is an embarrassment to us all."

"It was decorated not six years ago," Laurence argued.

Harriet took a bite of her potato and washed it down with a bit of wine. After dabbing at her mouth with a napkin, she replied, "Six years or six hundred, it does not matter." She snapped her fingers at one of the footmen and tapped on the rim of her glass. "If I am to host a party, I will not allow the guests to sit in such squander."

Isabel set down her fork with a clink. "Party?" she asked in shock. "No one mentioned to me we were hosting a party."

"Oh, yes," Laurence replied as his sister took a drink from her refilled glass of wine. "Harriet mentioned that a party would be a good way to introduce you to a few of our friends."

Isabel let out a concentrated breath, but before she could respond, Harriet said, "He never hosts anything. It is no wonder the *ton* believes he is a recluse."

"Perhaps he prefers to not have people traipsing through his house," Isabel replied evenly. "There are some who prefer to be left alone and not forced to be crowded together with their peers."

Harriet ignored her. "We shall go into town tomorrow and secure several workers to redecorate the ballroom. As a matter of fact, the drawing room needs attention, as well."

Isabel, realizing that she would have no say in the matter, turned to Laurence. "And what about you?" she asked. "Would you like to join us tomorrow? Perhaps Harriet and I can shop while you do something on your own."

She caught the flicker of a twinkle in his eye, but it fizzled at Harriet's snort. "He does not like to go into town," she said with a sneer. "Too many people would stare at him because of his limp."

Laurence reached under the table, and Isabel knew he was rubbing his leg, something she noticed he did quite often. Did his leg truly pain him, or had he developed a habit over time?

"Too much gossip for one to bear," Harriet continued. "It may be best if we plan on working on the entire house. Even your little hideaway."

Laurence blanched. "My hideaway?"

His sister laughed. "You believe I am naive to the fact that you spend time painting?" she asked still sniggering. "I do understand why you do so in secret, for if anyone learned of your particular interests, the embarrassment would be great."

Isabel glared at the marchioness. Family or no, she had had enough of this woman's harsh words and would not allow her to berate Laurence, or her for that matter, any longer. "My husband happens to enjoy painting," she snapped at the woman. Then she narrowed her eyes. "And I will redecorate the house when I feel it must be done and not a moment sooner. If a party is to be hosted, it will be because my husband and I have chosen to do so. Not you."

Harriet looked absolutely apoplectic. "I have never been…"

"Spoken to in this way?" Isabel finished for her. "I do not doubt it. This is our home, Harriet. If we wish for your aid or your opinion, we will ask for it. Otherwise, keep your nose out of it."

Harriet placed her napkin on her plate and pursed her lips. "To think I am being talked to like this in my own home," she said indignantly. "Laurence, how can you allow her to speak to me this way?"

Isabel pushed her chair back and placed both hands on the table and leaned forward. "Do not ever speak down to my husband again," she seethed. "Do not make mention of his leg or anything else he chooses to do or not do, or so help me…"

Harriet stood with such force, her chair toppled to the floor. A footman rushed to set it right, but the woman took no notice. "I will not be spoken to in such a manner any longer. I am going upstairs to pack my belongings and will leave first thing in the morning." She stared at Laurence for several moments, and when he made no comment, she huffed and then stormed out of the room.

Trying to compose herself, Isabel turned to her husband. "I am sorry," she said.

He remained silent, the only indication of his feelings about the interchange the frown he wore as he hurried from the room.

Had Isabel upset him to the point he would retract his offer to save Scarlett Hall? Or would he ridicule her for her actions and demand she never speak to his sister in that manner again? Had she taken an already difficult situation and made it worse?

She grabbed her wine glass and hurried to the garden, the only place she could sit alone to think.

***

Isabel stood looking over the rolling landscape as the rays of the sun lit the valley. Although she did not regret her words to Harriet, she did regret the manner in which she spoke them. Her stomach knotted with worry that Laurence was upset with her, and she hoped she would be able to appease him in some way.

The sound of footsteps made her turn to see Laurence approaching. His face was solemn, and Isabel braced herself for the scolding she knew was to come.

"It is still the most beautiful of views," he said as he came to stand beside her. "You asked me before if I ever wondered about the people who live in those cottages. I had not before that day we picnicked together, but since then, I find myself staring across the way and imagining what their lives might be like."

"Laurence," she whispered. "I am sorry…"

He raised a hand, and she closed her mouth. "I have seen people with very little, their hopes and dreams all they have to sustain them. Yet, here I am, living on a grand estate with much wealth, and many wish they could have what I have." He shook his head in wonderment. "They do not know the burdens put upon my shoulders. The fact is, the money they seek cannot bring them the happiness they want. I know this, for, although I possess much, my own sister still hates me."

Isabel wished she could calm the agony that threatened to overwhelm her. "If I have caused this distress, I am truly sorry. It was not my intention to speak as I did to your sister."

"But you meant your words?" he asked. The question hung in the air as Isabel considered how to respond. "Please, I must hear the truth."

She turned to him. "The truth?" she asked. "Very well. I do not regret the words, for I meant them. My only regret is the anger with which I articulated them."

Laurence nodded. "What do you wish me to do about Harriet? She is having her belongings packed as we speak. Do I stop her and ask her to stay, or do I simply let her go?"

"That is your choice," Isabel replied. "I cannot make it for you. You are the duke, and my husband; I will support whatever decision you make."

It was quiet for a moment, the only sounds the soft rustle of the tall grass in the light breeze and the twitter of nearby birds.

"Do you believe she treats me fairly?" he asked.

Isabel thought on the question for a moment before responding. "I do not," she replied with honesty. "She speaks down to you as if you were lower than a servant. She makes mention of your leg as if it was a burden she was forced to carry." Laurence winced, and Isabel's heart went out to him. "I care nothing about your leg, for it is the heart that I admire."

The man smiled. "Thank you," he said. "Those words mean much to me. I have but one more question, and I want you to remain honest."

"I will try."

"Do you like my sister?"

Isabel was taken aback by the forwardness of such an inquiry, and once again she wondered if she should be honest or not. She had lied before, and if her actions this night did not show that, something else would. Therefore, she replied, "I do not. She believes I am after your money, for one thing. And despite the reasons for our marrying, which has to do with money, that was an agreement you made with my mother. That is not the foremost reason for my dislike of her. Her manipulation of you is despicable. I see it, and I do not like it."

He released a heavy breath. "What you say is true, and I have known for some time."

"Then why do you allow it?" she demanded. "You are the duke; you should answer to no one, especially your sister."

"I..." His face was filled with anguish. "I hurt Harriet through the death of my parents. I have felt guilty since their accident, and I hoped that one day I could appease her by giving her gifts."

Isabel saw the pain in his eyes, and she placed a comforting hand on his arm. "You have been doing this for a while, I assume?"

"Yes."

"Doing so has not produced the results you sought," she said quietly. "And I do not believe it will."

"I am sorry," he replied. "For how she treated you and for me allowing it to happen."

"You owe me no apology. As I said before, you are my husband. I will support you in every decision you make."

"I believe it would be best to allow Harriet to leave. Her scorn toward me will still remain, but if you and I are to begin a new life together, then it must be just the two of us."

"I agree," Isabel replied.

"Would you like to return to the house?" he asked.

Isabel nodded, and the two walked back in silence, her arm in his. She never realized how low the man's confidence was until this past week, and his words moments ago only confirmed her suspicions. Now, as he affirmed his decision to remove Harriet from his life, or at least from his home for the time being, it was a new direction that would only help his confidence grow stronger.

When they returned to the foyer, Harriet stood beside her bags, a kerchief in her hand. As soon as she saw them, she dabbed at her eyes. "Have you come to ridicule me?" she said with a sniffle. "To berate me until I am a broken woman?"

"There is something you should know," Laurence said, placing his hand on Isabel's arm when she attempted to move away. "You are my sister, and I care for you. The way you speak to me and my wife will no longer be tolerated."

Harriet placed her hand to her breast dramatically and gasped. "I only wished to help," she exclaimed. "And this woman," she motioned to Isabel, "is filling your head with lies!"

Isabel placed a hand atop his for support and reassurance. From what she had seen, this was a large step for him, and she was proud he was taking it.

"Isabel has made me see where I have gone wrong," he said. "It is her wish that you leave, and I support it."

Isabel felt her heart drop to her feet. The decision to send Harriet packing had been his, not hers; she had agreed because she saw it as a way to build his confidence. Instead, he had passed the blame onto her.

"I see," Harriet said with a derisive sniff. She turned to Weber. "Have my bags placed in the carriage at once," she ordered. Then she huffed and strode out the door.

"Laurence, I did not want…"

"Do not worry. Harriet has learned an important lesson today."

Isabel gave him a skeptical look. "And what is that?" she asked.

"That I will do anything for you," he replied with a smile. "Even removing my sister from my home."

Isabel could not stop the racing of her mind. This step had not been meant for her, but for him. And now the burden of blame was doubly added onto her shoulders. She gave him a numb smile and then excused herself before hurrying to the drawing room and pouring herself another glass of wine.

Chapter Fifteen

The days became a week, and those became three, and each day the routine Isabel followed was unchanging. In the morning, she wrote at least one letter – typically to one of her sisters or her mother to assure them that she was happy in her new home – and then she would meet with Mrs. Atkins, the housekeeper, to discuss whatever household business that needed discussing.

Laurence had been happy, if not a bit surprised, how quickly she had taken on her role as duchess. Isabel reminded him that she had been married before and, although her husband had not been titled, they still had several servants and therefore she knew her duties. Of course, he had apologized profusely, which she had accepted without hesitation. Who was she to be angry with the man for something so trivial?

Once her morning tasks were complete, she breakfasted with Laurence, and as he worked in his study, she strolled through the gardens or returned to her room to read. At night, they dined together and then went to the drawing room to chat about their day and to have an evening drink of some sort.

Although she made every attempt not to, Isabel could not help but think often of Scarlett Hall. She missed her childhood home and wished to be there with her sisters. Granted, it was only a few miles away, but now that she was married once again, it might as well have been in Scotland for all the chance she would have to visit.

Laurence seemed to sense her melancholy, for he offered to accompany her if she chose to go riding, but she declined, complaining that her stomach was queasy. Then he had asked her to join him while he painted, but she refused such an invitation, as well. What could she possibly understand about the intricacies of painting? Furthermore, why would she find such an activity entertaining? He could have his painting; she would eventually find some sort of activity to consume all the extra hours in her day, she was sure of it.

As she sat in the field just beyond the garden that overlooked the cottages in the valley, Isabel's hair fluttered in the light breeze. She had taken a blanket and spread it upon the grass beneath a large shade tree, which allowed her to remove her bonnet. In her hand she held a glass of wine, the bottle lying open beside her.

Closing her eyes, she harkened back to a time when she and Arthur shared a bottle of wine together on a day much like this soon after they were married. They spoke of their future together and everything beautiful that was to come.

Isabel sighed. Those dreams ended before they began, and the hurt from that time still remained with her.

"May I join you?"

Isabel gave a yelp and opened her eyes to find Laurence standing over her.

"Forgive me. I did not mean to frighten you," he said with a laugh.

Isabel smiled. "Not at all. I was lost in my thoughts, is all. Please, sit." She indicated an empty space on the blanket.

"I hope you do not mind," he said, holding up an empty wine glass.

"Of course." She poured wine into his glass. He had such a kind smile that warmed her heart, and she found his company a pleasant change from the routine that had fallen into place.

"I received a letter from Harriet today," he said as he swirled the liquid in his glass. "She is offering me a chance to apologize." He chuckled and then took a drink of his wine. "She does not know it as of yet, but she will be waiting a while, for I will never send it."

A sharp twinge of annoyance entered Isabel. Even after three weeks, she had still not recovered from her vexation that he had placed the blame on her for wishing Harriet to leave.

Mentioning it, however, would do no good; therefore, instead, she said, "As I said before, I respect and will stand beside you whatever choices you make."

"And I appreciate that," he replied.

For a moment, they did nothing more than sip their wine, until Laurence asked, "What do you think about when you are out here?"

She sighed as a gust of wind whipped her hair into her face. Laurence reached over and pushed it aside, and she thought her cheeks would burn his hand if he touched her. What a silly thought!

How could she answer such a question without hurting him? He was so kind and had made no demands on her thus far, and she hoped he would not. Ever. It was more than she could ask, she knew, but she hoped this freedom would last for as long as possible.

"It is nothing," she replied. "Simply the thoughts of women."

"You miss him," he said, and her heart skipped a beat. "Arthur."

"Laurence…"

"I understand. I have not experienced the loss you have, but he was a good and strong man. It would only be proper to miss him." Isabel could not mistake the sadness in his voice, which only tormented her heart all the more.

"I am married," she said quietly, "to you. That is all that matters."

"Then why do you hide from me?" he asked. "We are to take the smallest of steps in this relationship, and I am willing to do so. Besides taking meals with me, you either escape out here or retire to your room."

Isabel wished to explain to this man the roiling feelings within her, yet how could one put them into words? And yet, the agony she felt at being unable to articulate what was on her heart only increased her overall melancholy.

Was she to tell him the truth? That Arthur was not the man of integrity so many believed him to be? That she had waited until all hours of the night for him to return home, until the candles flickered into darkness? His excuse had always been the same – that he was working late – yet his breath always smelled suspiciously of drink.

No, Laurence did not need to know about her past. "I do not escape from you," she replied finally. "You must believe that."

Whispers of Light

Laurence sighed. "I do not believe you an outright liar, but I cannot help but believe you are not speaking the full truth. That day we went riding together? Before we were married? I know you enjoyed that outing. I just find it odd you do not wish to do so again."

Isabel placed her hand on his. "If you wish to join me tomorrow, I would be happy to go riding with you."

"I only wish you to be happy," he said, pulling his hand away. "I am doing what I can to make that possible, but I cannot do it alone. I need your help."

The pleading in his eyes tugged at her heartstrings, and at this moment, she wanted nothing more than to please him, even if it meant doing something she did not wish to do. "Tomorrow, then," she said with a smile, "you shall teach me to paint. Unless you no longer wish to? I would not blame you if you did not. I know I have been...difficult."

"You do not need to do that just to appease me," he replied. "And you have not been difficult. Our marriage was sudden, and you clearly did not want it, but I will do whatever it takes to please you."

Why this man tried so hard to make her happy, she did not know, but she could not help but recognize how exceedingly gracious he was to her. If he wished her to paint, then she would allow him to teach her. Not only would she learn, but she would appear to find great joy in doing so.

"I do wish to learn," she replied with a smile. "I must admit, it was your paintings that kept me from agreeing before." When he gave her a confused look, she added, "You are a gifted painter. How will I ever compare?"

He laughed. "I am no great master, but I believe you have the capacity to be."

"Is that so?" she asked in surprise.

"Indeed. You have a strength about you, a strength that can be transferred from the brush and onto the canvas."

"In that case, I look forward to it." What he was doing for her was more than she could have ever expected, and a desire to do something for him rose inside her. "I have a favor to ask of you, as well."

"Whatever you desire," he replied.

"An invitation came today to a party my mother is planning for Juliet on Friday. She will be eighteen – a very important age – and friends and family are coming together in order to celebrate."

"That is wonderful," he said. He hesitated, his hand moving to his leg. "I wish I could attend, but a prior engagement for business has been arranged for some time now…"

Isabel took his hand in hers and smiled. "No one will judge you, I promise. Certainly not I nor my sisters." She could see the reluctance in his eyes. "Attending a party for one's birthday is much like painting."

"Oh?" Laurence asked with clear amusement.

"Indeed. You must take the strength from within and transfer it when you appear among the guests. And you, my husband, have that strength. I believe you will be the most welcomed of guests."

This made Laurence laugh, and Isabel felt a sense of relief wash over her when he agreed to attend the party.

And as they continued to talk as the sun lowered in the horizon, Isabel found that her worries were not as great as they had been before Laurence had joined her for that glass of wine.

***

For the first time in a month, Isabel returned to Scarlett Hall. As she stood looking at the building that was her childhood home, she found it all the more magnificent than ever before. The sun shone, its rays warming the dark gray stone and gleaming off its many windows. She closed her eyes and imagined her father returning home from one of his many business trips and she, as a young child, rushing out the front door to throw herself into his waiting arms.

He always returned bearing gifts, as well. A small trinket, a sweet known only to a local village, and although she always cherished whatever he brought her, it was seeing him again that lifted her spirits.

Yet, her father was dead, and she was no longer a little girl.

"Isabel?" Laurence asked, interrupting her thoughts, and she opened her eyes once again. "Is everything all right?"

She went to respond, but the front door opened, and her sisters burst through, squealing as they bounded down the steps to greet her. Juliet was the first to wrap her arms around Isabel, followed by Hannah.

"Oh, we have missed you so!" Juliet cried.

"I have missed you both, as well," Isabel said with a laugh. "And the most happiest of days to you," she added as she brushed back a curl that had fallen from Juliet's many hairpins.

The door opened again, and Isabel thought she would faint when she saw who stepped out.

"Nathaniel?" she gasped. Where was the young boy who would follow her around the house? In his place stood a young man of thirteen, his wavy blond hair and perfect smile staring back at her. Then he rushed down the steps and into her arms. "I cannot believe you are here! I have missed you terribly. How is school?"

He laughed as he stepped back from her embrace. "School is going well enough," he replied. "And I missed you, too." He glanced around at all of his sisters. "I have missed all of you. It is so good to be home."

"Are you not enjoying school?" Isabel asked as she threaded her arm through his. "They are not mistreating you, are they?"

"Oh, nothing like that," Nathaniel replied. "I just miss being home is all."

Isabel knew how he felt. She remembered spending time at Mrs. Downs' School for Young Ladies when she was Nathaniel's age, and she could not wait to return home. Hannah and Juliet had been lucky enough not to be forced to live away from home after their parents realized that they could teach their daughters what they needed to know themselves without the extra cost of a boarding school. Isabel did not hold any grudges for being forced to spend time away from her home and family, but it had taken her several years to recover from her annoyance her sisters did not have to go through what she had been forced to endure.

A clearing of a throat made them all turn to where their mother stood at the top of the stairs. "We have a guest; behave accordingly."

Isabel gasped. How could she have forgotten Laurence? Shame washed over her as she turned and smiled at him. "I am sorry," she said. "I suppose I have missed my family more than I had thought. Nathaniel, this is my husband Laurence Redbrook, Duke of Ludlow. You remember him, do you not?"

Nathaniel gave Laurence a deep bow. "I do. Congratulations on your marriage. I'm sorry I was unable to attend; I had exams."

Laurence gave a hearty laugh. "I remember those days," he said merrily. "I understand that you are attending Eton; that is the same school I attended in my day. Is Master Greenbriar still teaching mathematics there?"

"He is," Nathaniel replied with a grimace. "As a matter of fact..."

Isabel smiled as the two conversed about their school experiences, and soon everyone made their way into the house. When her eyes met those of her mother, Isabel's smile faded.

"I am glad you came," her mother said. "The guests will be arriving soon."

Isabel nodded. She had nothing to say to this woman, so she went to move around her, but her mother placed a hand on her arm. "I know you are angry with me. Please do not be."

"Today is Juliet's birthday," Isabel replied, her voice rimmed with ice. "There is nothing more to discuss beyond that." It pained her to speak to her mother in such a manner, but the hurt inside was too great to push aside. If they discussed what her mother had done, it would not be today, for to do so would only ruin Juliet's day, and Isabel was not willing to allow that to happen.

"If it makes you feel any better," her mother said as they stepped into the foyer, "all the debt was paid off yesterday. Scarlett Hall has been saved, and you are the person who saved it."

Isabel narrowed her eyes. "Then see to it that you do not bring about ruin again," she snapped. "Unless you plan on selling either Hannah or Juliet in order to cover those debts, as well."

Her mother winced, and Isabel felt a sense of satisfaction. The sensation was short-lived, for regret replaced it almost immediately.

To be so hurtful was not in her nature, and she knew she should apologize to her mother.

Before she could do so, Nathaniel called out to her. "Isabel! Please hurry. I want to have a piece of cake, but Hannah won't let me."

"I am coming," she said. She took one last moment to glance at her mother and then hurried to the drawing room, leaving her mother – and the bad memories – behind.

Chapter Sixteen

As a duke, Laurence was expected to be an articulate speaker, an avid conversationalist, and the man others held in esteem. Despite these expectations, he could not help but feel intimidated as he stood in the drawing room of Scarlett Hall surrounded by the dozen or so guests, most much younger than he and with whom he had never been acquainted. They laughed and whispered amongst themselves, and in those hurried words, he feared they spoke about him, of how he was half a man because he could not walk upright with pride and honor. Of the fact that he lacked the attributes that made him a duke.

Perhaps they wondered how a woman as lovely and outspoken as Isabel could agree to marry a man such as he. His reply could have been it was because she loved him, but that was simply not the truth. She had married him in order to save her family home, a marriage of convenience, and although it was not uncommon to marry for this reason, somehow it felt odious, for he had always wished to marry for love. For so many years, he worried that women only saw what was in his coffers and not what he had to offer, and, in the end, that is exactly what he received. Life was certainly ironic.

The fact of the matter was that Laurence could not recall many of the peerage who had married in love. Although that emotion had eluded him and Isabel, Laurence believed that one day they would at least gain a mutual affection for one another.

Isabel stood beside Nathaniel, and Laurence had never seen her smile so broadly or laugh so gaily. Perhaps they should have the boy over for dinner some night while he was home from school, for if he could make her smile where Laurence was unable, it would be worth the time spent.

Isabel laughed once more and then turned. Their eyes met, and Laurence could not stop his smile from growing. It had been the power of her smile that had captivated him that day of their outing, that drove away the fear that had gripped him moments before, and he silently swore that he would do what he could to make her happy. No expense was too great. No request too outlandish.

A moment later, she whispered something to her brother and then joined Laurence. "I apologize for leaving you alone," she said with a smile. "I was so absorbed in my conversation with Nathaniel that I am afraid I neglected you."

"No. He is your brother, and I would expect you to spend time with him. I imagine you have much to discuss since he has been away at school."

"Indeed," she replied. "Mother sent him off much too young, in my opinion. He has attended Eton only two years, and he returns home three times a year. It seems he has been gone much longer. For as long as I have been gone from here..."

Her voice trailed off, and Laurence had a better understanding of how much she missed Scarlett Hall. Then a thought came to him, one that he suspected would please her immensely.

"How long will Nathaniel be here?" he asked. Juliet and her cousin Annabel laughed in the corner, and when their eyes fell on him and they giggled once more, a flicker of fear went through him. Worry began to knot his stomach, and he worried he would sick up what little he had eaten.

"Another week," Isabel replied. "Why do you ask?"

Laurence swallowed back the bile that rose in the back of his throat and made a pretense of taking a drink of his wine. "Perhaps you should return for a visit before he leaves," he said when he was certain he would not be sick. "On your own, of course. Or he is welcome to come to Camellia Estates if you'd like."

The twinkle in Isabel's eyes told him her response before she spoke the words. "Oh, that is a wonderful idea!" she said. "Thank you. I will come to visit for a few days before he returns to school. Oh, he will be so pleased."

Suddenly, Laurence had a strange urge to kiss this woman. She was giddy with excitement, and her face glowed with pleasure, and all he could do was wonder what it would be like to press his lips to hers at this very moment.

The thought left him as Lady Lambert approached. "I hope you are enjoying yourself, Your Grace," she said.

"I am," he replied. "Although, I believe that it is Juliet's enjoyment of the day that is of consequence, not mine. And by her gleefulness, I would say you have exceeded her expectations."

Lady Lambert nodded. "I do not mean to burden you, but may I speak to you in private for a moment?"

"Certainly," Laurence replied curiously. Then he turned to Isabel. "I will return shortly."

"I will be with Nathaniel," Isabel replied, although she shot her mother a strange glare.

Laurence followed Lady Lambert down the hallway to the study that had once belonged to Lord Lambert. The baroness closed the door behind them and then went to the dark sofa, offering him the seat beside her. "I wanted to thank you for all you have done," she said. "To know that Nathaniel will have a home to inherit, that my daughters will one day..." her words trailed off, and she removed a kerchief from the sleeve of her dress and dabbed at the corner of her eye.

"I assure you," Laurence said, "the arrangement has been rewarding to both of us. I find my time with Isabel engaging, and I believe she does, as well."

"That is wonderful news," Lady Lambert said with glee. "I did worry...not that Isabel does not care for you, for I believe she does. Just a mother's worry is all."

Laurence studied the woman for a moment. "Is everything all right? Do you have other concerns?"

"No," the woman replied before giving a heavy sigh.

"You spoke of being willing to help me in the matter of business. Our adviser, Mr. Patrick, has gotten on in years, and I am afraid to say that he has become quite senile over the last few months."

"I see. Are you in need of a budget drawn? Or advice on your current business holdings and future investments?"

"I am afraid I am in need of assistance with everything," she said as she raised her hands as if in defeat. "I do not know what to do. I am afraid all will be lost if I do not do something soon." The worry she wore on her features matched that of her voice.

"You have nothing to fear," Laurence replied with a warm smile. "Have your ledgers sent over to me at your convenience, and anything else you wish me to review. I will look over everything personally and then search out a new adviser who I trust to take over the accounts."

She sighed with relief and rose from the sofa. "I do not know how to thank you!"

Laurence also stood, and a bolt of pain shot down his leg, and he was forced to grab a nearby chair for support.

"Your Grace!" Lady Lambert said as she hurried over to him.

"I am all right," he said, straightening his back, although his leg still pained him. The burning of his cheeks hurt more, by far. "It tends to give me problems from time to time. I suppose standing for so long has not helped."

"Would you like to rest? I am sure we can set you up in one of the guest rooms or you are welcome to use the sofa if you would like."

"No," Laurence said all too quickly. He took a deep breath to calm himself. "I appreciate your offer, but I believe it has passed. Let us return to the party."

"If you are certain..."

"I am."

He followed the baroness back out into the hallway, doing everything in his power not to reach down and massage his leg despite the fact that the pain increased with each step he took. On most occasions, if the pain was this harsh, he would be forced to lie down for several hours until it subsided, but he could not – no, he would not – do that now.

And as they reentered the room, it was as if every eye fell on him, and his embarrassment grew tenfold, for he could not keep himself from limping more than usual. He searched the room for Isabel and was surprised when he could not find her. He felt his humiliation deepen and his anger rise. He had not asked much from his wife, but the fact that she chose to leave him alone with a group of people he barely knew was uncalled for.

He searched the room for a chair, but the closest would force him to walk through the crowd of people. Therefore, he forced a smile, hoping Isabel would return soon. As the seconds turned into minutes, his anger only worsened, and all he wanted to do was return home.

***

Isabel had never been happier to be back home. It was as if she had never married and was still living at Scarlett Hall, and she listened intently as Nathaniel spoke of his days at Eton School.

"The headmaster is strict," Nathaniel was saying. "I must admit he is fair. I don't find myself reprimanded as often as other boys."

"That is because you are a good young man," Isabel said. She ruffled the boy's hair, and he grimaced and pulled away. "It has been truly wonderful to see you again. I wish you did not have to return to Eton just yet."

"But I must," he said in sudden seriousness. "If I am to take over the barony and all of Father's businesses, I must return and finish my studies." At times, the boy was as serious as their father had been, which made Isabel want to weep with joy. Coupled with his innocence, he was truly a remarkable young man, even at the age of thirteen.

As they continued their conversation, something in the back of her mind began to gnaw at her. The guests around them laughed and smiled, but one laugh seemed to be missing from the room.

"Juliet," Isabel whispered under her breath. "Nathaniel, I will return in a moment."

"Where are you going?"

"To find your sister," Isabel replied.

She walked over to Annabel, who stood talking with a young man Isabel recognized as Loftus Skettington, the son of Lord Skettington, Earl of Warrington, a young man whose reputation most decent people found questionable.

Why he had even been invited was a wonder, but Isabel suspected her young cousin might have had something to do with it. And by the guilty expression she wore, she knew she was right.

"Isabel," Annabel said in a shaky voice.

"Excuse us a moment," Isabel mumbled as she grabbed her cousin by the arm and pulled her aside with a faint smile for the boy to whom she had been speaking. When they were a decent distance away, she lowered her voice and hissed, "Is Juliet where I think she is?"

Annabel nodded, and Isabel turned and hurried away to warn her mother about Juliet. She had seen the woman and Laurence go into the study and close the door, so she pressed her ear to the door to listen. If they were there, she would hear their voices.

"I do not know what to do," her mother was saying. "I am afraid all will be lost if I do not do something soon."

Anger filled Isabel, and she gave a huff before making her way outside. Leave it to her mother to ask more of Laurence than she already had! Had Isabel's sacrifice not been enough for the woman? Her mother was going to foolishly lose everything her father and his family had worked so hard to gain if she was not careful. Laurence only had so much he could offer before he cut the woman off completely. And if he did, Isabel would not blame him.

Yet, it was not only the loss of the home that concerned Isabel, although it was the most important. There was also the fact that Juliet and Hannah relied on her to guide them. Here was Juliet, alone in the stables with Daniel, and where was their mother? Locked away in the study discussing the financial situation she had created.

As she neared the stables, Isabel heard hushed voices coming from inside.

"If you wish to please a woman," Juliet was saying, "you must try harder than that. My lips are not poison, so this time, do it correctly."

"Yes, Miss," Daniel replied.

Isabel opened her eyes wide and her heart skipped a beat. Of all the things Juliet could be doing on her eighteenth birthday, sharing in kisses with a servant should not have been one of them!

She rushed to the stable doors. "Juliet! You are a lady, not a common..." Her voice faltered as she tried to take in the scene before her. Juliet sat atop a pile of straw as Daniel held a small plate with a slice of cake on it. The fork, which held a small bite of cake, was aimed at Juliet's mouth.

"Isabel!" Juliet gasped when she noticed her sister in the doorway gaping at her. "I did not expect you." She smoothed her skirts nervously. The poor stable hand held his head in shame.

"What are you doing here?" Isabel demanded, hurrying to her sister and brushing away a piece of straw that clung to her hair. "Do you realize that there is a party going on inside the house."

"Of course I do," Juliet retorted haughtily. "And since it is my birthday, and one day I will have my own servants, I thought it best to practice by asking Daniel to feed me." Daniel's face reddened even further, and Isabel worried he would have a stroke or some other malady soon.

"You may leave us," Isabel told the young man.

"I'm sorry," he said with a bow.

"Do not apologize," Juliet said with a derisive sniff. "You are my servant, not hers."

Anger rose inside Isabel, a cumulation of all that had happened over the past month, and she grabbed her sister by the arm so tightly, the girl cried out in pain. "Do not speak to him in that manner again!" she shouted.

"Isabel?" Juliet asked in shock. "You are hurting me."

"No!" Isabel said through clenched teeth. "I am sick of the way you treat others. You act like Laurence's sister, Harriet, believing you are better than anyone else, and I will not put up with it a moment longer!"

"But he is only a servant," Juliet said with a whimper.

"He is a human being with feelings just like yours. Yet that is beside the point. You are a lady, and you should act like one. Not like a child."

Tears filled Juliet's eyes, but Isabel ignored them, her anger was so great.

"Your first season will begin soon, and you will not ruin our family name. Not after what I have done to save this family!"

Juliet's eyes went wide, and Isabel realized she had said more than she had intended. "What do you mean that you saved this family?" she asked.

"Nothing," Isabel replied. She took a deep breath to steady herself. "I suppose I am as prone to theatrics as you are." This seemed to appease Juliet somewhat, for which Isabel was thankful. "The fact remains that you cannot be left alone with Daniel – or any other man. This is not up for discussion. But I also cannot be here every day to remind you."

Juliet looked down at the ground. "I am sorry," she said in a low tone. "I did not mean any harm." Then she looked up at Isabel, tears now streaming down her cheeks. "I wish you were still here."

"I do, as well," Isabel said as she pulled her sister in for a hug. "There is not a day that goes by that I do not wish to return to Scarlett Hall." She sighed and kissed the top of Juliet's head. "I am married and happy in my new home." She was unsure why she had said the words, for they were a lie. Were they not? Regardless, they made Juliet smile.

"Will you tell Mother?" Juliet asked as they returned to the house. "I do not want her to be angry with me."

"No. I will not say anything."

They returned to the drawing room – after Isabel checked that Juliet did not have a blotchy face. No one seemed to have noticed their disappearance, which pleased Isabel.

That is until she saw Laurence. His face was a bright red, and his jaw was drawn tight. Hurrying to him, she placed a hand on his arm, and his eyes clouded with something she could not identify.

"What is wrong? What happened?"

"I…" He seemed unable to speak. "Nothing. Perhaps the cake was a bit too sweet for my stomach." A bead of sweat formed on his forehead, and Isabel scrunched her brow. Before she could voice more concern, he added. "A few more minutes, and it will pass."

Isabel sighed with relief and turned to look back at Juliet, who had joined Annabel as though nothing outside of the party had transpired.

"Scarlett Hall is full of laughter," Laurence said.

"Indeed," she replied with a smile. "My only hope is that it remains that way."

Although she did not speak the words, for she did not want to hurt her husband, she wished her laughter could reside in these halls once again. And for always.

Chapter Seventeen

I sabel remained at Scarlett Hall three days following the party, and each day was filled with the joy of being with Nathaniel and her sisters once again. They laughed and reminisced about days past. Of when their father chased them around the house when they were little – even Nathaniel experienced this, although less often than the girls – or when they played Blind Man's Bluff in the back garden. How they laughed when they recalled their father tumbling into a rose bush and emerging with multiple scratches on his face and hands, as well as a tear in the sleeve of his coat! All that so he could retrieve a ball that had bounced into the flowerbed.

Isabel returned to Camellia Estates with reluctance, but she had little time to settle back into her daily routine the following day when she came down the stairs in the morning to find Laurence returned home with a gift. It was not the typical present – no jewelry or flowers or some sort of trinket to please her. No, he returned with a young woman with dark hair and a fair complexion perhaps a year or so younger than Isabel.

"I would like you to meet Nancy, your lady's maid."

Isabel had forgotten that Laurence had conducted interviews in order to procure a woman to assist her, and she was unsure how she felt about that. At Scarlett Hall, everyone dressed themselves – their father had insisted that the expense was unnecessary, and their mother agreed. Now that she was a duchess, it would not be becoming of her not to have one, at least according to Laurence.

Nancy bobbed a curtsy as she continued to stare at the floor. "It is an honor to serve you, Your Grace," she said in a soft voice.

Laurence grasped his lapels with pride as if he had procured the Crown Jewels. "She was trained under the careful eye of the lady's maid to Lady Clancy."

"I am glad you are here, Nancy," Isabel said with a warm smile as she donned a kidskin glove. "I am certain that Mrs. Atkins will see you to your room. I am leaving for the day, but we will speak later when I return."

"Isabel," Laurence said in a firm tone, "I believe it is imperative you spend time with Nancy. She will be expected to begin her services as soon as possible, but if she is unaware of what those services are, today will be a waste of her time."

"I had thought that since Nathaniel..."

"He has seen enough of you already," he replied, his voice bearing a sternness she had not expected. "I have work I must complete." He stalked down the hallway, or stalked as well as he could with his limp.

Isabel felt a surge of frustration course through her. Nathaniel would be gone in just a few days, and her plans for the day were ruined. Yet Laurence was her husband, so she sighed and shook her head, removing the gloves once again.

"You served with Lady Clancy?" Isabel asked Nancy.

"Yes, Your Grace. Or at least I was trained by her lady's maid." She had a distinct Irish accent that Isabel found endearing. "Lady Clancy, she let me do some of Peggy's duties so I could practice." She still had not looked at Isabel. "I hope I meet your approval." The last was barely audible, and Isabel could see the girl was apprehensive. Despite her nervousness, she possessed a warmness that Isabel liked.

"I am sure we will get on beautifully," Isabel replied. She sighed and glanced down the hallway toward the study. "Follow me." She led Nancy up the stairs and down the hallway to her bedroom. "I believe the servant's staircase is through that door." She pointed at a nondescript door at the end of the hall and laughed. "I am afraid I am relatively new to Camellia Estates, as well, so we may be learning our way around together. As a matter of fact, we can tour the house now, if you would like, and we will see how much I have learned in the past month. Would you like that?"

"Yes, Your Grace," Nancy replied.

Isabel placed her fingers on the girl's chin and lifted her face. "There is no need to look down when you speak to me," she said kindly. "I might be a duchess, but I am also a woman."

Nancy gave her a shy smile. "Yes, Your Grace."

They toured the entire house, Isabel introducing Nancy to servants as they encountered them – Isabel was surprised she remembered all their names – and when they were done, they returned to Isabel's bedroom.

"You will be tending me most of the time, of course, but Mrs. Atkins will also have duties for you at times. Have I missed anything do you think?"

The girl's eyes widened. "Why, no, Your Grace. At least, I don't think so. But if I have any questions, I'll ask. That's all right, isn't it?"

Isabel took Nancy's hands in hers. "Never be afraid to speak to me or to ask questions." When she received a smile for her words, she added, "Now, Mrs. Atkins will be in the kitchen at this hour, so go search her out and she will show you to your room."

"Thank you, Your Grace," Nancy said with a quick curtsy before heading toward the door that led to the servants' stairway.

Isabel smiled when the woman was gone. It was strange how she had a heart for those who served, and yet Juliet acted as if they were subhuman. Yet, Juliet only acted as society dictated, and Isabel knew her own treatment of the servants was rare for one in her position.

The clock on the mantle showed it was just past noon. She still had plenty of time to go see Nathaniel, so Isabel set off in search of Laurence. When she entered the study, she found it empty. Neither was he in the library or the drawing room. After knocking on his bedroom door and receiving no reply, she went to the ballroom intent on going to the hidden room he had shown her.

She was surprised when she found him sitting upon a stool before a set of canvases on easels in front of one of the large windows in the ballroom, a tarpaulin stretched out over the floor to keep paint from staining the polished wood.

"Ah, Isabel," Laurence said without even a glance over his shoulder. It was not a pleased greeting but rather one a headmaster would give to a student sent to him for misbehaving. "Has Nancy become acquainted with our home?"

"Yes," Isabel replied as she walked over to him. "What are you doing in the ballroom?"

"I decided that it was time to bring my work out into the open," he replied as if it was a natural step to take. "I no longer wish to hide what I do."

She studied the canvas before him and was impressed by the bold colors he used to depict a field with a tree to the left. "It is beautiful," she whispered as she looked over his shoulder.

Laurence made no reply as he cleaned his brush and took another from the small table beside him.

"I did as you asked," she continued with determination. "May I return to Scarlett Hall to see my brother once more before he returns to school?"

Laurence dabbed at the canvas, adding lighter green to the rolling landscape, but remained silent.

"Laurence?"

"The party we attended for your sister?" he asked. "Did you enjoy yourself?"

"I did." She looked at the back of his head with suspicion. There was a strange tone in his voice, as if he asked but did not care what she answered. "Did you?"

He laughed as he cleaned the brush once more and then placed it in a cup. "How kind of you to ask." This time she did not miss the sarcasm in his voice. "My leg," he turned and faced her "pained me when I was speaking with your mother."

"I am sorry to hear that," she said. "I did not know…"

"No, you did not," he retorted. "You were nowhere to be found."

Isabel took a step back from the heat of his anger, although he had not raised his voice. "It was Juliet," she said, hoping he would understand. "She needed to be cared for."

Her hopes were dashed when he replied, "She has a mother, and that is not you."

Now Isabel grew angry. How dare he speak so crassly to her. Of course he would not understand the relationship she shared with her family. After seeing how he and Harriet treated one another, she could see he had no idea of what family consisted. "I am sorry about your leg," she said, attempting to keep her anger from her words. "Truly, I am."

Laurence shook his head and walked over to a window that looked out at the gardens. "It is not my leg, nor Juliet, that bothers me."

"Then what is it?" Isabel demanded, tired of this game. She had no desire to anger the man further, but he was infuriating! "Tell me so I can make it right."

"I want to be happy," he replied. "And you can do that for me. For you to do that, you must be here. With me. Not back at Scarlett Hall or in your room or in the garden drinking wine."

Guilt flooded her when she heard the pain behind his words. "I did not mean to be away from you. And I agree that I spent more time with Nathaniel at the party than I did with you. I apologize for that."

"And the painting you promised?" He turned to look at her for the first time. "Do you still wish to join me?"

She hesitated only a moment before replying, "I do." It was a lie, but at this point, she did not care. "I have been so preoccupied that I forgot."

This seemed to appease him. "Go to Scarlett Hall today and enjoy time with your family. Tomorrow morning, we begin your first lesson in painting."

"I look forward to it," Isabel replied before leaning in and kissing his cheek. This man's kindness knew no bounds, for all he wanted was to spend time with her. And although she should have been thinking of him as she hurried out of the ballroom, her thoughts were instead on returning to Scarlett Hall.

***

That night after dinner, Isabel and Laurence had their customary drinks in the drawing room. Isabel attempted to focus on what Laurence was saying, but her mind continued to drift to other matters.

She recalled when she was seventeen and had first met Arthur. They had attended a birthday party not unlike the one given in Juliet's honor several days earlier. He was the same age as she, but there was a maturity about him that had caught her attention as soon as they were introduced.

He had called on her several times before her eighteenth birthday, after which he began to court her. He brought her flowers and showered her with gifts, and Isabel thought him the most thoughtful and handsome man she had ever known.

Soon they were married, ready to embark on a journey of love and adventure. Yet what was expected did not take place, and she refused to recall the painful events.

Yet, a warning received just a month before her wedding to Arthur came to mind of its own accord. Mrs. Patricia Lentworth, an older woman prone to gossip, had insisted she had seen Arthur acting in a much too familiar manner with another woman, the daughter of a farmhand.

"Only those jealous of what we have would make such unfounded accusations," he had said, laughing when Isabel had confronted him about her concerns. How quickly had his sweet laughter turned sour.

With great effort, she pushed the thoughts back into the box where she had locked them away, hoping they would not return but knowing she had little control over when they decided to reappear to her. She was glad to have them gone, even if only for a short time.

Now, she had married again, and the thought of falling in love with Laurence terrified her, which in turn brought on a bout of guilt she struggled to shake. Laurence was a good man deserving of love, but she could not allow herself to be the one to give him such a gift. The fact of the matter was, she had walked that path before – an image of Arthur flashed in her mind again of its own accord – and what she had learned was that any relationship they could build together would destroy not only her, but him as well.

"Isabel?"

Isabel started. "I am sorry, Arthur." She gasped when she realized what she had said. "Laurence! I am so sorry. I did not mean to say his name. Please, forgive me!"

Rather than being angry, Laurence set his glass on the table and placed his hand on his hurt leg. "I suppose it will happen from time to time," he said. Then he sighed. "I believe I will retire for the evening." He stood, and although he attempted to hide it, the hurt from her words was etched in his features.

Isabel felt horrible. She had no intentions of hurting this man, but she did so time and again. "I must say something before you go," she said as she rose from her seat. She wrapped her fingers around her skirts; what she had to say would be difficult. Not for him, but for her. "You see, the truth of the matter is, I do not miss him."

He gave her a kind smile. "Only a fool would believe such a thing. I understand the man was your husband, and he was a better man than I. I have no anger toward you."

"You are a good man," she replied. "Not because you have a title or wealth, but because of your heart."

He smiled. "Thank you for saying so," he replied, although he did not sound as if he believed her. "I shall see you in the morning."

When he was gone, Isabel finished the remainder of the wine in her glass and then poured another. She hoped Laurence was not too upset, but she could not blame him if he was. Since they had married, she had not been a very good wife. Just thinking about what little attempt she had made since they spoke their vows made her guilt grow, and she grabbed the wine bottle and took it back with her to the sofa.

Her life had not proven to be what she had expected, and yet Laurence was relentless in his hope that their marriage would be successful. Although she suspected that she would never grow to love the man – a great affection, perhaps, but not love – she vowed to do what she could to make him happy. If that meant painting with him when he asked, she would paint. If it meant appearing content even when she missed her life at Scarlett Hall the most, she would smile. If it meant allowing him into her bed in order to give him an heir, she would turn down the covers for him.

She thought again about Arthur, the man who had promised her not only the world, but happiness as well. The young girl she was before had believed his sweet words, but the woman she was now understood the meaning behind those promises and how impossible they were.

The tall clock struck one, and Isabel started. She had lost complete track of time and had nearly finished off the rest of the wine beside her. The room tilted as she stood, but she was able to gain her bearings before retiring to her bedroom for the night. Although the hour was late, Nancy was there waiting with drooping eyes to help her into her nightdress.

She will be a wonderful lady's maid, Isabel thought giddily.

As Isabel lay beneath the covers and the moonlight created a pattern of boxes across her blanket, she closed her eyes and drifted off to sleep, wondering if perhaps Laurence was different and his promises of wishing her to be happy were true.

Chapter Eighteen

The following morning, Isabel dressed early – a lovely turquoise day dress she had purchased on one of her shopping ventures with Harriet – with the help of her new lady's maid. Having another to help her dress made working with the stays of her bodice much easier, for, in the past, she had only her sisters upon whom she could rely to give her such aid. It was also pleasant having someone else doing her hair, and despite her young age, Nancy had learned the craft well. It was not long before her hair was curled and pinned back, a ribbon holding it all together on top of her head. Although not elaborate enough for a party, it was so much better than what she could have done on her own.

"Do you have any sisters?" Isabel asked as Nancy tied a bow under Isabel's breasts.

"No," the girl replied. "That is...I did have a sister once, but she died four years this past May."

"I am sorry to hear that," Isabel said. The thought of losing either of her sisters was terrifying. "And your parents? Are they still alive?"

"Mother works near London as a seamstress," Nancy replied. "I can sew, but I never found it very interesting, so I decided to become a lady's maid instead."

"When did you begin your service? You did not become a lady's maid right away, did you?"

Nancy laughed. "Oh, no, Your Grace. I began as a scullery maid in the home of Lord and Lady Clancy. But I knew when I started I wouldn't stay in that position. I had my eyes set on higher places."

Isabel enjoyed listening to Nancy's Irish accent and found her much more engaging than she first thought. As a matter of fact, the girl reminded her of a combination of both her sisters – with a dash of Cousin Annabel thrown in for good measure. She had the articulation of Hannah and a bit of impishness in her eyes that reminded Isabel of Juliet. And her resilience was so like that of Annabel that Isabel would have thought they had both been raised by the same parents.

"And your father?" When Nancy gave her a downcast look, she added, "I am sorry. You do not have to tell me if you do not wish to."

"Oh, it's not that, Your Grace," she replied. "It's just that I've never met my father." Her cheeks turned a deep crimson. "I know I shouldn't speak ill of my mum but she and my father were never married, and he ran off with the butcher's daughter before he even knew about me."

Isabel's heart went out to the girl, and she took her hand. "There is nothing of which to be ashamed," she said. "You are an intelligent and beautiful woman, and you should be proud of that fact. Please do not take offense, but you seem well-spoken for someone of your background. Did you have lessons?"

"You're very kind," Nancy replied. "And yes, I did have lessons. I was fortunate because, when I was younger, my mother worked for a baronet who had several children, and he allowed me to join in on the lessons his children received. You see, he believed that all children deserved an education, not just the children of wealthy families. Of course, when I went into service myself, I had to give up the lessons, but I was glad to have received what I had."

"Well, I believe we are going to be great friends, you and I," Isabel said with a smile. Then she studied her hair once more. "I just ask that you do not run off and get married, for I believe I would struggle to find an equal replacement."

Nancy's smile broadened. "Oh, I'm staying here for as long as possible."

"Good. Now, I believe Mrs. Atkins has some work for you to do, but later, if you would press my pink and white dress for me – the one with the satin ribbons at the waist – so I am able to wear it to dinner, I would greatly appreciate it."

"Yes, Your Grace," Nancy said with a curtsy before leaving the room.

After one last glance in the mirror – Nancy really had done a wonderful job on her hair – Isabel went down to the ballroom where she was to meet Laurence for their first painting lesson. She had tried on more than one occasion to make an attempt at creating works of art, but somehow, she had never advanced past the stage of making everything she painted appear as if a child of five had created it.

If it were up to her, she would remain in her room reading, but she had promised Laurence she would do her best. Furthermore, the man needed help to build his confidence, and it was the least she could do in repayment for all he had done for her.

She waited in the doorway of the ballroom as she watched her husband, who stood in front of the window. The newly risen sun lit his face, and although she had always thought him handsome, for some reason, she thought him especially so today. His jawline seemed much more defined, and for the first time, she noticed how broad his back was. Despite the damage to his leg, the muscles in his arms seemed well-sculpted beneath his coat sleeves.

He seemed to sense her arrival, for he turned and smiled. "Good morning. I am looking forward to our lesson today."

"As am I," Isabel replied as she walked over to where the painting supplies sat. She stared at the blank canvases that rested on the easels. Oh, how she did not want to do this! "You do not mean for me to complete a portrait today, do you?" She gave him a small smile.

"Of course you must," he said, and Isabel could do nothing but stare at the man in shock. "I have already pledged to sell it by sundown."

Was he mad? Did he honestly believe she would become some master painting after a single lesson?

When he winked at her, she realized he was teasing her. "I would not put such expectations on you," he said with a smile. "I thought this morning we could familiarize ourselves with the paint and the brushes."

"That will be fun," she said, although the words could not have been further from the truth.

Laurence indicated the stool that would be hers, which she took, and he sat upon his. Then he handed her a palette that held seven different colors of paint and a wide brush. "One of the rewards of painting is that no mistakes can be made. If you pour all your heart into your creation, it is impossible to do any wrong."

"That is a fascinating way to look at it," Isabel said. "I never realized you were such a philosopher as well as a painter."

"There is much you do not know about me, Your Grace," he replied. He took a similar brush in hand and said, "I thought we could practice technique first. Therefore, dip your brush in the blue paint like this." He took his brush and moved it about in slow circles in the blue paint. Then he painted a straight blue line across the middle of the canvas. "The brush will go where you want it, if you use your entire hand to paint rather than relying on just your fingers."

With a nod, Isabel dipped the tip of her brush into the paint and touched it to the canvas. What was left behind was a thin blue line rather than the bold line Laurence had created. "Am I doing something wrong?" she asked. "Mine looks nothing like yours." She glanced at his canvas once again and cringed. If she had failed to make a simple line, how was she to create a masterpiece?

"That is good," he said, standing and stepping beside her. "Try again."

Determined to get it right, she dipped her brush into the paint once more and then raised her arm to paint, but this time, Laurence placed his hand over hers. It was as if his hand was a burning torch, for she felt heat move from her hand, up her arm, and into the pit of her stomach. It was a familiar feeling, although it had been several years since she had last encountered it.

"Now" he said, his breath on her ear, creating a pleasant tingling throughout her body, "press firmly. Do not be afraid of the canvas. Or the paint, for that matter. Remember, there is no wrongdoing when it comes to art."

He removed his hand from hers, and she found her breath once again.

"Look!" Isabel gasped when she pulled the brush away from the canvas. "My line is nearly perfect!" She smiled proudly. "You should beware; I may surpass you with my abilities. At least when it comes to painting lines."

He chuckled. "I have no doubt you will. You are strong, and I do not hesitate to believe you can accomplish anything to which you set your heart and mind."

His words hung in the air for several moments, and she offered him a smile before looking back at her pallet. She still had not recovered from their intimate moment, and his added compliment only heightened the sensation.

"Now we will clean the brush like so." He pulled the brush through a piece of cloth striped with dried paint. "When we have removed as much of the paint from the bristles as we can, we then place the brush into linseed oil, which will remove the remainder of the paint from the brush."

She followed the steps he had given her, and soon her brush was in a cup of amber liquid.

"This time, we will use a thicker brush and our green paint."

Isabel was surprised how fast the morning passed. Not only that, she was enjoying the lesson. By the time Laurence announced they were done for the day, Isabel felt a sense of disappointment she had not expected.

"You did well," Laurence said as he cleaned the oil from his last brush.

Isabel stared at her canvas. Streaks of blue above green with splotches of yellow and pink was all she was able to see, and Isabel knew he was being kind.

"I appreciate you saying so, but all I see is an eyesore."

"I see beauty," Laurence replied. "Perhaps you should look at it again."

After Laurence left the ballroom, Isabel studied her canvas again. She had to admit that she felt some satisfaction for the work she had completed, but she did not see the beauty of which he spoke. What was it about the man that he could see beauty where all she could see was a disaster? Would she ever learn to do so?

Frustrated, she hurried to the drawing room and poured herself a glass of wine. She took a drink and sighed. Perhaps it was not for her to learn to see it.

***

For eight mornings, Isabel met Laurence in the ballroom to receive her lessons, and he taught her new techniques in the art of painting – brush strokes, pigments, hues, and textures. At times, some of the language seemed overwhelming, but Laurence was a patient teacher. Although she had only been practicing for a short time, Isabel felt she had improved immensely. She would never become a Wilson or a Bonington, but she was pleased when sections of her canvas resembled what she had meant them to represent.

"You are hesitating again," Laurence admonished lightly as he stood behind her. "It is why the stroke is uneven." He pointed to the middle of the line she had added to the canvas just moments before. "If you maintain an even pressure and move the brush across the canvas with your entire arm and not just your fingers, you will not have something that resembles a fat man lying on the ground."

Isabel laughed and tried again, this time making a quick, but bold, stroke. "There. Is that more to your liking?" she asked playfully.

"Much more," he replied with a laugh. "You will be ready to attempt your first landscape soon. Far sooner than I expected."

Her heart skipped a beat when he placed his hands on her shoulders, and that once familiar warmness rose in her stomach, just as it had their first day of painting lessons. She took a deep breath to calm herself. It was merely an echo of the short former marriage that had brought about such a reaction.

Then Arthur appeared in her mind, and she feigned a cough in order to cover what had to be extremely red cheeks.

"Are you all right?" he asked, concern in his voice.

The image of Arthur did not disappear. As a matter of fact, it morphed into something else completely, and panic attempted to overwhelm her. She could not go down that same path! She would not!

Jumping up from the stool in order to be out of his reach, she replied, "Yes. I am not sure what came over me. My throat went dry."

"Can I get you a glass of water?"

Isabel nodded. Good. He had accepted her excuse. She would have to be more careful in the future or this marriage would become more than she had first intended, and she certainly could not have that happen.

She accepted the glass of water Laurence offered her, and a knock came to the ballroom door.

"Yes?" Laurence called out.

The door opened and Weber entered, a silver tray balanced on his hand. "Your Graces," he said with a bow. "A letter arrived for you, Your Grace," he said to Laurence. "The messenger gave an indication that there was some urgency behind it, and therefore, I brought it to you immediately. I hope that is acceptable."

"Of course. Bring it here."

Weber brought the tray to Laurence, who took the letter and returned to his stool as he ripped open the seal. He scanned the document, his brows rising. When he set the letter aside, he shook his head and smiled. "Urgency," he said flatly.

"What is it?" Isabel asked, now confused, and more concerned, than ever. For an urgent message, the man seemed to take it quite well.

As if he just realized that Isabel was there, he laughed. "I am sorry," he replied. "It is from Hugh Elkins, an old friend from my school days. He is hosting a party Saturday next."

"How wonderful!" Isabel said. "Will we be attending?"

Laurence shook his head. "Too many people will be in attendance. I do not wish to embarrass myself...or you."

His words caught Isabel off-guard. She knew the man had a great concern about the thoughts of others when it came to his leg, but did he believe she, too, looked at him differently because of it? She attempted to recall any time she had made a comment or a glance that would have led him to believe she found his injury a concern for her, but nothing came to mind.

The sadness he wore like a badge tore at her heart. He truly believed that people thought him less than a man because of his injured leg!

She walked over and placed a hand on his arm. "Laurence," she said quietly, "you could never embarrass me. Why would you believe such a thing? Have I ever given you reason to believe I think less of you because of your leg?"

He gave a heavy sigh. "No, but women want a complete man, a man who is strong and who does not suffer from a limp. I would be a wounded deer amidst stags. Surely that would cause you concern?"

Isabel shook her head. "I do not care how others judge, for one thing. And for another, how often have you gone to a party or any other gathering and had a person ridicule you?" She knew the answer even before he did not respond. Never. This man needed to leave his house and see he had nothing for which to concern himself. "Perhaps we should go."

"No," Laurence replied without hesitation. "It is not worth taking that chance."

"Chance?"

"There are times when the muscles in my leg...seize. I am unable to move, both as a result of the muscles not doing as they should but also from the pain. It is difficult enough to endure when I am at home alone, but to be forced to in front of others? It is too much to ask. I will not be made a laughingstock."

It was at that moment that Isabel's heart truly went out to Laurence. His burden was far greater than she had ever realized. She suspected it affected him in more areas of his life than he would ever admit. She might not love him, but she did care for him, and he needed strength to venture out into the world.

"There is no shame in having a wounded leg," she said. She took his hand in hers. "If it were to seize, as you say, what would that matter? Your leg does not define you." His awkward smile said she needed to say more. "A man is worthy based on his heart and soul. If the entirety of the *ton* were to laugh, which I assure you they would not, it would not matter, for I will be beside you always, and I hope that how I see you is your only concern."

His fingers closed around her hand, and he smiled. "You are truly an amazing woman," he said. "Your wisdom, your strength, they surprise me every day." He turned to stare out the window and then said, "We will attend the party. Promise me you will remain by my side the duration of the time we are there."

"I will never leave your side," she replied before realizing she had not needed to lie to the man this time. "You must promise the same."

His smile broadened. "Always."

Chapter Nineteen

S he would support him. The words Isabel had spoken the week prior continued to elate Laurence. A woman would not make such a statement if she did not have some affection for him. If Isabel cared, the chances of her feelings for him deepening were great. He was uncertain when it had happened, but it was a certainty that his feelings for her were growing stronger. She may not have the same affection for him as he had for her, but he would wait until the end of time if that was what was needed.

The carriage jostled as it moved down the cobbled street. The unease Laurence had harbored the previous week was amplified as he and Isabel drew closer to the home of Mr. Hugh Elkins. The younger son of an earl, Hugh was not titled, but he was a savvy businessman, and Laurence had shared in several ventures with him since they had left school. Not to mention, they had always gotten on brilliantly.

"You are not distressed, are you?" Isabel asked as she placed a comforting hand on his arm.

Laurence turned to his wife and was once again amazed at her beauty. Her hair had been expertly done up into an intricate coiffure, and two long curls framed her lovely face. It was as if the most brilliant of painters had composed her cheekbones, her perfect nose, and her deep blue eyes. He had never experienced love before, not the love a man has for a woman, but he could see himself being afflicted with such an emotion for this woman.

There was a joy in seeing her each morning, in hearing her words of encouragement, and in being able to help her in some meaningful manner.

He had sworn to himself that he would make her happy, and by attending this party with her, he was taking a step toward meeting that goal. One thing he had learned was that Isabel was very much like him in that she preferred to remain at home, and by pulling him from his isolation, she was forcing herself from her own, as well.

"Laurence?" Isabel squeezed his hand.

"I apologize," he replied, realizing he had not answered her question. "I am all right." He sighed. "Perhaps a bit nervous, if I am honest," he added with a small smile. He might be nervous, but her gloved hand on his brought him comfort.

"Honesty is best," she said, and he could not help but laugh. "You are brave for attending this evening. I understand that it is not easy for you to do so."

"Yes, well, knowing you are beside me has helped immensely." He gave her his best smile. "I speak as an artist, not as your husband."

She laughed. "You speak as a kind man, the man I married. If I wished to marry a brute, I would have done so."

They shared in another laugh, and then the carriage came to a stop. "It appears we have arrived," Isabel said, pulling the curtain aside and peering out. "The night is yours."

"The night is ours," he corrected.

The door opened, and Laurence waited as Isabel stepped down from the vehicle. Once he was out, he soaked in his surroundings. The house, a square brick building painted white with large windows on either side of the veranda reminded Laurence of wide eyes on a surprised face.

"Applewood Estate," he announced with a laugh. "And not a single apple on a tree for miles."

"Have you been here before?" Isabel asked.

"Many times. It has been years, but the place has not changed much. At one point, I thought Hugh would marry Harriet. Thankfully, the man had more sense."

149

Isabel laughed and the two walked up the few steps where a liveried man stood waiting. With his straight back and forward chin, he greatly resembled a King's Life Guard.

The man gave them a deep bow. "Your Graces." He collected their outer garments and hats, which he handed to a younger man, also in livery, although the older appeared more comfortable in his clothing than the younger. "If you will follow me."

He led them through a set of double doors, from which came the lively melodies of a collection of stringed instruments and the laughter of several people. Perhaps twenty couples in their finest clothing stood in small groups laughing and talking. For a moment, fear gripped Laurence as he scanned the array of familiar and unfamiliar faces. When he remembered Isabel beside him, his previous confidence, as minuscule as it was, returned.

A familiar face stepped forward with a cheeky grin. "Laurence!" Hugh said. "It has been too long since you have been here."

"Yes, much too long," Laurence replied as he shook the hand Hugh offered. "I would like to introduce my wife, Isabel."

Hugh's smile widened, if that were possible. "My pleasure," he said as he took her hand and kissed her knuckles. He then turned to the other guests and raised his voice. "Everyone, I would like to introduce my good friend, His Grace, Laurence Redbrook, Duke of Ludlow and his wife Isabel."

As all eyes turned to him, Laurence had to force himself to keep his back straight. What he wished he could do was hide in a corner behind one of the large ferns that dotted the room.

"I want to thank you all for being here for this celebration of my new business venture. Enjoy the food and wine to your heart's content, for it is the finest you will find anywhere."

"This room is beautiful," Isabel whispered.

Laurence had to agree. It was not as large as the ballroom at Camellia Estates, but it was much more lavish with its gilt etched ceiling and gold-trimmed panels on the walls. Although it had only one chandelier, it was large enough to light the entire room, the light intensified by framed mirrors placed at precise angles to illuminate even the corners of the room.

"It is," Laurence replied.

"It has inspired me to redecorate the ballroom at Camellia Estates," Isabel said, but then she stopped and worried her lip. "My apologies. That should be your decision."

Laurence smiled. "No," he said. "It pleases me you wish to do so. I look forward to what you do with it." He looked across the room and a familiar sight caught his eye. "I would like to show you something." He offered her his arm and the two walked over to a painting that hung on the far wall.

"Is that Applewood Estate?" Isabel asked. "It is very well done; every window and hedge are present. The painter is a master."

"Thank you," Laurence replied with pride. "I am that painter, although Hugh believes I commissioned it from another."

"You have not told him you painted it?"

Laurence shook his head. "I prefer to keep my abilities secret."

Isabel turned to him. "But why? You are a magnificent painter. You should allow the entire world to see your capabilities."

"It is better this way."

Her smile warmed his soul. "You are an amazing man," she said in a near whisper, or what could be considered a near whisper amongst the music and laughter. How beautiful she was – how perfect.

"And you are the most amazing woman I have ever known," he said with complete and utter honesty. "I am honored to be your husband, and I look forward to our many years together." When she replied with a smile, he added, "I must admit, I care for you deeply."

Her eyes widened and then she brought a gloved hand to her mouth and coughed. "I apologize," she replied in a choked voice. "My throat is parched."

"Allow me to get you a drink," he said. She nodded, and he hurried over to the refreshment table to pour them each a punch. When he returned to her, he handed her one of the glasses.

She took a small sip. "Much better," she said. "I fear the changing weather is affecting me."

Laurence could not stop the surge of doubt that came over him.

Did she feign the cough so as not to be forced to respond to his admission of affection for her? It was possible. When she smiled once more, his doubts retreated, but he wanted to learn if his instincts were correct or if he was simply seeing what he expected to see.

He did not get the opportunity to repeat his admission, for she spoke first. "Does my husband wish to introduce me to old friends?" she asked, her eyes sparkling.

What remained of his doubt disappeared. "I would be honored," he replied. He took her glass and placed it and his on a nearby table. Then he offered her his arm, which she took readily, the loveliest of smiles on her lips.

He led her to a couple with whom he was acquainted, each step taken in pride, and he realized that, for the first time in a very long time, he was truly happy. And the cause of that happiness was the woman beside him, his wife and the woman he now knew he loved.

***

Isabel was thankful when Laurence became engaged in conversation with an old friend, allowing her to slip away with a glass of wine and take time to compose herself. In all honesty, the evening was going better than expected. The carriage ride to Applewood Estate had been enjoyable, as had meeting Laurence's friend Hugh. She could understand why Laurence liked him, for he was pleasant and had a streak of humor in him that she found refreshing.

He did not carry himself as if he thought he was better than everyone else like so many of the *ton*. Granted, he had no title, but he was brought up in a titled home and therefore had been raised accordingly. Perhaps it was the fact he had no title that made him feel free to be himself.

As much as Hugh entertained, Isabel felt a greater joy as she watched Laurence overcome his fear. He had not only attended the party – with extreme reluctance and yet he had to be complimented for taking that step – but he interacted with others.

152

He held his head high, laughed, and replied to questions as if he had not been living the life of a hermit these past years. And Isabel could not have been prouder.

Yet, there was more than pride. They had spent these past mornings at their painting lessons, working closely together in the corner of the ballroom when the rays of the sun streamed into the room and directly onto the canvases.

Their evening meals were always shared now, and with each passing day, they became better acquainted as their conversations grew. It was when he had shown her the painting of Applewood Estate that had topped it all, for he had not a shred of conceit in his words. As far as she knew, no one else was aware that he was the painter of that artwork, and to be trusted in such a way said much of his feelings for her.

Not to mention his words. When he had said she was amazing, an odd thing occurred. Her heart soared, for that was the moment she saw Laurence as her husband. Oh, she was well aware that they were married, but thus far she felt he was more a friend and confidante than a spouse. And although her feelings could not be considered love, she found that she had acquired a great affection for him, and for some reason, that pleased her.

She had experienced those feelings before, when she married Arthur, but she had loved him from the beginning. Therefore, when Laurence had mentioned the many years they would be together, the emotions those words had brought about had both confused and excited her. Thus her reason for her feigned fit of coughing. Yes, it was childish and most unbecoming of a lady, no less a duchess, yet she had been unsure as to what to do.

Now as she stood in the corner pretending to admire another of the many paintings that hung from the walls, her mind raced. She was tempted to follow these emotions to see where they led. Would this time perhaps be different? Would her marriage be full of laughter instead of heartache? Worry consumed her as she sipped at her wine – her second glass since Laurence had given her punch – and she wondered if allowing this man into her heart was the right thing to do.

She turned just enough to see Laurence now speaking with Hugh. How happy he looked! Gone was the worry he had carried for what the *ton* would say about him, replaced by a radiance that made him glow. The man was clearly in his element, for which she was glad.

"Isabel?"

Isabel started and turned in shock to see Arthur's youngest brother standing behind her, a man she had not seen since her former husband's passing.

"It is you!" he said with a wide smile.

"Conner," she replied. "I did not expect to see you here this evening."

"I arrived only moments ago," the man replied. "It has been a while. Are you well?"

Isabel nodded. "I am." The man who stood before her reminded her so much of his eldest brother, she had to blink to remind herself it was not Arthur. "I have remarried."

"So I heard," the man said with clear enthusiasm. "I am happy for you. The duke is well respected."

"Indeed."

"And your family?" He attempted to appear nonchalant, but Isabel could see he had something on his mind.

"They are well."

For some reason, Conner's cheeks reddened. "And Miss Hannah?"

Isabel raised an eyebrow. "She is well," she replied, intrigued at his inquiry. Was there an interest there she had not realized existed?

He shifted on his feet and said, "I heard she was unwell during the London season this past year. Was it not to be her first season?"

"Yes," Isabel said, stifling a giggle. If only he knew her sister had feigned her illness. "She is expected to be of good health this year."

"I am glad." He took a drink from his glass, and the conversation turned to other news of her family – Nathaniel and his time at school, Juliet and her upcoming introduction to society, and her mother's continued good health.

It was inevitable when the conversation turned to Arthur.

"A man taken from us much too soon," Conner said with a sad shake to his head. "Not a day goes by that I do not think of him."

"He is greatly missed," Isabel said solemnly. It was the truth, and yet an uncomfortable sensation came over her. The elation she had been feeling over Laurence was seeping away like water through bedrock.

"Indeed. I never saw him as happy as he was when he married you."

Isabel said nothing. What could she say? The truth was, how could she be reminiscing with the brother of her former husband when she was now wed to another? Somehow, it felt...indecent.

Conner must have sensed her discomfiture, for he said, "I apologize. You are remarried, and here I am discussing your deceased husband. I do not mean any disrespect; it is just that I miss him terribly."

Isabel felt bad for her thoughts, even if this man could not have heard them. "Not at all," she replied kindly. "The past should never be forgotten, nor the dead who populated it."

Although she said the words, Isabel wished she could forget her own past. Too many memories brought on emotions she no longer wished to relive, but it was bound to happen when one spoke with the family of the one who had died. What right did she have to take away their memories?

They spoke for a few more minutes about nothing of consequence before Conner excused himself, to Isabel's relief. Conner was pleasant enough, but she had enough of her own memories, she did not need to add his to the mix.

She glanced around in search of Laurence, who was now speaking with another man who had joined him and Hugh. The smile she gave him was easily returned, and her mind thought of the conversation with Conner, and then subsequently of Arthur.

Without warning, the memory of the day Arthur's friend arrived with news of his death came to mind. She had been overcome with grief, which was to be expected. What she did not anticipate was another sensation that had plagued her that day. An emotion that she still carried today.

Guilt.

She took a drink of her wine and returned her gaze to her husband.

There lay too much risk, and a pain resided inside her that he would never understand. Although she was undecided not an hour earlier, she now came to a painful conclusion. She had allowed herself to open her heart to Laurence, and now she knew it was a foolish mistake.

Therefore, she made a resolution. She would continue to please him, for she was his wife, yet she also vowed to seal her heart and never open it again, for to do so would only invite pain, and she had endured enough for one lifetime.

Chapter Twenty

To say he felt elation was an understatement, for Laurence felt a happiness and confidence he had not felt for many years. The party at Applewood Estate, which had taken place just over a fortnight ago, had just been the beginning, and truth be told, he awaited the next with the eagerness of a child on his first journey to the seaside.

It was not only his excitement for returning to society that had a hold on him. After two additional weeks of early morning lessons, his wife was ready to venture off into the world of painting on her own. Yet, although it brought him joy to have her beside him participating in an activity that brought him such peace, he worried she did not share his enthusiasm.

Something had changed in the woman beside him since Hugh's party; more specifically when he had shared his feelings for her. Certainly, she had joined him for her lessons with a smile every day since, but her behavior toward him was somehow different, a bit more reserved. Yet, he could not put his finger on what exactly had changed.

He glanced at her canvas. She had been painting a landscape of a field with numerous trees, but now her brush rested in the cup of linseed oil, her pallet on the table beside her as she stared at her creation.

"It is coming along quite nicely," he said, hoping to encourage her. "Your first painting will soon be done, and we will display it in a place of pride."

"Thank you." She spoke barely above a whisper, and when she picked up the glass of wine beside her, he bit his tongue in order to not make any comment. Her drinking had increased since their wedding, he noticed, and she was rarely seen without a glass, even in the early mornings.

"I have thought about the party Hugh held," he said in an attempt to launch a conversation. Where they had chatted as they practiced the various types of strokes he had taught her before the party, they now sat the majority of the time in near silence; the only words spoken were questions she asked of him concerning her learning or words of encouragement from him.

He added a touch of brown to a tree and awaited her response, and when she made none, he continued. "It has been some time since I have had such a marvelous time." Still, she made no comment, and he stopped and turned to her. "Perhaps it is time to host our own party. A celebration of our marriage and our new life together."

"That would be lovely," she replied before taking another sip of her wine. Was her enthusiasm forced?

"I am sure your sisters would enjoy attending. You will invite them, will you not?"

A small smile found her lips, much to his relief, and she replied, "Yes, they would. I would like to see them again." Her ardor was short-lived. "I do not wish to continue with this painting. May I begin another?"

Laurence wished to encourage her to continue with the one she had begun, but, instead, he nodded. "I have a few unfinished works myself," he replied. He did not add that they were very few. "Do you know what you wish to paint? Perhaps an animal or an ocean setting might do."

Isabel sighed sadly. "I am unsure. Somehow, I feel...overwhelmed." She looked up at him, and a dispiritedness rolled off her in waves. "You are a brilliant painter, but I am afraid I cannot do this anymore. I will never complete a painting."

"That is not true," Laurence said as he reached out and took her hand in support. When he had done so before, her hand was always welcoming. Now he could feel her reluctance, and his worry increased. "Paint from your heart. Whatever you desire, put it onto the canvas. Allow the brush to speak what your heart is not able to say, and you will be surprised by the results."

Although Isabel nodded, she removed her hand from his, and Laurence returned to his painting, a foreboding he could not explain coming over him. There was no doubt, something had happened in the last two weeks, and he knew in his heart it had begun during the party Hugh had given.

He glanced over at her. Was it his confession of his feelings for her that had brought about this metamorphosis? He believed that was part of it, but he suspected there was more to it than that. He had seen her speaking to Conner Barnet, brother to her former husband. Had seeing the man resurrected memories of Arthur?

What a fool he was. Of course, speaking of her former husband would bring back memories. It was clear she had loved the man; how could he expect her to not be reminded of him at every turn, and even more so when she is confronted by his brother? Yet, how does one compete with the memory of a ghost?

Frustrated, Laurence dipped his brush into the green paint and pressed it to the canvas as he continued his recollection of that evening. Perhaps seeing the man had not only resurrected memories of Arthur, but also her love of the man. The fact that lack of love was not what had separated them but rather because the man had fallen in a tragic accident also played its part.

As he continued to paint, a pastime that had once eased his mind, that lovely confidence that had returned began to slip. The woman who sat staring at the blank canvas before her had gone from a man she loved to one she did not, and the more he considered this, the truer his suspicions became. He could never have a place in her heart, for it belonged to her former husband, every bit of it, and as much as he hated to admit it, she was not willing to open it up once more.

The pain in that thought forced him to realize that he truly loved his wife. It crushed him to know she did not return the sentiment.

Perhaps Harriet had been right after all; he had been responsible for the death of their parents, and now he failed to win over the heart of his wife. The truth throbbed as much as the pain in his leg. He was undeserving of his title, and it appeared he never would be.

But no. He was not willing to give up just yet.

"I am sorry," Isabel said, breaking him from his thoughts. "I do not feel well and wish to return to my room. Is that all right?"

"Yes, of course," he said with concern. "Would you like food sent up to you? Or perhaps I can call in Doctor Comerford."

"No, that will not be needed."

With a heavy heart, Laurence watched as Isabel walked away. He returned his tools to their places and then walked over to the portrait of his parents. Guilt plagued him, and he hung his head beneath their fixed gaze.

"Father, I thought Isabel would bring me happiness, and although I have felt it at times, I am riddled with shame." His hand moved to his leg. "It may have been too much to hope that Isabel would be my repentance for all my wrongdoing." He waited for a response he knew would never come.

Sighing, he turned his back on the portrait. His parents were long gone, and nothing would bring them back. He would receive no redemption. Not now. Not in the future. He was destined to live in contrition until he, too, joined his parents. If Heaven would have him.

As he stared at his half-finished work, he no longer wished to resume painting. Instead, he went to his office, wondering what the future would hold and guessing he would more than likely not like it.

***

As the week continued, Laurence believed Isabel grew unhappier with each passing moment. He made attempts to speak on subjects that would be of interest to her – their upcoming party, the redecorating of the ballroom, her love of the rolling hills beyond the garden gates – but whatever he proposed or brought up for consideration was met with a simple nod or short replies. It pained him to see her in such a state, but nothing seemed to bring her out of her melancholy.

One particular morning as they sat in their regular places in the ballroom, Isabel heaved a heavy sigh and rose from her stool. "I cannot continue," she complained. She had begun yet another painting, her fifth in as many days, and like the others, it was not completed. "I am sorry. Perhaps If I observe you over the next few mornings, I will gain a bit more understanding of the steps required." She grabbed her customary glass of wine and clicked her tongue when a few drops splashed on her hand.

Laurence had had enough. He stood and took the glass from her hand. "We must talk," he demanded.

"About?"

"You are drinking more than is proper," he scolded. "And you hardly speak to me anymore."

"I apologize," she said as she cast her eyes to the floor. "I will make attempts to do better."

Laurence sighed. "I do not want you to make attempts."

She raised her head, and he took a step back from the coldness that came from her eyes. "Then what do you expect?" she demanded. "I have done everything I can to please you, and yet it appears I am still unable to do so."

"You speak as if it were a task assigned to you," he said, taken aback by her words.

Isabel shook her head. "It is not that," she said as she walked over to the window.

"It is not a task?"

She did not look at him when she replied, "No."

"Very well then, what is it?" He knew he sounded as if he were begging, but he had to know the truth. "Is it my leg?" She shook her head. "It is more than learning to paint. You have been this way since the party at Applewood Estate." He walked up to stand behind her. How he wished he could wrap his arms around her and hold her, to comfort her, but he did not. "It is Arthur," he said when she made no indication to respond. The drop of her head told him he had spoken the truth. "I suspected as much since you spoke to his brother. I assume the love for your former husband has returned."

"It is not that," she whispered.

"No. That is it. He was a better man, more complete than I. If that is the truth, then do not deny it. I would rather have my heart broken by the truth than to hold joy over false words."

When Isabel turned to face him, she looked at him with reddened eyes. "I am not happy here," she said simply.

"I see. Have you felt this way since our marriage?"

"Yes," came her whispered reply. "Do not doubt that I care for you, for I do. I cannot care for you in the way you desire. Or need."

Anger boiled inside Laurence. "I have done everything I could possibly do to win your heart. I have purchased new dresses and gowns for you, new jewelry, hats. Yet, nothing I do seems to have any effect on you."

"I want none of those things."

He barely heard her words as his ire built. "And Harriet! I removed my own sister from my home for you. And yet, even that does not make you happy! What I want...what I need is to understand why."

"Because I cannot make you happy!" she shouted, her hands clenched at her side. "Harriet needed to be removed for you, not for me or anyone else."

Laurence shook his head, unable to believe what he was hearing. "Then I shall never do so again."

She met his gaze without wavering. "Do what?" she demanded.

"Remove my sister for your sake."

"I told you that it was your choice, and yet you laid the blame on me. That is not fair! The decision was yours, not mine."

He gave a derisive snort. "Apparently a bad one at that, but that is of little consequence now. You are not happy, and like many things in life, I have failed to bring you even the smallest amount of joy. What do you wish, if I might ask?"

"Nothing. You have done more than enough for me and my family."

He took a deep breath and let it out slowly. His anger was great, but the sadness in his heart blew past it like a wind coming in from a storm over the ocean. "You do not wish to remain here. With me." He said the words, and as they left his lips, it was as though he was condemning himself.

And as he looked into Isabel's eyes, he knew the answer before she spoke. It pained him more than anything, but having her remain where she was so terribly unhappy pained him more. A caged animal could not have pained him to this point.

"Laurence," Isabel whispered, "perhaps we can..."

He raised his hand in defeat. "No. I will not listen any longer. I have houses in London and throughout the country. We will find a place you prefer, and you can live there. I can tell people I travel on business often, and that is the reason you prefer that home to Camellia Estates."

For the first time, a single tear rolled down her cheek. "I am sorry. I did not mean for this to happen."

He was tired of apologies, but he could see in her eyes she spoke the truth. "I believe you." He turned back to the canvases and sighed. "Perhaps you should return to Scarlett Hall for a few days."

Isabel walked up to him and placed a hand on his arm. "Is there anything I can do?"

How he wished to ask her to remain here, to give him one more chance to prove his love for her. Then, as his eyes scanned the unfinished work, an idea occurred to him. "I make but one request," he said. "When you return, I want you to complete a painting, but you must swear it will come from the heart. Whatever it may be, it must come from deep within you."

"You have my word," Isabel replied. "I will do that."

He nodded and returned to his stool. Isabel stood behind him, watching for a moment, and then soon after left him alone in the ballroom. He tried to focus his attention on the canvas, but he found he was unable to. His heart had taken over his thoughts. Isabel was returning to her family home, and once she completed the painting she had promised him, she would leave him. His house would be empty once again, her laugh and promise gone. And even worse, the love he had for her would never be uttered, not now or ever in the future, for he could not endure such rejection once again.

Chapter Twenty-One

Numbness. Isabel had felt nothing but numbness for some time now. In fact, it had been well over a year since she had experienced any true emotions. To the casual observer, one might believe she was simply another lady amongst many, for, at various moments, she could be seen smiling or finding joy in a particular activity. The majority of the time was spent in complete apathy, both in mind and soul. That was how she found herself now as she entered Scarlett Hall, hoping that happiness would come to her once again.

"Forbes," Isabel said, "it is good to see you again."

The old butler did not shy away from her embrace as some butlers would, for which she was glad. The man had been a part of the staff at Scarlett Hall for so long, he was close to being a member of the family, and Isabel was honored he was so kind to her.

Forbes took her bag from her and said, "And it is good to see you again, Your Grace. I will see your bag taken upstairs to your old room."

"Thank you," Isabel replied with a smile.

When he was gone, she stood in the foyer staring around with appreciation. And yet, something was missing. She was glad to be home, to be certain, but the joy she had expected was lacking, and that did not sit well with her. Well, it was not as if she returned under the best of circumstances.

An image of Laurence came to mind. She had not meant to hurt the man, and although she had tried to speak about her feelings with care, her words had only increased his ire. Yet, it was more than that; it was all too clear that his heart had been broken by her words, and for that, she could only feel regret.

"Isabel?"

Isabel turned as her mother came down the staircase. "Hello, Mother."

"I was not expecting you."

Was there more gray scattered through her mother's hair? It was difficult to tell with her light coloring and the swatch of fabric that covered it, but there did seem to be more at her temples than even the last time Isabel had seen her. Regardless, if her hair had changed, her strength had not.

"Laurence will be occupied with business matters this week and suggested I return for a few days' visit."

Her mother studied her for a moment as she stepped off the staircase. "Is that all?" she asked. "There is nothing more that brought you back here?"

Isabel had no desire to tell her mother the truth, for she had been the cause of Isabel's current predicament. "No. There is nothing more."

"Your sisters and your cousin Annabel are in the garden," her mother said. "If you would like to join them."

For a brief moment, Isabel considered speaking with her mother about her troubles with Laurence. How she missed the closeness they had once shared! It would do no good, for the woman would never understand the pain Isabel endured. Yes, she was a widow just as Isabel was, but the pain Isabel carried went deeper than her grief over the loss of her husband. Furthermore, what could her mother do if Isabel did tell her? Not a thing.

"I often wonder why Annabel never remained with us," Isabel said in order to make an attempt at conversation with her mother. There was no denying that Isabel still loved the woman despite the fact she had been forced to clean up the mess her mother had made. "Scarlett Hall is more a home to her than her own."

Annabel's parents often left her at home with a chaperon, or a governess when she was younger, or allowed her to stay with Isabel and her sisters. Many nights, the poor girl wept, and Isabel did what she could to console her, assuring her that she was loved.

"Annabel has known she is always welcome here," her mother replied. "If the time comes, and she wishes to remain, she will do so."

Isabel pursed her lips. "Unlike me, you mean," she said.

Her mother went to speak, but Isabel jutted out her chin and strode past the woman without allowing her the opportunity to respond. Once she was outside, Isabel leaned against the railing to rein in her emotions.

Her world was falling apart. Her new marriage, for all intents and purposes, was over, and now she had to decide where to live. Although she wanted to return to Scarlett Hall once more for good, she could not for two reasons. First, it was much too close to Camellia Estates, and thus too close to Laurence. The rumors of the *ton* would bring forth unnecessary embarrassment for the duke, and she could not do that to him. He was not the one at fault for her shortcomings.

The second reason she could not return to Scarlett Hall was much more heartbreaking. Although she loved the place where she was born and raised, and she missed her sisters terribly, the truth of the matter was that she could not stand to look at her mother on a daily basis. Yes, thinking in such a way about the woman she had loved all her life was terrible, but the anger Isabel had for her mother was that great.

"Isabel!" Hannah cried as she came running down the footpath. "It is you!"

Isabel returned her sister's smile and then hugged her and kissed her head. "My sweet Hannah," she whispered. "I have missed you."

"And I have missed you," Hannah replied. "I believe Juliet is ill, for she has been behaving herself as of late."

Isabel laughed as she and Hannah walked in the direction from which Hannah had just come. "That is wonderful to hear. And Annabel? I hear she is with us once again. How is she?"

"She is well, as usual. I have a feeling she does not share with us how she truly feels."

Isabel nodded. She understood all too well the girl's situation. And her propensity to hide her feelings from others.

"You are upset."

The statement caught Isabel off-guard, and she stopped beside a large well-trimmed hedge. "I?" she asked with a forced laugh. "I have never been better."

Hannah sighed and took Isabel's hands in hers. "You have always looked after me," she said. Then Juliet and Annabel came around a corner and joined them. "You have looked after all three of us."

Isabel smiled as the other two girls added their hands to those of Isabel and Hannah to form a circle, and it reminded Isabel of the night before her wedding when they had escaped into the night to drink brandy around a campfire. If only they could repeat that night forever.

"You have encouraged me to do the things I like," Hannah continued. "Even when others laughed or thought it odd."

"And I," Juliet said. "You were patient when you corrected me, demonstrating always how to behave properly."

Tears welled up in Isabel's eyes. How she loved these girls so much!

"You are the big sister I have always wanted," Annabel added. "One who listens to my problems with patience and understanding, and one who gives me sound advice."

Hannah sniffled. "You have been there for all of us."

Isabel looked at each of her sisters – Annabel was included in that moniker – and smiled. "Thank you," she said as she blinked back tears. "I love you all and will continue to help in any way I am able."

Juliet glanced at Hannah, who gave a nod. "We are worried about you," she said. "We know you carry some sort of burden, and you can share with us if you would like. It might make you feel better."

The words were innocent and heartfelt, and Isabel could not stop a tear from escaping her eye and roll down her cheek. As she looked over the three faces before her, her heart swelled with love for them. Although she wished she could bare her heart to these young women, she would not, for they did not deserve to be burdened with what were her problems.

"You are correct when you say that I carry many burdens," she replied, choosing her words with care. "There is no reason for me to speak of them now." When the girls went to argue, she stopped them with a raised hand. "All you must know is that I am doing what I can to resolve these issues, and if I believe you can lend me aid in some way, I will ask."

This seemed to appease them as they smiled. Then Juliet took a half-step in and whispered, "Laurence. Does he hurt you? If he does, Annabel and I will march right over to Camellia Estates and shoot him!"

Isabel gaped at her younger sister. "Never say such things about him," she said with a shake to her head. "He is a good man and would never hurt me."

As the last words left her lips, a feeling came over Isabel, a near-peace she had not known was there. In her heart, at that moment, she realized that she had spoken the truth; Laurence would never hurt her, and that realization somehow made the day a bit brighter.

"I am sorry," Juliet said with her head bowed. "I have heard rumors of men who strike their wives, and I did not want you to be in such a situation."

Isabel hugged Juliet, and then Hannah and Annabel insisted on another hug, as well.

Soon, they were all talking and sharing in what they had been doing since Isabel had last visited, and by the time the circle broke, Isabel's heart had lightened significantly.

When the girls returned to the house and whatever activities they had planned for the day, Isabel continued her walk through the garden. As she neared a flowerbed filled with a variety of roses, she looked toward the direction of Camellia Estates. Perhaps she had been wrong to leave as she did, or maybe she should have told Laurence the truth about how she was feeling.

And, like many times in her life, Isabel could not unravel the confusion that had turned her life on its head.

***

Laurence entered the ballroom just as he had many times before, but this time Isabel would not join him. His footsteps, although not particularly loud, echoed in the empty room, now left emptier by her absence. He had grown accustomed to her sitting beside him, even if they did not speak to one another, and that only made the room that much more vacuous.

He turned and studied the row of unfinished canvases that lined the wall. Half-finished paintings of landscapes, various animals that lacked tails or manes, all incomplete. When Isabel had agreed to join him in painting lessons, he had been overjoyed, and during their time together, they had bonded, sharing in stories and laughter with each stroke of the brush.

He had hoped that she would soon care for him as he cared for her, but that dream came to a sudden end. Their argument the previous day still weighed heavy in the air. He regretted that he had grown angry when she informed him that she no longer wished to remain at Camellia Estates, but her words about Harriet concerned him more. Laurence had requested that his own sister leave, and he had done so for Isabel.

That made him pause, for Isabel's words returned. What had been his true motivation for asking Harriet to leave? Had he done it for his wife or was there another reason?

Frustrated, he sat on his stool and stared at the empty canvas as images of Harriet came to his mind. The years of belittling he had endured from her. Her propensity to hang the guilt of their parents' death over him. And he had welcomed that guilt as easily as a lamb suckled its mother's teat, for he believed it was his burden to bear. Yet was that burden truly his?

Releasing a sigh, he stood and then groaned as pain shot through his leg. Would this pain never leave? No, it would not, for it was a more constant reminder of the burden he carried, his reward for the part he played in the death of his parents.

He walked over to the painting of his parents and stood before it. Memories flooded back of that fateful day, and closing his eyes, he hoped to shut them out. They returned in his mind's eye, and his heart turned to lead.

"Have I not suffered enough?" he whispered. When he opened his eyes, his mother's smile greeted him, as did his that of his father. Their look held no grudge. Instead, their faces held peace. And was that forgiveness?

No, not forgiveness but something else, something he could not name, which only increased his frustration.

"Laurence."

The whisper made him jump, and he turned hoping that Isabel had decided to return early. Yet it was not Isabel who stood at the door but his sister.

"Harriet?" he asked as the woman slowly approached. Something was different about her. Where she always held her nose high so she could look down upon everyone else around her, she now hung her head. "What are you doing here?"

"I realize I am not welcome," she said, her voice unusually soft. "But it is imperative I speak with you."

Then he saw the redness in her eyes, as if she had cried recently. Never had he seen his sister so distressed.

"Please, come in," he said as he returned his gaze to the portrait.

"I miss them," Harriet said as she stood beside him. "For so long, their deaths have haunted me." She turned to face him. "I could not grasp that they had left us." To add to his confusion, tears rolled down her cheeks. This was not the Harriet he knew, and he could not help but wonder if it was a ruse. "Ambrose and I had an argument."

So, the perfect marriage is not so perfect after all, he thought, but he found that it did not give him as much pleasure as he would have expected. Instead, he felt pity for his sister. "I am very sorry to hear this."

She snorted. "There is no need to be. What he said was extremely hurtful, but that is not the worst of it."

"Oh?" Laurence asked.

"No. We...that is, I discussed having children, and he told me he did not wish to have any."

Laurence could not stop his jaw from dropping. A man who did not want children? And a marquess to boot? That was unheard of.

"And do you know why?" she asked, that same quiet tone in her voice. What he would have expected was anger and resentment, but he heard no traces of either.

"I cannot imagine why. He is a good man, and I know he loves you as you love him."

Harriet nodded. "That is true; we do love one another." She wiped at her eyes before lowering her head once again. "But his reasoning is sound."

"And what reason is that?"

She sighed. "He fears bringing a child into a world that would be as cruel-hearted as their mother." With this, she began to sob into her gloved hands. She took the kerchief Laurence offered her and wiped her nose. "At first, I was angry. I collected my things and returned to Margaret's house. Then I wrote Ambrose a letter much like the one I had written to you. I demanded an apology for him treating me so horribly."

"I am sorry," Laurence said.

"No," Harriet said with an avid shake to her head. "Do you not understand? Ambrose was right! I am cruel. To the servants, to my friends, to my husband, and even...to my own brother."

The suspicions Laurence had felt upon her sudden arrival now dissipated. Never before had he seen his sister in such a state, and to hear her speak so freely and honestly astounded him.

"When they left us," she continued as she looked up at their parents' portrait, "I was shocked and did not understand the gravity of death. What it meant for us and how it would change our lives. I refused to accept they were gone. Therefore, in that hurt and grief, I attempted to place blame for their deaths. I blamed you, my brother, who did no wrong. My brother who wrote to me whenever he was away at school and did his best to encourage me."

"It was because I have always cared for you," he said. "I still do."

"I understand that now," she said as she turned to him and gave him a weak smile. "I know now what I became over the years, and I do not like that woman. Therefore, I ask...no, I beg your forgiveness. The old Harriet is now gone, and the new one wishes that you accept her apology so we can be the siblings we are meant to be."

Laurence did not hesitate as he pulled Harriet into his arms. As he embraced her, she sobbed into his shoulder. "I am so sorry," she whispered. "You are not responsible for the death of our parents; you never were."

Those words left him with such a sense of relief, he thought he would rise from the floor. For years, she had ridiculed him, blamed him, hated him, and for years, he did what he could to appease her, to no avail. At least one of them no longer believed him guilty.

"Thank you," he replied. "You are my sister, and I love you. You are welcome at Camellia Estates at any time." He sighed. "I look forward to our new relationship."

"As do I." She paused. "I have one more request before I return to settle things with Ambrose."

"Yes, of course," he replied. "What do you need?"

"Isabel. My words and actions were so cruel toward her. I must apologize and seek her forgiveness, as well."

Laurence sighed.

"What is it?" she asked.

"Isabel is not here," he replied. "And I am afraid she will never return."

Chapter Twenty-Two

A lthough Scarlett Hall offered Isabel warmth and the love of her sisters, the pain she had brought with her when she had returned four days prior had not eased. The walls contained laughter, yet they did not echo in her heart as they once did. In fact, the home now seemed to push her away, as if she were some sort of thorn it wished extracted from its surroundings.

Soon, Isabel would be forced to return to Camellia Estates and fulfill the promise she had made to Laurence, to complete a painting from her heart, and she vowed to keep it. She had given the subject much consideration, but still she had no idea what the subject of her work would be.

Her other paintings had been complete disasters, and every time she thought about it, she grew more and more frustrated. In order to obtain permission from Laurence for her to live wherever she chose, she had no choice but to complete this task, as ridiculous of a request as it was.

The thought of living in another home added to her remorse. She could not fathom hurting the man further, but she knew she would regardless. How could she not when she was unable to return his affections?

Shivering, she drew her wrap closer. The sun had not yet set, but the breeze was cool as the summer drew to a close and autumn woke from its slumber.

She had slipped out of the drawing room earlier with a glass of wine and now stood overlooking the garden in which she had spent so many hours of her childhood.

"No matter how much wine you drink," her mother said from behind her, "the pain will not ease."

"I have no pain," Isabel stated before drinking the remainder of her wine in one go. "I have come to enjoy a glass of wine in the evening, which is common for many people." She placed the glass on the stone railing as her mother stepped up beside her.

"And yet you enjoy a glass in the morning and after lunch, as well," her mother stated. "You are my daughter, and I recognize when you are hurting."

Isabel stared at her mother in astonishment. "You know when I am hurting?" she asked flatly. How dare this woman, who had mismanaged the finances to such a point that Isabel was forced to marry a man she did not love, say that she understood anything that Isabel was feeling at any given moment. "You know nothing of me! You know nothing of the chains that bind me into this life to which you have sold me."

"I know far more than you suspect," her mother replied. How did she remain so calm? It was as if Isabel's ire did not affect her in any way whatsoever, which only fueled Isabel's hurt that much more. "I know that the woman who stands before me was once a girl full of love. Many times, I ask myself where that girl has gone."

Like a dam bursting from the stress of too much water pressing against its walls, words tumbled from Isabel's lips, and she cared nothing for what damage they would cause. "She was forced to marry and live at Camellia Estates," she said with indignation. "Her laughter, her love, remained behind." She motioned to the house behind them. "That is where that girl is now. Hidden away in some dark corner of the house she loves."

"I do not believe that," her mother said. She placed a finger to Isabel's breast. "She is still inside you. Despite the hurt you have endured, she is there, buried beneath a mountain of pain and anguish. That is where that girl is."

"Then why did you bring about that pain?" Isabel demanded.

"You asked me to do the impossible and marry a man I did not love." She clenched her fist as she looked at her mother with scorn. "I had planned to live at Scarlett Hall forever, for I do not wish to love ever again! Now, not only am I destroyed, but Laurence is, as well. That poor man," Isabel tried to catch her breath between sobs, "The poor man tries every day to love me, to care for me as a husband should." Oh, how she wished she had another glass of wine! It would help ease this torment that wracked her body and soul.

"Why do you reject it, then?" her mother asked.

"Because I am afraid to love again," Isabel replied, tears now streaming down her cheeks unabated. "Do you not understand? I once loved and I do not wish to experience it again, for it ends in heartache."

"Your heart will not be healed by Scarlett Hall. Not even if Laurence gave you his blessing to return. You would soon come to realize that the pain you carry cannot be contained within walls, for it is attached to you and will go wherever you go."

Isabel sniffed derisively. "I will never know," she replied tartly, "for I will never be able to live here again." She narrowed her eyes at her mother. "And it is all because of you!" She shook her head in frustration. "All my life, I saw you as a strong woman, but you hid away these last years as I looked after my sisters. Then I learn that what you were truly doing was bringing this house to near ruin." A sliver of guilt entered her when her mother sniffled, but she straightened her back and pushed it away. These words were long in coming; she could no longer keep back the truth of her anger.

Her mother sighed. "What you say is correct. I hid away too long. Like you, I have carried pain and guilt over many things." She turned toward the house, staring at it as a mother stares at her newborn babe. When she returned her gaze to Isabel, she had a sense of certainty behind her eyes. "You are no longer a child, Isabel, so I will speak to you as an equal." She pointed back at the house. "What do you see?"

Isabel looked up at the home she loved. "Our home," she replied after some contemplation. No, it was more than their home. "The house that had been in our family for over one hundred and fifty years. A house built with pride and held together with love."

Her mother nodded her agreement. "Some of that is true, but that is not all it holds."

Isabel frowned. "What do you mean?"

"Scarlett Hall holds secrets so deep that they are embedded within the very layers that hold it together. It was because of one of those secrets that I asked you to marry the duke."

"Secrets?" Isabel asked in astonishment. "What secrets?" She had always thought her family open and honest with one another. Had she been deceived all her life?

Her mother sighed. "Come, follow me. There are things you must know, although I prayed this day would never come."

Isabel frowned as she followed her mother to the house. Once inside, her mother spoke to Forbes in a hushed tone, and although Isabel strained to hear their words, she could not. For several moments, they carried on until, with great reluctance, the butler dipped his head and hurried away.

"He appears upset," Isabel mused.

"Not at all," her mother replied. "This way." She led Isabel to the library, where she closed the door and walked to the bookshelf containing the tomes encased in glass. "You are familiar with what lies behind this glass, are you not?"

Isabel nodded. "Of course. They are the journals of the former Lady Lamberts. Father said they are filled with gossip and other such nonsense." Her cheeks heated when she saw her mother's jaw tighten. "Not that I believed him, mind you."

"For one hundred and fifty years, Scarlett Hall has stood far above other estates. Yet, this did not happen by chance, for the writings of every Lady Lambert, including myself, contain not gossip but rather secrets that have held this home together."

Isabel gaped as her mother produced a key from the pocket of her dress. "Secrets?" Isabel asked. "What sort of secrets?"

Her mother sighed. "I fear even mentioning them, for if others were to learn the truth, it would destroy everything the Lambert family has built. I will, however, share one with you, for once I do, you will come to understand much."

Isabel's heart began to thud in her chest. What secret could be within the pages of those tomes that she needed to know?

"Mother," she whispered, for some reason wishing to turn and run, "perhaps it would be best if – "

"Your father was not the man you believed him to be."

***

Scarlett Hall 1802

Lady Eleanor Lambert looked out the window of the study belonging to her husband, although it was she who had been assigned to balance the financial affairs of the estate.

On the desk behind her lay the latest ledgers for Scarlett Hall. The accounts listed inside detailed every holding the estate possessed as well as the everyday running of the household. The story they told was not of coffers of overflowing wealth but rather an estate that lay in near ruins.

Her gaze fell on a gardener as he walked down the cobbled path, stopping beside a rose bush with a pair of snips in his hand. What tore at her heart was the fact that the man performed his duties unaware that soon she would no longer be able to pay his wages.

Curse that man for the state in which he has put our home! she thought of her husband. Now his spendthrift ways had finally caught up to them and now threatened their children's very livelihood!

The door to the study opened, and Forbes entered. "My lady," he said with a deep bow, "Lord Lambert has agreed to join you in a few moments."

"Is he drunk?" she asked.

Forbes gave a nod, and she sighed. When was her husband not drunk? When they were courting, he had promised he would give up the drink, yet that had been one of many vows he had been unable to keep.

"Then I shall prepare myself for him accordingly." Her hand went instinctively to her jaw. "Thank you."

"My lady – "

She raised a hand to silence him. "Thank you," she repeated, this time with a note of clear dismissal.

Again, he bowed and then exited the room.

A moment later, Charles entered. "I was packing for my business travels," he snapped, his face a thunder cloud as he leaned on the desk, "yet you summon me like I am some sort of common servant? What do you want?" His breath reeked of spirits.

Eleanor, aware that his temper could explode at any given moment, and likely would once she said what needed to be said, braced herself for his wrath. "I would advise you not to take this journey," she said. She was well aware that he was not traveling for business, but it was the term she had become accustomed to using to explain to her children their father's many absences.

"Since when do you dictate my comings and goings?" he demanded.

"We are nearly bankrupt, Charles," Eleanor replied as she slid the ledger across the desk. "There is no more money. The loans are in default, and we have borrowed against every piece of property we own besides Scarlett Hall itself. Our friends rarely speak to us, and when they do, they cover their pockets in our presence. Your gambling debts have ruined everything." His breathing had become heavy, but she continued her prepared speech, even as her heart pounded with terror. "We have no choice. We must begin to sell – "

Charles reached out and grabbed her by the arms. "Do not blame me for the problems you have caused," he hissed. "The money has always found a way back into our coffers, so do whatever you can, but see that it is done."

Eleanor shook her head. "I have done all I can. There simply is no more money."

"Lies!" he bellowed as he shoved her so hard that her head bounced off the wall behind her. White speckles clouded her vision as she tried to remain standing. "I do not care how you do it," he growled, "but you will repair what you have done. Do you hear me?"

Closing her eyes and bracing herself for his fist, Eleanor whispered a silent prayer. Then she heard the sound of the slamming door, and she opened her eyes to find the room empty once again, yet his ranting voice echoed through the corridors of their home. A home that was soon to be lost forever. She was unsure from where the funds would come, but by some miracle, she would do as he requested.

Chapter Twenty-Three

Scarlett Hall, 5ᵗʰ of June 1805

Johnathan Brombley, debt collector, stared out the window of Eleanor's study, a scar running from the corner of his right eye to the tip of his chin making her stomach churn. The man had inquired about the gardens, but she knew very well where his gaze lingered.

"I'm afraid that I can no longer offer any more extensions, my lady," he said before turning toward her. "I can't extend even a farthing of mercy. Not any longer."

"What if we were to arrange more interest?" Eleanor suggested. "I believe I could then – "

The man's laugh cut off her words. "I know I'm not the only person you are indebted to. Do you not realize the peril you are in at the moment? Your home is collapsing, the stones are swaying, and your family will soon be crushed beneath them." He narrowed his eyes. "When I return for my money, I expect it to be paid in full. I will accept no more excuses, and don't ask me what'll happen if you don't have the funds, for you know quite well already, I'm sure."

Indeed, she knew, for the man's terrible reputation was well-known. It sickened her that she had been forced to do business with him, but what choice did she have? The smaller debt Charles had with the man had compounded into a larger one over the years, and

179

Eleanor had no choice but to beg for an extension when it came due.

Unfortunately, over the past year, she had learned of other debts that existed, all of which she had never been made aware. The list was far longer than she would have thought possible.

"Your eldest, her name is Isabel, correct?"

Eleanor nodded. "It is."

"Such a beautiful woman," Mr. Bromley mused. "I imagine she's lonely now that she has a bed all to herself, but there's no need for her to suffer at all." He chuckled, and Eleanor's skin grew cold. "Perhaps we can make an arrangement that can suit both of us. After all, I'm in need of a companion and you have a widowed daughter who is much too old to put back on the market."

Anger rose in Eleanor. Oh, how this man disgusted her! Well, she would not stand for it. "I will not give you my daughter as a form of payment. That is nonnegotiable."

Mr. Bromley's eyes bore into hers as he took a step closer, his breath hot on her face. "You may soon learn that what you refuse as payment," he glanced out the window, "may end up being what I will take in interest." When he smiled, the scar on his cheek looked more frightening than ever.

This was no veiled threat; she knew exactly what he meant. Yet, the thought of him laying a single finger on her daughter sickened her. It took every ounce of strength to keep from collapsing.

"You will leave my home at once," she said, her voice firm as she stepped aside.

"Just remember this, Eleanor," he said, pointing a finger at her, "Charles understood my terms when he came to me. He mentioned another daughter, one with dark hair. Is she the one – "

Eleanor lifted a hand to slap him, but the man grasped her by the wrist. "I wouldn't try that again if I were you," he growled. "When I return, have the money or have Isabel ready for me. I will not leave until I have one or the other. The choice is yours." He released her and walked to the door. "I'll see myself out."

Eleanor closed her eyes, her stomach knotted in worry. She would never hand over her Isabel to a man such as Johnathan Bromley. Turning to the window, her eyes fell on her eldest child, who stood with her arms wrapped around herself as if she were standing in a winter storm.

What Charles had done to their family was unforgivable and inviting the likes of Mr. Bromley into their lives made it all the worse.

"My sweet Isabel," Eleanor whispered. Much like her, her eldest daughter had suffered greatly through no fault of her own. Yet, Isabel had far greater strength than she realized.

"A man wishes to have you in lieu of payment, but I cannot allow that to happen. But there is one who will have you, may even come to love you, I am sure of it. The Duke of Ludlow has a good heart, and I trust that not only will he save our home, but he will save you, as well."

Returning to her desk, Eleanor drew in a deep breath. There was a letter already prepared, but she first needed to write another…

***

Isabel's head spun as her mother continued.

"That, my sweet child, is why I asked you to take on this burden, one that was not yours to bear. I could no longer carry it on my own. I just ask that you do not hate me, for I could not live another day if you did."

Everything Isabel thought she knew about her father, her parents' marriage, and even her marriage to Laurence, became clear. It was as if a veil of innocence had been torn from her. When she looked at her mother, she recognized her strength, a woman who never hid away from fear but instead faced it head-on. Now it was time for Isabel to do her part.

"I could never hate you," Isabel said, tears streaming down her cheeks. "I see now why you wished me to wed Laurence; you did so to protect me. I am so sorry for my actions as of late. I was so angry. I do love you, Mother, and I am glad Laurence and I have married. You were right all along; he is a man who has come to love me."

Her mother pulled Isabel into her arms. As they held one another, Isabel sobbed, releasing the anger and hurt that had once tormented her.

When the embrace ended, and Isabel's tears had subsided, her mother took her by the hands. "I know I have asked much of you, and now I place a question before you. Where is that girl who was filled with laughter and love that I knew so well? I miss her terribly."

"I miss her, as well," Isabel whispered. "I believe I know when I last saw her, but I must admit that I am uncertain how to find her again."

"Perhaps I can help."

Isabel smiled. "I would like that, for I do not know where to begin."

"But you have already taken the first steps," her mother replied. "I believe if you search very hard while you are here at Scarlett Hall, you will find those memories you have hidden away."

Isabel stared at her mother's hands, hands that had brushed her hair, that had nursed her when she had scraped her knee. Then she thought of Scarlett Hall and the memories that resided within its walls. Yes, she knew where to begin her search.

"Mother," she said slowly, "I have my secrets, as well. That girl who was so full of love? She disappeared soon after I was married."

"Then you must go in search of her at once," her mother said. "Do what you must because I miss your wonderful smile."

Isabel kissed her mother on the cheek and then went to the door. "Thank you for telling me the truth," she said. Then she set out in search of the woman she once had been.

Chapter Twenty-Four

Laurence stared into the empty fireplace, a glass of brandy dangling from his fingertips as he slumped down in the chair. Isabel was gone, and he doubted the woman would ever return. She would return to collect her belongings, to be sure, but then she would leave him as alone as he was now. Harriet had returned to her husband, and, for the first time in many years, she had left on good terms with Laurence. It was a good feeling, and he looked forward to seeing where this new bond they had reconstructed would lead them.

Even today, he wondered at the change that had come over the woman. When he had expressed his concern over Isabel and the possibility – the great possibility – that she would leave him, Harriet had comforted him and even gave him advice. She did not berate him, nor did she place all the blame on him as she would have in the past. No, this time, she was the sister he had not seen in all too long.

Sighing, he sipped at the brandy. Time moved without care for those around her, and soon winter would be upon them. Yet, would he have a companion with whom he would share a fire? In his heart, he hoped Isabel would be with him, but he feared that would never happen, for she did not love him as he had grown to love her.

How strange life was. When Lady Lambert had approached him about marrying her daughter, he had thought it barbaric. Granted, even his parents had married for convenience, but times were changing, and more people married for love than they had in the past. He had thought he had taken a step back in time when he decided to agree, but he could not imagine Scarlett Hall in the hands of anyone but a Lambert.

It had to be due to the loss of her husband that Isabel could not love him. She had loved Arthur, and Laurence knew it was impossible for a heart to have love for more than one. If she did decide she did not wish to reside with him, he would allow her to leave, just as he had said during their argument. If he forced her to remain, the agony he failed to remove would only worsen. And he could not bear to see his wife suffer more than she had already.

Footsteps stopped outside the closed door, and Laurence glanced at the clock on the mantle. It was just after midnight, and Weber had retired for the night. Perhaps the old butler had decided to check on him. Or maybe Mrs. Atkins was doing some late-night work. It could be any number of servants who fell behind in his or her duties.

Laurence had not expected the person who stood in the hallway when the door opened.

Isabel's blue dress matched her eyes and her face was bright. As handsome as he had seen her in the past, at this moment, she was beautiful.

"Isabel," he said and went to stand. "I did not expect you. Not tonight, at least."

"Please, sit," she said. "I would like to speak with you."

"Yes, of course," he said, and he joined her on the sofa. "Speak whatever you must." Although he gave her permission, he wished he did not have to know what she wanted, for this was it. This was the moment she would inform him she was leaving. Forever.

"My anger during our argument," she said, "it is imperative you know that you are not the cause of it, despite the fact you were the recipient. For that, I am sorry."

"You are forgiven," he said readily. "And for my actions and words, I apologize, as well."

Then she surprised him by taking his hand in hers. "That is kind, but you owe me no apology. You have done more for me than any could ask, or even wish." Her smile was much different than any he had seen from her, and he was curious to what decision she had come concerning her place of residence. "I would like to begin the painting tomorrow, if you do not mind."

The painting? He had expected her to return with an excuse as to why she was unable, or unwilling, to keep that promise. "Yes. I would like that." That did not change the fact she would leave once it was completed. Yet, he did not speak that thought aloud, for what difference would it make in her decision? "Do you know what you wish to paint?"

"I do," she replied with a firmness that surprised him. When she rose from the seat, he followed suit. "You have asked me to paint from the heart, and that is what I shall do."

"Then I look forward to seeing your completed work," he said. He could see the exhaustion in her features. "You should retire for the night. Will you remain here or return to Scarlett Hall?"

"Yes, I am tired," she replied. "I will remain here. But know this. I will finish this painting. It may not be a masterpiece worthy of a fine gallery, but it will be mine."

"Good. I cannot wait to see it."

She smiled and then leaned in to kiss his cheek, and his hand remained where her lips had touched his skin long after she left the room. What had come over her? Whatever had happened, tomorrow, Isabel would not be the only one creating a new work of art, for, in the morning, he would begin his most magnificent piece as he sat by her side.

Chapter Twenty-Five

Isabel rose the following morning in the best spirits she had experienced in some time. To be able to speak to her mother and share with the woman the very secrets that plagued her soul began a cleansing of sorts. Now, rather than wallowing in what she realized was her self-pity, Isabel had a sense of determination. She would put her secrets to canvas and ease the pain that resided deep inside her once and for all.

"You seem spirited this morning, Your Grace," Nancy said as she adjusted the final ribbon on her dress. It is good to see you smile."

Isabel looked at the woman's reflection as she sat before the dressing table. "It is good to smile," she replied. "I must admit I have not done so as of late."

"I wouldn't worry about that, Your Grace," Nancy said as she put the curling iron to a strand of Isabel's long blond hair. "You being a duchess and all, well, that lets you be however you want to be."

"That does not mean I should be unhappy."

Nancy gasped in horror. "Oh, no, Your Grace! I didn't mean to tell you how you should feel…"

Isabel laughed. "It was not a reprimand," she said, and the girl relaxed visibly. "What I meant to say was that it is my right to control how I feel, and it is about time I took back that control."

Nancy gave her a puzzled look but did not comment. How could she understand the agony Isabel felt if the young woman had yet to marry?

Had yet to live through the atrocities of life? Had yet to become a widow? Granted, almost everyone experienced the mountains and valleys of life, but she hoped that, if this girl was forced to endure them, they did not come tumbling down around her as they had for Isabel.

As Nancy continued on Isabel's hair, babbling about this and that as she worked, Isabel looked at the woman staring back at her. Her mother had been correct; a girl existed inside her who was once happy, and Isabel believed she would find her and release her from the prison she, herself, had created. And the painting she created would be the first step in that rescue.

"There," Nancy said as she stepped back from her finished work. "Does it meet your approval?" Morning dressing was much easier than readying for dinner, and the girl had formed large curls from Isabel's otherwise straight hair, pulled it all back with pins, and finished it off with a strip of fabric that matched Isabel's morning dress.

"It is perfect," Isabel said as she rose from the stool.

Nancy beamed with pride, and Isabel was glad. "I am so pleased that you are with us, Nancy," she said as she placed a hand on the girl's shoulder. "You are a wonderful addition to our staff, and I do not know what I would do without you."

The girl blushed at the compliment. "I'm so terribly happy to be here, Your Grace," she said with a curtsy.

Isabel made her way to the ballroom. She did not know how many days it would take her to complete the painting, but whatever it took, she would do it. What she wished was that she could complete it in one day, but what she had learned was that paint needed time to dry between layers. No, she could not be impatient with this piece of art, for it was to be her redemption – and her salvation.

When she arrived at the ballroom, she caught the movement of a figure outside in the garden. Laurence stood alone, staring in the distance, and Isabel readily joined him. The sun beamed down on them, and the sky was a deep blue with just a hint of clouds scattered across the horizon.

"I did not know you visited the gardens in the morning," Isabel said as she came to stand beside him.

Laurence chuckled. "This is the first time, or rather the first in some time. Either I am busy painting or I have work that needs completing, both of which keep me away from the crisp morning air." He sighed. "Now, I realize that I have missed many enjoyable things in life that cost not a single farthing."

Isabel smiled but said nothing, enjoying the light breeze that rustled her skirts.

"Harriet came by to see me while you were gone."

"Oh?" Isabel asked. What did that woman want now? That was another item on her long list of things to repair. The woman might be her sister-in-law, and sister to Laurence, but she would no longer be allowed to create predicaments in Isabel's family. Either she – Isabel – would set the woman straight, or she would see that Laurence did.

"We have mended our relationship," Laurence said.

Isabel groaned inwardly. What lies had Harriet told him to get him to agree to a reconciliation? Yet, Laurence had a peace about him that was not there before when speaking of his sister. Perhaps Isabel should allow him to finish, for now her curiosity was piqued.

"I will not go into details at the moment," Laurence continued, "but we were able to iron out our differences. I realize I have been a fool in the past when it came to my sister, but this time I know she spoke the truth. Never has she outrightly apologized, and yet, that was exactly what she did."

Isabel was shocked. She did not know the woman well, but what she had seen of her was enough to show the type of person she was. And that person did not apologize. Not for anything. If that is what Harriet did, the tale would be good indeed, and she was anxious to hear it. When Laurence was ready to share it and not a minute before.

"I am happy for you," she said. "She reminds me a bit of Juliet, or rather Juliet of her. Either way, their hearts are good, but they are consumed by mischief."

Laurence laughed. "I have heard tales of women leaving for grand adventures and for faraway lands. I never believed them, yet Juliet strikes me as the type of woman to make a go of it."

Isabel joined in his laughter. "Indeed. I can certainly see that," she said. She reached up and adjusted the lapel of his coat.

"There we are. I cannot have a duke who wears his coat with a rumpled lapel." She gave him an impish grin.

"I should hope not," he replied with an amused smile. "Very well, if you are finished dressing me," this made them both laugh, "and if you are ready, we should begin painting. Unless you wish to eat something first?"

"No," Isabel replied firmly. "I am ready."

They returned to the ballroom, and Isabel noticed that the easels, which in the past had sat side by side, now sat apart and faced each other.

She raised an eyebrow at him, and he chuckled. "I thought it would be nice if we did not see one another's work until they were completed."

"That is a wonderful idea," Isabel agreed. "May I begin now?"

"Yes, of course," he said. He sounded surprised, but Isabel did not wish to relinquish even the tiniest of moments; she had too much to do.

They went to their prospective stools and Isabel slipped the apron over her head. Then she collected her tools, organizing them just so, and with a brush in hand, she sat on the stool before the empty canvas. For a brief moment, panic overtook her.

Where did she begin? She closed her eyes and recalled the conversation she and her mother had shared the night before. She had shared her heart then and it was time to do it once again.

In her mind, she pictured Scarlett Hall with its dark gray walls and tall height. The hedges that grew to either side of the front door rustled as Juliet rushed through them, and the large trees Hannah could often be found reading in the shade they provided stood tall. It was not the bushes or trees she had to paint; it was herself. Therefore, opening her eyes, Isabel knew exactly where to begin.

On her pallet, she mixed the perfect gray. She dipped the tip of the brush into the new color and brought it to the canvas, and her heart pulled. As the brush moved in a solid stroke, it was as though a small chain that had bound her heart loosened. It was the most wondrous of feelings, which only increased with the next pass of the brush.

For some time – Isabel was unsure how long – she focused on her artwork, ignoring everything around her. The ballroom no longer existed, nor did the windows. Nor did Laurence across the way. Just she, the canvas, the brushes, the paints, and her emotions. Each stroke was perfect, the colors mixed with care.

Finally, after what seemed like forever, exhaustion forced her to stop, and she wiped her brushes and placed them in the oil before observing her work thus far.

The painting was far from complete, but Isabel could already see traces of what it would become, and that brought her joy.

She glanced over at Laurence, who was also cleaning his brushes as he studied his canvas. He looked her way, and although they sat separate from one another, she felt closer to the man than she ever had.

"I do not believe I can paint anymore today," he said with a sigh.

Isabel laughed. "You are not alone," she said as she joined him in the center of the room. "I never realized how tiring painting could be."

He chuckled. "Painting from the heart takes much more effort than copying what we see in front of us." He paused. "Shall we eat, or would you rather paint through the remainder of the day and starve ourselves instead?"

Isabel laughed at his joke. "It will do us no good to starve. What would people think of finding us thin and dying beside our paintings?"

"I would not care," Laurence replied as they made their way to the dining room. "Let them think what they wish."

Isabel loved the answer her husband gave, for it expressed her thoughts, as well.

"If it is not too much to ask," Laurence said, "I would like to breakfast in the garden. Would you care to join me?"

"Yes," Isabel said without hesitation. "I would be honored."

It was not long after that they sat at a table in the middle of the garden. They ate in tranquility, sharing in pleasant conversation, and Isabel found that she enjoyed it so much that it saddened her when Laurence said he had work to complete.

After he returned to the house, she remained at the table, her mind not focused on the past as it had been when she first arrived at Camellia Estates but, for the first time in many years, she thought of the future.

***

"It was at that point," Laurence was saying as he sat beside Isabel on the sofa in the drawing room, "I realized I had one of two possibilities. Either I sell the pigs or keep the land."

"And what was your decision?" Isabel asked, intrigued by his tale.

"To keep both of them," he replied with a laugh, which Isabel echoed. "A local man was in need of work, and to this day he runs that farm. He now has a family, who has joined him in the cottage, and they have been wonderful tenants ever since."

"How amusing," she said. "I do wonder..."

Her thoughts were broken off as the door opened and Weber entered, Nancy following behind him.

"Your Graces," Weber said, bowing his head as Nancy curtsied, "forgive my intrusion and rudeness, but I thought it imperative I speak with you."

Laurence sat up and placed his glass on the table. "What is it?"

Isabel wondered why Nancy wrung her hands. "What is the matter?" she asked as she hurried to her lady's maid. "Nancy?"

"I am sorry, Your Grace," the girl said, and then she began to sob. "I did not mean to hit her! I thought she was a thief and only wanted to protect your property."

"What is this?" Laurence demanded.

"Who did you hit?" Isabel asked, keeping her tone even. The girl was scared enough without shouting at her. She glared at Laurence with that thought.

"Her-her Grace's sister," Nancy sobbed. "Please do not dismiss me! I didn't mean to, I promise!"

"You are going nowhere," Isabel promised. "My sister? Is she still here?"

"We all are."

Isabel turned to find Juliet, Hannah, and Annabel standing in the doorway. None seemed injured in any way, although Isabel looked for any signs of blood or bumps.

"She hit me with a pillow," Juliet said. "Do not be angry with her; it was my own fault for startling her."

Isabel had two distinct thoughts at that moment. One was that never in all the years she had known Juliet, which was since the girl was born, had she ever heard the girl take responsibility for anything she had done against a servant. It was much more typical of her to place all blame on those she considered beneath her, even if the fault was her own.

The second thought that occurred to Isabel was that she had never felt such embarrassment in all her life, and she wondered what Laurence must think of her. She had a sobbing maid to contend with and therefore could not worry about Laurence, at least not yet, anyway.

"Nancy," she said in a quiet tone meant to sooth the girl, "return to your quarters. Sleep well knowing you did no wrong and that you will not be dismissed."

The poor maid gave a heavy sigh of relief and then dropped into a quick curtsy. "Thank you, Your Grace," she said with a sniffle.

The door closed behind the maid, and Isabel turned on her sisters. "What are you girls up to?" she demanded. "Have you any idea what trouble you have caused? And why have you come here? And sneaking into the house, no less! What has gotten into you?"

Hannah and Annabel lowered their heads, but Juliet was the one who replied, "We found an open window near the servants' quarters, so I peered inside. I suppose my footsteps were not as silent as I thought, for the next thing I knew, a pillow came down on my head."

Isabel groaned inwardly as Laurence turned his back on them. Things had been going so well and now this! He had to be as angry as a hornet!

"That still does not explain why you are here at such a late hour," Isabel said through gritted teeth. "And the servants' quarters? I am ashamed and embarrassed; you are all ladies of society, not vagabonds or burglars!"

Laurence stalked from the room. Oh, he was angry indeed! Not only did she have to deal with her sisters, but she would also have to mollify her husband.

"You had better have a good explanation for all this!" Isabel said. "You have embarrassed me in front of my husband. Do you not see? His anger is so great at this moment, he cannot even look at me!"

"I am sorry," Annabel whispered, and Hannah and Juliet echoed her words. "We did not mean to be caught by your servant."

"It is not a matter of being caught," Isabel snapped. "I assume this is all part of some scheme Juliet concocted?"

Juliet jutted her chin. "It is true that the idea was mine, and I will take the flogging come sunrise instead of my sisters."

Isabel groaned. Always the dramatics when it came to Juliet. "No one is to be flogged. Now, before I become angrier, what are you doing here?"

"Yesterday," Juliet said, "I went to the gardens and I heard you yelling at Mother."

Isabel stared at her sister in shock. "You heard?"

"I swear, I only heard a few words," Juliet assured her. "I may have eavesdropped before, but I do not do so any longer. I am not the child I once was."

"What exactly did you hear?" Isabel asked, hoping what little Juliet overheard did not include the confession she had shared with her mother.

"That you were chained here at this estate," Juliet replied.

Isabel sighed. "There are phrases that are used as expressions. I am not literally being chained."

"I told you," Hannah whispered. "You would not listen."

"I am sorry," Juliet said. "I did it because I care."

Isabel had never seen her younger sister so contrite, and she realized that, although Juliet was now of age, she still was as naive to life as she ever was. That did not excuse her actions, nor that of the other two.

"I appreciate your concern," Isabel said. "But let this be a lesson to the three of you. Do not eavesdrop and always ask before assuming the worst."

All three girls nodded, and Isabel was uncertain what to do next. She looked from one girl to another and finally came to a decision. "You will apologize to His Grace immediately. Wait here while I go in search of him. You had better hope he chooses to accept it."

Isabel left the room intending to go to the study only to find Laurence standing but a few steps away. His face was as crimson as a ripened apple, and she feared he was close to unleashing his anger on her. Regardless, she had to make him see reason, to make him understand that her sisters meant no harm.

"No words can express how sorry I am for the actions of my sisters," she said as she hung her head. "I am embarrassed. My family is shamed, and I will have them apologize and whatever else you deem necessary to punish them."

It was silent for a moment, and Isabel worried the situation could not be resolved. She did not blame him; knowing anyone had attempted to enter the house through a window would have tested the patience of any man.

It was not anger that was loosed, for he snorted instead. "Can you imagine their shock," he asked, "of being hit by a pillow while trying to climb through a window?" His shoulders shook with laughter. "That is perhaps the most comical thing I have ever heard."

"You are not angry?" Isabel asked in shock.

"Angry? Not in the slightest. I am amazed at the lengths your family will go to call over to one's house."

It was with relief that Isabel relaxed, and her previous peace returned. "I am unsure as to what to do. The girls have good hearts. Yet, they frustrate me. Why do they not listen and behave?"

"Such is the way when one gives advice to others," Laurence replied. "You celebrate when it is taken and groan in frustration when it is not."

Isabel chuckled. "Yes, there is much truth in that statement. What do you suggest I do?"

Laurence stepped forward, leaving only a few inches between them, and Isabel felt an odd sensation move through her body, a warm, pleasant feeling. "Do you trust me?" he whispered.

Isabel smiled. If he had asked that question even a week earlier, she would have been unsure as to how to respond. Her heart guided her now, and she replied with a fervent "Yes."

"Good. We will return to the drawing room and I will threaten to punish them. You will then ask me to spare them. That should be enough to put them in their places so they never do something like this again."

"That is a brilliant idea," Isabel replied. She reached out and took his hand. "Thank you for your kindness once again."

"Always," he said. They looked at each other for several moments, until a maid gave a small gasp before scurrying away, which only made Isabel giggle.

They returned to the drawing room, Laurence wearing a stern glare and Isabel a worried one. All three girls quickly dropped into perfect curtsies as apologies tumbled from their lips like waterfalls.

"Silence!" Laurence commanded, and they all went quiet. "Your apologies have not sat well with me. To trespass on lands belonging to a member of the Royal Family has very stiff punishments."

Isabel had to stifle a giggle. The Redbrooks had not been members of the Royal Family for several generations, but she made no move to correct him.

"To enter my home as you did," he continued, "may be met with hard labor in the sheep fields for a dozen years or more."

The girls stood staring at each other with wide eyes and gaping mouths. "Please," Juliet sobbed, "we beg for your mercy."

"I wish I could," Laurence replied as if he had no choice in the matter. "Yet, as a duke, I have a responsibility to the Crown, which means I must report this crime at once."

Tears ran down their cheeks, and Isabel placed a hand on his arm. They had suffered enough. "Your Grace," she said, "Might I ask one favor of you?"

"Yes?"

"I can assure you they have learned their lesson. If you were to extend kindness to them, I believe they will behave after today."

Laurence pursed his lips and appeared to study each girl with deliberation.

They nodded emphatically to Isabel's words.

"Is this true?" Laurence demanded. "For if I show mercy, you must never speak a word of this to anyone lest I remand my decision."

"We swear," Hannah replied. "We will return home at once and never do anything like this again." The others nodded their agreement.

"Very well," Laurence said with a sigh. "You should be thankful your sister is kind, for, in such matters as these, I am not." He then walked over to the window, his back to them.

Isabel ushered her sisters out of the room. "I hope you have learned your lesson," she said as they made their way to the foyer.

"Oh, we have," Juliet said. "I cannot imagine being forced to work on a sheep farm!"

"I would not enjoy that," Hannah agreed.

Annabel nodded. "Neither would I."

Each girl gave Isabel a hug, assuring her that they would behave from this day forward. Isabel suspected they would have a terrible time keeping that promise, but at least it would put them on the straight and narrow for the time being.

"I love you all," Isabel said. "And thank you for your concern, but rest assured that I am happy here."

"That is all we ever wanted," Hannah said.

They said their goodbyes, and Isabel watched as the girls headed off to the horses she now saw tied to a tree at the edge of the drive. She sighed, relieved the drama of the night was over. It was the words Laurence had said that came to mind. He had asked for her trust, and for the first time in a very long time, she had trusted someone. By doing so, she found that it brought her great happiness.

Chapter Twenty-Six

The following nine days passed much like the first upon her return to Camellia Estates, each day beginning with Isabel and Laurence painting together in the morning and ending with the two sharing in a drink in the evening after dinner. Minus the surprise visit from her sisters, of course.

As Isabel studied the canvas before her, a sense of satisfaction filled her. With the stroke of her brush, her emotions had transferred to the canvas, and the results were better than she could have expected. She had not shared with Laurence what she had told her mother, but now that her painting was complete, she realized the day had come when she would do just that. She glanced over at Laurence, who had completed his painting the day before. The patience the man possessed spoke volumes, and he deserved to know the truth.

She walked over to where he sat gazing at his canvas. "I have finished," she said. The clouds that had covered the sun moved away, allowing rays to highlight his smile. "Would you like to show me yours first?"

"I would," he replied. He took a step back and extended his hand toward the easel before him.

Isabel, filled with enough curiosity to kill a cat, stepped around the easel, the skirts of her blue dress rustling around her ankles. She was immediately taken by his work, which depicted a forest with a road running through it. A carriage traveling with two occupants lumbered into the depths of the trees, leaving behind two figures – a man in a long dark coat and a woman in a white dress.

"Laurence," Isabel gasped as she brought her hand to her breast, "I cannot lie; it is beautiful. Would you explain its meaning to me?"

Laurence took a deep breath. "Many of my works have not come from the heart," he replied. "But this one did. It tells the story of a young boy, and I wish to share that story with you now."

Isabel nodded and instinctively reached for his hand. In return, she received a shy smile.

"For years, I have been ashamed because of the injury to my leg. I saw it as a hindrance to being the man I wished to be. Whenever I seemed ready to move on, either my leg or Harriet would remind me of the guilt I carried."

"Guilt?" Isabel asked in surprise. "You have nothing for which to be guilty."

"Not anymore," he said with a small smile as he looked at the painting. "Do you know how my leg was injured? And the story of how my parents were killed?"

"I had heard it was a carriage accident," Isabel replied. She recalled when her mother had told her the horrible news that the duke and duchess were killed and the leg of their young son had been crushed in the accident.

"My parents had come to see me at the boarding school," Laurence said, his voice distant. "While others had been sent carriages to retrieve them, my parents wished to journey with me; such was their love." His voice broke, and Isabel's heart went out to him. "It was late when we left Cambridge despite the fact the rain fell in a steady stream and the wind was not kind to the carriage. The driver misjudged a turn, and I remember that, as the carriage tipping to one side, I was thrown from it."

"Oh, Laurence," Isabel gasped, unable to imagine the terror that young boy had to have felt. "I am so sorry."

"When I woke, my leg was broken in several places, and I felt such pain as I had never experienced before. It was dark and I was scared and alone."

Isabel wiped tears from her eyes as he continued.

"Unable to walk, I crawled through the mud toward where I thought the carriage would be. I do not know how long it took me, but it seemed an eternity." He turned to look at her, and although the man shed no tears, the pain of his memories showed in his eyes. "When I finally found the carriage, I found my father dead and my mother on the verge of death. I told her I would find help, and I began to crawl in the direction from whence we came. The pain worsened to the point that I fainted. When I awoke, I was in an unfamiliar bed and my parents were dead."

Isabel embraced him. "I am so sorry," she whispered. "I never knew."

"How could you? I have not told anyone." He sighed. "Harriet, of course, was devastated. When I returned to school the following year, the boys teased me that I had been the cause of my parents' death. When I returned to Camellia Estates, Harriet was even angrier with me. Of course, it is not fair to place all the blame on her, for I had already accepted the guilt for their deaths." He turned to look at her. The pain was gone, replaced by something else. "Now I am ready to let that go."

"I am pleased for you," Isabel said as she kissed his cheek. Then she looked at the beautiful painting. "Is that them in the carriage?"

"It is," he replied. "I have accepted that I am not to blame for their deaths, and therefore, I have allowed them to go on to the next stage of their lives in peace."

Isabel was overcome with emotion, but she swallowed the tears. He had moved on, and so should she.

"You told me when we argued," Laurence continued, "that you could not make me happy. At first, I was hurt, for I did not know what you meant. Now I understand."

"Tell me," she whispered.

"My refusal to attend parties with you, thinking myself a lesser man. You could never heal those wounds. You helped and guided me, which was what I needed. Yet, in the end, I had to find my own peace.

"Yes. That is important."

"I have found that, in forgiving myself and realizing that I am a man – a full man, one who is no longer ashamed to venture into town or to attend a party." Isabel followed his gaze to the painting. "I will not lie; I did not wish to do those things alone."

"And the couple there?" Isabel asked, pointing to the images of the man and woman behind the carriage.

"They are the two of us. That is the man I have become, and that is the woman for whom I care deeply – the woman I love. I want her to know that, as I say goodbye to the past, I continue to desire a future with her."

"What a beautiful sentiment," Isabel whispered.

He took both her hands in his and pressed them to his lips. "I will never ask anything of you that will make you unhappy," he said. "I believe we have planted a seed and together we will grow it into something wonderful."

Isabel could not stop the flow of tears, and she accepted the kerchief he gave her. "I have an answer to your request," she said when she was able to speak again. "Before I give it, I wish to show you my painting, for I believe it will also answer many of your questions, as well."

With an exchange of smiles, they walked over to Isabel's easel. "Your painting," Laurence said as he stared at the canvas, and for a moment, Isabel thought he did not like it. "It was as I suspected. I knew it would be breathtaking. Is that Scarlett Hall?"

Isabel nodded. "It is."

"You have captured it perfectly. And the faces in the windows? Are those your sisters?"

"They are," she replied. "And my brother, as well."

She had indeed painted Scarlett Hall, including her siblings peering out the windows. A young girl stood at the front door, and in the drive stood a man and a woman.

"You asked me if I still loved Arthur," she said as she turned to Laurence.

"I did. I feared you could not share your heart with two men. Although that thought hurt, I understand why you might still love him."

"My answer to you that day was truthful," she said. "I no longer love him. Nor had I loved him that day I learned of his death."

***

The Barnet Home, eighteen months earlier.

Two years. That was how long it had been since Isabel had spoken her vows to love, honor, and obey the man she loved. Arthur Barnet had been the perfect gentleman, had been the man she had always dreamed of marrying, and he had won her heart and soul.

When they had met just before her eighteenth birthday at a party held in honor of a mutual friend, they had engaged in a lively conversation about Abraham Crowley's poem The Change.

"How can you say that anything Crowley wrote was 'metaphysical'?" Isabel demanded. "I find his writing expressive and eloquent. That is nowhere near metaphysical."

Arthur laughed. "That is exactly what metaphysical entails. It is the idea that love is something other than a physical reaction of two people speaking to the reader at a spiritual level."

They had spoken for hours, and when the London season began two months later, he was calling over to her parents' townhome on Buckley Street on a regular basis. With each conversation, her admiration for him grew, and it was not long before he asked for her hand in marriage.

Although he was the younger brother of a titled man, and therefore not titled himself, he came from a family who had wealth, so her parents had readily agreed, and she and Arthur were married as soon as the season ended.

The vows she had spoken that day no longer meant anything to her two years later. The more she tried to deny it, the more her heart plagued her. The truth of the matter was, she no longer loved her husband.

Their first month together had been perfection. They had honeymooned on the coast for two weeks, and then he brought her to his home, the place that was to be her home, as well. It was not long after when the illusion of what she had imagined her life to be had begun to unravel.

It all began when Arthur began spending late nights with friends, oftentimes not returning home until just before sunrise. Isabel said nothing, of course, for it was her duty to obey her husband and, therefore, never question him. Yet, when he returned home from one of his late-night outings and crawled into bed beside her, the fragrance of a woman's perfume overtook her senses, and she knew that he had been lying to her.

Initially, she had been hurt that he had been in the company of another woman, but the more she thought about the man to whom she had given her heart, she assured herself that Arthur loved her and would not do such a thing. Perhaps what she had smelled was not what she suspected. And, by the time he awoke late the following morning, the scent was gone. Yes, she had imagined it.

Yet, the late nights continued, and she spent hours fretting over where he was. That is, until she learned about his accounts.

As it turned out, Arthur did not hold as many properties and businesses as he claimed. It was the visit from the accountant that unwittingly apprised her of that fact, and within six months of their wedding, they were in debt, a debt so massive that she feared it could never be repaid.

Her lady's maid had been dismissed first, followed by at least one servant each week until only the butler, the cook, and the housekeeper remained. When no more servants could be dismissed, all the properties were sold, leaving them with only the house in which they lived. At least they had that.

Yet that was not enough. As their troubles grew, issues in their marriage increased.

"You have caused this," he had screamed at her one night after the butler had been dismissed. "If I had not married you, I would have been better off! At least I could have married an heiress or someone with a decent dowry. I had several by the ear, you know. They all wanted to marry me, but I chose you, and look where that got me!" He pulled dresses from the wardrobe and threw them on the floor before her. "Go sleep in the guest room! I cannot stand the sight of you!"

She had gathered up her things as tears rolled down her face and did as he bade, moving into the guest room, where she remained for the rest of her marriage.

Isabel leaned against the window frame as she gazed down at her sisters in the garden. They would never understand, and she refused to burden them with her problems. She could only pray that they were luckier than she when they finally married.

Arthur had sent her away to Scarlett Hall. She was to remain a week with her family in order to allow him some time alone, or so he said. Her joyous visit was interrupted by worries for her husband. His drinking had reached levels of near madness, and, although she was angry and hurt, she still loved him. Therefore, she decided to return home two days earlier than planned. One way or another she would take care of her husband; had that not been what her vows had been about?

When she arrived home just before sunrise, she found him sleeping in the arms of another woman. Her cry had awakened him, and he cursed her for entering his room without permission. She had run to her room, slamming the door behind her, and thrown herself onto her bed to weep. Her heart was shattered, and yet she still refused to yield. He was her husband, and no hussy would take him from her!

The thoughts of a naive woman, she thought as she recalled the days that followed. She had entered his study in order to confront him about his infidelity, but he had sneered at her as soon as she entered.

"I told you before," he had snapped, "my office is prohibited."

"I am sorry," Isabel whispered, "but it is important that I speak to you."

"And what could be so important that you interrupt me in the midst of saving our home?" He reached for the drink he had sitting on the desk and took a hefty gulp. "Well? Speak up. You are wasting my time."

"The woman in your bed?" she said in a near whisper, for she was so filled with terror, she could barely speak. "I have decided to forgive you, and I hope..."

Arthur slammed his fist on the desk. "Her name is Collette," he said with a glare, "and I do not need your forgiveness. It is my privilege to spend time with whomever I please."

"Do you care for her?" Isabel asked, afraid of his reply.

"Does it matter?" he asked with a malevolent smile. He finished the remainder of his drink. "Now, is there anything else?"

Isabel almost replied no, there was not, but as she turned to leave, she stopped and looked at the man for whom she had given up her life. "I want you to know that I still love you. I believe we can survive this. I do not understand why you feel the need to seek the arms of another woman. Is it because you do not love me?"

It was the pause before he answered that hurt worse than the words that followed, for the man she saw at the desk was not the same man she had married. And even before he spoke, she realized that he never had.

"Love is a word for fools and poets," he replied finally. "Your duty is to birth me children and to obey my every word. Now, leave me be."

He returned to his work, and Isabel left the room. Despite his hateful words, she refused to allow their marriage to fall apart. Not when he came home drunk and kissed her in the night calling her by the name of another woman. Nor when he grew angry and took her by the shoulders and shook her. No, Isabel fought to love the man, to save him, until she came to a point when she stopped. The last six months of their marriage she had grown numb; she felt no joy, but she also felt no sadness, just a heaviness on her heart.

It was on that fateful day when she resigned herself to tell her husband that she no longer loved him. They both needed to be free of one another, for she could no longer endure another day living as she did. She would ask for a divorce, and then he and his harlots could drink themselves to an early death for all she cared. Although she wished the man no harm, she no longer cared what he did.

Voices from the hall had her turn toward the door. She smoothed her skirts, ready to present herself to her husband perhaps for the last time. As the door opened, it was not her drunken husband who entered, but her brother-in-law Connor.

"Isabel," he said, hurrying to her side, "I have some horrible news."

"Arthur," she whispered.

"Yes, Arthur," Connor said as he took her by the hand. "I am afraid he was found late last night. Apparently, he had fallen from his horse…"

Isabel did not listen to the rest of the explanation, for her head felt as if it were filled with cotton wool. When he pulled her into his arms, she wept, but they were not tears of losing a man she loved, but rather of what might have been.

***

By the end of her telling, Isabel had tears streaming down her cheeks, but her heart felt ten times lighter. "That same night after learning about his death, I returned to Scarlett Hall, hoping to find solitude within its walls – and within myself. As my despair deepened, I swore I would never love again."

"I can understand why," Laurence said as he handed her a clean kerchief. "You went through much."

Isabel nodded. "Then my mother came to me with a request – to save the home I loved."

"Your story explains why you were so distant when we married. I can only imagine what you thought our marriage would be like."

"I was terrified, to be honest. In my mind, marriage was a trap and I the prey."

Laurence gave her hand a squeeze. "I know you miss your family. If you remain here, you may go there as often as you wish. I will never stop you."

"I appreciate you saying so," Isabel replied, "but this last time I ventured down those halls, I came to realize something; Scarlett Hall cannot take away my pain, for its walls hold many secrets, including mine. I will never reveal what happened when I was married to Arthur to anyone else, but because of you, I was able to put all my pain and hurt onto that canvas."

"Tell me about your painting."

Isabel turned to her work, which held all her fears and worries from the past three years. "That young girl at the door is me," she explained, "as I once was. A girl who believed that her home was a place of magic that, once a person entered it, he or she would never be hurt again. If you were to listen to the secrets it holds, you will learn that the hurt stays with us." She sighed with a shake to her head.

"And them?" Laurence asked, pointing to the pair at the top of the drive.

"That is us. And like your painting, I wish to say goodbye to the past. To say goodbye to the childish belief that my old home would keep me safe."

Laurence pressed his lips to her fingers but made no comment, for which she was glad. If she stopped now, she would never be able to continue.

"I once vowed to keep my heart sealed, for to suffer heartbreak again was something I could not fathom. Who could survive such anguish in a single lifetime? As we spent time together and learned about one another, I also became afraid. What if what I was feeling for you was love? And if it was, would it not result in the same ending?"

"I could never hurt you," Laurence said. "I know it may be difficult to believe, but I can assure you, I never will."

"Yes, I know this now," Isabel replied. "Over the past week, I have learned to open my heart again. I have learned to accept the feelings inside me, and I am no longer afraid of them. Oh, Laurence, I cannot keep it inside any longer. I love you, and I wish nothing more than to remain here with you at Camellia Estates."

She fell into his embrace, crying tears she had built up for the past year and a half. And Laurence said nothing, only whispering terms of endearment until she pulled away.

"I am sorry," she whispered with a light laugh. "I am afraid I am a blubbering mess."

He pushed back stray hairs that tickled her face. "You have no need to apologize. And you are no blubbering mess. This is our new beginning, and tears are just the cleansing of the soul."

She smiled and then pointed to a streak of sunlight that highlighted the couple in her painting. "Those rays of sunlight? They are the whispers of light that represent the new beginning we will have, for I see nothing but brightness in our days ahead."

He pulled her to him once again. "I love you, Isabel Redbrook," he whispered. "It was you who showed such strength that made me look inside myself to find mine."

When the embrace broke, Isabel looked into the eyes of her husband, the man she loved. And for the first time, they kissed, and it was beautiful and passionate. She did not compare what she felt to what she had once had for another, for that was long gone. In its place was something far different, something much more real.

When the kiss ended, Isabel smiled with joy, for she realized that many more would follow, and like the life ahead of them, if their steps were like each stroke of the brush that came from the heart, the possibilities of their life together were endless.

When he lifted her chin and looked down at her, she felt as if all the bones in her body had turned to mush. "I believe we have the most wonderful of futures ahead of us," he said before he kissed her again – thoroughly.

Chapter Twenty-Seven

The ballroom had been cleared of all their painting supplies and was now filled with people Isabel and Laurence had invited to their first party. One reason for this gathering was a celebration of the upcoming season, which they planned to attend, of course. The main motivation for throwing this party was to celebrate their love for one another. It had been a month since Isabel had completed her painting and confessed her love for Laurence, and with each day, that love grew, reaching new heights she had never known.

Now, looking around at her guests, she was pleased to see they all wore smiles, just as she did. Her gaze landed on her husband, a man who had doubted himself but now held no resemblance to that hermit he once was. For now, he stood in the center of a group of men, his voice filled with confidence. He no longer cared what others thought of him, for which Isabel was glad.

They had visited various shops together numerous times since the reveal of their paintings, often to simply walk amongst the people. Laurence had become a new man, and Isabel a new woman. All the hurt she had endured was now gone, not just buried away inside her but truly gone, left on a canvas now put away, never again to see the light of day.

"Why is the most beautiful woman at this party hiding away?"

Isabel turned to find her mother standing behind her and laughed. "I am uncertain," she replied. "Would she not rather speak to her daughters?"

"Oh, you," her mother replied, although her cheeks reddened from the compliment. They both turned to watch Isabel's sisters. Hannah and Juliet stood beside Annabel by the refreshment table, their heads together.

"They cannot be up to any good," Isabel said.

"Some things never change," her mother replied. Then she sighed. "I now have two daughters who will have their first season this year. Then Annabel. It feels like just yesterday when you were all children."

"We will always be your daughters," Isabel said warmly. "No matter how old we grow or who we marry. You will never lose us."

Her mother nodded in agreement. "Yes, of course," she replied. "It is the empty home in London at night while they are away that bothers me. Although, I suppose I shall keep myself busy waiting to hear of their stories when they return."

Isabel thought for a moment. "I will speak with Laurence, but why not join us in our home? There are more than enough rooms, and I would love the company during the day."

Her mother hesitated for a moment and then smiled. "If he allows it. I do not want to become a burden to the man more than I already have."

Isabel laughed. "You could never be a burden to either of us, I assure you."

They spoke for several moments before the string quartet began a new set. Then two guests entered the ballroom. Harriet wore a sweeping green gown with gold thread and white lace. Her husband Ambrose looked dashing in a dark blue coat and tan breeches. Or Isabel assumed it was her husband, for they had yet to meet.

Laurence walked over to them, giving Harriet a kiss on her cheek and Ambrose a firm handshake. Then he nodded to Isabel.

"Forgive me, Mother," she said. "I must speak to someone."

When she reached Laurence, he introduced her to Ambrose, who bowed deeply before kissing her hand. He seemed a kind man with a good wit, but she was unable to speak with him long when Harriet asked to speak to her alone.

"The day of your wedding to my brother," Harriet said after Isabel closed the door to the drawing room, "I spoke the cruelest of words to you. And I did not stop. My time there was spent in anger and hatred, and for that, I wish only to seek your forgiveness. I understand if we do not become fast friends, and if you wish to never speak to me again, I will be forced to accept it. You must know that I am truly sorry and hope that one day you can find it in your heart to forgive me."

Laurence had told her his sister had changed, but she had never expected to find an entirely different woman in her place. How could she not forgive someone who would humble herself so completely? "Of course I accept your apology," Isabel replied. "I hold no grudge against you. I am happy you are finding your way in life, and it serves you well."

"It will, Your Grace," Harriet replied with clear relief. "I know it has only been a short time since I have come to realize my many mistakes, I find it much better to be kind and listen than to be harsh and always speaking." The woman giggled and then looked down at the floor. "Forgive me, Your Grace."

Isabel smiled as she took Harriet's hand in hers. "At one time you mentioned that we would become great friends."

"Yes, but..."

"Allow me to finish. Friends, and especially family, call each other by their Christian names. So, I must ask you, Harriet, are we friends? Better yet, are we not family?"

Harriet broke into a wide grin. "Yes, Isabel, we are. We are both family and friends."

"Good," Isabel replied as she hugged her sister-in-law. If anyone had asked her if this day would come several months earlier, she would never have believed it, and yet, here they stood embracing one another.

"I truly am sorry," Harriet said as she dabbed at her eyes with a kerchief.

"All is forgiven, so no more talk of apologies. Now, we should return to the party or everyone will think we have sneaked away to drink."

This brought on a bout of giggles that reminded Isabel so much of her sisters. She was thankful their relationship had been mended.

They returned to the party, and music played, guests laughed and drank, but only one man made her heart leap. Laurence said something to his friends and walked over to stand beside her.

"How is it I have been so fortunate to marry the most beautiful woman in all the land?"

"I often ask myself how my husband is the most handsome," she replied. "He is such a great painter, among many other traits." She gave him a cryptic smile that made him grin widely. "Some may call it luck, but I believe what we know it to be."

"Indeed," he replied.

They both turned to gaze over the crowd, for what they shared was love. The very foundation of what had brought them together and had been able to heal them of troubled pasts. It was the same love that some who had attended their party already possessed and what others pursued. It was not always an easy journey; in fact, it was as treacherous as any expedition to a faraway land could ever tout.

Yet, it was also the finished painting much like the one that hung behind them that was the goal. For that work of art had been completed together, and it depicted Laurence and Isabel standing at the doors to Camellia Estates, the children to come at their side.

Epilogue

In three days, Isabel and Laurence would leave for London, ready to attend the season. Numerous invitations had already been sent and received, and Isabel could not wait. She had checked and rechecked their belongings, and Laurence, who watched as he leaned against the door jamb of their bedroom door, laughed.

"I will be forced to buy another carriage to carry all the clothes you wish to take," he teased.

Isabel joined in with his laughter and then looked at the many bags and trunks that surrounded her. "I suppose you might, at that," she replied. "It is just that I am excited about our first season together as a married couple." She walked over and took his hands in hers. "I want to show off my husband to everyone who will allow me to do so."

"And I will be watching in awe as you grace every home."

Isabel smiled, and then their lips met, which happened several times a day. It was beautiful, soft yet filled with passion.

Much to their annoyance, a timid knock on the door brought the kiss to an end.

"You do not have to answer, you know," Laurence whispered.

Isabel laughed. "I know, but it may be important."

She opened the door to find Weber with a tray in his hand. "A letter arrived for you from Scarlett Hall, Your Grace," the butler said with a bow. "The rider said it was urgent."

Isabel took the letter from the tray. "Thank you," she mumbled as Laurence joined her. She hoped all was well, but as she read the letter, that hope was dashed.

"What is it?" Laurence asked. "Is your mother all right? Or your sisters?"

"Yes, Mother is fine, but it is Hannah. Apparently, Mother asks for our aid."

"Of course," he replied. "Whatever they need, we will help."

Isabel nodded as thoughts rushed through her mind. Could it be true that her beloved and meek Hannah had been doing the things of which their mother accused her? It was something she might have thought Juliet to do, but not Hannah.

"Isabel?"

"We must leave for Scarlett Hall at once," she said, grabbing only one of the many bags she had packed. "I will explain everything on the way.

Author's Note

I hope you have enjoyed the Secrets of Scarlett Hall thus far, beginning with Isabel's Story in *Whispers of Light*.

More secrets are revealed in the next installment of the Secret of Scarlett Hall Series, *Echoes of the Heart*, which will recount Hannah's story of finding love.

Jennifer

Other Series by Jennifer Monroe

Those Regency Remingtons

Sisterhood of Secrets

Victoria Parker Regency Mysteries

Regency Hearts

Made in the USA
Middletown, DE
16 March 2024

51627961R00132